Shoal Waters

A Carolina Coast Novel

Normandie Fischer

SLEEPY CREEK PRESS

For hurting mothers
For babies unborn
For the silent, the fearful, and those longing for grace.

For you have formed my inward parts;
You have covered me in my mother's womb.
I will praise You, for I am fearfully and wonderfully made.
Marvelous are Your works,
And that my soul knows very well.
My frame was not hidden from You,
When I was made in secret,
And skillfully wrought in the lowest parts of the earth.
Your eyes saw my substance, being yet unformed.
And in Your book they all were written,
The days fashioned for me,
when as yet there were none of them.

Psalm 130:13-16, NKJV

PROLOGUE

THEN

The sun has hidden, dark draws nigh, no mask of smiles can sweeten her sigh.

Hours had passed, and still they wouldn't let her search. Didn't they know Olli could have been kidnapped on his way home? Maybe beat up? Maybe *worse*?

Jeminy bit her lip until she tasted blood. She was past crying as the fear grew and lumped in her belly.

Maybe—*please, please*—he'd only wrecked his bike. Twisted his ankle, gotten stuck.

But then he'd be lying out there somewhere, his jacket stiff with ice, his skinny body shivering. His glasses would be wonky, his sneakers unlaced. By now his voice must have drained to a whisper, if he could speak at all.

That image only made her insides hurt more. She shifted position, knocking her scabbed knee in the process, but who cared about a bleeding knee or bleeding lips or anything stupid when Olli might need her? And they wouldn't let her go out to find him.

On the kitchen counter, birthday cakes waited, hers and Olli's, twelve unlit candles on each. Gifts were piled in the living room, hers and his.

By dawn, the rain and hail had stopped. All evening and night, Mother'd wrung her hands like the crazy lady in that movie, and she'd yelled at their nanny, as if it had been Rose's fault. Mother'd kept Jeminy inside, shooing her from the living room to a corner of the kitchen, not listening to her words, never hearing *her*, the secondary twin—the girl, not the boy, the daughter who looked like her daddy, not the son who shared his mother's hair and his mother's eyes. Shaking, Jeminy'd huddled and prayed through the hours of dark that Olli was holed up somewhere, maybe hurt, but waiting, waiting for rescue, for her to find him.

Then, when the dark finally turned light and no one paid her any mind, she raced out the door, not pausing when her sneakers skidded on wet leaves, just picking herself up and trudging on, impatient of the methodical pace the adult searchers set.

Last night, she'd tried to tell them where to look. Crying his name into the woods now, she plowed forward on the rough terrain, up one leafy slope, across the trail, down, searching, calling, frantically listening for an answer. When she spotted his red mountain bike flipped near a bush and then his jacket—him— lying there by the path, she fell in a heap at his side, oblivious to the mud that squished where she stepped and rocks that dug into her shins and knees. Around her, bushes reached out, their tentacles fanning, waving, taunting. She grabbed his boney shoulder above where his jacket had fallen open.

"Olli, Olli, look. See, I'm here, come on, wake up. Please, please, wake up."

He didn't move, not even when she shook him, and she turned wildly, screaming for the others. Voices called her brother's name, but they sounded far away in the woods, lost in a tunnel that excluded her and Olli.

"Here! He's here! Please, I found him. Please, Daddy, somebody, help. *O God, please.*"

She needed her daddy. Daddy would fix things. He always fixed things, whatever was broken. Why didn't he hear her? She called for him again as her fingers touched Olli's once silky, now matted dark hair and traced his too-gray, too-cold cheek. If she hadn't felt the cold or seen his color—like a rag dunked in Rose's bleach—she could have imagined him sleeping. After all, his eyes were mostly closed. Not wide open like in the murder movies they weren't supposed to watch.

Behind her, finally, feet pounded and twigs snapped. They were coming, but too late, too late.

She alone had searched this little-used path, knowing Olli would have picked the wooded trail home from school to avoid the bullies. She'd tried to tell everyone, anyone, but her mother hadn't listened—because she never listened—and her daddy had been out looking with everyone else. And Rose was told to stay out of the way. Like her. Like a kid.

She'd heard Rose crying out to God, on her knees or from a chair all night long. God hadn't bothered with one boy, though, had He?

The path wasn't the easiest, not one Olli should have taken in the rain when his bike's wheels could have skidded, *had* skidded in the mud, had thrown him to the ground, laid him flat, and somehow killed him.

Why hadn't he waited? He was supposed to wait for her to get out of chorus, for Mother to pick them up if it rained because their nanny, Rose, had the day off. Mother had promised to be there, and, fine, she'd been late, but not *that* late, a little wild like she was sometimes, and Olli'd already gone when Jeminy had skipped out of the chorus room, glowing from the choir master's praise.

He'd left and taken his bike. In the rain.

The wrong way home.

She'd never seen real death before, never been touched by it. Her tears fell, dripped onto his jacket, and sobs curled her over him.

Someone's soft voice finally spoke. "Come, love." Her daddy tried to lift her away as she clung to her brother's limp hand.

"Olli, Olli, c...come back." Her words stuck on a sob, broken and barely audible. "Ple...ease, don't leave me!"

But he'd gone. And she was a twin without a twin, the live one, and Olli, her beautiful, sweetest-boy-ever brother was no more.

JEMINY

Ups and downs and all arounds;
It's time to go, it's time to flee.

Jeminy Buchanan tried to ignore the drunken prattle, but the woman beside her in the cab—what *was* her name?—kept asking inane questions and offering sympathy that was about as sincere as her puffy lips and silicone curves. "What a *pity* Rand left." The woman leaned much too close, her breath potent enough to blister paint. "I bet you miss him."

Jeminy only shrugged. She no longer had the energy for words.

Rand had moved out months ago to live with a man, but maybe Barbie here hadn't noticed that piece of gossip in the music industry rags.

Jeminy'd known she shouldn't have gone out, but Maggie had insisted. "Girlfriend, you've got to get off that couch and have a little fun. You worried about your music? Then quit staring at those walls, get your mind off your troubles, and write."

"You imagine a party's going to stimulate my creativity?" Jeminy'd laced her words with all the sarcasm she could muster. She hated parties where she barely knew anyone. Cocktail talk? Two-minute conversations and air kisses? No thank you.

"Pretend," Maggie'd said. "Besides, your birthday's tomorrow."

Birthdays weren't worth celebrating, but she'd let Maggie persuade her anyway. And then Maggie'd had to duck out early, and Jeminy'd been left with the wispy, gossipy types like this woman, who'd snagged her to share a ride home.

Now, too-thin, too-manicured fingers latched onto Jeminy's arm. "You want to meet for lunch next week?"

Never, thank you very much, but she subdued the shudder and merely said, "I'm leaving town soon." She rather liked the sound of escaping a city that had nothing to offer except a multitude of regrets.

Finally, the driver pulled up in front of her building. She uncurled her legs from the cramped space, said, "Goodnight," and meant goodbye. Then she headed down a flower-laced walk to the entrance.

The scent of bougainvillea combined with something else, something she recognized from back East but rarely noticed here, assailed her. She could almost believe she smelled a storm brewing.

But this was Los Angeles, where summertime rainfall averaged zero inches. Maybe she was imagining it, but the fragrance followed her to the door, where someone's cigar smoke lingered, layering itself over the lovely.

2

GEORGINA

Quiet pervaded the Beaufort waterfront, except for the occasional squawk of a gull or the plop of a fish. Sunshine doused Georgie's bones in a warmth that fought off all her old-person aches. Fighting off was good because, honey, those aches were just part of what had worry settling in.

Sometimes it was there, swooping like a buzzard after kill, and sometimes she was herself, Georgina Warren, her thinking clear as the drips from the hose snaking through her flowers.

The horrible thing that would steal her self from her and make her vulnerable had begun, and that thought shamed her. Only she had no time for shame. Or for anything else.

She lowered herself onto her porch rocker. She had too much to fret about, plans to make, things to see to. Dee's visit wasn't supposed to happen today, but now it was coming. It didn't bode well, not for Dee's mama.

Georgie smoothed the skirt of her simple day dress—and wasn't that pattern pretty, the blues and grays with that hint of rose weaving in and out? Closing her eyes, she breathed in the sweetness of wisteria. Behind the sweet should have been the tang of salt from Taylor Creek, but the flowers masked salt and marsh mud. Lots of flowers, wisteria vines all over the place, taking over, pretty much, and blooming, loving the warmth. She ought to do something about the taking-over, but instead she lifted her face to the sky and breathed a thank-you to the heavens.

Why was she sitting outside and thinking about flowers? The question took a moment to settle, and then the answer floated close enough to the surface for her to grab it. Dee was threatening to upend her life. Fix things, Dee had said, for Georgie's good. To ease her mother through old age.

Georgie pressed her lips together. She didn't want Dee fixing anything. No, sirree. Dee could just hightail it back home to Chapel Hill because Georgie wasn't going to do what her daughter said. She wasn't batty or, anyway, not near enough to need managing. She wasn't. Fine, she might be slipping some, but she wasn't on the verge of becoming another Auntie Lorraine, who'd rocked away her last days in a back room at her mama's house, sputtering and muttering and needing her pull-up diapers changed. *Please, Lord.*

Georgie waved her hand to push the thought away, as if to brush off impending doom. She wasn't old enough or ready enough for either crazy or mind-empty. She wasn't.

Right after Dee said what she'd said about selling Georgie's beloved house, Isa'd promised to take Georgie to see a lawyer. They thought there'd be time before Dee would start on her, trying to get her to move into one of those places, only now Dee was on her way to Beaufort, so it had to be fixed today, to get that lawyer to protect her from her stepping-all-over-a-person daughter.

Right this minute, right now, sitting on her front porch and staring across at the sun-speckled water, with her mind running clear like the creek on an incoming tide, Georgie knew she had to act, and act fast. Dee was coming, and Dee's fixes weren't the same as Georgie's would be.

Isa said they'd be ready.

"Hang on," she told herself and those fleeting thoughts. "Don't go."

One of her books rested on the table between porch rockers. She picked it up and opened it to the bookmark between pages 51 and 52. She began to scan the words, enunciating them aloud to help them stick. But for the life of her, she couldn't remember a single thing that had happened before page 51. All those words seemed to have slid right on through and landed in some black hole. She turned back to the beginning, praying this time she could hang on before poof, it was all gone.

In and out, in and out. Her life. Her world. Her words.

———

Tea always helped her focus, tea and a quick nap in her chair. Indeed, indeed, focus was all she needed.

She drew the front sheers back and stared across the yard to the road and then the water. A stone fell, not into the creek but smack in the middle of her stomach as the worry grabbed hold again. What would happen, where would she go, what would she *do* when her mind went all the way into the abyss of nothing but a ten-second *now*?

No one wanted to imagine the end of memory, the end of being able to know the whens and whys. She'd thought she'd make it for a good while yet. She'd prayed she'd make it all the way 'til her eyes closed for the last time. After all, she was only seventy-nine. And, according to Isa, seventy-nine was the new sixty. She was healthy, active. But she guessed her brain cells had it in mind to age right on past the rest of her.

The phone's peal stirred her to action. She hurried to the kitchen. "Hello?"

"Georgie, it's Isa here. I wanted to remind you, your appointment with Eric Houston's this afternoon."

"Appointment?"

"Yes. You said you needed some help. A lawyer."

A lawyer. Georgie tried to grab that notion as she squinted toward the outside. Something was there, dancing around with the dust motes.

Isa's voice interrupted. "You said something had happened to your money. The bank called? And your daughter?"

The bank? And then the memory clicked into place. "Oh, yes. I remember. That nice Mr. Patterson phoned. Do you know him? He told me there'd been a couple of large withdrawals from my money market account."

"And you didn't withdraw anything."

"No. I'd have known, wouldn't I?" Wouldn't she have remembered going to the bank? "I've known Holland forever." The more Georgie considered what Holland had said, the more puzzled she grew. "I didn't spend more than I always do. There should be plenty of money for me to live."

"We'll talk to Eric about it."

She had to stay home because of her daughter. She couldn't leave. "Dee's coming. I have to be here."

"What time?"

"I don't know. She's on the way." When had Dee phoned? Hours ago? "It wasn't supposed to be today, but she decided."

At Isa's sigh, Georgie hunted for a better answer. Isa was her friend. "I don't want Dee to come."

"I know. That's one of the reasons we're going to meet with Eric."

"Eric?" Did she know an Eric?

"Your lawyer, Georgie. You asked for a lawyer."

"Okay. When?"

"At three o'clock. Do you want me to stop by at two to pick you up? Help you get out of the house?"

Did she? "Maybe." But Dee? "Dee won't let me leave without her, especially to see a lawyer."

"Don't tell her."

"I won't. But how do I leave?"

"If you can't find a way, call me. I'll help you manage."

"I don't know what you can say."

"We'll think of something."

Georgie wished she knew what that could be. But then the doorbell rang, and her conversation with Isa flew right out of her thoughts. She dropped the landline's handset on the counter and hurried to answer the door. Dee had come.

Dee sidled in around her, bag in hand. With a sigh that held absolutely no joy at seeing her daughter, Georgie stepped out of the way.

"Mama, look at you, lovely and spry as ever. You go to the hairdresser recently?"

Georgie patted her gray curls and made a sound that was supposed to mean assent. She couldn't say the same for her daughter. What was with that girl, styling her hair in that hoity-toity fashion, reddish highlights her black had never known naturally? Mighty pretentious for a woman who'd grown up right here in Beaufort. Dee also had dark circles under her eyes and a few extra pounds. Not pounds enough to be called fat, but her bosom pulled on her black sleeveless dress so it showed more of her underarm than she ought to like, and there was a tummy pooching out where it didn't used to be. It was bound to be bothering Dee, the way she always went on as if being anorexic were the next best thing to godliness.

They hugged. Or bussed cheeks. It seemed Dee had grown too sophisticated to hug her mother. Really? She'd rather kiss nothing?

Georgie turned away, waving toward the stairs. "You go on and get settled while I fix you a cup of tea."

"You sure, Mama?"

"Of course. You go freshen up."

"I'll be right back down as soon as I splash a little water on my face."

Georgie put the kettle on and glanced around. She must have imagined making tea earlier because there was no evidence of a cup, no saucer, no teabag. She got down the supplies.

The toilet flushed, and Dee's footfalls sounded in the hall above the kitchen and then on the steps. By the time she got to the doorway, Georgie had the teapot on the tray and cups lined next to it.

Dee had changed into something that gave her more breathing room. It was a good color, sort of like the inside of a ripe mango—the orange, not the yellow, kind.

"Nice shirt," Georgie said, because it was. "And flattering, honey."

Dee's smile flipped on and off so quickly that Georgie wasn't certain it had happened at all. "I'll get that, Mama," her daughter said, with a glance toward the pantry. "You have any of those good oatmeal raisin cookies?"

Did she? Had she bought any when Isa took her shopping last? Georgie checked in the pantry, and, yes, there was an unopened box. She handed it to Dee, who opened it and set several on a plate on the tray.

"And maybe a dollop of something in my tea, just to help me relax after that long drive." Dee seemed to know exactly where she'd find the bottle left over from her last visit. She drew it down, unscrewed the top, and added a good bit to one of the cups.

Georgie pretended that hadn't happened and followed her daughter toward the front of the house. But she couldn't imagine ruining a good cup of tea that way.

There, next to her chair, was the cup she'd used earlier. Georgie fussed with it, trying to get it out of the way so Dee could set down her newly filled one. The replacement cup. She should have cleaned up after herself. Dee would think so. Dee always complained about her clutter. But Dee didn't live here, did she?

"I was distracted," Georgie said, which she supposed was obvious.

Dee's lips only thinned.

They sat in chairs facing the long windows looking full on to Taylor Creek. Next to her bedroom, this was Georgie's favorite room because of how the light danced around, chasing itself as the hours meandered forward and boat traffic passed one way or t'other.

Gerard used to have himself a fishing boat, nothing fancy, but he sure loved to take off work and go play on it. When Dee was little, she'd head out with her daddy, and he'd let her hold the rod while he helped reel in a dolphin fish or a mackerel.

Then Dee got too big, too interested in other things. Their boy, Andrew, tried to take Dee's place, but Georgie remembered the hard look in his eyes, showing he figured he never measured up. The look was gone along with Andrew. Georgie supposed she missed her son.

She sipped her tea as Dee munched one of the cookies. "These are delicious," her daughter said, a tad too heartily.

Georgie closed her eyes, suppressing the worry about Dee's purpose, the why of her coming.

"Mama." Dee paused, and Georgie looked over at her. "Mama, I've been thinking. You know how lovely Chapel Hill is. Well, there's this wonderful place they've built, right on the edge of town, surrounded by woods and gardens. Lawrence's aunt just moved in, says she loves it, all the activities they have. The food's good, too, she says, and you know how much Lawrence's family loves good food."

"How delightful for her," Georgie said, but her fingers tightened on the handle of her teacup. She loosened them. She didn't want to break one of her mama's bone china cups with the little blue flowers painted all around.

"Yes, well, I've been thinking, Mama, that it's time to sell this house and move you nearer to me. So I can take care of you."

"Sell my house." Georgie didn't make it a question. She'd've thought Deborah and her brother would want to keep this place. Her daughter used to love being here. Loved the water. Andrew, too. Only Andrew had died of cancer, so it was only Dee.

"You're getting on in age, Mama. You're letting things fall apart here."

Dee kept saying "Mama" with every sentence, like she imagined Georgie might forget who she was talking to. Who else was here for her to be addressing?

"And, Mama,"—there, she did it again—"there's all that money Daddy left you. Somebody needs to manage it. I mean, it is my inheritance. Now that Andrew's gone."

Georgie felt her brows hike at that. Seemed like Dee was getting a little ahead of herself. Georgie kept her lips tight. Dee didn't need to know where the bulk of the money'd come from, that it hadn't been from Dee's daddy. He'd had a hefty insurance policy and cash put away, which Dee'd heard about when the lawyer'd sent her a copy of his will. But the big dollars and her stock portfolio had come from Aunt Ida.

Why hadn't Georgie mentioned that before? She let that question bounce around a couple of minutes while Dee pretended to study the front view, and then the memory skidded to a halt. She hadn't told because Auntie Ida had died after Dee and Andrew had already found their own path to plenty, and she hadn't seen any need to make them lust after more.

"I'll take care of you, Mama."

The lump solidified in Georgie's stomach. It sure seemed like Dee meant her mama was supposed to roll over and do what Dee wanted. Who cared if it was what Georgie wanted for herself?

"You know how much I love you." Dee's voice was a purr. Made Georgie not trust it. Too sweet, too sugary. "I just want what's best."

Georgie squinted at her daughter. What was best for whom? Dee or her? Because, honey, Dee wanted. Dee always wanted, always had.

Her daddy used to pull her on his lap and call her his sweet thing. She'd wiggle in, her head on his shoulder until he gave her anything she wanted, and now Dee thought her mama was going to just keep on doling out, filling her daughter's hands.

No. Georgie'd done that way too much already.

Dee was fifty-five years old. Her husband, Lawrence Melthorpe Buchanan III, could fill her up. Maybe not fill the Oliver-hole, but the greed one? Yes, sir.

"What's Larry doing these days?" Georgie asked.

"Gone down to Houston to make some new deal. You know Lawrence, always busy with some new way to make money or move it around." Dee rubbed her fingers across her forehead as if she wanted to smooth away something she didn't like.

"Truth, Mama? He's a philandering, no-good mess. He lied— again—but I saw him at the club with that floozy, that big-breasted, loose-lipped Carole Philips of the liposuctioned thighs and padded upper. Carole, who's been leaning over Larry and letting those *things* dangle near enough to make him bug-eyed."

"Oh, my. I'm so sorry. Are you sure, honey? I mean, he never seemed to me to be that kind of man."

"Oh, he said it meant nothing. She'd put out lures, but he hadn't responded. Sure, like I believe him." Dee huffed a breath. "He must think I'm a fool."

Georgie didn't know what to say because this picture of Larry was so hard to imagine. Larry had stuck by Dee even at her worst, and he'd been a good father to Jeminy. No, those had to be more of Dee's concoctions.

Georgie smiled as her daughter droned on about the benefits of her moving to Chapel Hill. But while Georgie still had some brain cells left, she figured on making a few plans of her own.

Dee set both empty cups on the tray and rose. "Now, Mama,

you and I both need to have a lie-down. So, you just go on up to your room, and I'll go to mine. Maybe tonight we can head to Front Street Grill for dinner. How's that sound?"

Dee had this habit of assuming everybody should want what she wanted when she wanted it. It had to have come from her daddy spoiling her. It had been different with Andrew. Gerard always told the boy he had to toughen up, so that was what he'd done. Then he'd gone off to college and married a New York girl named Aeriel. You'd think with a name like that she'd have something more than stiff and hoity-toity about her, wouldn't you? Maybe a penchant for art? Dance? No, she was a banker, just like Andrew had been. Money. Oh, how they all loved money and power.

Amazing how Georgie and Gerard had raised one who'd turned herself into a Carolina socialite, while the other had molded himself into a New York banker. Not a one of them with the values they ought to have had. Andrew and That Woman had been childless by choice—and now there was no do-over for him. Thank the good Lord, Dee and Larry had given her Jeminy and Oliver, even if they no longer had that precious boy child. It had been hard on them all, that death, but Georgie wondered if it might have been hardest on the twin left behind. Maybe. Or maybe on the parents? Hard to say.

At least Dee didn't try to help Georgie walk up her own stairs. But she did shut both doors after scanning Georgie's room. "What are all those piles of stuff, Mama?" Georgie didn't answer and soon heard the click of the lock on Dee's door, a habit she'd begun when her little brother used to pester her. No telling who she imagined would break in now.

Georgie sat down on her bed to think. Dee'd gone and opened herself up to wrong-headedness, and that couldn't be allowed to prevail over right. Something was working on her daughter's brain, making Dee believe untrue things while she tried to convince everyone else her beliefs were truth.

Calling white black and black white didn't make it so. And it was up to Georgie to fix things. Keep the white white and the evil far away.

Fix things. See Isa. She had to remember the what and the why. Focus, Georgie, just focus.

She waited to be sure Dee had settled herself before changing her dress and tiptoeing down the stairs and out the door, her purse under one arm. She paused for a moment to check to make sure all was in order and she hadn't forgotten anything she might need.

She could remember what had to happen before she went to town. And the way to town. They said a person doesn't forget the things repeated from youth, only the minute-ago things.

She hoped they were right. If she ever forgot Gerard, she might as well up and die.

The sun warmed her as she turned toward town, past the old Ware house where that cute little girl and her mama lived. Had she heard their story? She couldn't remember. They had to have one, though. Everyone has a story, certainly everyone who'd picked to live here from somewhere else.

Sunshine and water had brought Gerard back with her to Beaufort fifty-nine years ago. Gerard had his law degree and didn't want the rat-race of Raleigh, so he'd been happy to settle in her hometown.

She'd made new friends and rekindled old ones, although some had moved and some had died. She prayed she'd never forget a one of them, especially not Isa who had become dear in the years since she'd come home. Isa was the one she'd find today. Isa would know how to do this thing that needed doing.

3

ERIC

Somewhere in South Carolina, a Mrs. Finley wanted to reach Eric badly enough to keep on plaguing him with please-return-this-call voicemails, starting around ten when he'd been with a couple of clients and just now, during a meeting. As far as Eric knew, he hadn't left behind an untethered piece of his life when he'd moved north from Charleston to Beaufort. Well, hardly any.

He only half-listened as one of the partners droned on and on about things that barely touched him. While staring out the conference room window at the back gardens of Smith, Smith, and Welty, Attorneys-at-Law, Eric remembered the one unreachable, unclaimable bit he'd left there. He shut his eyes against the image of curly black hair, mahogany skin, and big brown eyes with lashes that would someday slay the ladies. From the first moment he'd held that squalling infant, those lashes had wowed him and everyone else who came close. What baby boy had killer lashes? None, they said.

Only Danny.

For four years, Eric had been a dad. Danny's dad.

Now he was only a support check. Money in, money out. He'd

fought hard in the beginning, pressing for custody, only Gabby's lies and her sugary drawl had been believed over his truth.

Eric heard his name and refocused his attention on the meeting. "Sir?"

"I'm giving you back-up responsibility on the Jones case. Dig a little deeper into that before the hearing, will you?" The senior Smith glanced at his watch. "We're scheduled to appear before Judge Cantor in a month's time."

"Yes, sir."

"Ask AnnaLouise for the files."

Eric nodded and stood as the others began to leave. At least they'd given him something he could get his teeth into during this week's meeting. He wandered back to his office, trying to focus on what was happening to Baron Jones, who was contesting a divorce that was threatening his livelihood. Unlike Eric's divorce, which hadn't been able to touch family assets, Baron's farming business and other wealth had been acquired during the marriage.

Divorces could be so ugly. Gabby's shyster lawyer had gone barreling into court, accusing Eric of abusing her and her son. Eric had denied everything. Then he'd countered and accused and filed enough paperwork to have decorated all the walls of the courthouse. It hadn't been enough. In the end the judge had awarded her full legal and physical custody of the boy and ordered Eric to pay child support. How, he'd have liked to know, had she paid her legal fees before he'd had to hand over a sizable settlement check? At least South Carolina hadn't made him touch the assets he'd held before she'd conned him into marriage and then divorced him out of it.

He poked his head into AnnaLouise's office. "Can you get me copies of the files on the Jones case?"

"Sure. I'll bring them."

While he waited at his desk, he tried to focus on his notes. His voicemail from that South Carolina woman couldn't be anything requiring immediate action. He no longer had to worry about the big Charleston family home; he'd sold it. The beach cottage was managed by a very capable agent. His divorce had been well and truly final for a couple of years. His support payments were direct deposit, so he didn't have to think about them or deal with Gabby. He'd left his former associates on good terms, but not friendly enough to maintain more than Christmas-card contact.

It was an hour later before he checked his phone messages again. This time South Carolina left more information. Avelina Finley of the Charleston County Department of Social Services asked him to confirm that he was the Eric Houston who had been married to Gabrielle Benson. If that information was correct, would he contact her as soon as possible.

Gabrielle? Why?

He returned the call, but was only able to leave a message. Fine. Gabby'd been gone three years. Not gone-gone, but gone from his life, except for that last hair toss after she'd affixed her signature to the papers. Of course, *her* gone had also meant Daniel gone.

Because visitation rights had been mere suggestions to Gabby, and he'd been too angry—and, yes, too worn down—to fight for the child. After six months of trying to connect with the boy, Eric had decided to let them go. Maybe one day Danny would remember him and come looking for the man who'd promised to love him forever.

Occasionally, guilt surfaced, but, hey, he was trying to live a good life. He gave money to one of those charities that fed and clothed children. He'd even volunteered at a soup kitchen when he lived in Charleston. Sure, he'd cared about Danny, but that hadn't worked out. It was what it was. Right?

Danny, the innocent babe who'd started it all and who'd ended Eric's naive assumptions about love and fidelity.

Blond-haired, blue-eyed Gabby had been pregnant, supposedly by him, but the little guy who'd emerged from her womb hadn't resembled either of them, not with all that curly black hair or that skin tone Eric would never have been able to achieve if he'd sunbathed on purpose every day of the year. He'd sat by her side in the birthing room, holding her hand as he asked the hard questions. She'd tearfully confessed that she didn't know who the father was, but she'd picked him because she loved him. "You lied to me, Gabrielle. You knew he wasn't mine from the beginning."

She'd shrugged those beautiful shoulders. "He might have been."

"No. Who is the father?"

"I don't have a clue."

"Well, he's a baby. He's not at fault. You are."

"There you go, shifting blame again."

Had he been so caught up in studying for the bar and writing for the Law Review that he'd missed her escapades with too many men to remember who might have fathered the child? He'd been with her sexually one time before marriage, a slip-up on his part because he hadn't been ready for long-term commitment and had never wanted to lead a woman on or make promises with his body he didn't intend to keep with his brain and his heart. But Gabby had known how to entice him to the point of no return. She'd probably already been pregnant when she'd seduced him because she'd needed a better baby daddy than the one who'd done the deed. And he'd been sucker enough to have taken the bait—forgetting his moral compass, forgetting his faith.

Still, with all the love his broken heart had left, he'd adored her son. He still did, really, only it was now from a distance, a zero-contact zone that pushed Danny into the recesses of his heart and mind except when some twist of a little-boy head, some laugh from little-boy lips reminded him and brought the hurt back, front and center. All he could do was push it down again and go on with his life.

But, yeah, that had been the beginning of the end, in spite of his efforts. And he had tried. He'd stepped up to the plate for the first years of Danny's life. If only Gabrielle had been able to remain faithful, they might have learned to love each other. He'd been too naive to recognize the issues that drove her to multiple beds, issues beyond his ability to solve, issues she seemed unwilling to address.

If a social worker was calling him, Gabby must have gotten herself in some kind of trouble. He sighed. He'd know soon enough.

He snatched up his desk phone when it rang. It wouldn't be the call he wanted, but it would be a distraction.

"Eric," the receptionist said, sounding slightly apologetic, "Isa Wellington and Mrs. Warren are here. They're early but wonder if you have time to see them now."

"Sure, send them back." Anything to change the tenor of his thoughts.

Eric thought of the woman he'd met a time or two when he'd been looking for a gift at Downeast Creations. Isa'd also been at a picnic at Will and Tadie's, hadn't she? Anyway, he pictured her waving be-ringed hands, tossing her mane of silver hair and dangly earrings, laughing easily.

Isa walked in, set her purse on a chair, and stared at him. Behind her trailed a small, elderly woman with curly hair that still held hints of yellow-blond. He thought he recognized her from the church he'd visited with his friend Clay.

"Ladies." He ushered Isa's companion to the second chair. He was about to introduce himself when Isa cleared her throat and then cleared it again. He turned her way and grinned. "Got something to say, Isa?"

"I do. This is Georgina Warren. You may have heard of her. She owns a house along Front Street, couple of doors from Tadie's. And we're hoping you're a good lawyer because she needs one."

He flashed a grin toward Mrs. Warren. "I'm happy to meet you. You attend All Saints, don't you?"

Mrs. Warren smiled and nodded. "You, too?"

"I've been a time or two."

She relaxed back in her chair, still grinning. "See, Isa? God picked this young man to help me."

Isa moved her purse and sat down. "Glad to know it." Although she looked anything but pleased.

"Why don't you tell me what sort of help you need, Mrs. Warren?"

Isa answered for her. "Georgina has some money. Well, she has a lot of money. But she's getting older, and now she's worried her daughter is trying to dictate her future, including what happens to that money, along with where she lives." Isa pulled out a bank statement. "And, this just happened."

He took the statement. It showed a hefty balance and two rather large withdrawals in the last month. "And?"

"Georgina didn't withdraw that money." Isa slid another few statements across to him. "As you'll see from her checking account, she receives regular payments from her deceased husband's retirement account, which is more than enough for her regular expenses. Most of her bills are on auto-draft, which I helped her set up last January so she wouldn't have to worry about remembering to pay them."

"Mrs. Warren, do you have any idea where that money from your other account might have gone?"

"No, sir. But my daughter, she has one of those powers of

attorney so she can take care of things. Only now she wants to make me move near her, like Isa said. I want to stay in my home."

"Have you reported this to the bank?"

"The bank is how we found out about it," Isa said. "Georgina got a call from them because the withdrawals didn't fit her pattern."

"Holland Patterson knows me. He was looking out for me."

"Excellent. Was he able to tell you at which branch the withdrawal was made? Or if it was an online transfer out?"

"Online?"

"By computer."

Isa shook her head. "I guess Dee went to one of the branches and flashed her POA. Then she set up online access. Holland said her actions weren't illegal, but they were concerning, which is why he phoned Georgie."

"Right. Can you tell me what sort of estate planning you have in place?"

"You mean, like a will?"

"Yes, ma'am."

"Well, I have one from a long time ago, but I'm not so sure I like it anymore."

"That's why we're here," Isa said, flipping that long hair over her shoulder. "To see what else you can do for her beyond just fixing her will. So no one can make her do what she doesn't want to do or take her money without her permission."

"I understand that. But bear with me."

The older woman stretched her hand to take Isa's and held on. "My daughter is in town. Dee says I have to leave Beaufort soon and go with her, but even if I'm losing my mind, it's not all gone yet. I figure I'd better do something to fix things while I can."

Eric leaned back in his chair and listened as first one woman spoke and then the other. By the time they'd finished, he had a pretty good idea of what needed to happen, but it wasn't going to make her family happy.

"Let me just check something." He excused himself and went out of the office.

It didn't take the secretary any time at all to access the database, print out the information, and hand it to him. He carried it back to his desk.

"Mrs. Warren, it looks like you did sign a power of attorney for your daughter about five years ago."

She glanced down at her lap and took a few moments while he and Isa waited silently. "She said she wanted to take care of me. In case I couldn't."

"Yes, but now you say you don't want her to have that power over you, am I correct?"

Isa patted Mrs. Warren's hand. "We're here to do whatever you want, Georgie."

"Dee wants to put me in an old folks' home. She wants to sell my house. I don't want that."

"Do you have anyone else you'd like to have help you? Anyone you trust to take care of you?"

"You mean like someone who won't take my money?"

"Yes, ma'am. And perhaps someone who can take care of you as you age. Do you have any other family?"

Her brow furrowed. "There's Jeminy."

Isa filled in the gap. "Jeminy is Mrs. Warren's granddaughter. She lives in L.A."

"She's a good, loving girl."

He caught Isa's eye roll but didn't know what that meant. "If your granddaughter lives in California, do you think she can be of much help here?"

Mrs. Warren glanced fearfully at Isa. "I don't know."

Isa smiled. "We'll call her, shall we? You and I?" The older woman nodded. Then Isa turned to Eric. "Can you protect Mrs. Warren in the meantime? Keep her daughter from using that power of attorney again?"

He waited for Mrs. Warren to speak. She seemed to realize she was supposed to, which was a good sign. He couldn't do anything to help her if she didn't ask for that help or if she weren't capable of knowing what she wanted.

"I need to stop her from taking over. I'd like you to fix that. Can you?"

"I can. But do you have anyone else to put in her place?"

"You mean, like Jeminy?"

"If that's who you would trust. Perhaps you could find someone local also. To deal with things here."

Mrs. Warren clutched Isa's hand again. "It's a lot to ask."

Tears filled Isa's eyes. "I love you, Georgie. Anything I can do to help, you know I will."

Eric looked from one to the other before going to the door and opening it. "Isa, would you mind stepping out for a few minutes?"

Isa bent over Mrs. Warren, who had that worried look back on her face. "I'll be right outside. You just answer Mr. Houston's questions, okay? We're going to take good care of you, don't you worry."

"That's good. It's what I want."

He waved Isa toward a small waiting area and asked AnnaLouise if she'd join him.

"Mrs. Warren, this is AnnaLouise Fulton. I wanted her here while I ask you a few questions. Is that all right with you?"

"Yes, sir. That's just fine. You ask me whatever you want. Isa seems to trust you, and I trust her. Besides, you go to my church."

Not that church attendance should weigh much in the balance. His father had attended one of the big Charleston churches, and he'd certainly not been a man of faith. Just the opposite.

Eric pressed that memory back where it belonged. "Okay. Now, for the benefit of our records, would you again tell us your name, your address, and your reason for coming here, including your thoughts about the power of attorney now held by your daughter, Mrs. Deborah Buchanan of Chapel Hill, North Carolina?"

Mrs. Warren didn't answer immediately, and Eric realized he probably should have simplified his question and asked for the information one piece at a time. But she surprised him and spoke calmly and firmly, giving her name, date of birth, Social Security number, and address. AnnaLouise took notes, smiling over at him when his new client rolled out more information than he'd requested.

After a short pause, Mrs. Warren continued. "My daughter wants to move me into an old folks' home near where she lives in Chapel Hill. She wants to sell my home out from under me because she figures she'll be a whole lot better at managing my money than I am. And, honey, she doesn't even have a clue how much that is."

"Now, I know I'm repeating myself, Mrs. Warren, but I need you to tell me this so AnnaLouise can record it."

"That's fine." She smiled at AnnaLouise, who smiled back.

"Then, Mrs. Warren, do you wish to have Mrs. Buchanan continue to be your attorney-in-fact, holding a power of attorney for you with the ability to act in your stead in any business dealing you might otherwise perform for yourself?"

She squinted across at him. "Like selling my house? And taking my money?"

"A power of attorney gives her the right to do things in your name. Normally, she shouldn't go against your wishes, but she would have the power to do those things, yes."

"Then, sir," she said, leaning toward him, "I don't want her to have one of those because I am no good at fighting her."

"Do you have anyone you trust enough who could take her place?"

"My granddaughter. And Isa. I trust them."

"Mrs. Warren, are you aware that if you give a POA to either of them, they could sign documents as if they were you? Do you trust them enough to give them that power?"

"Young man, I've known Isa Wellington since she moved to

this town, which was a good long time ago. That's been enough years for me to learn to trust her. She may seem flighty to some folks, but she's been a faithful friend to me. You just ask Hannah Morgan—or Tadie Longworth. I've known Tadie and Hannah all their lives. And they both know Isa."

AnnaLouise piped up. "Hannah and Tadie, Mrs. Will Merritt, used to be business partners at Downeast Creations. Now Isa and Hannah are."

Eric nodded. "I know them some."

"And I've known Isa since she moved here," Mrs. Warren repeated. "A long while ago now."

His paralegal looked over at him. "Yes, ma'am," AnnaLouise said at his nod.

"Am I to understand that you would like me to write up a new POA for you, Mrs. Warren, making Ms. Wellington the one who can sign checks and paperwork for you?"

"And Jeminy. You add Jeminy, too."

"Yes, ma'am. I'll need her full name and address. Do you have it?"

"I do." Mrs. Warren beamed at him and dug around in her purse.

Good. She could manage to find an address book and locate her granddaughter's place in it. And AnnaLouise could attest to that.

"My daughter, Deborah—we call her Dee, but she doesn't like that—she named Jeminy after somebody rich in Larry's family. Jemima Day Buchanan. But Jemima's too stick-uppity to my way of thinking. Gerard and I started calling her Jeminy when she was barely big enough to crawl."

"It's a lovely name." Eric jotted down the granddaughter's information and turned to AnnaLouise. "Will you ask Isa to come back in, please?"

Mrs. Warren stood, clasping her black purse in front of her, as Isa came in the door. "You're going to help me, aren't you, Isa?"

"You know I will. Always."

"Mrs. Warren," Eric said, "I'm going to need you to see your doctor and have him write me a letter attesting to your competency to make these changes. Can you do that?"

She nodded. "Yes, sir. Isa here can take me to see him. But you need to get on this today. My daughter's pushing."

"I'll have AnnaLouise draft a document taking away your daughter's Power of Attorney. You're sure that's what you wish to do?"

"I said so, didn't I? That's why I'm here. You do that right now, please. Before I go back home. My daughter's waiting at my house, and she may not let me come out again. She'll say I'm too crazy to be on my own."

Eric glanced over at AnnaLouise, who nodded back. "We can do that. Would you like to go next door to the café and wait?"

Isa gave her friend's forearm a light touch. "I think Georgina would be happier if we didn't go anywhere until we have something in hand. Is that okay with you?"

"Dee may come looking for me," Mrs. Warren said. "I've got to fix this first."

Isa leaned forward. "And, Eric, it's important you know Georgina came to me all on her own. She walked out of her house this afternoon when her daughter was napping and came to the shop to ask for my help, remembering that we had an appointment to see you."

Mrs. Warren nodded. "That's the God-honest truth. I couldn't worry what time it was. I had to get to Isa while Dee was down for a nap, and I did it."

"You certainly did, Georgie."

"My husband used to be a lawyer, only he's been gone a long time. Isa here knows me and knows I want to stay in my own home. And I have the money to stay there if no one takes it away."

"We'll try to make sure you can remain there, Mrs. Warren, for as long as it's feasible." He stood, nodding to his paralegal.

As AnnaLouise led the women out to wait in a conference room, he ran his fingers through his hair. He could tell this was going to be a mess. He could just tell. A small-town mess with everyone knowing the business in spite of his best efforts at confidentiality.

The scene in the conference room where Isa and Mrs. Warren waited caught Eric's attention when he emerged from his office. The women had their backs to him, and Mrs. Warren must have thought she was whispering, but her words carried past the doorway.

"We need to call Jeminy. We've got to fix this."

"They're fixing it, honey," Isa said. "Right now, I'm going to call Dr. Walford's office and get you an appointment. How about that?"

"Good. Dr. Walford is a good man."

"He is. And he's known you a long time."

"A very long time. He'll tell them I'm not too crazy to fix this, won't he?"

Isa patted Mrs. Warren's hand. "He will because you're not crazy. A little forgetful is all, and we're each headed in that direction."

"I'm more so. I know it. But I've still got enough of me left to fix this." Their hands rested on the table, and Mrs. Warren laced her fingers with Isa's. "I can still think, can't I? That's what matters. Thinking. That's what's important. Knowing what's right and what's got to be done."

"That's what you're doing. Getting the right thing done."

"I am." She shook her mop of silvered curls, making Eric smile. It was such an endearing gesture because it emphasized the worry he heard in her voice. "I'm not being too selfish, am I? Wanting this? Doing this?"

"Why would you think that, Georgie? Your daughter has plenty for herself, and the money you have is to fix things for your life, not hers." Isa paused for just a moment. "Relax. You're doing what needs to be done to protect the rest of your life."

He shouldn't be eavesdropping, but he did want to be certain he was doing the right thing in helping them change Mrs. Warren's earlier intentions. Isa's words encouraged him.

Isa held up a hand. Obviously the call had gone through to the doctor's office. She explained why they needed an appointment right away. "One o'clock tomorrow? That would be great. Thank you."

Mrs. Warren's head bobbed again, but when Isa ended the call, Mrs. Warren said, "I don't know what Dee will say."

"We'll work it all out. Don't you worry."

Eric turned away when AnnaLouise cleared her throat. He grinned sheepishly at the paralegal as she handed him the prepared paperwork.

"You want me to bring them to your office?"

Eric nodded and returned to his desk. "Just Mrs. Warren. I'll need a second witness."

"I'll ask Ruth."

Eric smiled encouragement when Mrs. Warren took a seat across from him. He explained that they would go over what they'd discussed, this time with a recorder on, and then Mrs. Warren would sign her name.

"Papers that will fix things?" she asked.

"Yes, ma'am."

They'd do that, and AnnaLouise would have them recorded across the street at the courthouse.

"And it will be fixed?"

"Almost. You'll see your banker and your doctor, and Dr. Walford will send me a letter. Then it will be fixed more permanently."

"We'll call my granddaughter to find out if she can help Isa."

"That will be good. Isa may need help."

He nodded to AnnaLouise, who turned on the recorder, and he went over the statements Mrs. Warren had made, asking her to repeat her requests and her reasons for making them. She was unhesitating this time, and she smiled proudly when they'd finished. She signed her name where he indicated, and the two witnesses did the same.

Then AnnaLouise gathered the paperwork. "Be back soon," she said.

He was about to escort Mrs. Warren to the conference room when another lawyer poked his head in to ask if Eric was almost finished. "I've got a closing and the other conference room's occupied."

"Not a problem. We can use my office." After all, Eric didn't have any other appointments that afternoon.

Isa joined them. "Is this okay?"

"Sure. AnnaLouise won't be long, and perhaps it would be a good idea to look at other steps we can take to help protect Mrs. Warren. Have you ever talked about setting up a trust and moving her accounts and her house into it? It would be an extra layer of protection for her assets. Why don't we discuss that?"

"We could. But I don't imagine you can make that happen today, right?"

"No. But we should be able to get things in motion fairly quickly if that's something Mrs. Warren would like to consider."

Isa pulled up a chair next to Mrs. Warren's. "Georgie, we're going to talk to Eric about setting up a trust for you, but I promised we'd call Jeminy. Can you give me her number?"

She turned to Eric. "That okay?"

"Of course." Eric pretended to study his computer, but he might as well admit it, if only to himself. He was curious, nosy even. Georgina Warren was his first elderly client and the first who'd wanted to undercut her daughter's power over her life. Oh, he knew family squabbles resulted in all sorts of control issues, but this was his first glimpse into a client's world beyond what he did for her.

Mrs. Warren dug through her purse and handed Isa her little book. "Under Jeminy."

Isa thumbed her way through the pages. "After this, shall we surprise Dee and invite her to meet up for dinner? She won't cut up if we're at a restaurant, will she?"

"Oh, glory. I'm not so sure about that. Dee can make a scene anywhere, especially if she's had a drink or two—and she had one soon's she got to my house." Mrs. Warren sighed. "I must have done something wrong in the raising of that girl. It couldn't have all been Gerard's fault."

"There may have been other causes, Georgie. Perhaps things that happened in Dee's life after she left home?"

"Maybe. But Larry's a good man."

Eric would like to know who Larry was. He'd guess the husband, but if so, he was obviously a husband who had no control over his wife.

Or maybe he just didn't care.

Isa had the granddaughter on the phone, and she handed it to Mrs. Warren. Although Eric leaned in a little closer, he could only hear one side of the conversation.

"Hey, little girl. I know you were just here not so long ago, but I need you, if you have the time to come. And if you want to, that is. You listen while Isa explains it, okay? She can do a better job. She's been helping me."

Isa took the phone back and began telling the granddaughter what had happened, leaving out a few things Eric would have mentioned. Then Isa said, "Say that again, honey, so your grandmother can hear you. I'm putting you on speaker."

Eric perked up.

"Nana? Nana, you won't believe this, but I'd already decided to leave California. I'll just change my ticket to New Bern."

"Oh, my," Mrs. Warren said. "Change your ticket? You have other plans?"

"Sweet Nana, no, none. I just wanted out of here. Of course, I'll help you in any way you need. It would be my privilege."

Eric's gaze focused on his client as she wiped her eyes.

"Precious girl." Mrs. Warren sniffed and then spoke to the phone, her voice louder than before, as if her granddaughter needed loud to hear across the space between Mrs. Warren's lips and the phone. "You don't do anything you don't want to, hear? If you're needed out there, I'll understand. I can make other arrangements, you know."

"I don't have a single thing keeping me here. I'll board a plane as soon as I can."

"I'll buy you a ticket. Isa will help me."

"Not needed, Nana. Thank you, though."

Isa leaned in. "Text me your flight information as soon as you have it, and I'll pick you up at the airport."

"Thanks, Isa."

Isa clicked off her phone, and Mrs. Warren beamed at her. "You see? My girl wants to come home." She turned toward Eric, as if he ought to be included in this. "Did you hear that?"

"I did."

Isa agreed. "Jeminy sounded thrilled. Interesting that she was already planning to leave L.A. I wonder why." She said the last in an undertone, which it looked like Mrs. Warren missed.

"And you'll pick her up?" Mrs. Warren asked.

"Happily."

"You're a good friend, Isa. A very good friend."

"As you are to me." Isa held the phone, ready to dial. "Dee now?"

The older woman looked down at her hands. "I'm frightened."

"I know you are, but Front Street Grill will be open. We'll call them and then we'll call Dee. Courage, Georgie. Courage." Isa raised her brows as she asked Eric, "That okay with you, Counselor?"

He grinned. No hiding his interest, obviously. "Perfectly fine with me. When AnnaLouise gets back, you may want to make sure the bank has a copy of the revocation of Mrs. Buchanan's POA. You can also give her one when you see her."

"Indeed."

4

DEBORAH

For a moment, after she slid the sleep mask off and plucked it from her head, Deborah squinted at the unfamiliar four-poster and the sheer curtains, and then she remembered where she was. Her mama's house. Her old room.

The afternoon sea breeze made the sheers fly, and she wished she might have wings to carry her out of this mess that was her life, the mess her *husband* had made of it.

But she would fix things, and her mother could help with that. Deborah was owed, wasn't she? All these years of putting up with the life she'd been dealt. She would be the dutiful daughter again in her mother's time of need, and everyone would see the truth that she knew how to step up to the plate, to protect her aging mother from herself.

She slipped into a light bathrobe. She had time for a shower, seeing as how her mama's door was still closed. Her hair could use a wash, so she took the time to pamper herself under the stream of water.

Hair dried and styled and a little make-up added to hide the circles Larry had given her, Larry and the bimbo, she opened her door to see if there was any sign of Mama having awakened. Then she went back to finding the right clothes for dinner.

Her elegant chemise was a tad on the tight side. Really, those cleaners must have used some sort of chemical that made clothes shrink. It had happened before, but when she'd complained, they'd denied all responsibility. Of course they had. No one took responsibility for his actions anymore. Look at Larry.

She waved off the thought. No, she would not think that way. She took a deep breath, released it, another deep breath, another release. All was well, or it would be once she got back to Chapel Hill with a plan and could confront her husband.

He'd deny it. He always denied it. But this time it wouldn't matter. She'd have the backing she needed and the excuse to use it.

Slipping into a pair of sandals, she wondered if the restaurant would be cold. Should she change into slacks?

Maybe so. Okay, the white ones were a little snug, but she would wear the silk overblouse that hid a multitude of sins. She checked herself in the mirror, added a touch more spray to her hair, and headed toward her mama's room. It was time to wake her. Then she'd fix a cup of tea so Mama would have the energy to go out.

She sighed, admitting she was the one who needed a pick-me-up. Mama had twice the energy she did these days. A little dollop of vodka in her tea? She'd be set.

No one answered her knock. She opened the door. Her mama's bed was empty, unmussed. Maybe Mama had gone downstairs while she was in the shower.

But the downstairs hid no one. Still, she wouldn't panic. Her mother wasn't that bad off yet, and this was Beaufort. Everyone knew Mama here. At least everyone on Front Street.

The backyard was empty. The side yards. She didn't see anyone she knew on the street, and there weren't so many folks loose that her mama would become invisible.

Back inside, she grabbed her cell phone, tried to think of someone to call. She didn't have a clue because it had been years since she'd lived here. Years since she'd spent more than a few days at a time in the town of her childhood.

She'd have to call the police if Mama didn't come back soon. But how embarrassing.

She needed that cup of tea, and she needed it badly.

She set the kettle on, reached up in the back cupboard for the bottle of vodka and poured a dollop in the bottom of her cup.

What would one shot hurt? She drank that, and by then the water'd come to a boil so she filled the cup to the halfway mark, dunked in a teabag, and topped it off with another shot. And then one tiny bit more to take the liquid to the cup's brim, just to get her through the wait. Her stomach began to warm and finally to relax. She put her bottle away—in case Mama came home—and carried her cup to the living room. Another glance out the front door to an empty street, and she flung herself into one of the ancient wingback chairs.

Her curse was muted by alcohol, but she didn't stifle either it or the one that followed.

Her mother wasn't a missing person, not a person lost or hurt, not one who'd fallen and hit her head, not on Deborah's watch. Not again, never again.

No, no, no.

Her hand shook as she lifted the cup to cold lips. She closed her eyes and tightened her grip. This time, all would be well. She'd fix it all, make her mother safe with people who wouldn't let anything happen to her.

Because never again.

And then her phone rang with a number she didn't recognize.

5

JEMINY

Dark clouds poofed before the sun, the baking warmth, awakened light;
And just like that, the rain was gone, dried were the tears, a new day
dawned.

Jeminy didn't—wouldn't—care that her life had been reduced to a moderate savings account and the plans she now had to make. Nana's call precipitated her decision to move out of Los Angeles, and that was no bad thing. It was past time.

This place of promise and glitter had captivated her until she'd looked more closely at its underbellies, from enclaves peopled with the untouchable elite to Skid Row's un-helped homeless. Many of those living in between stumbled around on the verge of bankruptcy as they clawed toward access to the gated communities. Once upon a time, she'd been on the fringes of money and fame.

She didn't—wouldn't—care about the trappings of her big-city life she'd be leaving, not the BMW she'd thought hers, not this apartment.

In Beaufort, she'd have her grandmother. Nana was the one who'd paid for her trip to Europe and who'd been so supportive of her music. Nana'd listened to her early songs and applauded her successes. Along with Daddy and Rose, Nana'd helped her survive without Olli in those days when Mother had tumbled deeper and deeper into a darkness of her own, a darkness that had changed her from a disinterested mother to a demanding and judgmental one.

The only available flight to New Bern was an overnight out of LAX to Charlotte, and then a quick dash to catch a puddle jumper to the coast. She texted the information to Isa. Almost immediately, her phone dinged with a *See you soon.*

In Beaufort, she'd have time to figure out how she was going to support herself—and time to find a decent lawyer to help with those stolen royalties. The police had all the information she could give them about her dealings with Rand. All that remained to her were regrets.

Weak and stupid, thy name is Jeminy. "But," she said with a toss of her hair, "you don't have to stay that way."

One step in front of the other. She picked up a few boxes from the local market, not many, because she cared about very little from this life. There was too much shame wrapped up in the things Rand had insisted they couldn't do without. He could either take what she left or have it hauled off.

Tomorrow, it would be off with the old and on with the new, whatever that was and wherever it would take her and her guitar. A few more hours and this place would be on the way to being forgotten.

Please.

She'd wasted too many days and months and years—yes, years —with a man who...

Who what?

Who'd been...

How had she ever let him have such power over her? Take so much from her?

On that thought, she picked up her phone and called her landlord. When he heard why she needed to be released from the lease, he said, "You gotta take care of family. I get that."

"I'll text my ex-boyfriend to tell him to move the rest of the stuff out, but you can call him if he dawdles." She recited Rand's number. "I'd be very grateful if you didn't tell him where I'm going."

"Not a problem. He on the lease too?"

"He is."

"Then you don't got to worry about nothin'. I'll send him the bill, he don't move the stuff first."

Wouldn't that be a treat? To worry about nothing? Although, she suspected her worry was just changing locales from West Coast to East.

She had five hours to declutter and shred personal papers she didn't want to take with her. And then Maggie, who hated Rand more than she did and didn't trust him further than she could spit, would pick her up and take her to FedEx and the airport.

For the first time in weeks, Jeminy's smile felt real.

6

GEORGINA

Georgie wilted as she returned the phone to Isa. Dee had sounded so cold, so angry. "That was hard."

"I know, but don't worry." Isa's voice was soothing as she ushered Georgie out of the lawyer's office and to the sidewalk. "No one yells at Front Street Grill. Not even Dee."

"I hope not." She wasn't convinced, because her daughter liked to get her own way, but she followed Isa across the street.

"First off," Isa said, "we're going to take this paper to that nice Mr. Patterson at the bank, and then Dee won't ever again be able to use that power of attorney against you."

"If only she'll be nice." But Georgie knew her daughter, and nice had flown away years ago.

When they handed the paper to Holland Patterson—what a kind young man!—Georgie felt a little better, a little more courageous, which lasted all the way to the steps leading up to the restaurant. If her mind were going to wander in and out, she wished it would toddle off about now and let her forget their purpose tonight.

The hostess seated them at a back corner table with a view of the creek and all the boats heading in and out of the channel.

Georgie concentrated on one in particular, a boat driven by some young person who knew what he was doing. It wasn't a big boat, but she bet it would be a fast one. And they were heading to the dock outside the window.

How lovely, coming by boat to dine. Gerard would have liked that. She wished he were here with her now because he could control Dee. He wouldn't let Dee take over.

She glanced at the hand Isa squeezed. Isa smiled and said, "You look beautiful in that dress. I love the roses in the print, and you can sit proudly here. You're doing what's right, that's the big thing. And you're going to be great."

She wasn't supposed to worry. Isa was here, and Isa said she looked good. Georgie had to admit that having a nice dress on made all the difference. Her mama'd always said that half the battle was looking good when you had to face someone mean. Mama'd never have imagined the mean person would be Georgie's own daughter.

And, oh my, there came that daughter, barreling toward them, weaving around tables. When Dee opened her mouth to speak, Georgie took a deep breath and said, "Sit down, Deborah," in her mother-voice. Hearing it, she let go of Isa's fingers, reminding herself that her daughter could do nothing to hurt her now. Isa and the lawyer had promised.

Dee's face had a sheen to it, as if she'd been running, but she wouldn't have run anywhere and certainly not in public.

Isa patted a chair. "Hello, Dee."

"Deborah." Dee always did get huffy when someone used her nickname, except for when her daddy had.

Georgie turned back to looking at the water. Gerard shouldn't have died and left her alone.

"Georgie?" Isa's voice brought her head around. "You still want iced tea?"

"Yes, please."

Dee ordered a vodka martini. Had her gait been a little

wobbly? Seemed so to Georgie, but what did she know? Georgie'd never liked martinis, even in the days when she'd drunk alcohol. Years ago, Dr. Walford'd said it wasn't good for her, so she'd quit.

"Mother." Dee had dropped the familiar *mama* and opted for formal.

Georgie sat up a little straighter. She could do formal. She had Isa, and back at that office, she had the lawyer.

Those puffs under Dee's eyes made them look squintier than usual. She cleared her throat, a habit that showed she was nervous, and then she rushed into speech. "I have been frantic with worry. Where have you been all afternoon?"

"Here comes your drink," Isa said.

That had been quick. Thank God for quick and for Isa.

Look at that, Dee accepting the drink without even a thank-you to the server. Georgie'd taught her daughter better, so she said the thank you in Dee's stead.

The waiter smiled. "Yes, ma'am. And here come your teas," he said as someone else set drinks in front of her and Isa. "Are you ready to order yet?"

"I would like the flounder," Georgie said.

Isa nodded. "Make that two."

Deborah didn't even glance at her menu. "The salad special with filet."

"How would you like your filet cooked?"

"Medium rare. Pink, not bloody."

As he collected their menus, Isa drew an envelope from her purse. Georgie kept her focus on her friend, imbibing strength from Isa, because that envelope held papers Dee would hate.

Isa smiled at her, then turned to Dee. "Your mother was concerned about some of the plans she felt you were making for her without her consent, not to mention some rather large withdrawals from her money market account that she hadn't made." Isa kept her voice neutral. Neutral was soothing, especially when she sent Georgie a quick smile. "After her banker alerted her, your mother asked for my help."

"Why didn't you ask me, Mama?" Dee asked, stirring her martini with the tooth-picked olive. She looked beseechingly up before extending her hand toward Georgie. "Why, Mama, would you go to Isa instead of your own flesh and blood? All you had to do was tell me what you wanted. I am here to help you. I'm your *daughter*."

That last was true, but not the rest. "Yes, but you didn't ask me how you could help me do what I want. I still have brains enough to know you had your mind made up. I don't want to go to Chapel Hill. Or anywhere. I want to stay in my own home."

"And that doesn't explain the withdrawals, Deborah. They were managed using your power of attorney, and they were taken without your mother's knowledge."

"You don't know anything, Isa Wellington. Besides, what business is it of yours? I was making arrangements for my mother's accommodations in Chapel Hill. For her benefit."

"Can you provide documentation to that effect?"

"What are you? The police? My mother's keeper? That's not your job; it's mine. She's *my* mother." Dee swigged a huge gulp of her drink and waved toward the waiter for another. "Mama, you're getting on, and your memory isn't what it was. How can you possibly stay home alone?"

Georgina remembered they'd talked about this with that lawyer. She caught Isa's nod and her smile and finally said, "I will pay someone to stay with me. I have the money."

"That will cost twice what you'd pay in a nice retirement home. And who knows if the person you hire can be trusted? I've heard stories. They could rob you blind, and you wouldn't know the difference."

"Jeminy's coming."

"Jeminy?" Dee waved one hand dismissively. "She lives in L.A. Why would she come to Beaufort?"

"She and Isa are going to make sure I'm fine." Saying so gave Georgie a surge of happiness. Nothing could happen to her. Not with Isa and the lawyer and Jeminy. Who'd promised, all of them.

Dee upended her glass and swallowed the last drop, licking her upper lip, and smiled in a not very nice way with barely a nod at the waiter as he set a new drink in front of her "No, they're not. I can't allow it. I think I know what's best for you." She glared at Isa. "A whole lot better than some casual friend. Certainly better than my flighty daughter, who went off to California with her loser boyfriend." Her voice dripped disgust. "To work in *Hollywood.*"

"She's coming home. She's not going to be in Hollywood."

A few strands of Dee's hair flew out at the shake of her head. "I'm sorry, Mama, but that's just not going to work." She smiled that little smile in Isa's direction, the one that didn't have a speck of truth behind it. "This is the sort of help you've given her? Convinced her to invite a child to come here? A child who will probably stay a month or two and then hightail it to who knows where when the next boy comes along?"

"It's what Georgina wants. And if Jeminy leaves, we'll find someone else to move in. Your mother has the resources to choose how she wants to live. And she has the right."

Dee swiveled away from Isa, back toward Georgie. "You seem to be forgetting that I'm your attorney-in-fact, Mama, and that gives me the right to take care of you and make decisions for you when you're not capable of making them for yourself. Which has obviously come sooner than any of us expected."

Isa pushed the envelope across to Dee, and Georgie's nails dug into her palms. She welcomed the discomfort, which was better than thinking about Dee's mad.

"What's this?" Dee asked.

When no one answered, she opened the flap, spread the paper out in front of her, and turned a very unfortunate shade of red before she ripped the document in two pieces. It took her a minute to get her lips to stop sputtering. Little wrinkles lined their edges, like an old lady's, but Dee wasn't old. The wrinkles shouldn't have been there, not on her daughter's lips. Georgie patted her own.

She couldn't feel lines, but that didn't mean she didn't have any. "Did you know your lips are crinkling up, Dee?" Georgie pointed to the edges of her lips to demonstrate. "Right here. You're not old enough for that to happen, are you?"

"Mother." Dee sounded disgusted as she turned to Isa. "You see? You think she's capable of making sound decisions?"

"She knows what she wants."

Dee glared. "You won't get away with this." She extended the pieces of the paper she'd ripped. "I won't stand for it."

"That's only a photocopy of the original, which has been filed with the Clerk of Court and given to the bank. Your mother met with her lawyer, who drafted a new power of attorney according to your mother's wishes and, as you read from that notice, canceled yours."

"My mother, I'll have you know, is not capable of understanding what she wants or what is best for her. I'll take you to court. You will not win."

Georgie stretched her hand out. "Honey, this isn't about you. It's about what *I* want. How I want to live the rest of my life."

Dee leaned across the table. "You don't know what you want."

Georgie backed away from the hissing voice.

Dee continued. "You, Mother dear, don't know what's best for you. This is not my last word. Larry will fix things, Larry and our lawyer."

The waiter approached with a tray of plates.

"Pack mine up," Dee said. "I'm leaving."

"Yes, ma'am." He set two plates of fish on the table and took Dee's back to the kitchen.

"We will see about this, Mother." Dee finished her drink and stood. "This woman has unduly influenced you. And I'm not going to stand for that."

She walked purposefully to the end of the bar. When they handed her a to-go box, she held her head high and headed to the door. The slight wobble in her gait ruined the effect, but Georgie couldn't laugh.

Her heart hurt. She stared down at her food. Her stomach had gone all fluttery. "She's so angry. I said she'd be angry."

"Yes, we knew she would be. Pick up your fork, honey, and let's enjoy our dinner."

"She's spoiled, Isa. That's the trouble with Dee. She's used to getting her own way."

"I know."

Georgie did what Isa said because getting upset about Dee wasn't going to help.

"I'm glad you're seeing Dr. Walford tomorrow," Isa said.

"I know. He'll say I'm okay. That I can choose."

"I'm sure he will. You did very well at the lawyer's today. You spoke clearly about what you wanted, and you did it without me in the room. AnnaLouise was a witness."

"Dee tore up that paper."

"She did. But it doesn't matter. We have another copy of it, and the original's in the courthouse. She can't undo what you chose to do."

"She's going to try."

"I know she is. But I'm here, your lawyer is here, and Jeminy will be here very soon."

"When?"

"Tomorrow morning. I'm to meet her."

"You don't think it's too much, asking Jeminy to come?"

"I think it's perfect."

"She likes it here. She always has."

"I know."

"But what if Dee's right, and it's too much? What if Jeminy doesn't want to stay?"

"Then we'll do what we told your daughter. We'll hire

someone else." Isa laid her hand gently on Georgina's. "What you need to remember is that your money is there to take care of you, not to enrich your daughter or anyone else. If there's some left at the end, great. If it takes every penny to make sure you have the life you want, then that's fine, too."

"Dee has money."

"Yes, so you don't need to worry about her."

Georgie looked out over Taylor Creek as the boats came and went, and she smiled. "And Jeminy's coming home."

7

ERIC

Eric's pens were aligned in a neat row at the right side of his desk blotter, and he'd locked his files away before the Charleston Social Services woman, Mrs. Finley, finally got back to him. She repeated her question. "Are you the Eric Houston who was once married to Gabrielle Benson and is stepfather to Daniel Benson?"

"I am. Although that should be Daniel Houston."

He couldn't wait to hear the whys of this call. He hadn't seen his son since the final settlement meeting in spite of asking for his rightful visitation. Instead of granting that or answering any of his letters, Gabby'd moved away. Disappeared—except for that link via the bank. He supposed he could have gone after her, but...

"I'm afraid I have bad news about your ex-wife, Mr. Houston. Gabrielle Benson died in a motorcycle crash that left no survivors. It took us a while to track you down as the child's only living relative."

"Danny." He didn't make it a question.

"The minor child has been placed in foster care in Summerville until we can reach a relative. That means you. As you can imagine, he's very confused and hurting."

The thought of foster care made Eric want to yell at his self-indulgent, self-absorbed ex, the beautiful, broken Gabby, who'd taken herself completely out of reach of his anger—or anyone else's. "Where was Danny when his mother was killed?"

"With a babysitter. A teenage girl who lives in a neighboring trailer."

"They live—lived—in a trailer?" With all the money he gave for Danny's support?

"In a trailer rented by the other victim."

"Well, Mrs. Finley, I'm going to need you to send me more information. I'm not exactly in the best position to have him with me, but I would think the support payments I make should allow something better for him than foster care."

"You'll need to make the arrangements."

What a mess. A seven-year-old child dumped in foster care. It made his throat tighten to think of it. "Can you email me what you have, documents, the foster family's information?"

"Text your email address to this phone, and I'll take care of it."

"Thank you. I'll be in touch."

He disconnected the call and sent her the requested text. And then he sat there, remembering the boy who'd been four when Gabby'd driven off in the car he'd bought her, with everything she could possibly cram in it, minus the furniture they'd lovingly chosen for the child who was supposed to be theirs. The child he'd fallen for in spite of Gabby lying that he'd fathered him.

"I'll tell you where to ship the kid stuff," she'd said by way of goodbye.

Now Danny needed rescuing, but how could it be by a once-upon-a-time father who was single and lived on a boat?

He opened his email app. While he waited for word from DSS, he cleaned out his cluttered Inbox and checked his Instagram account. He'd uploaded a total of five images, mostly scenes of wild ponies and dolphins because those gave away nothing but his affinity for nature. By having an account and following his new circle of friends in Beaufort, he could keep up with their activities without actually having to engage with them on a regular basis. And, no, he wouldn't wonder what that said about his state of mind.

Okay, most of those friends had posted dog pictures, a few with kids in them, along with scenic shots of sailboats from Will and Clay, and foodie photos from Agnes and Eric's brother, Henry. Agnes would be thinking wedding food—as well as wanting to show off Henry's creations. Eric could appreciate how good she was for his brother.

For all Hen's issues, he was the one who'd chosen wisely. Not his supposedly perfect twin. Nope. Not Eric.

A ping sounded on his phone, and there it was, the information about Danny. He moved to his computer.

Eric didn't want to open the attachments. He was responsible, he guessed, but how could he help the child more than monetarily? He doubted Danny even remembered him. Three years was, after all, a long time in a little boy's life, especially when it amounted to almost half of that life.

Eventually, of course, he had to read what she'd sent. He downloaded the files and hit *Print*.

The foster home looked decent on paper, but paperwork could lie. People lied. Besides, the state wasn't going to let Danny stay there now they'd found him, the next of kin.

Worry niggled at him. He'd loved Danny. For four years, he'd acted as the boy's father even if he hadn't been by birth, and even if Danny'd forgotten him, Eric hadn't stopped caring about the innocent being who'd stolen his heart.

He needed to drive down to see for himself what kind of place Gabby's death had left the child in. Maybe the home was one of the good ones, a loving family wanting to help others. Maybe he could work something out with them.

Summerville was what, maybe six hours by car? He could go over the weekend, not miss anything here.

Gabby's death barely touched him. Forgiving her had been hard, but he'd recognized her brokenness and his need to let her go. In spite of Gabby's deception, Eric hadn't been able to toss her and her child out. Instead, he'd taken over fathering Danny.

When he'd nearly fallen apart because of the sudden loss of Danny, a loss that felt like a death, he'd sought counseling in a grief support group. There, he'd come to grips with his need to rescue and his guilt over failing his twin when Henry'd needed saving. Stepping up to the plate for Danny had eased that guilt. He'd imagined he could save the little boy and make up for not being able to fix Henry, the one person who'd been his to protect all the years of their boyhood.

Danny was, and then Danny wasn't—at least not in Eric's life.

Why couldn't life be simple—get up, go to work, do good for others, see friends, go home to his beautiful boat, rinse and repeat?

He was only Hen's elder by a matter of minutes, but somehow the first-born caretaker role had taken hold and extended beyond his brother. He'd rescued his twin countless times, then he'd rescued Gabby and her child—although he'd thought the baby his —and now?

Had he learned nothing in the years since then? Henry, praise God, had saved himself with the help of his faith. But what about Danny?

A seven-year-old child.

Escape was docked off Front Street, not far from the marina office, down a few slips to the third-from-last finger pier. He climbed onboard, unlocked the companionway door, and flicked on the converted kerosene lantern. A soft glow illuminated the boat's gorgeous teak, perfect for sitting back and listening to music, which is what he planned to do now.

His laptop stared morosely from his nav station. His laptop and his unfinished novel.

He ought to write. The novel had become a joke between him and Henry, the Great American Whatever he fell back on when things got tough. And they were tough now.

He wished he could talk to Henry about Danny. Did his twin even realize he'd once been married to Gabrielle? Eric couldn't remember where his brother had been in his in-and-out-of-the-hospital, in-and-out-of-rehab journey when Gabby and Danny had happened. Hen hadn't made it to Eric's law school graduation or to the quick wedding shortly after that, and his twin certainly didn't know why the marriage had ended. Or why it had begun. If he remembered it had even happened. What a strange thought that was.

Four years a father and his own brother unaware? That was sad, but whose fault had it been, after all?

By the time Henry got away from the restaurant and had said a proper goodnight to Agnes, it would be too late to bring him up to speed.

Eric's thoughts kept returning to Danny, a child with no place else to go. No maternal grandparents. No aunts and uncles on his mother's side. An unknown sperm donor. All Danny had, it seemed, was the man paying for his support. The man who'd loved him and cared for him until he'd no longer been allowed the privilege.

Back then, he'd imagined deserving what had happened, the consequence of failed choices. He'd wiped his hands, kicked off the dust, and moved here.

"I live on a boat in another state," he said to the walls of that boat, to the empty spaces that were perfect for him but wouldn't accommodate a seven-year-old boy. "I have no backup system, no wife, no safety net for a kid."

What was he supposed to do?

"I get that people like Will Merritt take their daughter sailing, but I can't go off." Will had worked remotely during those years. Eric had an office he had to go to and no backyard other than a dock.

And, no, he couldn't imagine letting a little kid loose on a dock even if he swam like a champ. Taking the child wouldn't work.

It couldn't.

But he had to find out. Wherever that finding out led him.

⸻

Eric hadn't discussed Danny's situation with anyone in Beaufort, mostly because he didn't exactly know what the child's situation was. He couldn't take the time to get into a long conversation with Henry—and explanations would be long. Instead, he left a message on Henry's phone saying he'd have to postpone dinner at *Agua Verde* and was sorry to miss his brother's planned menu. He was headed to South Carolina on business.

That would have to do for now.

He'd given AnnaLouise a heads-up on a few pending cases should he be late returning. "I may have to be out on Monday, so watch for anything that needs attention, will you? You can always text or call."

He packed a few things and headed south that evening after he'd arranged to meet the social worker.

⸻

The next day, Eric followed Mrs. Finley's directions to a small diner south of Summerville. She was already seated, a cup of coffee in front of her, when the waitress led him to her table. He slid into the booth across from her. "Thank you for coming out on a Saturday," he said after he'd introduced himself.

"Honey, it seems I work all hours. Would you like something, coffee, a slice of pie? They make the best peach pie anywhere." She said this as the waitress slid a small plate in front of her.

"Same for me," Eric said. He hadn't thought he could be hungry again, but that pie looked delicious.

"Heated?" the waitress asked as she turned over Eric's cup and filled it with coffee. "You need more cream?"

"No thanks, but heated pie would be great."

"Be right back."

He wasn't sure he was going to be able to drink the coffee, but he stirred in one packet of sugar, hoping for palatable. His first sip confirmed his fears. Perhaps the pie would be better. He loved pies, and peach was a favorite—or it had been when their cook at home had fixed it, years and years ago.

He turned his attention to Mrs. Finley. "What do you know about the foster parents that wasn't in the report?"

"Not much, really. Today, you and I are going to make an unannounced visit so we'll have a clearer picture of how they manage."

"Good. That's what I was hoping for."

"Have you had any contact with Daniel since your divorce from his mother?"

"I haven't. The support payments go directly into a bank account we set up, but I don't have access to it other than that. Gabrielle always cast blame on everyone else so she wouldn't have to accept any for herself."

"I've met Daniel. He's a sweet boy, but he's bound to have some issues with trust, seeing as how his mother moved around so much. She was an educated woman, though, wasn't she?"

"She had a degree in education, but she quit teaching after the baby came. I was fine with that, and it worked until she took up with another man. That's when things fell apart, and she ultimately left with him."

A steamy slice of pie slid into place under his very appreciative nostrils. "Smells incredible," he told the waitress. "Thank you."

After the waitress left, Mrs. Finley said to Eric, "When I interviewed Daniel, he said he didn't have a daddy. Said he'd had one, but that didn't work out because you hadn't wanted him, so his mama had rescued him and taken him away."

Eric bit back the word he wanted to say. "Of course that's what she'd tell him."

"You said she had a habit of transferring blame."

"She wanted to be gone."

Mrs. Finley shook her head. "No understanding some folks, is there?"

"I guess it's going to be hard, then, seeing him. Or rather, him seeing me."

"Probably. When you're ready, though, we can get it over with and find out what's what."

He scooped up his last bite. "How many kids are in this home?"

"Five, if I have it right. I didn't do the placement, but I did check on him after I took over the case."

Eric finished his pie and stood, leaving bills enough to cover both their orders and a generous tip. "Let's do it."

He followed her as they drove south and out into the country where a lot of the homes were small, old, and poorly maintained. The foster parents' house was down a rutted dirt lane, the second of two double-wides. There was an old swing set and a couple of rusting bikes in the front yard. A dog yapped out back.

Mrs. Finley approached the screen door and stopped, waving at him to be silent. Someone in there was yelling. Another voice added to the first, and then a child's cry could be heard, followed by more yells and a "Git yourself cleaned up and go do your chores. Now."

A small voice answered. "Yessir."

Eric wondered why only adult voices were making a racket. With five kids in the house, there ought to be children's voices somewhere.

Mrs. Finley had yet to knock on the door. Footsteps came into the living room. "I'll have my lunch in here. And get me a beer!" the man called before springs settled as if he'd dropped down into a chair.

Mrs. Finley seemed to brace herself. Then she knocked. The man called out, "One of you come see who's at the door!"

A girl, probably around twelve or so, approached and opened the door all the way. "Yes?"

"Hello. I'm Mrs. Finley from DSS. May I come in?"

The girl turned away. "It's Mrs. Finley."

"I don't know any Mrs. Finley. Mary!" the man called.

"Mary's the wife," Mrs. Finley told Eric.

"You want me to let her in?" the girl asked.

"Mary!" came the man's voice again.

"She's with the baby," the girl said.

"She's supposed to be fixin' my food. Drat the woman."

"Mr. Jenkins," Mrs. Finley called through the screen door. "I'm from DSS and am here to do a home inspection."

"We didn't have no appointment for today."

"No, sir. We often do them spontaneously. May I come in, please?"

"I suppose if you gotta, but you shoulda called."

"Thank you," she said, opening the screen door and nodding to Eric to follow. "I need to see your wife and the children, please."

A rail-thin man with a narrow face that had an oversized nose, easily twice what his face should have to bear, waved her on to the back of the house. "She's back there someplace." He turned to the girl who'd first answered the door. "You, there, go get my lunch. Hand me the remote first."

Mrs. Finley looked at the girl. "What's your name, honey?"

"Gretchen, ma'am." She bent to get the TV remote off the floor and handed it to Mr. Jenkins.

"Gretchen, where are all the other children?"

"In the children's room, ma'am."

"Can you show me the way?"

Eric wanted to yank that man off his easy chair and shake him, but he kept his mouth closed and his fists at his side as they followed Gretchen down a dark hall. When they got to the room Gretchen indicated, an overweight woman who must have been Mrs. Jenkins handed a baby to one of the older girls and told her to keep him happy.

Then she turned. "Who're you? And who let you in?" She squinted at them before rolling her shoulders. "Oh, yeah, you're the new social worker. We didn't have no appointment today."

"No, you didn't. This is one of our unannounced visits. We need to see how the children are doing."

"Who are you?" The woman inspected Eric, head to foot.

"He's with me," Mrs. Finley said.

Eric looked around at what Gretchen had called the children's room. It had a table and a couple of small chairs, a crib, and a TV. A few books were stacked in a corner, but all the children were glued to a cartoon. Eric didn't think they should be indoors watching TV, especially on a sunny day. Why weren't they outside playing?

He didn't see Danny among them. Mrs. Finley must have noticed his absence at the same time. "Where's young Daniel?"

Mrs. Jenkins shrugged. "Probably in the bathroom. He had spills down his front. Husband told him to change."

Eric looked for the bathroom in question. A closed door at the end of the hall must be it. "Maybe he needs help."

"I wouldn't," the foster mother said.

Eric ignored her. He knocked quietly on the door. At first there was only silence, then a tentative "Yes?" that he answered with a gentle push to open the door and a quiet "Danny?" He stepped inside.

The boy's eyes were red-rimmed, his nose a little runny, and his shirt halfway off. But the quick light of gladness when he saw who was there nearly knocked Eric over. He sat on his haunches and looked the boy in the eye. "I've missed you, son."

Danny gulped hard and turned away. "No."

"Yes. I hated that your mama took you from me."

"You never ever wanted me. She told me."

"But I did, Danny. You were my son."

"Not your real son. Not white like you."

"White, black, purple, who cares?" He felt the boy's tension and saw the little-boy muscles clench in those skinny arms. "Come here, let me help you with that shirt."

There was a button in the back—it was probably supposed to be in front—that Danny hadn't been able to release. Eric didn't ask how he'd put it on in the beginning but went about unfastening it and helping Danny get out of a shirt that smelled an awful lot like baby spit-up. When he had the child free of the shirt and into a clean one—a little grayed from being washed with dark colors—he smiled and said, "Did that baby barf all over you?"

"They yelled at me, but it was Timmy. I picked him up because he was crying and nobody would hold him."

"You did a good thing, helping the baby. I'm sorry you got yelled at."

Danny didn't look up when he whispered, "And swatted."

Eric stilled. "Where?"

Danny touched his thigh.

"Show me."

"You okay in there?" Mrs. Finley called through the door.

"Show me, Danny."

He was wearing elastic waist pants, and when he didn't move, Eric took hold of the waistband and paused. "May I?"

Danny bit his lip and closed his eyes, which Eric took as permission. The welts were huge and raw, from a switch of some kind and not done through clothing.

"Mr. Houston?"

Eric pulled up the boy's pants and opened the door. "We're leaving. Right now."

"What happened?"

"There are welts on his legs. They swatted him and yelled at him because the baby threw up on his clothes." Eric waved toward the so-called children's room. "And that is appalling. My son is not going to be subject to these people, not while I have some say in the matter."

"Now just a minute here. You hold on," Mrs. Jenkins said. "Children need discipline. Mr. Jenkins and I don't believe in sparing the rod and spoiling the child. We take these children to church with us, and we feed and clothe them. You can't go taking this here boy just because he was disobedient."

"I can and I will," Eric told her, unwilling to argue with her.

"He was placed here with us!"

"He's just gotten unplaced," Eric said, carefully lifting Danny into his arms and striding to the front door as three pairs of eyes stared from the doorway of the children's room.

Mrs. Finley spoke to Mrs. Jenkins and her husband as she followed Eric. "I'll be in touch."

Eric marched to his car, opened the door, and placed Danny in the back seat. The boy looked stunned. Then Eric turned to Mrs. Finley. "What do I need to sign so I can keep him?"

She grinned. "I just happen to have it here with me, Mr. Houston."

"You do, do you?"

"Let's put it this way. Soon as you called saying you were going to come check on Daniel, I figured I'd better get things ready for you because you didn't sound like a man who was going to turn your back on a boy you'd raised for four years."

Eric chuckled. A real laugh would have to wait until he undid some of this anger he had building.

Mrs. Finley unlocked her car, reached in for a folder, and spread it open on Eric's trunk. Then she pulled out a pen and offered it to Eric. "I imagine you're familiar with those yellow tabs. Just sign everywhere you see one. I'll get this to the judge on Monday. We should have approval for you to take him home with you by Tuesday. Do you have someplace you and Danny can stay until then?"

"I'll find us a place."

"May I recommend one? There's a great little motel over on the beach that has a pool and playground for kids. You give them my name, and they'll give you a deal, I'm sure."

"There's something on the beach this time of year?"

"Well, seeing as how my sister and her husband run it, I made a call and secured a room. Just in case."

"You, Mrs. Finley, are a credit to South Carolina."

"Name's Avelina."

He extended his hand. "Eric."

"Here's Beatrix's card. You go on and call her. Then you may need to go shopping. You remember this area well enough to find your way to a kid's store?"

He laughed. "I probably do."

"Okay, now let's make a photographic record of those welts. You think you can get him to let you do that?"

Danny's eyes were round and frightened, but he nodded when Eric told him what they needed. "So I won't ever have to go back there?"

"That's right. So the judge will let you come home with me."

He took the photos and handed the phone back to Avelina Finley. "You know how to reach me if you need anything more. Will the judge want to interview Danny?"

"He may. I'll let you know."

"Thank you so much."

"You boys go on and have a fun weekend."

"Yes, ma'am."

As Eric buckled the boy in, he experienced a moment of panic. What had he just done?

8

MR. JENKINS

Gripping his Bud longneck, Dalton Jenkins pushed open the screen door and stepped onto the trailer's cement stoop. That man who'd grabbed Danny and the paycheck that came with him headed to one car, while the social worker went off to another. She grabbed something from the front seat, bunch of papers looked like, and the man went about signing in places she pointed to. Probably to shift the money from that boy's legal caregivers over to...

Dalton squinted to see the plate on the man's car. Read North Carolina.

They weren't even keepin' the boy local. That was just wrong.

Dalton rubbed a finger along side of his nose. The heat was gettin' to him, no cover on the stoop. Only good thing about bright sun was how it illuminated what you wanted to see.

He'd keep quiet and he'd bide, on account of there being more than one way to skin a raccoon. Those varmints and this man in his fancy-schmanzy shoes, drivin' that fancy car, had thievery in common.

Soon's they started up, Dalton noted the man's plate number and committed it to memory. Being smart like that had paid off more than once, and numbers… well, they could lead you pretty much wherever you needed to go. Plate numbers, phone numbers, bank numbers, even government ID numbers.

Maybe the boy going off like that was just fine. With the plate number, Dalton could find him.

He fished out his phone and dialed. When the call was picked up, Dalton said, "That boy you wanted, the one with the pretty eyelashes? I can bring him to you for the right price."

9

JEMINY

Tears sluiced the hours away,
Until it was time to leave, to be up and about, to head on out,
To flee.

Jeminy took one last look through the apartment before locking the door behind her and heading to Maggie's car. "All set." She had what she needed in her two suitcases. The rest, including her beloved guitar, she'd have to trust to FedEx.

Maggie handed over a tall cup and a bag of pastries. "Latte's decaf. Muffins for now or for the trip. Midnight snack, breakfast, whatever." Maggie put the car in gear.

Jeminy sipped gingerly. "Perfect. Thanks for making it decaf. I'm hoping to sleep on the flight."

"So," Maggie asked as she steered through the busy streets. "How'd you leave things with what's-his-name?"

She couldn't blame Maggie for refusing to say Rand's name. She'd like to expunge him from her memory that easily. "I'm going to tell him now. By text message."

"Good idea. Then you can't hear him yell. By the way, I looked up FedEx, and there's one a block off the freeway."

"Thanks." Jeminy's fingers flew over the tiny keypad. *I moved out. You remember all those things you said we had to have? They're yours to deal with now.*

He responded almost immediately. *?Huh? What am I supposed to do with any of it?*

She wrote: *Sell it? Give it away? I don't care. The rent's yours too.*

A ping sounded almost immediately. *No way. You've cost me too freakin much already. You better call off your hounds, you lying b—*

She turned off her phone.

The plane had taken off from LAX only fifteen minutes late. Fifteen minutes was nothing when you were crossing a continent.

While this had felt like a retreat from what Jeminy'd naively called her Grand Adventure, it didn't have to be. It was all in how she looked at it.

The power of positive thinking, right?

She wasn't a failure. She wasn't running *from,* but rather *to,* her destiny.

Right?

She squeezed her eyes shut as the word "wrong" seemed to answer her. Right/wrong, yes/no…

She rubbed her temples. Sleep. She needed sleep, that was all.

She reclined her seat as far back as it would go and tried to breathe tension from her body, but not even an antihistamine shielded her from the wail of an unhappy baby or the jabbering of two women who imagined midnight the perfect time to raise their voices above the engine noise.

With scratchy eyes and a full bladder, she made her way to the lavatory just as the announcement came that they were ten minutes out from Charlotte. She was really doing this. Moving, running, but the question remained. Was she running toward or away?

She was still in worry mode when she boarded her flight to New Bern and during the hour it took to get there.

By the time they landed and she collected her luggage, she was dragging her feet and her attitude. She wanted two things—breakfast and a nap, in that order.

She found Isa out front in a miniature black and white car, one of those fuel-efficient toys that would crumble to nothing in a collision. At least this one had four doors. "Was it a good flight?" the older woman asked as she opened the trunk for one of Jeminy's suitcases.

Jeminy loaded it in and rolled the other toward the back door on the passenger side. "Okay, I guess. I was pretty numb during the last leg. Sorry I had to drag you out at this hour."

"Those red-eye flights are aptly named." Isa slid behind the wheel and, when Jeminy had settled next to her, asked, "You need coffee?"

"Maybe something else? I'd love something to eat, a bagel, anything. I ate the last muffin I'd carried on board at around two this morning."

Isa pulled away from the curb. "We can stop just a few miles up the road."

On a sigh, Jeminy said, "There may be a God after all."

"You'd better be careful around your grandmother with talk like that."

"Are you? Careful, I mean?"

"Of course." Isa glanced over at her. "She knows how I feel about religion, and I respect how she looks at life. We don't have to agree in order to remain friends, and we don't preach at each other or ridicule the other's point of view. I've learned to keep my mouth shut."

They passed parking lots and signs advertising everything from tire dealers to Botox practitioners, and, in between these, green grass showed off after a recent rain. Soon, the roadside would need those big tractors out with their mowers, something she'd never seen in Los Angeles.

After a pit stop that included a bottle of Cran-Apple juice and a slice of pumpkin bread, she began to feel human again, even without caffeine. "Tell me more of what's going on here."

Isa flashed her a quick grin. Jeminy was struck again by the almost ageless beauty of the woman. She had to be in her late fifties, maybe even early sixties, but that smile wiped away any vestige of age in spite of her almost silver hair, which she wore long and straight, usually tucked behind her ears to show off dangly earrings. When Isa gestured with her long-fingered hands, the bangles at her wrists jiggled.

"Your grandmother's incredibly grateful you were able to leave your exciting Hollywood life to do this for her. You don't really have to stay long—we can hire someone to be with her—but I'm hoping you'll remain until everything settles down. She needs protecting."

Jeminy focused on the highway ahead and bit the inside of her lip. She would not let tears win. She would not. She didn't want to tell Isa the humiliating news that there was no exciting life waiting for her anywhere. At least, not until she made one happen.

Finally, she spoke. "Why does Nana need protecting? You said my mother's up to something." She rubbed her forehead. "I'm still groggy. Sorry."

"Your mother's determined to sell your grandmother's house and put her in an assisted-living facility in Chapel Hill."

"My *mother* wants to do that? But why? Does Nana need that much care?"

"She will. She has the beginnings of dementia."

"Alzheimer's?" The weight of that word hit her like a punch to her gut.

"Not yet," Isa said. "Maybe never, but she knows something's happening to her memory. We'll see her doctor today. Her lawyer said he needs a letter attesting to her having the mental acuity to do things like sign papers and choose the people she wants to take care of her so you and I will be able to manage her investments and discuss her situation with him when necessary."

"Yes, she'd need that."

"Absolutely. When we saw your mother last night, she claimed I'd exerted undue influence over your grandmother. I assume she will also accuse you of doing the same thing."

"Me?"

"It's mostly because your grandmother gave you and me her power of attorney and took it away from your mother."

"Power of attorney." Exhaustion must have fogged her thought process as well as her memory because all Jeminy could think about was what form her mother's retribution would take. Her mother did not have a forgiving bone in her body. "She's going to hate me."

"She's already decided we're the enemy, but at least she can't take away your car keys or lock you in your room." Isa glanced over with another grin.

Jeminy snorted. "She can't, can she?"

And, really, what could her mother do other than yell? Jeminy hadn't been dependent on her parents in years.

"She did go home, didn't she? I mean, I won't have to see her."

"You can hope." Isa sighed. "She stormed off last night, but you never know. She may have thought better of it."

Jeminy lowered the visor to check her reflection. "Oh man, and I look a mess."

"You're fine," Isa said. "If she shows up, you just hold your ground. She's powerless."

"And that will make her mean."

"It already has, but you just need to smile and nod and do what you've come home to do, and that's to make sure your grandmother feels safe."

Jeminy closed her eyes and tried to release some of the tension she'd hoarded, but it had lodged too deeply to be breathed out. Isa punched a button on her dashboard, and the sound of stringed instruments... oh, and a flute... filled the car. Jeminy sighed.

She awoke with a jolt when the engine stopped. "Wow. I actually slept."

Isa smiled. "I don't usually play something so soporific when I'm trying to drive, only when I have insomnia."

"I bet not."

Jeminy squinted at a car parked in the driveway. "Is that my mother's?"

Isa shrugged. "That would be my guess." She popped open the trunk and hefted Jeminy's bigger bag as far as the back porch before leaning in, giving Jeminy a quick hug, and whispering, "Better you than me, honey. I coped with Dee's antics last night and needed two glasses of wine after the scene she put on at Front Street Grill. Your grandmother was mortified."

"I'm so sorry. I hope she doesn't create another one. I'm not up to it."

"You'll manage for your grandmother's sake. It's time for you to put on Teflon skin."

"So Mother's words will slide off?"

"Your grandmother's fragile, but you're not. You just stay quiet and be the non-stick surface."

Jeminy laughed at that image. "I'll try. Thanks again for meeting my plane."

"Georgina has a doctor's appointment at one. If your mother's still here, we'll just work around her. I'll see you shortly after noon."

Isa bent to pet one of Nana's rescue cats. "I hope she remembered to feed them this morning. There's usually a food bowl or two out here."

"I'll take care of it," Jeminy said.

"Okay, I'm off."

Jeminy waited until the other woman had backed out the drive before she opened the door and shuffled her two cases inside. Those and three boxes contained all her worldly goods, not including her guitar. Pitiful at the age of thirty-two to own so little.

Or maybe it was a blessing.

Less to carry. Less to lose.

She rolled the cases, one at a time, to the far end of the kitchen. Before she could duck into the powder room, her mother's voice filled the hall all the way from the front room.

"Jemima Buchanan, is that you?"

Who else did her mother think it might be? "Yes, ma'am. I'll be right there."

"We're waiting for you. Please come now."

Jeminy curled her fingers. How could her mother's tone still paralyze her after all these years? "Need a pit stop first."

She took care of business and then closed her eyes and practiced those deep breathing exercises she'd learned as a teen on the verge of trouble. Let it go, let it slide off and out and past.

"Jemima!"

"Jeminy, my name is Jeminy," she mumbled to the bathroom door as she closed it behind her. And then she raised her head, squared her shoulders, and pasted on a smile. Not a big one, but one designed to ease her nana's worries. Nana hated it when anyone argued.

And Nana'd had the courage to take control of her future.

Now it was up to Jeminy to stand guard and protect the sweetest woman she knew.

Teflon, she told herself. She'd be Teflon.

She stepped through the doorway and hurried to the wingback chair to give Nana a hug. Was there less flesh on Nana's shoulders, on her arms? She crouched low and sat back on her heels, eye-level with her grandmother. "Nana, how are you?"

"Out of her mind, that's how she is." Mother spoke from behind her. "She has completely lost touch with reality. And you, I see, ignored my message. You should have paid attention."

Jeminy glanced over her shoulder. "Hello, Mother." But she didn't stand up, and she didn't ask what message. She hadn't even thought to turn on her cell phone after the flight. Oh well, it didn't matter. Her mother never had anything nice to say anyway.

Nana patted her cheek and spoke in her soft voice. "I'm fine now you're here, sweet girl."

Mother sputtered. "Jemima, I'm sorry you came all this way for nothing. My lawyer will soon have your grandmother's ridiculous decisions overturned. This just goes to show that she needs to have someone responsible take over."

Jeminy stood up and glanced around until she found a straight-backed chair she could move next to Nana. Then she sat down and took Nana's hand in hers. "Isa assured me all is in order."

"Isa Wellington is a fool."

"Isa is my friend," Nana said. "She's protecting me."

"From *me*?" Mother said. "Your own daughter?"

"From having to move." Jeminy spoke quickly to keep her grandmother from having to answer.

"Do you expect me to believe you're willing to give up your career on the West Coast to move to this dinky little backwater town out of the goodness of your heart? That you don't expect to get rich from it?"

Nana's fingers tightened around hers. "Mother," Jeminy said, "you're upsetting Nana."

"Don't you think she has upset *me*? I come all the way here, cancel important meetings of my own, all so I can help her, and *this* is how she repays me? By insulting me?" She looked around, following her gaze with the sweep of her hand. "Do you plan to take on this messy place? The piles everywhere?" On a humph of disgust, she continued. "The faucet in the guest bath leaks, and there's a water stain on the ceiling, so the roof might have a leak. You up to fixing those things?"

"We'll do what needs doing," Jeminy said, her voice low and soft. She closed her eyes. This was her mother. Nana's daughter. It was really too bad that she'd been taught to show respect because she had a lot to say if only she dared.

"Your grandmother has the gall to suggest I don't have her best interests at heart!" Mother dabbed at dry eyes while her voice spat angry words.

"I don't want to move," Nana said, her voice just above a whisper. "I want to stay in my own home. I like my house just as it is."

"And you shall stay here." Jeminy stood. "Nana, why don't we go back to the kitchen, and I'll fix a nice cup of tea? I see your cup is empty. And I'm starving."

Nana smiled up at her. "That would be lovely."

Her mother had become the regal Deborah Buchanan again. "Fine. I'm going home now. But you haven't heard the end of this."

Of course not. When had Mother ever quit harping on any subject that tied her gut in a knot? Sometimes Jeminy questioned her father's sanity, that he hadn't up and left his wife years ago.

"Goodbye, Mother. It was great seeing you, too." Jeminy didn't even try to keep the sarcasm from her voice. Her mother only increased her pace, her heels clicking sharply on the hardwood of the front hall.

When the front door slammed, Jeminy whispered, "It's okay."

And then they shifted to the sunny kitchen, where they sipped tea and smiled at each other because talking was too hard. For now, their smiles said enough.

Eventually, though, exhaustion took hold. "I need a nap, Nana. How about you?"

"You come on up. I think it's time you moved into the bigger guest room. The bed's all ready for you."

"Isn't that where Mother stays?"

"I don't think she'll be visiting much."

Jeminy sighed. "I guess not."

Once Nana was settled in her own room, Jeminy returned to the kitchen to fetch one of her suitcases. Her mother had been right about the clutter everywhere, as if Nana couldn't bear to part with a single envelope of junk mail or a single issue of a magazine or newspaper.

And dust had settled on all the surfaces. It had only been a few months since she'd been here. How had it degenerated to this?

Mother'd been right about the drippy faucet. Jeminy washed her hands, splashed water on her face, and determined to find a way to fix it after her nap. Until then, she set a dry washcloth under the drip to keep the sound from plaguing her sleep.

She undressed and climbed between cool cotton sheets. She was here, and everything would be okay. Really.

Nana had almost finished her lunch before Jeminy remembered her silent phone still tucked in her purse. "Be right back, Nana."

But her grandmother was wiping her lips and didn't seem to be paying any attention. "My cats," she said.

"I'll check them in just a moment." Jeminy dashed upstairs and retrieved her phone, powering it up as she took the steps more slowly this time. And there was her mother's text. She almost deleted it without reading.

Almost.

If all you plan to do in visiting your grandmother is to aid and abet her in this ridiculous scheme against me, stay where you are. It won't pay you to come all this way because my lawyer will make short shrift of whatever document my mother made to take away my inheritance, and you'll just have to fly back to L.A. again, with nothing to show for any of it. You will not be in charge of your grandmother or anything here.

She could hear her mother's voice as if she'd spoken those words—the anger, the disdain. Again making Jeminy feel worthless. Again spitting her out like some foul-tasting food.

She breathed deeply and wrapped up what was left of her sandwich. She couldn't eat it. Instead, she picked up a dishrag and wiped off crumbs and a dollop of mayonnaise. She'd sprayed down the sink and immediate counter before fixing their lunch, but now she moved further afield with the cleaner. Checking to make sure her grandmother was out of sight, she stacked the opened and unopened mail and shoved it out of sight to go through later.

The floors needed a good scrub, too.

Whatever.

Her gut hurt. Rose used to tell her, "Your mama isn't angry at you, honey. She's angry at herself, and that's something she's got to work through with the Lord on her own." Maybe true, but those words didn't wipe away the hurt.

Outside, a cardinal swooped over the empty bird feeder. This time of year, the birds could fend for themselves, but Jeminy knew her grandmother loved to watch them peck just outside the back window. She dropped the dishrag in the sink and searched for seed in the pantry. There, at the back, behind a large container of cat food, was an opened grain sack with grain scattered everywhere. She picked up the cat-food scoop and dug it carefully into the birdseed—carefully because an open sack under a shelf seemed like the perfect hiding place for mice or roaches or who knew what. Birds she liked. Rodents or insects she could do without. Only Olli had relished creepy crawlies.

With a sigh she lifted a remarkably vermin-free scoop and emptied it onto a small plate, heading outside where Nana was talking to her cats.

Jeminy pushed open the screen door. "Hey."

Her grandmother reached toward the tabby. "I don't know where his food bowl is. I'm afraid someone took it. You didn't take it, did you? I always leave it out here."

"I didn't. No, but what time do you usually feed the cats?"

"Early morning and dinner. I feed them both times. Breakfast and dinner. Two bowls."

After repeating herself, Nana went back to mumbling. Jeminy took a deep breath. "Let me check inside."

"The bowls wouldn't be inside. They'd be right here. I feed them in the early morning, and then I feed them at dinner time."

"Maybe my mother washed the bowls. You know how she is." A habit that had driven Jeminy and her daddy to roll their eyes at each other. They'd set a glass or a cup down, and before they could pick it up again for a refill, it would be gone, snatched for the dishwasher.

"Dee wouldn't touch anything for the cats. She doesn't like them. She says they're messy."

Well, that was certainly true. Mother called them dirty creatures who shed all over furniture and clothes. But she might have thought getting the bowls clean was one step in the war against clutter.

Jeminy darted inside and checked the counters, then the dishwasher. Water pooled on the bottoms of upended glasses and cups, signaling that the dishwasher had gone through a wash cycle. And there, on the bottom shelf, were two small stainless bowls that looked like they belonged to the animals of the house.

Jeminy carried them to the porch. "Nana, are these the ones?"

Nana came close. "Oh, my, yes. Where did you find them?"

"In the dishwasher."

Nana squinted from the bowls to her. "The dishwasher? Why would they be in there?"

"Perhaps someone decided they needed a bath."

"Must be, but who?"

Either her mother or Nana herself, but suggesting either of those possibilities would only upset her grandmother. "I guess the only thing that matters is that we've found them. Now, do you think those cats have been fed already?"

"I always feed them first thing."

"I know you do, but you've had a lot going on."

"I have?"

"Yes, ma'am. Forgetting would be easy to do."

"It would, wouldn't it? I guess it would be better to give them too much than not enough."

"I think you're right. I don't think cats will overeat and make themselves sick, and that tabby sure looks like he'd be grateful for a meal about now."

"I keep the food in plastic containers just inside the pantry. A little dry and a little wet, about half a can for each bowl."

"I can do that. I'll be right back."

Jeminy filled the bowls and carried them out, setting one near the tabby, the other closer to the steps. The huge black and white male was checking out this new person. She backed away. "It's okay, kitty. I won't hurt you. Come on and eat."

Hunger eventually overrode the cat's scruples, and he slunk up the steps to the bowl. It was fascinating to watch him check over his shoulder every minute or so as if he'd had to fight for every bite in his early days.

Nana sat down on the swing and smiled happily. "Aren't they beautiful? They were hungry. My sweet boys were hungry."

"They were."

A yoo-hoo followed the slamming of a car door, and Isa came around the side of the house. "Ladies."

Nana looked up and smiled. "Isa, how lovely to see you again."

"You, too, Georgie. I came early in case you need help getting ready."

For a moment, Nana seemed puzzled, and then her smile widened. "You're here to take me to the doctor's, aren't you?"

"I am indeed."

"I remembered." Nana sounded so pleased with herself that Jeminy wanted to applaud.

"Do you need to do anything to get ready first?" Isa asked. "We have time."

"I do. Thank you for reminding me." She stood and brushed down her linen slacks. "I will be down soon."

Jeminy and Isa followed Nana inside, and Isa nodded toward her retreating form. "I'll check on her in a few minutes if she doesn't return. She may forget why she went upstairs."

"Is it that bad?"

"Sometimes it's not bad at all. Her understanding isn't impaired, only her memory, hence her efforts at self-protection."

"Which is where we come in."

"Indeed." Isa opened the cupboard where Nana kept her glasses. "You mind?" she asked as she took one down.

"Of course not. I'll join you. Water?"

"With ice." Isa settled on one of the kitchen chairs. "How'd it go this morning?"

Jeminy slid in across from her. "Mother was as you'd expect and wasted no time hightailing it out of here once she'd threatened me with legal action." She took a sip. "Isa, how long has it been like this? The house, I mean?"

"Not long. She gets bogged down with indecision because she doesn't remember what she's supposed to do with everything. I helped her set up automatic payments for all her bills so she won't be in danger of having anything cut off, but she sometimes doesn't remember that and begins to worry. You'll need to remind her gently and distract her, if possible." She smiled. "I once told her I could be her computer storage—her hard drive—for recent memory but she was still brilliant at the long-ago memories and could tell me her stories."

"Did that make it easier for her?"

"It did. She actually laughed—after I told her what a computer hard drive was." Isa braced both palms around the icy glass and then patted her cheeks. "My car's air conditioning hasn't had time to lower the temperature inside. Felt like I was having a hot flash."

Jeminy grinned. "The one thing, probably the only thing, I liked about California was the lack of humidity."

"Yeah, well, Delaware was worse because Wilmington didn't have sea breezes, not like my place at the beach here. Speaking of which, you and Georgie need to come visit, sit on the balcony, at least."

"I'd like that. I know Nana would, too."

"Georgie loves the water, which makes me wonder what your mother was thinking, trying to take her away from it."

"Mother wasn't thinking. Only reacting to feeling out of control, I'd guess."

"Dee's a very unhappy woman."

"I hate it, you know? I can't reconcile my mother's attitude with her own mother's kindness. I wish I knew what made her into the person she is."

"What's your dad like? I've never met him."

"I feel sorry for him because Mother isn't nice to either of us. She's been accusing him of having an affair, but I don't believe it."

"That can't make for a happy marriage, either way."

"No, it can't." Jeminy glanced toward the front of the house, where footsteps sounded on the stairs. "Nana and I each had a short lie-down, so I think she's in good shape. Don't you want me to come with you?"

"Not necessary," Isa said. "I'll report what the doctor says, and I'll give his office a copy of our health care power of attorney."

Her grandmother shuffled in with her purse in one hand and

tissues in the other. She beamed when she noticed Isa. "You're here. And I'm ready."

"First, water." Jeminy handed her a glass. "You need to keep up your fluids, Nana."

Her grandmother sipped delicately.

"Drink it all, if you can."

"That's enough." Nana set the glass in the sink.

With a sigh, Jeminy let it go, but she refilled her own glass. "Nana, if I need to run an errand or two, may I take your car? Does it still work?"

"Of course, it works. It was out just last week."

"You drive yourself?" The image of Nana behind the wheel was mind-boggling.

"Oh, no. The boy who does my grass starts it for me and takes it out sometimes, but now that you're here, you can do that." Nana pointed to several hooks just inside the door. "Keys and opener thing for the garage."

"Maybe I'll pick up something for dinner while I'm out."

"We'll stop at the store." Isa pointed to her wrist. "Time to go, Georgie."

Two hours or so later, Jeminy pulled Nana's car next to Isa's and carried in several sacks of groceries to augment whatever the two older ladies had picked up at the store. She set these on the counter and followed the sound of voices to the front of the house.

Nana and Isa each occupied a chair on either side of the long front windows. Jeminy'd always thought those chairs and their chintz covers in lavender and blue perfect for her grandmother but less than easy on a person of her height. She preferred big and enveloping, a chair she could curl up in, or even Nana's high-backed couch with lots of pillows.

"How'd the doctor's visit go?" she asked, glancing from one to the other.

Isa answered first. "Georgie did a wonderful job. Dr. Walford said she passed with flying colors, and he's going to draft a letter attesting to her competency."

Nana beamed.

"I'm so glad," Jeminy said. "Let me put away the groceries I bought, and I'll join you."

Isa followed her back. "She's supposed to eat apples and bananas to counteract what your grandmother called a bit of stomach upset. We picked up a few on our way home." She indicated the fruit bowl. "Anyway, the cognitive test wasn't easy, but she was as sharp as I've ever seen her. This memory thing is certainly fluky."

"It seems to scare Nana." Jeminy set a rotisserie chicken on the counter and tucked veggies in the refrigerator.

"Confusion like your grandmother experiences would scare anyone. Not knowing when you'll be you and in control and when you won't."

"I'd be terrified."

"I'm so glad you decided to come, Jeminy, but there's a lot we'll have to go through, you and I, to figure out the easiest and best way to help your grandmother. We'll see the lawyer first and then the banker. Hopefully, Georgie will be alert, but it doesn't really matter much now that she has the doctor's word and we have the paperwork completed."

Nana yoo-hooed from the front of the house. "You both still in the kitchen?"

"Nice." Isa smiled and said quietly, "She's with us."

"Coming, Nana!"

Jeminy took a seat on the couch facing the two ladies, and they chatted easily about what had been going on in town since last fall, including the upcoming wedding of Brisa's mother, Agnes, to Henry Houston.

"He's Eric's brother, and Eric is your grandmother's lawyer," Isa explained. "You haven't met Agnes yet, have you?"

"I haven't, but if she's anything like her daughter, I know I'll like her."

"Georgie," Isa said, "why don't we take Jeminy out to *Agua Verde* for dinner one night soon? Let her meet some of the younger people in town."

"Who do you want her to meet?"

"I was thinking Agnes and Henry, though he's usually busy in the kitchen. He's a sous chef there."

"Do I know them?" Nana's brow furrowed.

"You may have met Agnes. She's mother to that cute little Brisa." Isa pointed east. "They live in the next block, in the old Ware house."

"Judge Ware. I knew him."

"Agnes is the judge's stepdaughter."

"Oh."

"Would you like to go for dinner where she works? We've been to *Agua Verde* before, and you liked it. Maybe tomorrow night."

"Could I go lie down first? I'm tired." Nana pushed herself up from the chair. "I think I'll go lie down. Thank you for coming to visit. It was lovely to see you both."

Jeminy jumped up. "Do you need help, Nana?"

Her grandmother waved her off. "Of course not. I know the way to my own room."

After she saw Isa out, Jeminy loaded their glasses in the dishwasher and dried her hands. She felt wrung out and put away wet, and her state wasn't only physical.

Upstairs, she peeked into her grandmother's room. The door hinges needed oiling.

"Hey, sweet girl," Nana said, rousing enough to beckon her in. "I was just talking to my Lord and thanking Him for you."

"It's always good to give thanks."

Nana's smile widened. "Now, you go take a rest, too, honey. You look wiped out."

Jeminy leaned down to kiss the smooth cheek. "I love you, Nana."

With the touch of her grandmother's fingers lingering on hers, Jeminy smiled and left, tears threatening to leak onto her cheeks. Maybe she wasn't yet ready to claim a relationship of her own with God, but having a praying grandmother—and a praying daddy—only increased her longing.

She'd have liked to trust fully in a God who had the power to reorder her universe. If only that were something a person could just decide to do, like choosing an outfit. "Oh, hey, I think today I'll believe." Knowing that you might change your mind the next day? Not a great plan.

And yet it wasn't that she didn't have faith that He existed. She did. But she hadn't bothered following Him and didn't know how to begin. Especially after all she'd done.

Hindsight put everything in stark relief, didn't it? The regrets, the what-ifs in a life badly lived. Her steps were leaden, her heart hammering as she fled to her bathroom.

A hot shower washed her outside, but it didn't cleanse the awful choices she'd made. Nothing she could do would remove the stains from the parts she'd allowed Rand to touch. Like the unreachable part that was her womb. Once upon a time... Once... *O God...* once that womb had made life, started a life, a... a...

O God, please!

Standing there, with the hot water pelting her skin, her arms crossed and her head fallen forward, a sob burst from her. She rested her forehead against the tile walls until the water chilled and matched her heart before turning the knobs to off and pulling her towel close.

The memory didn't weaken. Once upon a time, not long ago, part of her had produced life. It might have been in the embryonic stage, but still a life. A being.

No matter what Rand or the doctor had said.

A potential baby, one that would have grown into full babyhood if she'd let it be. Then into her arms and her life and her heart.

Hers.

O God, please.

Her womb might never produce life again.

Might never… never… never.

O God, please.

She'd been weak. A coward. She'd let Rand dictate, let his fears become hers. She'd believed his threats. Let him take her. Let him stand there. Let him.

Her choice.

Her doing.

Her guilt.

Her daddy used to call her strong, fearless, able to do anything she set her mind to. Rose had taught her truth and the preciousness of life.

Her imagined strength had puffed away like a tumbleweed across the desert floor. Rand's words had been the wind, and she'd bowed, rolled, fallen in a heap.

And then he'd nailed her coffin shut with his disparaging words. "You're nothing."

It was true.

Rose would be so disappointed in her. Her daddy would look at her with mournful eyes and blame himself. Her mother would probably flick her off like dandruff flakes on a dark sweater.

By rote, she toweled dry and stepped onto the bathmat. She wrapped in a robe and headed for the bed.

She had no one to tell. No one to ask. No one who'd listen.

Closing her eyes, she longed for sleep but had to content herself with whispers heavenward. "I'm so sorry. So very sorry."

She was, and she probably always would be.

She could hate Rand for contaminating her, for pressing and pushing her, but she had to hate herself for the thing she'd done, for the thing that meant she deserved whatever punishment God meted out. Sickness in her body was nothing compared to what she'd done.

If only she'd listened to her daddy's truths, to Rose's, instead of her world's. Instead of Rand's. If only she'd stood up and said no.

Tears came again, tears of shame and loss and pain.

Rand wasn't to blame for what she'd chosen, for the yeses she'd said to him. Those were on her.

She was to blame for her empty arms. She hadn't been forced into that clinic. She hadn't been held down while they assured her it was her body, her right, her choice. No one had picked her up and put her on the table or forcibly touched her.

Touched her? Be real, Jeminy. No one had forced her to be an accessory to murder.

But then, no one had warned her she'd feel forever empty.

A scream woke her. As Jeminy opened her eyes in the semi-darkness, her panic ebbed along with her cries. She'd been dreaming.

Again.

She shouldn't have been surprised; after all, she'd dreamt of Olli weeks ago on the advent of her—their—thirty-second birthday, and then there'd been those reminders of that other death. First Olli, then her baby—one an accident, one her fault.

She sniffed and wiped her cheeks. Perhaps if she'd stayed upright and out of bed—although falling asleep on her feet would have brought its own risks—but if she'd been able to do it, maybe the twenty-four hours of risk from birthdays or pointed fingers would have passed uneventfully.

Although she'd still have the memory of each loss begging for attention.

Dawn came and went. The sunshine-yellow paper on the walls seemed to have morphed into a metallic gray, closing in, pressing her into a tight ball. Her eyes remained unfocused and overflowing. She brought her hands to her chest. Rain pinged the roof, spattered against the windows, running in trails down the glass, rivulets of tears.

She swiped again at her damp cheek. *Enough.*

Please.

That first loss, she'd only been twelve. The second, she'd been old enough to have thought through the decision, to have researched her options, old enough to have said no. To have stopped things before she'd gotten on the table. She'd pressed the memory of that choice down and back and under until she no longer thought of what might have been, *who* might have been if she'd chosen differently. If she hadn't let Rand, the promise-master, weave a spell with words she should never have believed. Had part of her been relieved at the choice? To have her self back without an encumbrance?

That must be truth, if she could bring herself to confront it. She wasn't just a weakling, led by a nose ring into obedience.

O God.

O God.

Mea culpa.

Not a choice, unless it had been a choice to ignore what she knew. To become what she hated. She'd known better. *She'd known.*

Her daddy would be so disappointed in her. Her nana, Rose. Olli would have... would have...

Don't go there. *Don't.*

She, Jeminy Buchanan, had given Rand power over her life and then she had been too weak to run from the decision. She'd tried to ignore his language, but words are catching if they're too often repeated. Nana—not to mention Rose and Daddy—would be horrified by her living in a world that cursed God. And more.

How had she not recognized the slippery path? Or that she was so weak-willed and morally shattered? She'd never thought of herself as spineless.

How wrong she'd been.

10

DEBORAH

No lights burned from inside their Chapel Hill house when Deborah pulled into the driveway. Obviously, Larry was still away. That was fine as it would give her time to contemplate her lawyer's words.

She'd bought Dave a couple of drinks at the club, and they'd discussed her options for dealing with the mess in Beaufort. He was happy to serve her, willing to draft any demand letter she wanted, file any kind of lawsuit. Of course, he was. Those billable hours kept him in the kind of house, driving the kind of car he was certain he deserved. His wife had taken off for greener climes, but Dave didn't seem to be hurting post-divorce.

As for her own marriage? No matter what, she wasn't going to let Larry find out if the climate would be permanently better in Carole's loving arms, even if he begged her for a divorce. Oh, maybe he could get one eventually, but she'd make the process as uncomfortable as possible. He'd been out of town for a week on business, or so he said. He was always out of town or out somewhere. She ought to have him followed, but he was getting mighty cagey with money, and investigators cost.

Her keys jangled as she tried to fit one into the lock. When it eventually clicked, she pushed on the heavy oak door and stepped into the marble-floored entry. Instead of dropping her keys on the hall table, she slid them into her purse, then flipped on enough lights to find her way into the kitchen. There she reached into a cupboard for a wine glass and then into the refrigerator for the chilled bottle of chardonnay. Best to stick with what she'd been drinking earlier.

She took a sip. Much better than the wine she'd shared with Dave, smoother, richer. She carried her glass into the living room and reached toward a table lamp. A voice spoke from the darkness.

"Did you have a good time?"

She jumped, stumbling as she fell onto the deep cushions of the sofa. Fortunately, she'd gone bottom first and only a drop spilled on her hand. "Why are you sitting in the dark?" She set her glass on the side table and reached up to click on the lamp next to her. "I didn't know you were home already."

She tried to slow her erratic heartbeats. She should have parked in the garage where she might have seen his car.

"I was watching the sunset. The garden is beautiful at this time of day."

She couldn't imagine enjoying the dark with only a little light filtering into the room from outside. She swallowed another, larger sip to steady her nerves. "How was your trip?"

"Excellent. How was yours?"

"I told you on the phone. It was terrible. But Dave is going to help me fight this, so we should have it cleared up in no time."

"How does he recommend you fight?"

She considered not answering because she didn't like his tone, but eventually she said, "Dave agreed it may take a lawsuit."

"And you'd sue your own mother? Our daughter?"

"I'd sue Isa Wellington for undue influence."

"Right. And you're supposing there'd be no fallout for your mother or Jeminy?"

"I have to protect Mother. She's being used."

"By whom, other than her friend Isa? Your daughter?" He never took her side, and now he was intent on his twenty questions.

A scowl was the best she could do, when what she wanted was to haul off and hit him or toss her wine in his face. She could picture it now, Larry letting her blacken his eye. He never fought back, so what fun would that be?

She took a deep breath before speaking. "Jeminy's shown how unstable she is, running off to California to follow some pipe dream and shacking up with a smooth-talker who only wants what's best for him."

"And you know that how? Have you talked to Jeminy about her choices?"

"We met Rand. He looked shifty. I mean, he wouldn't even make eye contact when you talked to him."

Larry sighed. "I happen to agree about Rand, so we should both rejoice that she moved away from what I can only assume was a toxic relationship. It certainly wasn't a godly one."

She flicked that off because godly or ungodly didn't play into anything as far as she was concerned. The greed of her daughter and her mother's friend did. "I tell you, Jeminy is in this for what she can get. And that Isa?" Deborah shook her head in disgust. "She has never liked me. I could tell from the very beginning she was out to sabotage my relationship with Mother. Now see where it's gotten us. Having to go to court to protect my mother and her assets."

"Dee..."

"Deborah. My name is Deborah." She used to like being called by the diminutive, but no longer. Never again.

"Is your worry for your mother's sake or for yours?"

"Don't you go making this about me, Larry Buchanan." She upended her glass and stood. "Do you want dinner?"

"Only if you have something ready."

"I ate at the club."

"Then, no, thank you." He paused a beat. "But, just out of curiosity, how do you plan to pay for this lawsuit of yours? Do you have enough in your bank account to cover the costs, which, with Dave running things, will mount up?"

She ignored him. He'd always covered her overdrafts, and she couldn't imagine him quitting now. Her allowance—she almost choked on the word; who'd ever heard of a *wife* being given an allowance instead of access to a joint account?—would just cover her credit card bills, but Larry wouldn't leave her high and dry.

As she filled her glass with the last in the bottle, he spoke again from the living room. "I won't advance you a penny toward a lawsuit. Not a penny."

His words cut like a knife. It was his *job* to take care of her, to make her happy. When had he quit caring?

She loosened her hold on the fragile glass. It wouldn't do to break it and slice her fingers. He'd like that. He might even let her bleed to death on the kitchen floor. She could imagine him talking to the paramedics when he finally called them. *I didn't know,* he'd say. *I didn't hear.* She wouldn't give him the satisfaction.

Taking a deep breath, she carried the half-full glass with her up the stairs and to the master suite. Larry was gone so much, he could use the bath next to his office. Why should he care? She was the one who needed the master bath's luxurious tub and separate shower stall.

This might be a good time to suggest he use the guest bedroom, too, so she wouldn't have to listen to his snores. She'd given him information about ways to quit, treatments, machines. The memory of waking herself up when she'd spoken aloud in the night flashed into her thoughts, but she quickly suppressed it.

They weren't the same thing. Besides, Larry'd never complained. He probably hadn't even noticed.

Her room, her bath, and none of his cold judgement like a wall erected stone by stone between them. She grinned at the first thought of it being *hers* and immediately wanted to slap away the second when she pictured Larry's cold eyes.

Because, really, where did he get off judging her? He was the one carrying on with another woman.

11

JEMINY

Hands out, palms up, let worry fly
Straight up to the sky.

Jeminy could almost hear Rose's voice speaking words she needed to hear. "Don't worry about tomorrow, sweet girl. Tomorrow? Well, that'll surely take care of itself." There'd been something more tacked on, hadn't there? Something about each day having enough trouble of its own?

Jeminy could certainly attest to the troubles.

Sunlight bounced off the glass-topped dressing table where her mother used to sit and smooth creamer over sun-bronzed skin. Jeminy remembered watching from the nearby bed when she'd been little and they'd still visited Nana's as a family.

She picked up a silver-framed photo of her mother, model-thin and preening for the camera. Changes from the years post-Olli had erased most memories of a softer Deborah. Jeminy ran the tips of her fingers across an unfamiliar face. "Come back," she whispered to that barely remembered woman. But longing would never be enough to shift her mother from the person she'd become to the one Jeminy—and Nana—longed to know.

All she could do was keep busy, concentrate on her nana, and take life one day at a time. As soon as her guitar arrived, she'd reevaluate, refocus. She was fine—or, she'd be fine. She'd learn to breathe again.

She stacked her few books on the desk by the window, shook out, refolded, and arranged her clothes in the chest of drawers that had been her mother's. Lavender and hints of cedar assailed her, and she remembered her mother taking lingerie from a lace bag and the scent coming with it. When she pulled open the bottom drawer to add her sweaters, something slid forward. She crouched low and reached in.

There, tucked out of sight, was an old picture of herself and Olli, taken on their grandfather's boat. They must have been around seven or eight, all knobby knees and elbows and huge grins. Olli's glasses had been too big for his face, and his hair stuck out wildly, but he looked so happy, so carefree.

He'd been her best friend, her other half, the smaller one born minutes after she'd come sliding out. According to their daddy, Olli had emerged with barely a whimper compared to her robust howl. But then, Olli'd never been a fighter, had he? She'd been the stronger twin, the one nobody wanted near when they tried to pick on the frailer, kinder, gentler soul. The boy who'd never hated anyone, who'd always made excuses for others, even for the malicious ones.

Jeminy didn't bother to wipe away the tears that leaked out as she clasped the picture to her breast.

She'd loosed so many tears in the years since his death. So many. And now there were more. Eventually, though, she blew her nose and swiped at her cheeks, kissed the picture, and set it on top of the bureau. "I love you," she whispered to his image.

Next to it she set the black-framed picture of her with her daddy from his visit to her when she was studying music in

Greensboro at UNCG. Only he had come to see her there, to applaud her progress and listen to her recitals, never her mother. Jeminy couldn't wait to see him again.

It would be soon, now that they were in the same state. She smiled as she headed downstairs to scrounge up something to drink. Her grandmother was enjoying the morning on her back porch. Jeminy poked her head out the screen door.

"Nana, do you have any cranberry juice?" Nana used to keep bottles of it, and the tartness appealed to Jeminy.

"Oh, dear. Cranberry juice... I might. I just might. In the pantry?"

"I'll check. You want any if I find some?"

"Any?"

"Juice."

"No, no... I don't think so."

Nana's pantry held an interesting assortment of foodstuffs, including some jams and canned goods that looked as if they were at least a decade old. Culling the out-of-date items would be a job for her to tackle soon. But there, on the bottom shelf, were bottles of various juices. And yes, along with some interesting looking mango and pear juices, there was a lone bottle of cranberry.

She filled a tall glass and carried it out to join her grandmother. No sooner had she stepped outside than a "yoo-hoo!" from the front caught her attention, especially when it was followed by a dog's happy bark and the giggles of children. "Be right back, Nana."

"Mmm..." Nana started the rocker moving and kept on smiling.

The mailman was bending over to pat one of the dogs, and four kids stood around him, chattering. By the time Jeminy got all the way to the sidewalk, he was saluting with a wave and heading to the house next door.

She'd heard Brisa was home with her mother. "Brisa, hey!"

All four kids turned toward her. Brisa bounced up and down,

crying, "Look! It's Jeminy! From California! Hey, Jeminy! You came back!" Brisa followed a gorgeous Golden Retriever who seemed to be leading her on the leash.

The boy in the group held an Irish Setter in check. Both dogs had decided to investigate, along with the little redhead—Jilly, if she remembered correctly—and another girl.

"I'm so glad to see you again," Jeminy said. "Will you introduce me to your friends, including those beautiful animals?"

"This is Link. He's mine," Brisa said of the Golden. "And that's Harvey with Louis. Harvey likes to walk us, instead of us walking him, so Miss Hannah thought he might get some better manners if we took Link along to show him how to behave."

Jeminy raised a brow at that until Link obeyed Brisa's point and the click of her fingers to sit quietly at her side. She smiled at Louis. "Pleased to meet you." And then she turned to the other two.

"You know me," Jilly said. "We sang with you last time you visited. And that's Linney. She's Louis's big sister."

"I do know you, Jilly. And hello, Linney," she said to the grinning girl whose eyes indicated Down Syndrome. "Manners are important in a dog, so it's good you're working on Harvey's."

Louis nodded. "Yes. I've been trying to teach him things. So has Ty. Do you know Ty?"

"I'm afraid not."

"He's our friend," Louis said. "He belongs to Miss Annie Mac and Mr. Clay. Katie is his little sister. Katie and Linney sometimes hang out together. We, Linney and me, belong to Miss Hannah and Mr. Matt."

Jeminy grinned at the group. "Isn't belonging a wonderful thing? I belong to my nana, Mrs. Warren." At least she could name someone. She supposed her daddy would count, but she couldn't use him with this group. They'd then wonder about her mother. And no one belonged to Mother.

"Miss Georgie's real nice," Jilly said. "She used to always give us cookies. And I know all about you, on account of Brisa and her daddy singing your songs and you being Miss Georgie's granddaughter. Also, my mommy loves your music. She grew up here. Her name is Tadie Longworth Merritt, and my daddy and I married her when I was seven, almost eight."

Jeminy bit back a laugh. "So you're Tadie's girl. I remember Tadie from visits here. She was the older girl who was always sailing or out on her dock."

"When she married us, we all went sailing on our boat, the *Nancy Grace,* and we went all over the place, but then she got pregnant. Did you know I have a little brother? His name's Sammy."

"I didn't know. You'll have to bring Sammy to visit us someday."

"Maybe you and Miss Georgie could come to our house. I'm not allowed to take Sammy off by myself on account of all the tourists in town in the summertime. Mommy says you never know."

"You never do. That's absolutely right. How old is Sammy?"

"Oh, he'll be three real soon, so it's hard to keep up with him. He's fast."

This child was a hoot. "I'm not very familiar with three year olds, but I can imagine." She glanced toward the back. "Nana's feeding her cats right now. Do you want to come say hey?"

"I think maybe we ought to keep the dogs away. They might scare the cats," Jilly said.

"That's smart." Jeminy tried not to grin. "Perhaps another time when the dogs aren't with you."

"Are you going to stay here a while?" Brisa clucked her tongue when her dog got up from his sit. He sat back at her side.

Jeminy wished she could cluck obedience into people. "I am. I moved here to take care of Nana."

"Oh no, is she sick?" Jilly stretched as if to peer around back.

"No, but she isn't young anymore, and sometimes when we

grow old, we need people to help us remember things and to take us to the doctor or to the store. Nana doesn't drive now, so I'm here to help with all of that."

"What about your music?" Brisa sounded worried.

"I'll still write songs. And maybe you can come by sometime and help me."

"That would be cool."

"Can I come, too?" Jilly asked.

"Of course. My guitar will be arriving next week. I didn't want to bring it on the airplane."

"Okay!" Jilly danced from one foot to the other.

What a cutie. But then, they all were, weren't they? All eager and pleased to be here and together. If only Olli'd had a pack like this.

But she wouldn't go there. Instead, she slid her smile back in place. "I look forward to seeing you all again soon."

They waved as they headed back down the sidewalk, dogs strutting on their leashes.

Dogs and kids, two things she never expected to have, and wasn't that the saddest thought?

She'd just finished loading the washer with delicates when her cell phone rang. Her daddy's name popped up on the screen.

"Hey, lovey," he said when she answered. "How's my favorite girl?"

"Still recovering from jet lag, but doing well."

"Your mother said Georgina'd asked you to come to Beaufort. Are you sure that's what you want to do, trap yourself there?"

Her mother's words in translation, obviously. With a sigh, Jeminy said, "I want to help. And Isa said I only have to stay until we make certain Nana's okay. Safe from threats."

"You mean your mother."

"What's up with that?"

His sigh was loud. "I'm not sure."

Typical. She loved her daddy, but he never had stood up to his wife.

His next question should have been expected. "And your career?"

It was hard to tell him even now, to admit how wrong she'd been. "There are some legal issues I have to straighten out, and I can do them from here as easily." Perhaps more easily. She tried to sound unconcerned, upbeat.

He made a noise of disgust that she could almost picture: her daddy leaning forward as he watched televised news and throwing up his hands at what he considered stupidity. Then he'd sigh and shake his head with a "You can't cure stupid."

"Honey," he said, his voice fiercely compassionate. "It sounds like you're still mourning that man. You're worth a hundred of him."

Her heart ached to climb into her daddy's embrace. "I wish I'd listened to you in the beginning."

"I never thought I'd say I'm glad you never married him. I didn't approve of you moving in together, but at least you don't have to worry about divorcing the scumbag."

"There is that," she admitted, loving his anger on her behalf. She wouldn't talk about the other loss. Not with her father.

"How are you holding up against your mother's accusations?"

"You heard them?" Of course, he had. Mother never kept her ugly thoughts caged.

"She's an unhappy woman, honey, and I'm not sure why. Right now, she's got some foolish idea I'm involved with another woman. I want you to know that's not true."

"I never thought it was, Daddy. Not for a minute."

"That... that means a lot to me."

"But you're going to stick by her, even now? Continue to make excuses for her?" Jeminy had a hard time accepting what seemed like his weakness. He'd always said she should stand strong for what was right, and Mother's behavior fell pretty far from that mark.

"Last I heard," her father said, "God hates divorce and calls us to forgive, to love others no matter how they treat us and to bless them to the best of our ability. As far as I'm concerned, he's called me to love your mother even when she's being unlovable."

"You're a better person than I can be. I'm so angry at her that I don't have much love left and barely any forgiveness."

"You don't mean that."

"Sure I do. You should have heard her accusations and threats. The things she said…"

"That wasn't your mama talking. That was meanness the enemy put in her based on the lies he's gotten her to believe."

"Why does she listen? Because no matter where her meanness comes from, it's hurtful. I sure hope it comes out of her soon."

Daddy laughed. "Oh, honey, I do, too. I'm praying for her and her release." He paused. "I know prayer works, but sometimes the waiting on answers is hard work."

She could only muster a very ungenteel snort. "You got that right."

He cleared his throat, a sure sign he wanted to change the subject. "I'm hoping to see you now you're here on this coast. You think you could manage to come home for a weekend?"

"Daddy…"

"Right. Sorry. Well, then, why don't I see if I can visit you in Beaufort?"

"I wish you would. It's been too long."

"I'll try to clear my calendar and make it happen."

"Thank you. As soon as you can." She paused, remembering her letter from Rose. "By the way, did I know Rose had gone on some missionary trip to Africa?"

"I don't think we talked about it. You did know she'd gone to work for a medical team that travels to places that need their help because you worried she'd catch some infectious disease."

"I got a letter from her before I left L.A. She'd been thinking of me."

"She's always loved you, and she's a woman of deep faith."

"Yeah. I remember."

"I'm glad she wrote."

"Me too." As she disconnected, she wiped at a stray tear. Her daddy... The dearest man who'd ever lived. And Rose, her surrogate mother.

12

ERIC

The drive to Walmart seemed to have wiped away Danny's joy in being rescued. Whatever Eric asked was met only by silence and a mulish pout. Maybe shopping would break the ice.

All kids liked stuff. And they liked the beach. So he let Danny push the cart as they loaded it up with clothes, including a swimsuit for each of them, and with toys, books, sunscreen, and other items Danny would need, such as a toothbrush and comb. "Have to keep the toys small enough to fit on my boat," Eric said, picking up a not-so-small squirt gun, and then grabbing a second one. Boys liked battles, didn't they?

Danny handled the red water gun with a glimmer of interest. "What's your boat like? You really live on it?"

"I do." He punched a few buttons on his phone and brought up pictures of *Escape*. "Here, take a look."

Danny examined the photos. "Pretty big, huh?"

"Big enough."

"You think it can fit two guys?"

"Two cabins, two guys. Why not?"

"Where's the TV?"

Eric lowered himself to kid level and said, "Real men don't need televisions. We do other things."

Danny squinted and pursed his lips, full of skepticism. "Like what? How're you gonna know about stuff without TV? And you don't even have a backyard for playing."

"That's true. It's a good thing I have a lot of friends with big yards. And kids."

"You don't have a dog."

"No, I don't have a dog. A dog needs a yard."

"A kid needs a yard, too."

"Everything's negotiable," Eric told him, sighing inwardly because he supposed that was going to be his new truth. "Let's finish here and go find the place we'll stay for a few days."

He paid and rolled the cart outside. "You want to ride?" He indicated the front of the cart.

Danny looked skeptical until he noticed another kid giggling as he hung on and let his Mama push him. Eric's pretended struggle—"How does she do that?"—when Danny climbed on brought a grin back to the child's face.

"Okay, off you go."

At the car, Eric unlocked it and clicked open the trunk. "Grab those things, will you?" He said, indicating a bag with the squirt guns. He'd also bought a ball and a couple of mitts, along with a life vest with a safety tether for the ocean and the boat.

"You really don't know how to swim?" he asked Danny when they were settled in the car. "I took you to the beach a lot when you were little."

"Mama didn't. She said she had better things to do."

Gabby, what were you thinking?

On the way to the motel, they grabbed tacos, which Danny said he liked better than hamburgers.

"All hamburgers?" Eric shot him a surprised look in the rearview mirror.

Danny shrugged. "Don't like ones I've had, all ketchup and yucky lettuce."

"Those, young man, do not qualify. We'll find a good one before too long. And some french fries."

Eric's GPS led them across a bridge to a turquoise-and-pink stucco building set behind dunes and relatively close to the road. Inside, Avelina Finley's sister greeted them.

"Welcome to Sunflower Motel. My name's Beatrix Gambacorta." She peered over the counter at Danny. "You know *gamba corta* means 'short leg' in Italian?" She pronounced that eye-talion. "Wild, aint't it? Anyway, my husband Tony's around here somewhere. You'll recognize him when you see him 'cause he's twice my size, and, honey, that's saying something." Beatrix's belly vibrated with laughter. "My sister Avelina was so excited about you coming here for your vacation, she made me give you a beachfront room. How you like that?"

Danny's fingers clung to his, and he'd affixed himself to Eric's side.

"We're very grateful," Eric said. "And you have a pool, which is pretty amazing."

"Tony, he don't like the sand in his swimming trunks, so he mostly uses the pool. Rest of the folks who stay prefer to mosey on down to the beach and stay there until they turn crispy."

"We, this lad and I, are going to have a few swimming lessons while we're here, and there's no place better than that pool of yours."

"Indeed there isn't. You got plenty of sunscreen? You both gonna need it." At his nod, she took his credit card, swiped it, and passed the paperwork across for him to sign. "Here's your key. We have coffee, tea, and juice here in the mornings, but most folks go across the road to our other sister's little coffee shop for breakfast."

Eric emitted a bark of laughter. "Another sister?"

"Yes, sir. That one's Jasmine. And her place is named for her,

Jasmine's. Also have a brother who rents dune buggies, bikes, and boards a few miles on down the road."

"Beatrix, color me impressed. I'd love to meet your daddy and mama."

"They would have loved to meet you, too, only they've both passed on. But they taught us to work and dream, so we done exactly that. Still doing it, yessir."

As they changed into swimming trunks, Eric had a chance to examine the welts on Danny's legs. The skin was still raised and probably tender, but he could find no open wounds, which would have precluded them from using the pool. Still, the chlorine might sting, so he slathered on waterproof salve.

"Grab your towel," he said after he'd applied sunscreen to them both.

Danny took to the water in spite of the initial cold, which might have kept his mind off any pain from the welts. Maybe his body remembered toddling on the beach, playing in the surf, building sandcastles with Eric. Once they got in that clear pool water, it wasn't long before the boy was ducking his head and mimicking Eric, swimming underwater as best he could with a doggie paddle. Having his face in the water made an easy transition to kicking behind a short board and floating on his back. By tomorrow, he just might be doing the crawl.

Too exhausted and hungry to go wandering on the beach, they dried off, put on shirts, and made their way across to Jasmine's. Her offer of fried chicken and mashed potatoes sounded about perfect. Turned out it was.

Danny didn't say much while they ate, but he balked at the green beans until Eric explained the rule of eating everything on your plate as the only way in to dessert.

"What're you offering?" Danny asked.

"That's a fair question. You need information to negotiate properly, don't you?" Eric signaled the waitress so Danny could ask her.

"Let's see, hon. We have ice cream, vanilla, chocolate, and strawberry, and we have peach and blueberry pies. Also a slice or two left of today's cake, chocolate. What d'you have in mind?"

Eric raised one brow. "Beans first?"

"Okay. Then ice cream." He looked hopefully at Eric. "Two scoops?"

"Sure. Beans and then two scoops."

"Chocolate and strawberry."

The waitress raised one drawn-on brow. "You sure you don't want vanilla with that strawberry?"

"Nope. Chocolate and strawberry. My mama liked them together."

"Honey, you just let me know when you're ready."

Danny scooped up a mouthful of beans, and Eric smiled. "Won't be long."

<hr>

After the dinner and dessert, Danny's eyelids were drooping, and they headed back to their room. He brushed his teeth and pulled on his new Superman pajamas.

"Which bed d'you want?" Eric asked.

Danny pointed to the one nearest the bathroom. Eric turned down the covers, and the boy climbed in.

"Shall we read a story?" Eric asked. "I always used to read to you at bedtime."

"Yeah. Fine."

Danny chose a book with a lot of pictures about a day in the life of a fireman. Eric watched as the boy studied the pictures. He'd need to find out what Danny's education level was or if

Gabby had ignored that, too. He hadn't asked which grade the kid was in, although he imagined second.

"Can you sleep if I leave the light on for a while?"

"Sure." Danny turned away from him and pulled his pillow close.

"Goodnight, son."

At that, Danny faced him. "I'm not your son."

"Maybe not biologically, but you were always my son in my heart."

Shifting away from Eric again, Danny said, "Not your son."

A loud cry woke Eric, a cry and then soft whimpering. He climbed from bed and moved to sit next to the boy, running his hand gently over his curly hair as he whispered, "It's okay, Danny, it's okay. You're safe."

"Mommy!" The child clutched Eric's thigh before coming fully awake and pushing away. "I want my mommy."

"I know. I know you miss her."

As the tears turned to sobs, Eric lifted the child into his arms and whispered soothing words while Danny's fists pounded against his chest. "I don't want you! Go away! I want my mommy."

"I know you do. I'm so sorry."

Finally, Danny wore himself out and slept, but it was many hours before Eric's thoughts slowed enough for sleep to overtake him.

The next day, Danny followed him to the beach and sat on the sand, listlessly digging and tossing and staring at nothing. Eric had trouble enticing him into the ocean. When he finally succeeded, Danny wouldn't go beyond his knees, even though he didn't seem to fear the waves and the water hadn't reached any of his wounds. Before long, the child retreated back to the beach.

They washed off in the outdoor shower and headed back to

their room when Danny didn't want to play in the pool either. "You must learn to swim so you'll be safe on my boat," Eric said.

The boy shrugged. Eric wasn't going to make it an issue now. There was time enough.

"Get dressed, then. We'll go get some food."

"I'm not hungry."

"Too bad. I am." Eric pointed to his clothes. "Put on something dry." He turned his back, stripped, and pulled on the clothes he'd worn yesterday.

Danny did the same, ignoring the new ones Eric had bought. Again, Eric let it go. He grabbed his keys and wallet and ushered the boy to the car. "What kind of food do you want?"

"Dunno. Don't care."

Maybe a pizza would cheer him up. Eric had seen a sign about a mile back toward the mainland.

Danny crossed his arms and wouldn't move when Eric pulled up in front. "I can't leave you in the car, buddy, so out you go."

"I'm not hungry."

"Out."

"No."

"Take a look at me, Daniel. Which one of us would win, do you think, if it came down to it? You think you stand a chance?"

"I'll scream. Then you'll get in trouble."

That was true. Where was the agreeable child of yesterday?

Probably locked in anger that had been buried by shock after they'd hauled him from that horrid house.

Eric should have taken parenting classes before he'd acted so rashly in coming here. His college psych courses seemed useless.

He climbed back in the car. *God, you there? I could use some wisdom about now.*

"Look, Danny, maybe you don't want to eat, but you can at least come in with me so I can order something. You know, think of someone other than yourself? Then we can go back to the room, and you can mope all you want." Eric waited.

Finally, Danny unbuckled his seatbelt. Eric went around to the other side of the car and let him out. Inside, Eric ordered a large pizza, half with cheese and pepperoni, half with Hawaiian topping and ham. He asked for bottled water to go with it, two.

Then he led Danny to a table to wait.

He could see the boy's frustration. If he remembered correctly from his own childhood, it was hard to keep up the I'm-not-hungry pretext when your stomach was empty and you were faced with mouth-watering food. Like pizza. Danny had liked pizza at four. His tastes probably hadn't changed that much.

Eric could introduce a healthier diet later, after he'd figured out how he was going to take care of a boy and keep up with his work. Granted, he didn't have a lot of clients, but more came in every day.

And wasn't it going to be interesting when he introduced Danny to Henry. Oh, and to Brisa, who would be Danny's step-cousin by marriage.

Brisa. Whoa. He hadn't considered Brisa's parentage before now. Brisa was mixed race—a quarter black. And Danny was who-knew-what, but he was at least half something that wasn't Gabby's pale skin and blue eyes. Soon, Brisa's white mom would marry Eric's white brother, as Eric (white) had married Danny's white mom, while the two kids were several shades away from cream.

He was going to get dizzy with all these connections, but wasn't it fascinating that both these moms had come with mixed-race kids. Stuff for a novel.

Maybe he could incorporate race-mixing into his great American, plotless, notes-only book.

An image of his father slid into his thoughts. Wouldn't the great Robert E. Houston blow a gasket if he could see his sons now? Maybe he'd never expected much of his second-born, but of his first? Of Eric? Oh, yeah. And the idea that the races might overlap and intermingle within his family would never, not in his entire miserable life, have occurred to the Charleston pillar of correctness and affluence who had been their father.

That thought made Eric smile. He couldn't wait to laugh with Hen about it. Surely, Hen had come far enough past unforgiveness to see the humor in the situation.

"What?" Danny asked.

Eric had almost forgotten the boy sat across from him. He glanced up. "Nothing. Just remembering some things about my father."

"You have a dad?"

"Had one. He's dead."

Danny paused a moment, then said, "How do you know for real he's dead? Did you see him after?"

"You mean after he died?"

"Un-huh."

"Yeah. I did."

"What'd he look like?"

Eric tried to remember. He pictured the gray of the lifeless body he'd found on the library floor, and then he pictured his father in the casket, all made up and fake. "You ever seen a dead body on TV?"

Danny nodded. "Not close up. But those were just actors pretending."

"My father had a heart attack, so he looked gray and pasty. He didn't look like himself."

"But enough so you knew it was him, right?"

"Yeah. I knew."

"I haven't seen my mama. So I don't know."

Ah, of course. "They don't usually let kids see when a parent's been in a bad accident. But they have ways to know for sure it was your mama and that she was dead."

Danny stretched his thin arms across the table and leaned into it. "Does dead just mean gone? So you're here and then you're nothing?"

"Who told you that?"

"One of the girls at that house."

"The Jenkins' house?"

"Yeah. One of the big girls said my mama didn't exist anymore 'cause she'd been erased."

A theological discussion with a seven-year-old wasn't something Eric felt up to. "I don't think anyone gets erased, Danny. Everybody has a spirit, and it's only the body that dies."

At least, he believed that was so. He didn't have first-hand empirical evidence, but he had faith that what the Bible said was true. Because of Henry. "You ever heard of God?"

"I kinda think so. Back when I was a kid."

"Well, my brother—"

"Wait, you got a brother?"

"I do. We're twins, only we're fraternal twins, not identical."

"What's fraternal?"

"We don't look alike, but we were born at the same time to the same mother."

"Okay, but how come you never mentioned him before?"

The cashier called Eric's name.

"Hold that thought. Let's get the pizza, and we'll talk while we eat."

13

———

JEMINY

A new day dawning, a new time begun,
New hope in the morning, rising with the sun.

J eminy hurried to answer the doorbell before it woke Nana from her nap. What she never expected to find on the other side of the door was a FedEx driver with an electronic pad in one hand and a guitar box at her feet.

"Oh, my goodness, you're two days early!" Jeminy looked behind the driver for her other boxes. "Aren't there more? You should have a few boxes to go along with this."

"This is all I got today. I guess they fit this on an earlier flight. You hit the perfect moment 'cause my truck was ready to go when the plane landed." The young woman's smile showed bright teeth contrasting with dark lipstick and spiky black hair contrasting with a pale face.

Jeminy grinned. "Perfect moment. I love it." None of the other boxes held treasure anyway, so she could wait.

The other woman tapped a couple of buttons on the touch

112

screen and extended the pad for Jeminy to sign. "Thank you, ma'am. Have a nice day."

"I will." Oh, she would. Gully, her Seagull guitar, had arrived.

Once she had her guitar free of the box and its case and on her lap, she smoothed her hand over the wood with a lover's touch. Her fingers slid across the strings, plucked, tuned, and then strummed, going immediately into one of her songs.

Songs someone else had made famous.

Which reminded her that she needed to find a copyright lawyer to help her renegotiate her royalty contract with Darling. Now that Rand was no longer involved, he shouldn't be collecting anything from either of them. It wasn't as if she'd signed an agency contract with him or agreed to an *in perpetuity* clause for a man who'd dump her. A fool she was, but not that much of one.

She ground her teeth against the ugly words that would have shattered her joy if she let them into the room. Instead, she picked random notes that spoke for her as the music turned into a melody. Random words of tears and shame might one day become a song, maybe even one to set her free.

Jeminy blew a stray hair off her forehead, but it refused to lift and stay gone. Which pretty much summed up her attitude this morning.

She carried the guitar to Nana's back porch and let out a sigh as she glanced upward. "I really am trying."

She could almost hear Rose whispering, "I know it's hard, honey. But don't let the hard win."

Caught up in the moment, Jeminy imagined it was Rose calling from inside the house, until the creak of the screen door was followed by Nana saying, "I couldn't find you. I couldn't find anyone."

Jeminy stood and touched her nana's arm, trying to erase the worry lines and the fear in Nana's deep-set eyes. "I'm here. I haven't left." Then, drawing her grandmother toward the porch swing, she whispered, "Guess what?"

"What?" Nana whispered back, excited now.

"I'm going to write you a new song."

"For me?"

"Yes, ma'am, for you. I don't have much of anything yet, but let's see what comes."

A beginning might not become anything, but she'd let her strumming speak, the words of music soothe them both. Notes filled the air, and then a few words came.

"The sun comes up and a promise comes with it, days to laugh and days to sing. You're my dear delight, you're my precious one, you are the reason for my joy. Sing with me and laugh with me and settle here right here beside me. Together we will live this life."

She strummed a few more notes because she needed a transition and didn't have it yet, a bridge of sorts before she went into the next verse, which she also didn't have yet. The notes and words rolled out and up, down and around. When the last one eased into silence, Nana had fingertips to her lips and tears filling her eyes. "Oh, baby…"

"I love you, Nana." She might only have an audience of one these days, but that audience loved her back.

And wasn't that enough?

Jeminy sat down on the swing and picked up her guitar as her grandmother bent over a rose bush. Her guitar was a Seagull, the perfect brand for this place where seagulls perched at the end of docks. She'd named him Gulliver, Gully for short, because Gulliver traveled. He'd gone with her to college, to her first—and last—job in Nashville, where Rand had heard her sing in a small club, found out she wrote her songs, and seduced her with praise and words she should never have believed.

She tightened Gully's strings, tuning him until he sounded rich and mellow, perfect for her voice, while Nana cooed softly over a lovely yellow blossom.

Jeminy closed her eyes, listening, waiting. The scents of honeysuckle and wisteria wafted from nearby, almost overwhelmed by the heady aroma of newly mown grass. She plucked and hummed, bringing back the beginnings of her nana's song, allowing the music to sink into her mind and down her throat, then out as the words took shape. And soon that was all—notes and words, vibrations, sounds. Nothing else, no one else.

Until she opened her eyes and saw the dark-eyed-doe look of Brisa standing where the side yard met the back. "Hey, there."

"I heard you from out front. I like your song," Brisa said. "Is it new?"

"It's just the beginning of a new one. Come on up. Maybe you can help me with it."

In answer, Brisa dashed to the steps and up. Jeminy scooted over and waved Brisa to the swing. "Have a seat."

She began strumming lightly and then loosed the words. "*The sun comes up and a promise comes with it, days to laugh and days to sing. You're my dear delight, you're my precious one, you are the reason for my joy. Sing with me and laugh with me and settle right here beside me. Happy in this, happy in this, happy together as we live this life.*"

The lyrics had changed slightly, better fitting the tune growing under her fingers. They'd probably continue to move around until the song was fully formed. She strummed through the pause and then found more words.

"*Together we will dance at the moon, together we will sing to the sun, up and down through all our days, down and up through the nights we share. Happy in this, happy in this, happy together as we live this life. Sing with me and laugh with me and settle right here beside me.*"

It was a wistful song of longing that spoke of coming home, of purpose and love. "I just started with thoughts I've been having about my nana. Songs can stay in our memory when we lose other things, so perhaps if I finish it and sing it to her often, she'll remember how much she is loved."

"Will you sing it again so I can learn it?"

"Just like that, eh?" Jeminy grinned and did as Brisa asked.

One more run-through and Brisa sang it back, note-perfect.

"Very nice. I bet we could harmonize, too. You sing the lines and the melody just as you did. I'll begin three notes up." She showed the girl, nodded her approval when Brisa remained with the melody instead of following her. At the end, Jeminy stilled Gully's strings. "Did you ever sing harmony with your daddy?"

"I don't think so. Maybe I did with the radio, but I didn't know the name for it."

"You're amazing."

Brisa grinned sheepishly. "I bet my daddy will like your new song."

"I don't know if he'll ever hear it."

"Oh, he will."

A voice called for Brisa from the street, interrupting Jeminy's question of how that might happen. The girl bolted up. "I've got to go. Thank you for the lesson." And over her shoulder as she hit the ground running, "Maybe we can do it again sometime?"

"I'd like that," Jeminy called to Brisa's back.

She would. She'd like it very much indeed. Having a singing partner would make living here so much more fun. Amazing, wasn't it, that Darling's only child lived just down the street?

Coincidence or meant to be?

14

ERIC

Eric rested his forearms on the steering wheel for a moment before turning off the car and waking Danny. It was about to begin, this adventure of living on board *Escape* with a young boy.

He took a deep breath, turned the key, and waited. "We're here," he finally said.

Danny sat up, rubbed his eyes, and looked around at the unfamiliar sights. "This it?"

"It is. You ready to go check out your new home?"

"I guess."

In spite of his exhaustion, Eric kept his voice calm, his smile pasted on, when all he really wanted was to sag onto his bunk and not think about the future.

He'd get the boy settled and then come back for the stuff they'd picked up at the Walmart.

"You need to hold onto my hand on the dock."

There was enough daylight left for Danny to see where they were walking and to check out the other boats. There was also enough for him to look over the dock's edge at the water.

Danny pointed below them. "That's how come I need to learn to swim."

"One of the reasons. There's lots of water around here and lots of places that could be dangerous for someone who can't swim. Until we get you certified, you'll have to hold my hand or wear a life jacket."

"Life jackets are for sissies."

"No. Life jackets are for everyone at sea and for non-swimmers anywhere near water. They can save your life." Eric stopped at the finger pier to which *Escape* was tied. "Here we are. This is home."

"Really?" Danny looked from the dark hull to the top of the mast. "It's pretty big, but not so big as that one." He pointed at a huge motor yacht tied up at the end of the dock.

"Not nearly as big as that." Touching Danny's shoulder to stop him, he said, "Stand right here." He unhitched the folding ladder and positioned it. "You think you can climb this?"

Danny puffed out his skinny chest. "Sure."

"One hand here, the other there. Good boy." Eric stood behind him as Danny climbed to the deck. "Great job."

Once they were on board and standing in the cockpit, Danny continued to thaw as he checked out the wheel and tried to see ahead. "It's real big."

"We'll find a stool for you to see over when we go somewhere."

"Can we? I mean, go places?"

"Sure. What good would it do to have a moveable house if you don't take it anywhere?"

Danny grinned, his big-boy teeth large in his face. Eric opened the companionway doors. "Come on. Let's check out below."

"'kay."

"Watch your step and hang on to this pole as you go. That's it. Good."

Danny turned around and looked at the space. "Kinda little inside here, isn't it?"

"How much room do you need?" Eric walked forward. "This little kitchen is called the galley, and I can stand here and cook and still chat with you if you sit there in the salon."

"Where do you sleep?"

Eric had been thinking about the safest place for the boy, and that wouldn't be closest to the exit. "Come on up here." He led the way to the V-berth in the bow. "This can be your room now. There, take off your shoes and climb that little step. Up you go."

Danny crawled onto the mattress. "This is pretty neat. I can see the sky up there. Does that window open?"

"It does." Soon Danny'd be big enough to climb out that hatch onto the deck. But not yet, thank God.

"Where do I put my stuff?"

"You see the netting there, and here's a cupboard that we can make yours." Eric opened it. There was an area to hang clothes as well as three drawers below that. "On a boat, we don't carry a lot of stuff, but there's room enough for necessities."

"Where do you sleep?"

"There's another cabin with a bunk for me in the stern—or back—of the boat. That'll work." It would have to. Good thing he didn't have to worry about fitting in two adults. "Why don't you hang right here while I go fetch our stuff from the car?"

The boy lay back with his hands behind his head, and Eric hurried to complete the unloading because there was no telling what a curious boy might get into if left alone for any length of time.

Fortunately, Danny remained on his bunk. When Eric had brought in the last bag, he peeked into the forward cabin and found the boy curled up and asleep.

He watched the sleeping child for a few minutes. He'd rouse Danny after he unpacked. He still had to show the boy how to use a manual flush toilet.

Turning away, Eric sighed loudly. *Lord, how am I going to do this?* Manage a child and work with no babysitter? He really hadn't thought things through before he'd left on what became a rescue mission. He'd have to make phone calls, but to whom? He certainly didn't want to put pressure on any of his friends to provide themselves as a solution to his problem, but maybe one of the kids was old enough to stay with Danny... but not here on the boat. Which meant hiring one of them would place an imposition on their family.

As he unpacked and organized what they'd brought with them, he went through the list of people he knew—again—and came up with no one who wouldn't make promises and offers they might easily come to regret.

Perhaps his brain would be rested enough tomorrow to conjure a solution. There had to be someone he could hire who'd take Danny to the park or playground—surely there was a playground somewhere in town—after school while he was at work. Someone who'd be safe aboard a boat, who could climb in and out and keep Danny from hurting himself or falling overboard.

The images from that thought nearly threw him into panic mode.

Bringing Danny here, imagining he could fit the boy into his life, had to be the worst idea he'd ever had.

He couldn't sleep. It wasn't just that he no longer had his comfortable berth. That was a minor issue. It was having to consider what to do with the occupant of his bed that crippled his sleep.

Eric had found himself praying more in these last two days than he had in his entire life, except maybe the day Gabby left him —and not because she left, but because she'd bundled his heart in a car seat and he'd been unable to stop her from leaving.

He'd been skeptical about his twin's faith as he'd watched

Henry wrestle with sobriety, but these last couple of years Henry had shown the strength of that faith along with his conviction that God was really at work. He'd certainly convinced Eric that *he*, Henry, believed.

Not that Eric had done much more than acknowledge Hen's truth in the beginning. Oh, he'd gone to church with his brother and Agnes a few times, but the church they loved didn't fit him. It seemed too exuberant, too loud, and he'd been very conscious of being one of only a few light-skinned congregants. That didn't seem to bother Hen or Agnes, especially because Brisa seemed so at home there after she and her famous birth father had sung together at that church.

Eric preferred the services he attended with Clay and his family. He wasn't sure why. Maybe the liturgy touched some memory of going to church with his mother before she'd been overcome by depression and the meds she took. He and Hen had walked up the aisle, hand in hand with her, to take communion. They'd knelt, one on each side of her, and been given a wafer and a blessing by the priest.

Clay's church, All Saints, was Anglican, while his mother's had been Episcopalian, but they seemed very much the same, at least from his childhood memories. Clay had told him there were theological differences and had gone on to explain them, most of which had to do with what Clay called "the whole counsel of God" and teaching biblical truth.

Eric had learned to question everything, but this God connection seemed to require that he step off a cliff and trust he'd be kept from falling.

Okay, maybe that wasn't a good analogy. A cliff suggested danger. What danger did faith in God pose unless it was to his ability to control things? His father and the world had taught him he could keep control through hard study, hard work, and determining to manage everything correctly. Purposefully. Hadn't his father said—

Eric steadied himself as images flashed of his father's squinting eyes or raised brow and straight lips, of his father's words, and of his father's abuse of Henry.

Abuse he, the elder twin, hadn't been able to stop. Protection he hadn't been able to offer, especially when his own world had turned in such different directions from Hen's. What else could he have done?

His eyes slammed shut. Truth, the full truth, had to be acknowledged, didn't it? For healing, for freedom.

But how did he do that?

He remembered going to a counselor after Gabby left. He'd been grief-stricken, hurting, and the counselor—fool that he'd been—had tried to dig through Eric's past to come up with psychological mumbo-jumbo to explain his marriage and his love for Danny, a child not his. Something about his own need for a parent making him cling to a parenting role that had never actually been his own.

Huh? Had the man been drinking laced Kool-Aid? Of course Danny had been his. Danny'd been the child of Eric's heart, no matter whose sperm had fertilized the egg.

Eric shook himself. How had his thoughts gone down such a rabbit hole?

He descended the companionway steps, grabbed his iPod and earbuds, and climbed back in his bunk. He'd listen to music. Maybe that would put him to sleep.

Tomorrow, he'd figure out his life.

There was always tomorrow.

15

JEMINY

Fix and fashion, turn and clean,
Busy the hands, still the brain.

Jeminy was determined to do things differently today. First on her list was to organize repairs. The roofer Isa recommended said he'd be around to check for leaks soon as he could grab a free moment. Jeminy wondered what that meant in the roofing world—a couple of days? Weeks?

The plumber would stop by later that day, if he wasn't held up by his other jobs. "Not an emergency, is it?"

"Just a drip I couldn't fix that's driving me crazy."

He'd laughed and said he'd do his best. She'd see what that meant.

The yard man agreed to a schedule to mow and clean up the overgrown brush out back. "I'll start Thursday, if that's okay with you."

"You don't have anything sooner? It's a real mess out there."

"Well…" he seemed to consider. "I guess I could give you a couple hours after lunch."

"Thank you. I'd be grateful."

All of that was a whole lot easier than dealing with the clutter in the house, but she did get through two piles of mail and magazines stacked next to Nana's chair in the front room before running the vacuum and dusting.

By three-thirty, she wanted to stretch her legs, but the idea of hitting the sidewalks at more than a stroll didn't appeal, not when the humidity meant droplets would form on her skin that came from the air as well as her sweat glands. A walk, though, would work, especially if she kept to a slower pace. At least she'd be out of doors, soaking up a little Vitamin D. She changed into a loose sundress, slid her feet into sandals, and went in search of her grandmother.

The yard man, Keith, had actually come, and his mower was making enough racket to deafen anyone who got too close. Jeminy waited until his path took him up the side yard before approaching her grandmother, who sat on her swing, petting the friendly cat.

"I thought I'd walk into town. Do you want to come?"

Nana straightened and looked around with an expression of surprised pleasure. "I would. We could go have a latte. Would you like me to treat you to a latte? And maybe some of those wonderful pastries."

"Are you talking about going back to *Samantha's*?"

"I'll take you. And I can treat you to a latte."

Jeminy held open the back door for her grandmother, then closed and locked it behind her. "A hat, Nana. Where do you keep them?"

"In the hall closet. Yes, I need a hat. You, too."

Jeminy handed her nana a hat that looked well-loved and then helped her search for her sunglasses.

"I don't know where I left them. I always put them on the table out there so I'll have them when I go somewhere. Have you seen them? Did you pick them up?"

"No, but maybe you left them in the kitchen. I'll just run and check."

She scanned the counters and was about to turn away to run upstairs when she saw them neatly closed on top of the sugar canister.

"Oh, thank you," Nana said when Jeminy delivered them. "I wondered where they were because they were supposed to be here."

"Is that everything? Do you have tissues?" Her nana always needed a tissue, or imagined she needed one.

"In my purse. I should have my purse."

"Do you remember where you keep it?"

"I always put it in my room. I'm sure it's there."

"Be right back." Jeminy bounded up the stairs and turned to her grandmother's room.

She checked in the closet, opened a few drawers, and then noticed a zipper pull sticking out from under a throw pillow on Nana's bed. She shook her head, imagining the thought process that would have tucked the purse out of sight.

She slid her own bag over her shoulder and headed back to her grandmother, who was now sitting on a hall chair, examining her fingernails. "I need a manicure," Nana said.

"I can give you one later, if you'd like."

"Thank you, honey. I'd like that. Or you and I could go out together to get one. Belinda does a lovely job."

"Whatever you'd like. Here's your purse."

"Are we going to Belinda's salon now?"

"I thought we'd walk to *Samantha's* for a nice latte."

Nana's expression turned from puzzled to pleased. "Wonderful, but you need a hat, too."

"Perhaps I could pick one up. I seem to remember there's a place that has a lot of hats."

"We'll get you a hat." Nana tilted her head and studied Jeminy. "A pretty yellow one. To set off your dark curls."

"That would be fun."

Jeminy could picture jaunty and yellow. She took her grandmother's elbow as they walked down the front porch steps and out to the sidewalk. Nana straightened her back and headed toward town with purpose. Across the street, a few folk wandered in a leisurely fashion as they checked out boats anchored in Taylor Creek. A little further on, visitors lined up for the tour boat that would take them on a dinner-time cruise. Other tours went all the way to Cape Lookout, but not usually at this time of day.

Jeminy remembered her grandaddy's boat, long gone now, its topsides sparkling with bits of teak he'd varnished until you could almost see your reflection in the shine. She remembered her pride in being able to go out on a family boat and not having to pay someone else to take her.

"Your grandfather used to love taking you with him, you know," Nana said, echoing her thoughts.

"Whatever happened to his boat?"

"Your uncle sold it." Nana's wistful tone made Jeminy miss childhood moments she hadn't considered in years. Maybe her grandmother felt the same.

"We used to love going out to the cape, didn't we?" Images of Olli's huge grin, of him pointing to the wild ponies, to dolphins, to sea turtles, flashed into memory. The two of them had made sandcastles, run down dunes, cavorted in tidal pools, dug for shells, and checked out sand crabs. Closer to home, their granddaddy had taken them gigging for flounder with lanterns and crab nets.

She swallowed hard against the lump those memories provoked.

Nana's voice broke into her thoughts. "We had good times there, your grandfather and I. The children, too. I thought they'd keep the boat for vacations here. But Andrew said it was too much work. And his widow never liked North Carolina."

"Does his wife—I mean, widow—ever come now to see you, Nana? Or call?"

Nana shook her head. "She likes the city."

So, no help for Nana from New York. Who cared, though? Really, who cared? She didn't. Her focus would be on Nana.

And on Nana's house. She ought to be able to bring order in a few more days, maybe a week—if she ignored the attic. Oh, and the fourth bedroom. She hadn't even peeked in either of those.

She wanted to hurry her grandmother toward a latte and bagel; instead, they moseyed as they approached Clawson's and then a shop Nana pointed to. "Hats?" But it had only nautical memorabilia. Three shops down, though, a display featured the perfect hat, big-brimmed and jaunty, the yellow Nana'd wanted for her. "I could never wear yellow," Nana said. "But on you, my sweet, it is like sunshine."

Jeminy leaned over to kiss her grandmother's soft cheek. Moments like this, when Nana seemed completely fine, had to be held close. She vowed to do whatever it took to protect and encourage and, well, just be here for Nana.

Hats shielding their faces, they continued into town, stopping at a hail from across the street. "Miss Georgie!" Jilly, the little red-haired bundle of energy, called.

"Girls, hello. Do you know my granddaughter?"

"We do!" Jilly said.

Nana seemed so pleased to see them that Jeminy said, "Well, Jilly and Brisa, what are you two up to? We thought we'd go over to *Samantha's* and get ourselves a latte or something. Would you like to join us? Maybe they have ice cream." She checked her watch. "Or have you had your after-school snack?"

The girls looked at each other and nodded. "No, we haven't." Jilly, the obvious spokesperson, said, "They have frozen yogurt that's real good."

"Nana, I've invited our neighbors to join us. They'd probably like something cool on this hot day."

"Oh, I would, too." Nana turned to the girls. "Will your mothers mind?"

"They said we could come to town. I have money," Jilly announced.

"No, no," Nana said. "It will be my treat."

"Thank you, Miss Georgie."

"That's so nice of you, Mrs. Warren."

Nana looked at Brisa with a frown. Jeminy had no idea why, except those were the first words from Brisa today. And then something settled over her grandmother. "You should call me Miss Georgie, too, young lady. If your friend does, I think you should, too."

Brisa beamed. "Thank you, Miss Georgie."

The girls held hands as they skipped down the sidewalk, pausing every few skips to wait for the older folks. They were the first ones into *Samantha's* and held the door open together—Jilly with her back against the open door and Brisa tugging on the handle. When Jeminy and her grandmother were safely inside, Jilly spoke to the woman behind the counter.

"Tootie, hey!"

"Hey to you all! Miss Georgie, how're you doing? I have your favorite yogurt here, that peach you like so much. Made it myself with peaches from Macray's farm." Tootie turned her bright smile on the rest of them. "And you three, what's on your mind for today? Frozen yogurt or a pastry? And maybe a latte for you, Jeminy? It's great to have you back."

"Lovely to be here, Tootie. You'll be seeing a lot of me because I'm here for a good long time."

"I know your grandmother is thrilled."

The girls leaned forward to peer in the freezer section. "Please," Jilly said. "I want the strawberry banana."

"Vanilla with chocolate sauce for me," Brisa said. "In a bowl so it doesn't go down my front."

Tootie laughed. "In a bowl. Perfect." She looked again at Jeminy.

"A latte and one of those chocolate croissants. And, Nana? Latte or peach frozen yogurt?"

"Both? Or maybe tea."

"Coming right up!"

Jeminy watched the girls lead Nana toward a table by the window. "I'll help carry everything."

"Thank you," Tootie said with what must be her signature grin, she flashed it so often.

The bell over the door rang as more customers entered. Tootie called to a girl in the back to come help before sliding the yogurt bowls across the counter. "Why don't you get Jilly to come fetch her cone?"

Jilly showed up at the counter before Jeminy could turn around. "Thank you," Jilly said, taking her cone and immediately licking it.

"I'm so glad you're prospering," Jeminy told Tootie. "*Samantha's* really adds to the waterfront area."

"We do fairly well, and it keeps me busy."

"Winters, too?"

"Less, but the locals like a good cup of coffee, and we sure have that. Selling kitchen supplies augments the coffee and pastry sales." She passed over Jeminy's drink and croissant.

"Thanks, Tootie."

Jeminy slid into an empty chair next to her nana and took a sip of the delicious latte. As the girls and Nana devoured their frozen yogurt, Jeminy bit into the croissant and let out a huge sigh.

Somehow Jilly managed to talk and eat. "I love the croissants, don't you, Miss Jeminy? I mean, it's hard to pick the best thing to have when you come in here, croissant or yogurt. Even the muffins are great. Don't you think so?"

"I do indeed."

And so the conversation zipped from one subject to another with surprising speed, mostly due to the little redhead. Jilly was a spitfire and full of stories, especially ones involving the sailboat her family traveled on before they came home to have Sammy.

Jeminy waited for a break when Jilly's mouth was full and turned to Brisa. "How's your dad doing?"

"He's great. I got to go visit his grandmother. She's my great-grandmother. Isn't that amazing? And I have more cousins than anyone. It was so much fun!"

"I bet it was. I noticed that he's working under his own label now. You know, with his songs?"

"I don't know much about that, but he sure seems happier."

How nice that one of them was.

Something... well, okay, some*one* caught Jeminy's eye. She wouldn't look, she wouldn't...

She certainly shouldn't stare at the man's face or let her eyes wander to those muscular arms. She certainly shouldn't notice his height. Or anything about him.

She wasn't ever going to look at a man again.

But, really?

Anyway, this guy had a kid with him, which probably meant a wife. Not that the kid resembled him, but mixed marriages weren't uncommon.

The man and boy approached the counter, and the boy peered into the glass to check out the frozen yogurt. The man ordered a decaf for himself and waited while the child chose.

"That one. The swirly one."

"Rainbow?" Tootie asked. "On a cone or in a bowl?"

"Cone."

"Danny," the man prompted.

"Please," the boy said.

"Tootie, this is Danny, who has come all the way from South Carolina to live with me."

The boy seemed to focus on the ice cream scoop that Tootie pressed into the cone. "I came on account of my mama being dead. I didn't get to see her, so I have to believe people who said so."

Jeminy surreptitiously wiped at her lips to make certain no chocolate croissant lingered. Sitting at a table close enough to eavesdrop had netted a lot of information. Interesting information.

"That's got to be hard." Tootie handed the cone across the counter. "It happened to me when I was about your age, maybe younger, and all of a sudden my granddaddy was gone, and I didn't even get to see him sick, although that's what they said had happened. He used to give me chocolate mints, but that had been our secret."

"So then you didn't get any?"

"I didn't."

"My mommy didn't give me chocolate mints, but she was real good with hugs and stories."

"I'm sorry she's not here to give you those, but I bet the people who told you about her dying knew how to tell if a body's dead, don't you think?"

Danny took a bite off the top of his yogurt. "That's what he said." This time the boy angled the cone in the man's direction.

By now, the two girls were also listening raptly. Nana continued to take small bites of her peach yogurt, wiping her lips often.

Tootie grinned. "Eric's pretty smart. I bet he checked things out for himself."

The man's name was Eric. Good name.

"I guess so." The child seemed unconvinced.

Brisa stood up. "Be right back."

"Hey, Uncle Eric," she said, sidling up to him.

"Brisa, hey to you. I'd like you to meet Danny."

"You said he's gonna live with you? Like be your kid?"

"Yeah, like that." Eric laid a hand on the boy's shoulder. "Danny, remember how I told you I have a brother?"

Danny nodded, but his focus was on Brisa.

"Well, this is Brisa. Her mommy is going to marry my brother, so you two will be sort of cousins."

"Is your mama a black lady?" Danny tilted his head, studying her.

Brisa grinned. "My real daddy is, sort of. My mom's white. What about yours?"

"I don't know my daddy, but he's like me, Mama said." The child pointed to his forearm, which was a shade darker than Brisa's.

Brisa nodded. "My mama pretended she didn't know who my daddy was, too, but then he found me. How old are you?"

"Seven and a half. I'll be eight soon."

"I'm twelve. You're kinda tall for your age."

"Yeah."

"Me, too. Me and Jilly—that's Jilly over there with the red hair. She's my best friend, and we know lots of kids in the neighborhood. You'll like them."

"You think?"

"Sure. Come on. You guys sit with us." Brisa led the way without waiting for a response.

Eric seemed slightly bemused, but he followed. Brisa made the introductions, ending with "Danny's going to be my cousin. Isn't that cool?"

"Step-cousin." The man named Eric smiled apologetically. He had a lovely voice. And eyes that mirrored his expression. And he was staring at her. She tried to smile back, but her insides were tumbling crazily, and she didn't like that. At all.

"Step-schmep, who cares?" Jilly waved away that distinction. "I've got a step-mom and a half-brother."

"Mrs. Warren. Nice to see you again." When Nana didn't seem to hear him, he glanced down at Jeminy. "You must be the granddaughter? Isa said you were flying in."

So this was Mr. Hunky Lawyer. A man that good-looking ought not to be allowed laughing eyes. It wasn't fair. He returned Jeminy's gaze with a fatally attractive eye-smile.

She tried to clear her thoughts so they wouldn't show. "I'm Jeminy. I think Isa set up an appointment for us to meet tomorrow."

"I think so."

"Grab a chair," she told him. The girls had already pulled one over for Danny and settled him between them.

"Mrs. Warren," Eric said, squeezing in next to her and touching her arm, "how are you today?"

Nana smiled happily. "I'm perfectly fine, thank you very much. All these lovely young people have been keeping us entertained, haven't they, Jeminy? That's my granddaughter there. Jeminy."

"Good afternoon, Jeminy." Eric's eyes twinkled again.

She wished he wouldn't twinkle anywhere near her. His eyes were a lethal weapon in her war against an attraction she was *not* going to feel. "Indeed," she said, glancing down at her almost empty cup. She would ignore the slight heating of her cheeks. Maybe he'd think she'd been too long in the sun.

When she looked up again, she'd regained some control. "There's a story here, I assume."

"A longish one."

"Ah." She wouldn't pry, but she'd certainly like to hear it. Nosy? Fine. Yes, she was. Who wouldn't be?

Besides, it seemed this was her grandmother's lawyer. She assumed that would make him hers as well. Maybe.

If this were a big city, they'd never run into each other at a coffee shop, never face each other as anything but attorney and client. Here, though?

Yeah, she wanted to know.

"This isn't the place to go into it, but I'm not trying to keep anything a secret." He'd shifted his attention to the three kids, but he obviously directed his words to her.

"Of course. You certainly don't owe anyone an explanation."

"No, but Danny's story's important, especially as I'm going to need help figuring out how to care for him."

"Why? Because you work?"

"Because I work and because I live on a boat."

"Really? That sounds like fun."

"It is. Or it was. I'm not sure it's going to be the best place for a non-swimmer who's only seven."

"No, I can see that might be a problem." She studied the boy who seemed to be loving the attention of two older girls. "Do you have any ideas?"

He turned to look at her, a worried frown creasing his brow. "I haven't a clue. It's not like I have a house where a babysitter can come, and he's too old for day care."

Out of the blue, Nana pointed across the table. "Who is that little boy?" Her voice was loud enough for even the children to hear.

For a moment they were too stunned to answer, and then Brisa piped up with, "He's Danny, my new cousin. Or almost," and Jilly said, "He's our new friend."

Eric leaned toward Nana to say, "Danny's my son."

Nana squinted up at him. "You have a son?"

"No." That was Danny.

Eric winked at the boy and didn't lose a beat. "I do. And I've brought him here to live with me."

Nana spoke to Danny. "You must come visit. I have two cats I bet you'll like."

Danny's big eyes beseeched Eric. Jeminy kept her attention on the boy when Eric spoke. "Indeed we will. Thank you, Mrs. Warren."

"Can we all come?" Jilly asked. "We need to take Danny to meet everyone."

"Really?" Danny said, his voice an octave higher with excitement.

"Uncle. Eric, will you let him come with us?" Brisa flashed her sweet smile at him. "Me and Jilly can show him Beaufort."

"Please?" Jilly asked. "We'll take good care of him."

"Yeah, can I?"

How could Eric resist his son's eyes, the dark depth of them pleading? And the child's lashes? Jeminy grinned. Those were going to be dangerous when Danny figured out how to use them —as Eric's smiling eyes already held enough power to slay a susceptible female.

Like you, Jeminy girl?

Her smile faded. No, not like her. She had no room for a man in her life.

Eric hesitated. Was he worried about letting a child Danny's age loose on the town with only two young girls to watch out for him? He turned to her. "What do you think?"

"This is Beaufort," she said. "Brisa and Jilly have been wandering it for a long time. Besides, their homes aren't far from Nana's. Perhaps you'd let Danny go with them to meet their mamas and then come back to hang out with Nana and me until you're ready to pick him up."

"I guess I could."

"Are you working today?"

"I thought I might stop by to check in, take Danny with me. We've registered him at the school and done our grocery shopping, but I have to pick up my messages and get back to any clients who're waiting for a return call."

"Aww..." Danny obviously didn't want to go to an office.

"Danny," Jeminy said, "would you like to go with the girls and then come to visit us and the cats?"

"Can we come, too?" Brisa asked. "Maybe we can all sing together."

"That's fine with me, and I'm sure Nana would like the company."

"Can I?" Danny was already pushing back his chair. "I'm finished."

The girls stood and picked up their trash. Danny noticed and copied them, carrying his to the bin when they did. Then they all returned to await Eric's answer.

"Fine. But don't get in anyone's way, okay? And do what the girls say." He thought a minute. "Hold hands crossing the street. I'll pick you up, say around five?"

Danny grinned. "Okay. See you later!"

"Thanks, Mr. Eric," both girls said, not quite in unison. "'Bye!"

He rested his forehead on his hands. "I'm not sure I'm cut out for this. Scenarios of disaster are already playing in my head."

Jeminy laughed. "They'll be fine. My brother and I used to visit Nana when we were little, and we roamed the streets and played with neighboring kids."

He looked over at her. "That was then. I don't know how Will does it. Trusts Jilly like that."

Nana's yogurt and tea were long gone. "Could I have a nice cup of tea? I forgot to get one earlier."

"Of course you may." She whisked Nana's cup away and started to rise.

Eric beat her to it. "I'll get it. What kind would you like, Mrs. Warren?"

"Kind?"

"Of tea. You often like the green tea." Jeminy looked toward the counter. "Or Earl Grey." She wouldn't mention that Nana had already had a cup of green tea.

"Green tea. Green tea sounds lovely."

It took only minutes, and Eric returned with a cup of tea and a packet of sugar. "Did you want anything else?" he asked Jeminy.

"Oh, no thank you. I filled up on that croissant. It's salad for us tonight."

He moved his chair back where it belonged and sat across from Jeminy. "So I can see you both. I was getting dizzy, all that back and forth."

"We don't want dizzy."

"Perhaps you'd let me explain how I came to have Danny."

"If you want to, of course."

"People are going to wonder, and if I'm looking for help with him, I'd better."

She waited.

"I married Danny's mother when she came to me, pregnant, and said I'd gotten her that way. Obviously, I hadn't, but I didn't know that until he was born."

"That had to be a shock."

He shrugged. "It was. But in spite of his parentage, I fell in love with him the moment he looked at me."

"He has killer eyes." She fluttered hers at him and grinned. "And lashes."

"I think he came out like that, the slight slant and those lashes. And so I forgave her, and we tried to make it work. I was, in all essentials, Danny's father for the first four years of his life. In my heart, he's always been mine."

"What happened after those four years?"

"She wanted out, and by concocting various scenarios, ended up with full custody. When she died, Social Services came looking for a relative. In the meantime, they had him in a wretched home. You wouldn't believe."

"Poor baby."

"I wanted to damage the lout's face for what he'd done to an innocent boy—although his wife was probably just as bad. Anyway, here he is, and I need to figure out how to make it work."

"Have you considered renting a place on *terra firma*? It might make finding a sitter just a tad easier."

"Frankly, I haven't had time to think that far ahead. I really love living on *Escape*. She's the perfect size, and I can change backyards whenever I want."

"Hard then."

"Exactly. But a matter of priorities."

16

MR. JENKINS

Dalton pulled a plastic toothpick out of his pocket and worked a mess of gristle from between two teeth. Hamburgers were barely worth the money these days, all filler, fat, and this hard stuff. Maybe he should have gone with that fish sandwich. Specialty of North Carolina, the sign had said.

Of course, it might have been full of bones that could kill him.

Dinky little town with too many out-of-towners trying to swank it up. Same thing in Charleston, which was why he only went there for special clients.

That made him chuckle. Special client had him here, too, sitting in his truck, shadowing that man and Danny.

Lookee there, the boy was let loose with a couple of girls. Should be real easy to snatch him, only Dalton'd have to be real careful. The girls would be witnesses.

Cute little redhead. And the brownish one? Oh, man, she'd bring a good price. Both of them would.

Only how would he grab all three, get them in his truck and to Charleston, unhurt and unmarked? He didn't have enough drugs for more than the boy.

Still, if the kid could run loose with no adult, all he, Dalton, had to do was be patient.

And find something a sight better to eat than that hamburger.

17

ERIC

E ric turned off his office computer and left the room. He'd been so engrossed in going through notes from his researcher that he'd lost track of time, and it took AnnaLouise poking her head into his office to remind him that he had more than himself to consider.

Clouds hovered on the horizon, hinting at an approaching storm, but the weather was still lovely as he headed toward the residential area to the east. Shouts and laughter drew him to the house he identified as Mrs. Warren's and then around to her backyard. Children of all shapes and sizes ran around laughing, and Danny was right in their midst.

A smile tugged at his lips as he watched.

From the porch, a voice said, "Hey, Eric. Come on in." It was Tadie, standing at the open screen door with a glass of tea in her hand. "Jeminy's upstairs making sure her grandmother has all she needs, and the rest of us have gathered up front. You want some iced tea?"

Puzzled, wanting to know who the rest of them were, he followed her. "I would, thank you."

"Here, take a glass, and I'll bring the pitcher. Go on through to the living room."

Agnes, Hannah, and Rita all stared at him as he entered. And they stared just a little too closely for his comfort. "Ladies," he said.

Agnes was the first to speak. "Interesting to know you have a son. Interesting also that Henry doesn't seem to know anything about this family addition." She didn't sound at all pleased.

"No. I was planning to introduce them today, but things got away from me."

"He's your twin. Why doesn't he know?"

Eric raised his brow at her, his left brow. He didn't appreciate the inferred judgement in her tone. "My twin was busy with his own issues during that period of my life." That ought to shut her up.

"But since?"

His inclination was to back up a step, turn around, and leave. Who was Agnes to get in his face about his relationship with his brother? Instead, he took a deep breath and released it slowly. "Since," he said, keeping his voice level, "there hasn't been anything to discuss. Danny's mother left and took him away three years ago, and I didn't see any reason to bring up what seemed like a closed chapter in my life."

"Your silence has hurt Henry."

"Did he tell you so?"

"No, but..."

Keep your cool, he told himself. Breathe.

"Look, Agnes, I know you mean well, but you might try not to make this into something it isn't. Danny was in need of rescuing, and it seemed like an emergency to me when I got there. I didn't plan to deceive anyone, and I certainly didn't think Hen would find out about Danny through you and Brisa before I had a chance to speak to him. " He stepped into the room, plowing his fingers through his hair. "Perhaps we could table this until then?"

Agnes turned with a shrug. He'd been so focused on her displeasure that he hadn't noticed Tadie stopping behind him or the interested stares from the others.

"Sorry." He shifted out of Tadie's way.

Rita, who'd worked with him on Brisa's case, spoke up. "Danny seems to be a delightful child. You have custody of him?"

"I do. I'm all he has."

Jeminy came in then. "Hey, Eric."

"Jeminy." Yep, there she was.

What did that mean? *There she was?* He tried not to follow her with his gaze, stare at her hair trailing down her back, at her length. Tall, elegant...

"You're wrong about being all he has," Tadie said. "Danny—and you—aren't in this alone. You have all of us. You know how this works." She refilled Rita's glass. "Anyone else need more?"

"I do," Jeminy grabbed an empty glass from the table in front of the couch. "This is mine, I think."

Eric forced himself to look from one to the other of the women. Agnes had either gotten over her snit, or she was willing to let him have the last word. Maybe she didn't want to keep showing herself in a bad light.

And maybe she felt better since she'd vented, but he didn't. Although he supposed he'd have to get over that, certainly before he spoke to Hen.

Agnes's words had triggered an old anger he'd been trying to cover up or sublimate—or something. Wasn't he the one who'd always been there for everyone, including his twin—mostly his twin? The one who'd tried to rescue Henry again and again? The one who'd lost the boy he'd loved as his own? The one who'd been dumped on by Gabrielle, always and again, for the final time, by her death?

So what if he hadn't told Henry about Danny? So *what?* Henry couldn't have been involved back when the child had lived with

Eric, not when he was using and more out of rehab than in. And then Danny'd been gone.

Eric would tell his brother now. That ought to be good enough for all of them.

He was pulled back into the conversation when Tadie spoke. "Eric? Brisa and Jilly said you need some place for Danny to stay when you go to work because there's the issue of him being on a boat."

He'd watched the town take action before, and Tadie always seemed at the forefront. Now he was seeing her at work. "Yes."

"I take it you didn't have time to think this through before you brought the child here?" Rita asked, a little too pointedly.

Again, Eric's brow shot up. "What about *emergency* makes that question even relevant?"

"Let's start over, why don't we?" Hannah spoke for the first time, waving a hand through the air as if to bat away all the tension. "Eric has done a good thing in rescuing a child in need. And we should be the ones helping him figure out how to manage now—not the ones castigating him for anything he's done or hasn't done."

Tadie nodded. "Amen. And, Agnes, your daughter—as she reminded us when she introduced Danny—is about to become his cousin by marriage."

"She is pretty excited about that." Agnes's smile seemed tentative, as if she were embarrassed by her earlier outburst. She ought to be.

"And," said Tadie, "it doesn't hurt that her skin tone almost matches his."

"I've tried to keep her from feeling the odd one out..."

"And so have we," Tadie said. "Because to us, she's not."

"She certainly isn't," said Rita, poking at her own arm. "We come in all shades."

"But a darker-skinned child in a white world does stand out, no matter how we pretend otherwise." This time Agnes couldn't hide the pain in her voice.

"Honey," Rita said, "we can either let stupid speak to our self-image, or we can let good surround us. You know my story, and you know how Tadie and hers were always there for me and mine. So, you just stop worrying about that girl of yours."

"Besides," Tadie said, her grin widening, "her daddy's fame gave her instant popularity at school, according to Jilly."

Agnes wiped below her eyes as if some of the words spoken had touched a sensitive spot. "It has, hasn't it?" Her posture seemed to relax. "I guess I still get defensive."

"No need. You've done a great job with that young lady," Rita said, "and Darling seems to be standing the test of time when it comes to being supportive without intruding too much."

Tadie seconded her words. "Eric, you need to remember how all that went down and your part in helping Agnes and Brisa."

"I'm sorry." Agnes looked straight at him. "I shouldn't have gone off on you like I did. I was just being protective of Henry, forgetting that's been your role for much of his life."

Well, that took him aback, to say the least. He nodded at her, grateful but not ready to answer with a smile.

Jeminy had quietly settled at one end of the sofa, flanked by Tadie and Hannah in armchairs and Rita at the other end of the couch. Agnes now took a seat near one of the long front windows. Eric remained standing, trying not to let this estrogen-laden room intimidate him.

"I wonder what Danny would like to do?" Jeminy asked. "Would he be comfortable going between houses until you can work out something more permanent? Nana and I would love to have him be here occasionally, but I think he might be very bored with just the two of us."

"You have cats," Tadie said with humor.

"But you trump me. You have kids. Playmates."

Agnes laughed. "We have a kid and a dog, so we trump all but Hannah. You beat me on the number of children."

"I guess we'll have to share." Hannah grinned at her.

"I guess so. Anyway, my biggest trump card is probably Becca Barnes, who still stays with us, except days the restaurant's closed. She helps with Brisa when I go to work."

"Doesn't she also still go to Annie Mac's?" Rita asked.

"She does. Once a week to clean and then whenever Annie Mac and Clay need a sitter. That doesn't get in the way of her helping with Brisa. We all coordinate."

Eric remembered the large, dark, and very amusing lady with the tight gray curls whose conversation was filled with biblical quotes and anecdotes. He'd first met her last fall when he'd been helping them deal with Brisa's famous biological father, Darlington Evermire.

"I have no idea what Danny'd like to do, but right now that has to come second to having him in a safe place when I'm at the office."

"I'm pretty sure," Tadie said, "that he'd like to hang out with the neighborhood kids, which means we could take turns having him stay for a few hours after school with each of us." She looked over at Hannah. "Wouldn't Louis and Linney like to be involved, too? Then there's Annie Mac and her two. Katie's not much younger than Danny, is she?"

Hannah nodded. "My two love the kids here, and they'll take to yours, I'm sure, Eric."

"I think Katie's seven," Rita said. "Or close to it."

"There you go. Most of the children are at the middle school, but Katie goes to the elementary school here in Beaufort because her mother teaches there." Tadie glanced around at each of them.

Eric kept silent. This was obviously one of those times when his input wasn't needed.

Rita checked her watch. "Sorry, all, but I have a new client coming into the women's center. Must run."

Eric nodded. "See you, Rita."

"Thanks for stopping by," Jeminy said.

"I'll be in touch. Don't get up." And Rita let herself out.

"Who wants to make up the schedule?" That was General Tadie. Was she always like this? All take-charge-and-take-names?

"I need to speak to Becca," Agnes said, coming to her feet. "I'll see how she feels about nannying Danny on her days with us."

"You know she'll be thrilled," Tadie said.

"I'll be happy to pay her extra," Eric said. "Anything you think appropriate." Was there light at the end of this particular tunnel? It was hard to believe the sitter problem could be solved with so little effort on his part.

"That's good," Agnes said. "Okay, Eric, we'll work out something for Danny. The kids have school tomorrow, and I suppose you'll register him then?"

"Already done. And I'll speak to my brother." At her squint, he heard his words and his frustrated tone. "Sorry. Of course, I'll talk to him. And thank you." That sounded better, more placating.

At the door, Agnes said, "See you all later. Tadie, I'll be by your house for Brisa in thirty minutes. That work?"

"Absolutely," Tadie said. "Any time. We're not doing anything special, except I'd better get home to relieve Will. He's manning the fort while Sammy naps. Hannah?"

"I'll walk with you."

"I'll tell the girls," Jeminy said.

He still stood in the living room, uncertain about what to do next. "I should—" he began.

But Jeminy interrupted him. "Let's go see how Danny's doing."

Right. Danny. The boy was his next thing. While the women planned, he still had to do and to decide.

This would be Danny's second night on *Escape*. They'd stopped at Clawson's for hamburgers and fries, and Danny had decided big and juicy with good things added made a cheeseburger yummy. Eric smiled at the memory of ketchup on the boy's chin as he stuffed in another fry. Danny's eyes had sparkled, and Eric had wondered if Gabby had ever let her son gorge on food treats. She'd been in charge of his diet even when they'd lived with Eric, but what had she given him since then? Ramen noodles, frozen whatever, and protein-empty non-meats? The boy seemed familiar with junk, but not with the well-prepared food Eric took for granted.

All that was going to change.

But first, they had to get Danny used to the boat and a routine. Eric showed his son where to keep his toothbrush and paste. And he gave him another lesson in how to flush a marine head. "I know it's hard work, but the more you pump, the stronger you'll grow. Right now, you start, and I'll finish. We have to get the toilet emptied and what was in it through the pipes into the holding tank."

"What's a holding tank?"

"It's where the stuff in the toilet goes so we don't pollute the water under the boat. When the tank is full, a special machine pumps it out."

Danny squinted down at the toilet, a worried look on his face. "What if I have to go in the middle of the night?"

"Then you go, and I'll help you pump in the morning."

"Will it overflow? You know, get all over the place on account of me not being strong enough to get rid of it?"

"Just don't use a lot of toilet paper, okay?" He had a macerator pump to take care of this, but he remembered having a guest on board, an adult, who hadn't been able to follow directions. The mess hadn't been pretty.

"Okay." Danny turned on the faucet at the sink and loaded toothpaste on his brush.

"One more thing. We need to get into the habit of not leaving the water running on a boat. Here at the dock, we hook up to city water, but when we go sailing, we only have what's in our water tanks, so we use it sparingly."

With his toothbrush still in his mouth, Danny turned to look at him, a question in his eyes. Eric laid a hand on the child's shoulder. "We carry everything we need when we leave the dock —our own water, our fuel—in tanks under the floorboards. We can even wash our clothes because we have a washer/dryer on board, but then we have to use a special engine that powers the machine."

Toothpaste dribbled to his chin, and Danny leaned over the sink to spit it out. "Can I turn the water back on?"

"Sure. Turn it on to use it, then turn it off."

"'kay."

"Wash your face, too." He waited while Danny took care of that and turned off the water, then he handed the boy a clean towel. "You hang your towel right here when you finish."

Tucking the boy into his bunk made Eric's heart swell, especially when Danny asked for a story. He wondered how well the child could read.

"Why don't I read one page and you read the next? That way we can both have a break and be listeners."

Danny shook his head. "No, you."

Fine, he wouldn't make an issue of it. But soon he'd need to know because at seven years old, Danny should be reading well, shouldn't he? Or maybe not. What did he know? He supposed they'd take care of it at school.

Which sounded like a parental cop-out.

But still...

The sky was brightly lit when he moved into the cockpit after he'd turned out the light in Danny's cabin. The boy had wanted the door open and a nightlight burning, and Eric had come outside so he wouldn't disturb his son.

His son.

He'd forgotten what it felt like to have a child with him, to have the one he'd loved here, and his.

Lost in thought, he didn't notice footfalls on the dock until a knock sounded on his hull. He stirred, turned, and there stood Hen. Here, under the bimini, Eric imagined himself invisible.

"Are you going to invite me on?" Hen asked, obviously sensing his twin's presence or perhaps seeing him in contrast to his surroundings.

"Of course. Come aboard."

"You asked me to stop by on my way back to *Harmless.*"

"I did. You want anything to drink?"

"No thanks."

"It's pretty public out here. Let's go below." Eric waved his brother to the companionway and followed him down the steps.

"Is he here?" Hen slid onto one of the seats.

Eric turned on another light. "Danny? Yes. But he's asleep in the forecabin."

"I'd like to meet him, this kid you call your son." His twin's voice sounded strained. "This kid you never told me about."

"I guess I should have, but back when it would have mattered, you weren't in a position to care about anything other than your own issues."

"I've been clean a while now, and we've talked since then."

"By the time you came to me, nine months after you'd left the halfway house and shown yourself completely sober, Danny and Gabby were gone. And I was trying not to care."

Hen glanced away. "And your focus was on helping me stay clean."

"It was. I also wanted not to remember my son, the boy I thought never to see again."

"I get it. I'm sorry I was so self-absorbed I couldn't be there for you, especially considering you were always around for me."

Eric released a sigh, letting go of the tension he hadn't realized he'd been holding onto. This was the Hen he knew.

"You have any coffee made?" Hen asked.

"It's a little late, don't you think?"

"Right. Just thought it might be the thing, you know, soothing? I still have to row out to *Harmless.*"

"Are you ever going to bring her to the dock?"

"My turn at secret telling," Hen said with a slight, almost sly, smile.

"O-ho."

"Agnes has applied for a permit to put in a dock in front of her house so we can tie up *Harmless.*"

"Really? That's fantastic."

"I know. It means I'll only have to walk out the front door to work on my old boat."

"Pretty cool."

"So that's my news. It's your turn. I want the whole scoop."

"Maybe I should make that coffee."

"I get it." Henry shook his head, not looking at all as if he had gotten anything from Eric's story. "But I'm back to being kind of ticked off by you keeping the kid and what happened with his mother a secret all these years. Especially when I thought we'd finally achieved more equal ground. Instead, I guess in your mind I'll forever be the failure who needs you, the strong, brilliant, successful brother, to be my trustee. Forever the twin who made a mess of his life and couldn't be trusted."

"That's not—" Eric tried to deny the words, but Hen interrupted him.

"It's sure the way it feels."

"I'm sorry. I can't fix how it comes across, but I didn't mean anything by it."

"Yeah, well, it's gonna take a while for me to move past this."

Eric had no idea how to respond. His brother was being totally unreasonable. "Before I told you the details of the boy and his mother, you seemed okay. Like you got why I hadn't told you. What changed?"

"I suppose it was inevitable," Hen said, ignoring Eric's question. "Close as we once were, it couldn't last, not with the inequities in our life, not with the choices I made. I get it."

Was his brother talking about how differently he'd been treated because of the cleft in his lip and their father's rejection? The choices, of course, involved Hen's letting his bitterness take him into addiction, an addiction he'd spent years trying to overcome. An addiction that had felt pretty much front and center to Eric, too.

At least Henry finally had broken free, even if it had taken him until his early thirties to accomplish it. They were almost thirty-six now, and Henry was over four years clean, but the effects of those lost years lingered.

"I think," Eric began, not sure what he planned to say and hoping he could sound conciliatory and not snarky. He felt snarky. On a deep breath, he started again. "I'm pretty sure my silence had a lot to do with habit. Your handicap was more visible, but that doesn't mean I came out of childhood unscathed. I felt handicapped by that whole 'perfect' son thing he forced on me. Have you any idea what sort of burden that was? I wasn't allowed to be less, to get anything but perfect grades, winning trophies. It was hell to pay if I didn't. Then there was the guilt I carried toward you because in your mind I got it all, when in reality, our father was incapable of loving either of us. He just had different ways of showing his disdain. You probably can't imagine the gut wrenching I went through, literally." Eric shook his head. "No, you've been too busy seeing yourself as the victim to consider you might not have been the only sufferer. The only one with issues to work through."

"Whoa."

"Fine. Whoa." Snark was back. "But maybe it's time we did some truth-telling."

Silence overtook the small space, interrupted only by water running through the refrigerator's cooling unit. Eric leaned back, his head resting against the bulkhead wall, his eyes closed. And he waited.

He could almost feel his twin wrestling with what must feel like a new reality to him, and Eric wondered why he'd never before voiced his need. Even considering Hen's issues, he might have said something in the days since his brother's final recovery.

Only, how? He'd had a lifetime of silence and of being the strong one. Lot of good that had done him.

Henry cleared his throat. "That's a lot to process."

Eric's only response was an exhausted shrug. Of course it was. His beloved brother was only now learning how to put others first. Oh, Eric got the reasons for that, but at least the emotional moves were being made, toward Agnes, toward Brisa. They needed Hen. Henry.

It was possible, of course, that Eric needed him, too, but a life of one response couldn't be unlearned in minutes.

Henry stood. "I'd like to meet your son someday soon."

"I'd like for you to."

"We'll talk later?"

"Sure." Eric followed his brother out the companionway. Then he stood on the deck as Henry climbed down to the finger pier and, with a wave, walked up the dock.

Later. Sure, why not?

18

ERIC

Thunder rumbled in the night, and lightning flashed across the sky. Eric watched out the Lexan hatch cover, wondering if Danny would be frightened.

He got his answer when a small hand touched his shoulder. A nightlight in the salon backlit the boy. "I can't sleep."

"Why don't you climb up here for tonight? I've got enough room." He remembered other stormy nights when a little boy had curled up next to him.

"'kay."

Rain pummeled the deck and hatch, but he and the boy were snug and dry in his bunk. At first, Danny lay rigidly on his side, but when a particularly loud peal made him jump, Eric pulled him close, hoping he'd remember doing this once upon a time. "It's okay," Eric said. "Just noisy."

Soon, the child slept, but it was a long while before Eric could relax enough to join him.

The next morning, they sat down to a breakfast of scrambled eggs and toast. Danny wasn't sure he'd like scrambled eggs "on account of Mrs. Jenkins making runny awful things with chunks like rubber."

"You try mine. If you don't like them plain, I've got hot sauce—"

"Ooh, yuck!"

"Or ketchup."

Danny looked skeptical, but when the eggs showed up, he ate them with a little cheese sprinkled on top and no ketchup. "Pretty good," he admitted around a big bite of toast and jelly.

"Now, drink up that juice, and let's get washed and dressed. I put out some of your new clothes."

"How come I have to wear new?"

"Because we're going to meet your teacher today. It's your first day of school."

Danny squinted at him. "Don't want to."

"I know. But you have to look at this from my perspective. If I hadn't enrolled you in some sort of school, I could get arrested and put in jail for child neglect. Then where would you go?"

"Brisa's?" he said, trying not to grin.

"Hah. You're hilarious." Eric pointed to the bathroom. "Go."

He checked the time. Obviously, they were going to have to start this eating and dressing process a whole lot earlier on school days, especially if Danny wanted to take the bus with the others. That wasn't an option today, but perhaps tomorrow.

He'd promised to find out about Danny's prior school so records could be requested, but he'd forgotten to take care of that yesterday. "I'll call the social worker today," he said to the principal as he and Danny waited for someone to show him to his new classroom.

"Please do. Now let's introduce Danny to his classmates and teacher." Mrs. Melborne looked down at the boy. "Why don't you come with me? I think you'll like Mrs. Lincoln. She's very popular with the students."

Eric hoped that meant she was also a good teacher. He bent to Danny's level. "How about if I pick you up after school today.

Tomorrow, we can figure out how to use the bus. Will that be okay?"

Danny's bottom lip was tucked tightly between his teeth, and he looked at the floor. His shoulders went into a slight shrug.

Mrs. Melborne laid one hand on his shoulder and said cheerfully, "We'll do just fine. Tell your dad goodbye now, Danny."

His eyes appeared stricken when he glanced up at Eric. "You'll have fun, son. And you can tell me all about it and your new friends when I come get you."

"You won't forget to come?" Danny's voice sounded small.

"Never. I won't ever forget you."

Eric waited in the hall and watched Danny shuffle beside the woman who looked quite young to be a principal.

As he headed back outside, he scrolled through his contacts and brought up Tadie's phone number. When she answered, he said, "Tadie, hey. I just left Danny at the elementary school. What can you tell me about the principal?"

"Not much, I'm afraid. She's new this year. The beloved former principal had to take a sabbatical because of illness."

"She seems really young."

"I know. She was hired out of a neighboring school, where she was a teacher, I think."

He hoped she knew what she was doing. "I have to get Danny's school records," he told her. "Gotta call the social worker. I don't even know where he attended."

"What do you plan for him after school?"

"I'll keep myself free today, you know, to help him get acclimated. Make sure he's okay."

"If he wants to come here, feel free. More than likely, Jilly will collect everyone and promise snacks. The others all ride the same bus."

"You're the snack fairy?"

"I've learned to keep lots of fruit and cookies here. And stock up on juices."

"Depending on how his day went, I'll let Danny know. Thanks for everything, Tadie."

"Any time."

Eric disconnected, left a voicemail for Mrs. Finley, and drove back into town. Time to get some work done.

AnnaLouise ushered Becca Barnes into his office. He'd come to know Becca when she'd gone to work for Agnes last year at the recommendation of what Eric had come to call the Beaufort Squad, consisting of Tadie, Hannah, Annie Mac, and Rita. Agnes, it seemed from yesterday's encounter, was rapidly becoming one of them.

He'd better watch out.

Becca had eyes that crinkled in joy more often than not. It was to Becca's church that Hen had been drawn, and he and Agnes still took Brisa there. Brisa loved the exuberant worship.

"Hey, Becca, take a seat."

"Mr. Eric, good to see you again. I hear you've got you a new son."

Eric returned her grin. "Let's just say I've reclaimed my son. He'd been lost to me for a few years."

"That's good he's got you back. Now, Miss Agnes said you gonna need some help minding him, so I came to say he's welcome to be under my care. Brisa seems tickled he's going to be her cousin soon's the wedding gets done."

"It will be wonderful to have him exposed to the kids here, see how well everyone gets on, no matter what they look like."

"Amen to that. It's not always the case, you know. I'm not sayin' racism is as in-your-face as it was in my day, but there's them that have their issues. Still, with us, he'll fit right in."

"I will pay you for your time, Becca..." He waved her protest off. "No, you can't say no. I won't allow it."

"It won't be much extra work, you know it won't."

"I don't know that. I'm assuming taking care of him will involve a lot of extra work, especially if he does extra-curricular activities. And then there's the whole bottomless pit of a growing boy's stomach."

"He going to be taking the bus home with Brisa and the other kids?"

"I assume so. Today, I'll pick him up, but we'll try the bus tomorrow."

"Okay. I'll tell Brisa. Have her make sure he knows where to go, how to get to the house. You'll see. Everything will be fine, on account of Brisa and Jilly, probably Louis too—that's Miss Hannah's boy—takin' him under their wing like they're gonna want to do."

"I do hope you're right, Becca. Thank you so much." He opened his desk drawer and took out a checkbook. When he'd made out a good-sized check, he tore it out and handed it to her.

She looked at it. "Mr. Eric, that's too much money. No way I'm gonna spend that much on one boy."

"Fine, spend it on Brisa too. On Agnes, on yourself. I don't care. You coming in here and telling me you're willing to help me when I so badly need help? That's huge. Worth a lot more than that paltry amount."

"Well, you put it like that, it will come in handy." She folded the check and slid it into her big purse. Then she stood. "You want to bring Danny by to meet me after school today, that'd be fine. I work for Miss Annie Mac on Thursdays, but I'm back in time to be there for Brisa's bus. Sometimes when Miss Annie Mac and Mr. Clay want to go out, I go stay with Ty and Katie. Most often, I take Brisa out there so she can hang out with Ty, too. Seems to me, Danny might like to join us."

"I bet he would. Thank you." Eric scribbled his personal number on a business card. "Here. You can reach me any time at this number. If I'm in a meeting, just leave a message and I'll get right back to you."

"Yes, sir. I'll look for you this afternoon then. Let Danny come have an after-school snack with Brisa." She gathered her purse and stood.

"Ah, you know the way to a boy's heart." Eric laughed and headed around the desk to open the door for her.

"Girl's too."

19

MR. JENKINS

Dalton parked along a residential street a couple hundred yards away from both the school and the man's car. So that's where the kid would be going.

While reconnoitering and cogitating on his next move, Dalton picked up his phone and hit speed dial. Might as well check in at home. "Stelle, you doin' okay?" He stared at the school doors as his wife ranted about one of the brats. Finally, he interrupted. "Look, I'm going to be a while more. Yeah, it'll be worth it, don't you worry none. Check from Social Services should be there in a couple days. You cash it down to the store, get what you need. You know what to do with the rest." And he disconnected.

The man came out of the school alone, got in his car, and drove off.

Think, Dalton told himself.

Stick with the boy came to him, like all his ideas did, dropping fixed and clear into his brain. He'd stick, maybe take advantage of a chance that might arise. You never knew when that might be.

He had to watch for that chance to make the snatch. There'd be other kids around when Danny got off the bus, assuming he'd ride it home. A town this size, where kids wandered unattended, parents trusting a school bus made sense. Stupid, but fit their pattern.

You wanted to get something done, learn the patterns. Use them. It's how you could get underneath the expected.

Dalton had trouble wrapping his mind around how careless parents were here. They knew better in cities. He'd once spent weeks trying to get a kid alone in Charleston, a high-value kid the man had picked out. Only, that boy had traveled in a pack of fancy-dressed kids, always with seven or eight others. That many in a posse, and one of them would be bound to make a ruckus, get the police.

Plus, kids had their own cell phones these days. Even little kids. They make a movie, post it all over, you're finished.

Dealing with a pack, you try your snatch, and a couple are fighting you, while there's that one, hits the emergency call button, and all you can do is get yourself out of there, pronto. If no one made a video to get famous.

Only smart to keep away from packs of kids.

Sure, he'd finally enticed that particular boy into a car he'd rented, a fancy Mercedes, made the boy think his own family had come for him. You know, new chauffeur?

There was always a way. You only had to be smart and patient.

Think, Dalton.

Best would be to see what he could see and take his time, not get caught.

He opened his glove compartment, drew out his pistol, fondled it. He kept it out of sight, just in case someone walked by. Not that anyone was around this time of day. Not here.

Maybe the man and the boy would take a drive out of town soon, visit one of those friends the kid was making. Dalton had the gun. He could take a shot to force the man off the road, disable him. Grab the kid.

Sure, he'd probably have to kill the man to keep him quiet, which was why he needed them to drive out to some of that empty space, maybe near the marshes. Marshes were great places to hide bodies, but there were woods too. Fields. Plenty of room to take care of things.

20

GEORGINA

A car horn's honk broke moments of clarity when she'd been remembering Gerard... or... or something. She glanced around and down at her feet. She was wearing the walking shoes she'd bought last year, the slide-on-no-laces type that were supposed to help her posture.

She'd come outside for some reason, hadn't she? Maybe with those shoes she was going for a walk?

That thought bounced around, but it didn't feel right. An image of her daughter slid in, and she remembered Dee would be here soon.

That she remembered brought a swift feeling of giddiness, which just as swiftly vanished. She didn't want to see her daughter, especially when she couldn't remember more than Dee's coming and her own not wanting whatever Dee was offering.

Or had that been last week? Had Dee come and gone? Something wanted to hook on in her brain.

Isa said she only had to relax, not worry about things. That she'd know what she needed to, and fretting on made the jumble in her head worse.

A slight breeze softened the sun's efforts to bake the day. She stood to get out of the porch's shade, walked down into her garden, and extended her arms. She kept her straw hat lowered to shade her face from the wrinkle maker, leastways to stop the wrinkles from worsening until old took over completely. Old took over everything at such a spanking pace it was nearly impossible to keep up.

But look there. Her dying plants needed pruning. Weren't shriveled and dying blossoms the saddest things? Of course, these days, dying had a way of stealing more than flowers. So did old.

Old and what it meant carried Georgie's thoughts straight back to her daughter, about to descend, probably with papers and a for-sale sign for Georgie's house. And that brought the worry, so much worry, enough to age her right into her grave.

But not yet. She had time, both for the dying and for the thing that twisted up her insides.

Didn't she?

She glanced past her yard as children's voices filtered over the hedge and two girls skipped down the sidewalk. A red-haired pixie waved, then moseyed toward her. The darker girl followed. They were grinning and licking the last of their ice cream cones.

"Hey, Miss Georgie." The redhead hopped from side to side, all energy. "How're you?"

Georgie could have done with some of that child's energy and —what was it called? The word was right there, tickling at her mind. Ah, yes. *Verve.* Yes, that was it. Hadn't she used it to describe Dee once upon a time? Her daughter had started with plenty of kick-up-her-heels enthusiasm, but, somewhere along the way, she'd spilled every last ounce into frowns and frets. The spilling had started with Oliver's death, hadn't it? It had always been Olli and Jeminy, twins, her grandbabies, who'd brightened everyone's life. Until there'd been only Jeminy, never enough for Dee.

Georgie tucked thoughts of Dee—and Olli—away for later. The Dee ones weren't going to stay tucked for long, not with that daughter of hers even now on the highway from Chapel Hill to

Beaufort, but right this moment a sweet little girl bounced in front of her. Waiting for something.

Had the child asked a question?

Surely there'd been polite words that would require a polite response. Georgie went with "I'm just fine. How about yourselves? You two having a good day?" At the girl's rekindled grin, Georgie relaxed.

"Yes, ma'am, we are. Brisa and I, we have a day off for teachers or something, and we just went to get these cones. Mama said we could on account of we helped out this morning. Do you like ice cream? I think it's spectacular, especially from The Fudge Factory."

My, the child had a vocabulary. "Spectacular?" Georgie smiled. "I think it is."

The one called Brisa licked her cone, then her lips, and said, "My mom works at *Agua Verde*. Did you know that? Have you ever had dinner there?"

Georgie shook her head. "No, I can't say as I have." Maybe she ought just to come out and ask the redhead's name now they'd told her the other's. Brisa. She needed to repeat names more than once these days. Way more than once. She was going to keep saying this one in her head so she'd remember. Remembering was important.

The redhead called her Miss Georgie and not Mrs. Warren. What if she'd known that child since birth, but her memory had gone and lost the name? Best just wait for them to say it.

Concentrate, she told herself.

"We picked up Brisa's swimsuit in case we get to play in the sprinkler to cool off after our cones. I have a water slide that's real fun." The child whose name had fled pointed to a plastic sack on her friend's arm. "Now we'd better get going, 'cause my little brother's awake, and we promised Mommy we'd let him play with us some. He can't have ice cream on account of it hurting his stomach. But we can."

"Will you say hey to Miss Jeminy for us?"

"Jeminy?" Georgie thought for a moment and remembered her girl was home, and wasn't that wonderful? "I will. Indeed, I will. Thank you for stopping by."

"Yes, ma'am."

They both spoke politely, and that soothed Georgie. "Come back again," she called to their retreating backs as she returned to her porch and her rocker. She'd been working in her garden long enough, hours even, and it was time to rest.

The child's name. She'd forgotten, hadn't she? Maybe she'd uncover it before they returned. Then again, maybe if she watched where they went, the pieces would snap into place.

She creaked to a standing position. At the edge of the porch, she looked after the girls. There they were, skipping down to… Ah, they were turning into the old Longworth place. She could remember going to that house when Caroline was a girl, before Caroline met and married Samuel Longworth. Before she herself had gone off to school and met Gerard.

She sure missed Gerard. She even missed his snores.

Caroline was dead, wasn't she? Had been dead a while. Everyone seemed to be dying.

With a sigh, Georgie opened her screen door and wandered inside to her kitchen. For a moment she stood there, squinting at the room. She was supposed to be doing something. It had something to do with Dee.

Dee. Something about Dee…

Ah, yes. Her daughter'd said she was coming to Beaufort. Georgie didn't want Dee here, fussing, making decisions, making her feel invisible. She found the phone and lifted the receiver.

And, in the process of bringing it to her ear, she lost her last thought. It had been there, hadn't it, because she was holding the phone in her hand. But why? Who had she intended to call?

Closing her eyes, she shuddered.

Her mind kept tripping off like this, willy-nilly, as if it had decided to go walkabout, leaving the rest of her behind. Feeling this, knowing it, made a spasm roil up from low in her belly. She swiped at a tear because this could not be happening. It *couldn't.* Yet look at her, staring at the phone, no clue as to why she held it. Was she about to call someone? Had she already made a call?

She couldn't remember. She could *not* remember.

And, oh, my, when had those veins started protruding right below her knuckles? Look at the brown spots.

What on earth was she supposed to do with the phone?

She put it down on the kitchen counter. Maybe enlightenment would come as she fixed herself a cup of tea. The heat of it would be good for her bones, and maybe it would unjumble her thoughts.

"Nana?" A voice called from the front of the house.

She was Jeminy's nana. Only Jeminy's.

Excitement skittered through her being, and she called out. "I'm here, sweet girl. Back here!"

Having her darling girl here made Georgie nearly burst with happiness. Jeminy had always been like sunshine sneaking in under the porch eaves on a winter's day. Winters could be cold outside and gray in the parlor, but when those rays from the sinking sun made it inside and showed off dust motes, Georgie's tension would just drift straight off. Like it always was with her grand-darling.

And wasn't that the best thing? Remembering the feeling? "Thank you, God," she whispered, "that I've still got hold of some beautiful memories." She'd sure hate all of them to leach out of her head like the calcium had been leaching from her bones. A brittle bone broke easily. A brittle brain, emptied of thought? Before that happened, she'd sure like it to break all the way and kill her because she knew where she'd be the moment after death, and it would be in the arms of her Savior.

21

JEMINY

Fixing one, fixing two, I'm just about ready to be fixing three.

A thunderstorm had rumbled through in the night, rain hammering the wood siding and window panes, lightning crackling and cannons seeming to explode in the sky. Limbs of an old magnolia scraped the porch's metal roof as Jeminy lay in bed, imagining lakes forming in Nana's yard. And the roof leaking.

She finally slept, though only after the storm abated and quiet settled on the house. Too soon, though, light filtering through the blinds woke her. She rolled to her side and ran fingers over the sheet next to her, fingers that touched nothing but soft cotton.

And there, outside her door, footsteps shuffled past, and Nana hummed. When had Jeminy last heard words telling of an old rugged cross? In her childhood, she decided, back in the day when they'd all gone to church. Now it was only her daddy who went, and she with him when she visited home, which had happened less and less over the years. Home with her mother was a hard place to be.

Nana humming was Nana happy, and that meant Jeminy didn't have to get up yet. She glanced, blurry-eyed still, at the bedside clock. Seven-something here was the middle of the night in California, and she was still so sleepy, so exhausted from the past days, from last night and feeling as if she had to be up and alert for whatever her grandmother needed.

She closed her eyes. Just a little longer. Another hour.

When next she woke, it was quarter to nine, and they had a ten o'clock appointment with the lawyer. Eric. She finished in the bathroom and slipped on a sundress before wandering downstairs to grab a bite of something and to see if Nana was dressed and ready. Through the screen door, Nana's soft cooing noises came, followed by the squeak of the porch swing's chain. Nana sure loved those cats.

Jeminy picked up an apple, washed it, and stuck her head out the door. "Nana, we have to leave for the lawyer's in ten minutes. Are you about ready?"

"Of course, honey. I just have to make a quick trip to the bathroom. I'll be ready in a trice." Nana stood, got her balance, and smiled at Jeminy as she came to the open door. "My, don't you look lovely."

Did she? She hoped it didn't look as if she'd primped just for this meeting.

"Are we going somewhere?" Nana asked.

"Isa's meeting us at the lawyer's office."

"Do you know why?"

They'd done this a few times yesterday, and Jeminy'd figured out that all Nana really wanted was assurance that, yes, she knew and all would be well.

"I do, and I'll tell you all about it as we go."

The lawyers Jeminy'd known in the music business had not looked like the man she'd met at *Samantha's* who now sat across from them. She smiled to herself at the image she'd created in her mind of someone bespeckled, balding, and old. Eric Houston was the opposite in his slacks and collared shirt, a light blue that worked perfectly with his eyes. It took all of Jeminy's willpower to keep her focus on his words, not on his jawline. His smile. The hair he kept having to brush back from his face, sun-bleached hair.

Hadn't she learned *anything* from her fiasco with Rand?

She tried to figure out what he was saying and what she'd missed of the conversation as he slid something in front of her.

She picked it up.

"That's your copy of the recorded power of attorney. I've already given Isa hers. You're going to need it when you go to the bank. I assume you've figured out the logistics of how you're going to handle things?"

Isa leaned forward. "Jeminy's going to handle the day-to-day finances. It looks as if Georgie has an excellent investment banker, and we'll try to develop a relationship with him. He's the one who alerted us to Dee's withdrawals."

"How are you handling those, other than cutting Mrs. Buchanan off?"

Nana spoke up. "Dee's angry with me."

"We think it's best," Isa said, "if we ignore those. Better for Georgie."

"Better for me? What's better?" Worry wrinkled Nana's forehead.

"Not fretting over spilt milk," Isa said.

"Oh, I agree with that." Nana's face relaxed. "You can't do a thing about it once it's spilled anyway, can you? Just mop it up and go on."

"That's what we're trying to do, Georgie. Move forward."

"Good."

Jeminy spoke. "I want Isa on the accounts, too. All of them. As protection, so no one can accuse me of mishandling Nana's money."

Eric nodded. "Wise idea."

"Do you think we need to send you reports?" Isa asked him.

"Unless we hear something from Mrs. Buchanan, you need only to keep good records with explanations for any big expenditures. If your mother causes problems, Jeminy, we may need to do more, perhaps set up a trust, to protect your grandmother. I spoke to her and Isa about that last week. If you need any information, you and I can go over it any time."

"Dee isn't happy," Nana said. "I don't want trouble."

Isa patted Nana's hand. "You've got your A-team here, Georgie. Jeminy, Mr. Houston, and me. Dee can't do anything."

"But I keep forgetting things."

"It's okay," Isa said. "You remember the important things. And you don't have any trouble thinking or reasoning."

"No. I can still do that. I still know what's right."

"And you know who has your back." Isa's voice may have been low and calming, but Jeminy could hear the fierce protectiveness in it.

Nana turned a tremulous smile on each of them. When she looked at Eric Houston, he grinned, but the wink he gave her grandmother sealed things for Jeminy. This was a dangerous man, a very dangerous man.

Still, she managed to pay attention to what he said and to nod in appropriate places. When Isa stood to help Nana to her feet, Jeminy managed to ask a question. "Mr. Houston—"

"Eric."

"Fine, Eric, do you know of a lawyer who handles copyright and contract issues?"

"What sort of contract do you need help with?"

Isa started toward the door. "Jeminy, honey, I'm going to take your grandmother to get a nice cup of tea. I'm thinking

Samantha's because it's on the way home. Would you like that, Georgie?"

"I would, thank you. You'll come, too, Jeminy?"

She hugged her grandmother. "If you don't mind, I'll meet you back at the house." She felt in no shape to sit at a cafè right now. "I have a couple of questions to ask Mr. Houston." She looked over at him. "If he has the time."

"Sure." He saw the others out before returning to Jeminy. "Now, how can I help you?"

"When I originally sold my songs to Darlington Evermire, I did so through his manager and mine. I'm pretty sure both of them took a hefty cut. They may still be taking cuts even though Darling fired his manager, Arthur Ames, and Rand, my agent/manager took off with Arthur, severing ties with me. Rand should be under investigation by the police for keeping fishy bank accounts and mishandling my money."

"Should be?"

"The detective—I assume he was a detective—who took the files from me didn't seem invested in doing much about them. My money troubles came low on his list."

"Do you have copies of what you gave him?"

"I do."

"Maybe you could let me see them." At her nod, he continued, "Are you looking to get money back from your ex-manager? To work directly with Darlington?"

"Yes to both."

"What about copies of your previous contracts?"

"I wouldn't be surprised if Rand walked off with them. They weren't among the papers I packed." She felt the blush rise and lowered her eyes. "I trusted him because we were involved." She had a name for the scumbag, and it wasn't one she could say here.

Eric set down the pen he was using for note-taking. "I can certainly take a look and see what I can come up with. We also have another excellent contracts lawyer in the firm."

She really, really didn't want to expose any more of that messy part of her life to this man. He already knew too much.

So, of course, she said, "I'd be happy to have you represent me if you can do the job."

Perhaps if he learned all her history, he'd quit flashing those eyes at her. There needed to be a barrier between them because she would never fall for another pretty man. Ever.

"Can you give me your former manager's address?" He raised the pen again. "I'll draft a letter asking for a copy of the contracts you have with him and with Darlington."

"Thank you. I don't know his address, but I've got his cell number." She recited it.

"Good. And yours?"

Jeminy gave him that as she stood. "Thank you. I'll look forward to hearing from you."

"And if you have any questions as you go forward with your grandmother, let me know."

"I will. Thank you."

He ushered her out, and she tried not to imagine him gazing after her retreating back.

They still had to visit the bank, which they'd agreed to do after lunch and a short nap. Nana was rested and eager when they set out—until they began to cross Queen Street, where she came to an abrupt halt and clutched at Jeminy's arm. "We can't go there."

"Why not?"

"Dee. I saw her car."

Jeminy'd noticed a silver Lexus pulling away from a parking space just ahead, but it hadn't been her mother's. "It's fine, Nana. A man was driving."

"Are you sure?" Perhaps fear had sharpened her grandmother's memory. The make of Mother's car seemed to have stuck.

"Absolutely. Besides, Mother can't hurt you, Nana. Really. You've got the protection of your A-team, remember? No one will take you away."

"She said she would. She said she'd get a lawyer."

"Let her try. She won't win."

"You're sure?"

"I am. So is Isa, and so is Mr. Houston."

"Is he my lawyer?"

"Yes, ma'am. He is."

Nana's shoulders relaxed visibly.

"It's a beautiful day, Nana, and we're going to enjoy it."

"Are we going to get a latte?"

"We can do that, but not until we've seen your banker."

"My banker?"

"Yes, ma'am. We have to fix things so Isa and I can help you with your accounts."

At Nana's puzzled expression, Jeminy continued. "We're going to keep you safe and make sure you have plenty of money to make you comfortable for the rest of your life."

Nana smiled mistily at that. "Thank you, sweet girl."

Isa approached as they entered the bank's impressive lobby. "Georgie, hey," she said, leaning over to kiss Nana's cheek. "Holland's waiting for us."

Holland Patterson, who had an impressive corner office, stood and came around his desk to greet them. Isa introduced him to Jeminy. "Holland's married to Tootie, that cute girl who runs *Samantha's.*"

"Really?" Having seen Tootie's flamboyant garb—so very *not* Beaufort—Jeminy couldn't wait to know more about the tall, lanky man whose appearance must make a fascinating contrast when he and Tootie went out together.

The twinkle behind Holland Patterson's glasses matched his smile. "You're wondering why she picked me."

She was, of course. Or perhaps wondering why he'd picked

Tootie, but who could understand attraction? She grinned back at him. "My guess would be that twinkle. You make her laugh?"

"She brings it out of me." He winked and turned to Nana. "Mrs. Warren, it's a pleasure to see you again. I hope you're well."

Nana beamed. "I am. Thank you. And I'm much better now that my granddaughter has come for a visit."

"How long do you plan to stay?" the banker asked Jeminy.

"As long as my nana needs me."

"Indefinitely," Isa said with a nod toward Nana, as if Jeminy's grandmother needed the encouragement.

Jeminy kept quiet. Indefinitely could mean short or long, right? Just undeclared?

Holland brought a third chair close to his desk and walked around to his seat near a computer. Pulling out a folder and yellow pad, he said, "Shall we talk about what Mrs. Warren presently has in her investment accounts as well as in her checking account? I understand that you've brought a power of attorney for each of you, so I'll need to know how you want the accounts structured."

RAND

Fingers jabbed into Rand's shoulder. "Can't lie abed all day. The agency's sending over a cleaning team at ten."

Rand grunted.

The scent of Arthur's aftershave didn't mix well with whatever remnants of last night remained in Rand's stomach, and he rolled over.

"You're a mess," Arthur said. "Get cleaned up before I come home."

Arthur's tone penetrated the fog that wanted to suck Rand right back under. Arthur had no right to talk to him that way. No right.

The next words seemed to come from a distance. "I've turned your phone back up. It's been vibrating all morning." It sounded like a door closed then opened again. "Take care of whatever's hanging over you before it threatens to become my problem, too."

The fog cleared enough for Rand to take note of the threat. But then it enveloped him again.

When Rand finally woke enough to climb out of bed, he stumbled into the bathroom and then to the shower. He was shaving his day-old beard when a message came through on his phone. He finished his ablutions, picked up the phone, and read the latest of three that had come from Jeminy's landlord, *his* former landlord. The man wanted rent money, overdue money. And if Rand didn't pay, the stuff in the apartment was going to be hauled to the sidewalk, and Rand would be charged for the clean-up on the way to court.

Rand cursed. He'd placate the man with some cash, and then he'd find Jeminy. She owed him. It was her mess, her stuff. And she wasn't going to stick him with it.

He'd called her friends, what ones he knew about, but no one admitted to knowing where she'd gone. Not that he trusted any of them, especially Maggie whatever-her-name-was. That woman hated him, and he just bet she knew more than she let on.

Maybe he should hire a detective. Jeminy wasn't smart enough not to have left some sort of trail. She wouldn't have gone to her parents.

Rand grinned. Oh, no, not the way her mother was. A more unnatural mother he'd never seen, like she was jealous of Jeminy.

No, Jeminy wouldn't have subjected herself to that woman's viper tongue.

He thought a moment, rubbing his fingers over his temples to quell the ache that built. On his way to the kitchen for coffee, he wondered if Jeminy had somehow found a direct line to Darlington. If she had, if she'd bypassed him and gotten herself back on the royalties payroll... If she'd managed that, she could have gone anywhere.

The cleaning team had invaded even the kitchen, and the coffee pot was empty. He collected his keys and headed out to his car. Coffee first, then he'd make a few calls from his car. Hunt up a detective. Find Jeminy.

He grinned as he conjured ways he could make her pay. And ways to get the honeypot refilled.

23

DEBORAH

Deborah sat down on her blue-and-yellow tufted bedspread, the one that matched the curtains and complemented the flowered chintz of her lounge chair on the other side of the king-sized bed. She'd adorned both chair and bed with throw pillows in yellow and shades of blue, with one in bright green to pick up the stems in the chintz pattern.

The decor was new last year, bought and installed after a few failed sessions with the counselor, and it had done her a whole lot more good than the counselor's "say this, do that, believe this" regimen. JoAnn had even suggested Deborah go into the business of decorating, but she wouldn't. Because there were fools out there who'd want to argue that *their* taste was superior to hers.

Hah. She knew better.

Who cared if Larry didn't really like it?

He could stay in the guest room. She hadn't yet suggested he move, but he could and he should.

By the time she roused herself enough to go downstairs, she'd focused her anger on her circumstances. She was the wife of a philanderer, the mother of a deceitful daughter, and never again would she have her perfect little boy. Oliver.

She swallowed back the sob that wanted to push its way to the surface whenever she thought of her boy and tucked it hard into the ball that filled her gut. Because it *hadn't had to happen*. The if-onlys could drown her if she let them.

Or they could explode in her belly and kill her.

Her foot hit the step awkwardly, but she caught the railing before her stumble carried her down the carpeted stairs and she broke her neck.

If only Olli had had a padded fall.

"You okay?" Larry's head appeared around the wall at the bottom of the stairs.

"Thank you, yes." She tried to make her voice composed, but it came out as merely haughty.

"We need to talk. Can you join me on the terrace?"

Larry wanting to talk never ended well for her. He'd demand something again. And she? She'd need a second or third drink just to sit there and nod.

Right now, she had no answers, no way to hold him accountable except her anger, which didn't seem to have won her anything. She filled a smallish glass with vodka and soda water and walked out to their flagstone terrace. If she were here alone, she'd be able to appreciate the well-maintained garden and the overhanging trees full of green. As it was, she noticed them without pleasure.

She settled on a *chaise longue* and adjusted a pillow at her head so she was sitting upright enough to sip easily. And she waited.

"I told Jeminy we'd meet her for lunch next week."

"We?"

"Yes, we. Her mother and father."

"And why would we do that right now, when she's being recalcitrant?"

"Not recalcitrant with me." Larry wiped his fingers down a sweating glass of tea. "But then, I'm not trying to tell her what to do."

Deborah closed her eyes and sucked in a breath. She had to keep the peace a little while longer, just until she had the resources she needed to shift things more her way. It would happen. All she needed was patience.

She curled her fingers more tightly around her glass and pasted on a smile. Her smile had been her secret weapon with Larry, but she hadn't used it much in the last years. Why hadn't she?

"I suppose," she said, "we could do that, but I'm not ready to go back to Beaufort. It's a long drive."

"I suggested we meet her halfway. In Goldsboro."

"Really? Goldsboro?" There couldn't be anywhere decent to eat there.

"Sure. I know a great little restaurant. The owners are clients."

"Clients." Of course, and he'd want to keep an eye on their business, wouldn't he? Their investments?

What did she know? As long as the income stream continued...

"The food is surprisingly good."

"Not greasy spoon?"

He laughed. "Not at all. Indian and well worth the visit."

"Indian." She said it reluctantly. She could be tempted with high-end cuisine, but not the mom-and-pop order of ethnic you could find near roadside motels run by foreigners of all backgrounds.

"I'll let Jeminy know we'll meet her at noon. That work?"

Already feeling heartburn, Deborah lifted her glass and shrugged.

Be nice, she reminded herself. Play along with him.

For now.

Larry had gone out, thank heavens, because she desperately needed a nap. Drawing the blinds and climbing under a light coverlet, she closed her eyes and waited for the alcohol to offer the oblivion she craved.

Sleep, oblivion, dreamlessness… Only, there she was.

She'd driven up to the school just after Olli had taken off on his bike, not long after, really. Boys had been chasing him, someone said, but she'd climbed back in her car after yanking Jeminy along, and they'd tried to find him. She'd yelled out the window that she was there, Olli should come back, get in, stay safe. She'd seen a bunch of boys, and asked, but they'd only shaken their heads, acting innocent. She hadn't forgotten Olli, really. She'd promised, and she'd come.

Only he'd been too far away to hear her, too far and out of sight and lost and…

Dead.

Because she'd been late. She'd gone to the club with JoAnn and they'd had a long lunch, too long, obviously, because when she'd looked at her watch, she'd realized she was supposed to pick up the twins almost an hour before because Rose was off, and it was raining, and she'd promised.

She'd promised.

But she'd been late.

And her little boy, her son, her precious Oliver was dead.

Her fault. Her fault.

She was a terrible mother.

Her fault.

O God, help!

On that cry, she woke herself. Light filtered under the door, which meant Larry was home. She hoped he hadn't heard her cry.

She didn't want him to know she still dreamed of her boy.

Her lost little boy.

Whom she had killed.

24

JEMINY

Pick up your feet, avoid the cracks,
Saunter down the sidewalk, wearing a hat.
Smile to the left, nod to the right,
Kick up your heels and dance in the light.

Jeminy focused on decluttering and tried to stay positive in her role as cook and housekeeper, chauffeur and grocery shopper. Oh, and finder of lost things, reminder of lost moments, and entertainer in ways she'd never experienced. Nights, she slept, but mental and physical exhaustion seemed to work against a peaceful or recuperative sleep, and the next day would be a repeat of the last.

At least the plumber had fixed the leaky faucet and the roofer had found the missing shingles and replaced them. The yard was looking a whole lot better, although the garden still needed help.

When she could keep her grandmother out of the kitchen, she discovered she actually liked to cook. But too often Nana wandered in and wanted to help, only what kind of help? The best

Jeminy could do was to sit Nana down at the table with a cutting board and knife and a vegetable to chop—one that didn't need to be first in the pot.

Occasionally, memories arose of days when all she'd had to consider was her music—what words to write and what notes to play. Days when she'd made enough money to dine out wherever she wanted or to spend a winter week in the mountains or a summer week at Cabo.

As she ran the vacuum wand over bedroom blinds that had needed cleaning years ago, other thoughts intruded. Perhaps the sound of the vacuum had triggered memories of over-indulgence in the forbidden and the just plain stupid, but suddenly her gut hurt and she began to shake. Nothing good had come from her way of life, her choices—especially not the politically correct choice that had forever changed her.

She hit the off button to shut down the vacuum's noise and sat heavily on the side of her bed. How did other potential mothers turned empty-womb carriers cope with the aftereffects?

Did they harden their hearts? Did they tell themselves the incipient person they'd been carrying was only a collection of nothingness when pulled from them? That the magical process used to grow a worthless collection of replicating cells into a person only worked if left unmolested in the womb? That they hadn't *murdered* someone?

What about the fully formed beings tossed on rubbish heaps? How did they fit the narrative?

O God...

Jeminy curled on her bed, trying to banish the images as she wept and the sun descended past its zenith.

———

She splashed water on her face and straightened her back. What was done was done, and she couldn't undo it. She headed downstairs.

Cleaning would get easier, surely, once she'd gotten the clutter sorted, surfaces polished, and corners vacuumed. She'd called Isa to find out who washed windows, because she really wasn't going to climb a ladder to get the top floor ones, and they looked as if they hadn't been touched in years.

"Probably haven't," Isa said. "I'm not sure your grandmother notices any longer."

"And what about the garden?" Jeminy asked, surveying the dead and dying plants. "I know Nana used to love to manage it, but it's too much, even for me."

"I know a couple of people I can send round. I'll give them a call and see if they're available."

Jeminy sighed. "I can't make myself work on my music if I see something that needs doing. And now that Darling's out of my future, I'm going to have to find another outlet anyway."

"Let me know if there's anything else you need from me, okay? I thought I'd come and take Georgie out to lunch tomorrow, and I've got a buying trip to Wilmington on Monday. Shall I ask her along?"

"That would be great." Nana craved variety, mostly because she often didn't remember what they'd just done together or where she'd last been. Jeminy, the newly minted housemaid, would love an outlet other than home maintenance. Please, please, please…

And the thought of time alone… the chance to hit the off switch on the need to be upbeat…

Nana wandered into the kitchen. "Hey, sweet girl. I think I'll sit out front and watch the boat traffic. It's such a lovely day."

"That sounds like a great idea. Why don't I fix something cold for us?"

"Do we have lemonade?"

"I can make some."

Nana glanced out the back window and paused, then headed for the back door. "I should go sit out back and talk to the cats. Do we have any lemonade?"

Jeminy reached toward her grandmother, touching her arm. She'd discovered that touch sometimes helped to ground Nana and bring her back to the moment.

"I thought we might sit out front, Nana." A breeze blew off the water but didn't make it to the back yard; they'd both be more comfortable out there, and she could use a break.

"Really?"

"I'll bring lemonade. You go ahead."

She squeezed lemons into a pitcher of water, added sugar, and stirred before pouring it over ice and heading to the porch. Nana was already rocking and took her glass happily. They sipped and rocked and were letting the afternoon quiet settle over them when the postman turned into their walkway and waved. "Afternoon, ladies. Gorgeous day, isn't it?" Billy'd been delivering Beaufort mail for years and always had a smile that lit his round face.

"It is indeed, Billy. Hope you're enjoying your rounds," Jeminy said.

"I am. And I have an important couple of letters here, look like they're from the same office." He handed one to Jeminy and one to Nana. "Need signatures here," he said, holding out a magic little machine.

Jeminy signed for each. Nana held the business envelope close to her face. "I seem to have forgotten my glasses."

He thanked Jeminy, nodded at them. "Maybe you both won the lottery."

"Maybe so." The letter looked like bad news, considering the return address on the envelope. How many law offices ever wrote anything positive? Or sent it registered?

"Well, ladies," Billy said, hopping back off the last step, "I'll see you tomorrow."

"Yes, thank you." Jeminy spoke absently as she tore open the envelope. Her mother, the darling, had instructed a lawyer to send a warning of intent to sue should certain things not change within thirty days.

Nana was squinting at the words in front of her. "I don't understand this, Jeminy. It has our names, yours and mine and Isa's, but it also talks about Dee. Why?"

"My mother intends to bring a lawsuit against us because she doesn't like the way you set things up." Jeminy continued reading. "She claims Isa and I have used undue influence to get you to turn things over to us. There's more, but that's the gist of it. She won't actually sue if we get her reinstated as your attorney-in-fact—and us un-instated, I guess. If that's even a word. Anyway, she claims she's the one who has selflessly taken care of your interests all these years, and the only way you would have made these changes would be if you'd been coerced."

Nana merely looked confused. "Why would Dee say such things?" She picked at the corner of the page. "I don't like this."

"It's okay, Nana. You don't have to worry about a thing. Really. Remember, you have Isa, you have me, and you have your lawyer, Mr. Houston. We'll take care of it all."

She hoped they could. If it came to a lawsuit, she'd have to have her own lawyer, she guessed, and how would she pay for that?

Against her own mother.

She shook her head. That Mother had threatened to sue both her own mother, Jeminy's grandmother, and her daughter, Jeminy herself.

The thought sliced like a knife to her gut.

It was after six before Isa called Jeminy's cell phone. "Your mother didn't waste much time, did she?"

"No. And poor Nana. I'm trying to keep her distracted enough that she doesn't dwell on it, maybe even forgets it happened, but you know how much she hates confrontation. She keeps picking her letter up and carrying it around."

"Did you talk to Eric yet?"

"Perhaps you ought to be the one to alert him. Do we all get to have the same lawyer?"

"I don't know. I certainly hope so, because paying for one to represent me isn't in this year's budget."

"Nor in mine."

"Jeminy," Isa said, her tone thoughtful, "have you spoken to your father about what your mother's doing? You told me he's a reasonable man. How can he let her sue his own daughter?"

"Good question, although I'm not sure it's a case of him 'letting' her do anything."

"She rules on the home front?"

It certainly felt like that, but was it? Was he a weak man? "I wish I knew, Isa. Maybe he doesn't know."

"Then tell him. Get him to call off the dogs."

"I'll at least tell him what's happening. He's a darling man, but he does tend to ignore what bothers him."

"I'll let Eric know."

"Thank you. Are you going to the wedding this weekend?"

"I'm not sure yet."

"Oh, come on. The weather's supposed to be great, and you know Nana will be glad to have your company."

"I'll come for her sake then."

Jeminy didn't bring up the rehearsal dinner as she said goodbye. Agnes and Henry were trying to keep the numbers under control because it was going to be held at *Agua Verde*, where they both worked. She'd been very surprised to find her name on her grandmother's invitation. Perhaps that had been Brisa's doing.

They would go to the dinner and the wedding. Nana was

excited, and that would go a long way to turn her mind to something other than her daughter's bad behavior.

Too bad you couldn't divorce a parent.

Even after all these years of disappointment, Jeminy still couldn't wrap her thoughts around her mother's actions against the sweetest woman in the world. Nana had only, always, shown love to them all.

That you know about.

Jeminy batted away that voice in her head. The old cliche of a leopard's spots fit here: Nana's spots had been inked in, and all who knew her spoke only of her love and generosity. Even Deborah the Great used to send Jeminy and Olli off to Beaufort for a month every summer saying, "Your Nana will give you a wonderful vacation. She adores children."

So which of the two had gone rogue? It certainly wasn't Nana.

Jeminy checked the time. Her father should have finished work, wherever he was, so she punched in the numbers to his cell and waited for him to answer.

It went to voicemail, but as she was leaving a message, a call came in from him.

"Sorry, honey, I'd left the phone in the bathroom. Took me a while to get to it."

"Where are you?"

"I'm in Atlanta for meetings." It sounded as if he were settling himself on a bed.

"I wanted to talk to you about Mother's latest move. Do you know about it?"

He sighed. "No. What's she done now?"

"We—Isa Wellington, Nana, and I—all got letters from Mother's lawyer threatening us with a lawsuit if we don't comply with her wishes." She went on to outline the demands and accusations.

"Oh, honey, no."

"Oh, honey, yes. She's gone off the deep end now, Daddy."

"How long is she giving you to comply?"

"Thirty days."

"I'll be home tomorrow. I'll speak to her then."

"I sure hope you can talk some sense into her. I don't have cash lying around to hire a lawyer for this on top of the one I have trying to straighten out my royalty issues."

"What royalty issues?"

"Rand has been diverting royalty payments and said our contract with Darlington ended on Darling's departure from his father's company. Rand seems to have been behaving badly with other firms, too, and police are looking into it."

"Who do you have representing you in this?"

"Eric Houston. He's Nana's lawyer."

"He any good?"

"I sure hope so."

His sigh was again loud, and it somehow comforted her. Then he said, "How's your grandmother taking it all?"

"I don't think she realizes the full extent of what's happening. Oh, she knows when she reads the letter from Mother's lawyer, and I can see the shock and hurt in her eyes. But I've been trying to distract her with happy and peaceful."

"Which is what your mother ought to want."

"You'd think."

"Okay, sweet. I'll do my best to rein her in. I have a few aces I can play."

She hoped her father would be able to control his wife. His wife, not her mother. Not Nana's daughter. Because Deborah Buchanan had withdrawn her membership in the mother-daughter club.

Jeminy chose a dress of vibrant green that brought out the greenish tint of her eyes and worked well with the white-blond of her hair. She hesitated before slipping into a pair of heeled sandals, but then pooh-poohed her worries of standing a head above everyone else. There were tall men who'd be at the restaurant. "Just stand up straight," she told her mirrored image.

When she finished primping, she went across to Nana's room to see if she needed help. "Nana, may I come in?"

"Of course." Her grandmother had the shades drawn and was lying on her bed.

"Oh, Nana, we need to get ready for the party!"

"Party? What party?"

Jeminy had already helped her grandmother pick out the dress she would wear, but it hung where she'd left it on a hook inside the closet door. "There's a dinner tonight to celebrate Agnes and Henry. They're getting married tomorrow."

Nana sat up. "I forgot."

"That's okay," Jeminy said brightly. "I didn't."

She waited while Nana used her bathroom and then helped fasten the hooks on her dress. Then she sat her grandmother down and brushed out her hair.

"Now, you look lovely." She pulled a light sweater from the closet. "Why don't you go ahead and wear this. It may get just a little cooler before we come home, and you never know about restaurant air conditioning."

They drove to the restaurant and parked in the small lot across the way. Other locals would probably walk, but she didn't want to push Nana too far this late in the day.

Agua Verde had limited capacity, but the temperature was balmy enough that overflow could spill into the outside seating area. They'd pushed tables together for larger groups, and folks could sit in booths along two sides and at the bar.

Jeminy's pulse quickened as she helped her grandmother through the door. This would be the first party of any size she'd attended as a resident of Beaufort, which must account for her excitement. It couldn't be because she'd spotted Eric Houston laughing with Darlington Evermire. Her lawyer and the man who'd made her songs famous. Of course her pulse went into overdrive.

She hadn't seen Darling in a while and still resented him cutting her off when he'd tossed out Arthur and company, but she was determined not to let her emotions show tonight when they were here to celebrate Agnes, Henry, and Brisa.

Glancing past that distraction, she spotted their host and hostess, chatting with a group that had to be Brisa's Georgia relatives. An elderly black lady sat in one of the slightly elevated booths, which brought her almost to conversation level, at least with the shorter Agnes. Henry waved Jeminy and Nana over.

"Come meet Darling's Mama Bea."

"Mrs. Warren," the elderly woman said, "why don't you jest make yourself comfortable here with me. I'm not one for wantin' to stand around anymore, are you?"

"No, ma'am," Nana said. "I'd be grateful to sit here with you." She turned to Jeminy. "Honey, will you get us both something to drink? I'd like a nice hot cup of tea."

"And you, Mrs. Evermire?" Jeminy asked.

"They're bringing me a lemonade. You don't need to worry yourself about me."

Jeminy spent a few minutes making sure her grandmother was comfortable and enjoying herself before wandering over to speak to Darling. Deep breath, she told herself.

As she approached, he turned from Eric and gave her a big smile. "Hey there, Jeminy! I've been wonderin' where you'd gone off to."

"Right here. How're things going for you since you went on your own?"

"Great, only I need more of your music. You've got more songwriting talent than anyone I've worked with yet, and I was real disappointed when you didn't get back to me."

Jeminy squinted up at him. "When did you try to reach me?"

He looked surprised at the question. "Why, right after I got the legal end of things in place. I wrote and asked if you'd be willing to negotiate new terms with me."

She didn't know what to say. That was months and months ago. Back when Rand had still been negotiating for her.

"I didn't get your letter."

"There was more than one. And my new manager talked to yours about terms, but he never heard back."

"He never told me. He stopped being my manager around that time. As a matter of fact, he chose to go over to Arthur Ames' team instead. Last I heard, they were living in the same house."

Darling raised his brows and let out a low whistle. "Then it's a very good thing he didn't try to negotiate with me. Sounds like they deserve each other, and it leaves us able to work out details without them."

She laughed. For the first time in months, she actually felt a burden drop. "Amazing."

Eric entered the conversation. "You two seem to have gotten back on track."

Jeminy agreed and then spoke to Darling. "I asked Eric to find out what was happening to my royalties and to check out the contract I had with Rand, so maybe you two can talk—or maybe your manager can negotiate with him?"

Darling slapped Eric's shoulder. "No problem. This man and I have negotiated together before. He'll take care of you."

They had? "Oh?"

Eric nodded. "We worked on a trust Darling set up for Brisa."

"Good to know," she said, uncomfortably aware of Eric's proximity. She took a slow breath and reminded herself to relax.

"Do you have anything new I can use?" Darling asked her.

"Almost. I went through a period when I stopped writing, but I have a couple of songs in the works."

"Maybe while I'm here we could get together so I could hear what you have?"

"Of course." Pressing her palms against her thighs, she told herself to breathe as the giddy feeling of relief washed over her.

She could do this. She could. All she had to do was finish the songs—the words and the music.

And then let them fly.

ERIC

There'd been talk of rain or at least of clouds obscuring the sun on this, his brother's wedding day, but as Eric donned his suit and helped Danny dress, they'd seen only a bright sky.

Darling Evermire had sent his jet to Atlanta, and two carloads of Brisa's Georgia relatives had arrived in town, including Brisa's great-grandmother and a slew of aunts, uncles, and cousins.

"Pays to have a celebrity for a grandson," Mama Bea, Darling's grandmother, had told him at last night's party.

Agnes had made peace with the man she'd dubbed Brisa's sperm donor because both she and Henry knew having Darling in Brisa's life was a positive thing for a girl who'd spent her first almost-twelve years not knowing who'd fathered her. And then to find out he was a famous singer?

Sure, there'd been hurdles to leap, but Darling's conversion to decent human being had surprised them all, including Darling himself. "I found love," he'd told them. "Seems she came in a little-girl package, and she led me back to my spiritual roots."

"Amazing" was all most of the Beaufort folks could say.

Danny hadn't yet seen the crowd that would be gathered today. He walked backward down the sidewalk and asked non-stop questions. "Brisa told me her daddy's gonna be there. Her real daddy. And her real great-grandma. She said his skin is the same color as mine and the rest of her real family's even darker. Real black, she said."

"Those aren't her only 'real' family. Her mama's real."

"But not Uncle Henry. Like you're not my real dad."

Eric reached out to steady the boy. "Watch out. You almost walked into a hydrant. And we're coming to a curb."

Danny checked over his shoulder and pivoted. "How come Brisa gets to know her real daddy and I don't?"

"Probably because I have no idea who yours is."

"Brisa said her mama used to tell her that, only it wasn't true."

"I'm afraid it's true for me. Your mama never told me, so I have no way of finding out." He led them across the narrow street and up onto the sidewalk before speaking again. "But, Danny, in my eyes, you *are* my real son. You were from the moment I held you after your birth and your little eyes looked into mine."

"But you left me."

"No, your mama took you away with her."

"But you let her."

"I had no power to stop her. But if I could have had you with me always, I would have. I would never have let you go."

They only had another block to go before Tadie's house, and others were also arriving by foot, some behind them, some from up ahead.

He stopped Danny and crouched in front of the boy. "You are mine, Danny. Forever. I chose you then and I choose you now."

Danny didn't look at him, but the boy's lower lip trembled. And then the mood was broken as Matt Morgan's children, Linney and Louis, came dashing up, leaving Matt to follow in their wake.

"Danny! Hey!" called Louis.

Linney, with her round cheeks and epicanthic eyes, grinned

widely, her face glowing with excitement. "A wedding! I like weddings!"

"Absolutely," Eric said.

"Brisa gets a daddy. Linney and Luse have a daddy." And she hugged Matt's midsection as he stopped next to them.

"You do indeed, sweetheart," Matt said, pulling her shoulder close. "Hey, Eric, Danny. Hannah's already helping set up. I suppose we ought to see if they need any manpower."

They followed Matt's crew up the driveway and to the backyard of Tadie and Will's big house. At the edge of the yard, Eric paused to look around, surprised to see a tent and what looked like a dance floor to one side. Someone was checking the speakers and microphone. On the other side were tables with white tablecloths and people setting up platters and drinks.

He hadn't realized the thing was going to be catered. He guessed he'd been so busy worrying about his own life that he hadn't paid that much attention to the details of his brother's, except that the women were organizing something fun. He'd thought covered dishes, not a meal with servers.

He was to stand up for his brother, and he'd made arrangements for Danny to hang out with some of the other families. Danny tugged him forward as Tadie's husband waved them to his side.

"Afternoon, Eric, Danny," Will said. "I have instructions to round you up, Danny, and point you to where we'll be. Jilly's over there. You see her?"

"Yes, sir."

"Okay, you head to her, and I'll catch up with you in a minute." To Eric, he said, "Tadie and Rita are in with Agnes, and your brother's in my library—the first room to the right of the front door—waiting for you. I think you might need to do some steadying there."

"On my way."

Eric took the porch steps two at a time. He wasn't late, he

decided as he checked his watch, and yet he could picture his twin pacing the room, nervous that something would go wrong.

Nothing would. Eric had the ring in his pocket. He was pretty sure he'd seen the pastor chatting with some of the Atlanta folks. And the women didn't look worried, which meant all was well with the bride.

He knocked and entered the library. At first, he didn't notice his brother. Then he spotted him sitting with his head bowed over his knees.

Shutting the door quietly, Eric moved to the chair opposite Hen's and waited.

Moments later, he heard a soft "Amen," and Henry stood.

"You okay?" Eric asked.

Henry smiled his sweet smile. "Now I am. I was having a few panic moments before I remembered I should pray."

"Ah, yes. Good." And then, "Everything okay between us?"

Hen reached over and laid a hand on Eric's shoulder. "I love you, brother. I'm sorry for being so wrapped up in myself that I missed being there for your hard times."

Eric bit the inside of his cheek to keep the tears in check. "We're good." He cleared his throat. "Now, let's get you married."

"How are things outside?"

"Lining up. Fancier than I'd imagined."

"Tadie convinced Agnes we needed a dance floor and caterers. As long as we're married at the end, I don't care how they manage it."

Eric checked his watch again. "Five minutes. You want to head on out?"

"Sure. I'm trusting you have the ring."

Eric grinned at his brother. "And if I didn't?"

Henry grinned back. "I'd beg, borrow, or steal one—or make a temporary one out of foil."

"Hah! That almost makes me want to lose this one."

"Come on, bro. Keep it focused." Henry slugged him gently on his upper arm and led the way out.

Focused. Good plan.

He'd focus on today and his brother and leave worries about his relationship with Danny alone. For now.

26

JEMINY

Knots and links and rings and kisses,
One for two and two for one.
How do we leave them, how do we go?
"None for me, honey, none for me."

Agnes and Henry were married with a ringing "And now I pronounce you husband and wife!" Jeminy had always felt a lilt in her spirit at those words, and this time the joy from everyone in the audience seemed palpable.

Agnes was a radiant bride, dressed in a cream-colored cocktail-length chiffon dress with a matching hat to shade her eyes when she wasn't looking up into Henry's, and he'd gazed at her in apparent adoration.

And then there'd been the food, yummy local shrimp and scallops, along with some interesting chafing dishes piled with various Southern fare such as collards, shrimp and grits, and barbecue. There were salads and a to-die-for cake layered in different colors from chocolate to red velvet.

Jeminy'd made sure Nana and Isa had plates and drinks before she circulated to speak to other guests. She was leaning over Agnes to admire her rings when attention focused on the microphone and the man standing behind it.

"Ladies and gentlemen," Darling said. "My daughter—whom I will now be sharing with her new stepfather, Henry—asked me to sing a couple of songs in honor of the bridal couple." He smiled over at Brisa. "And she promised to sing at least one with me."

Applause and hoots followed Brisa as she joined her father and they began to sing one of Jeminy's songs. Then, Darling leaned into the mic. "Brisa told me she had the privilege of hearing Jeminy Buchanan's latest piece. Jeminy even taught her a couple of the stanzas. So, Ms. Buchanan,"—and here he extended his acoustic guitar in her direction—"will you be so kind as to sing it for us here?"

"Please," Brisa said. "I'll help you."

"Oh, but..."

"Come, please," Darling said. "It would mean a lot to everyone to hear your newest from your own lips."

There was a burst of applause. Jeminy glanced around before nodding. "How can I say no to that?" She walked toward them and took the guitar. "Brisa, we'll sing the two stanzas I taught you."

"There's more?" Brisa said, her foot tapping in her excitement.

"Yes. And next time you come over, we'll work on them. For now, they can remain something to look forward to, okay?"

"Sure!"

Jeminy played through the melody once and then began.

"The sun comes up and a promise comes with it, days to laugh and days to sing." Brisa picked up the words and joined her, the girl's rich voice complementing Jeminy's. *"You're my dear delight, you're my precious one, you are the reason for my joy. Sing with me and laugh with me and settle right here beside me. Happy in this, happy in this, happy together as we live this life."*

Jeminy strummed a few bars as an interval and nodded for Brisa to join her again.

"Together we will dance at the moon, together we will sing to the sun, up and down through all our days, down and up through the nights we share. Happy in this, happy in this, happy together as we live this life. Sing with me and laugh with me and settle right here beside me."

They repeated the first stanza again, and then she let the notes die out. The applause was loud for both of them.

Darling draped an arm around his daughter. "You two sing beautifully together. And I can't wait until we have that contract taken care of, Jeminy." He winked at her. "Besides, I have a new proposal for you. I'll be in touch."

She smiled back and turned as Agnes held out her arms for a hug, first for her, then Brisa. "That song was perfect for today. Thank you so much."

"Indeed," Henry said. "Perfect." And to Darling, "And thank you so much for sharing your incredible talent with us today."

Jeminy studied Henry, who, surprisingly, seemed to mean what he said to the man who'd father'd Brisa without Agnes's consent. And wasn't that a PC way of saying the man had date-raped her?

This must be what forgiveness looked like. Only, how did one do that?

Jeminy closed her eyes and took a deep breath. She would not react to the conversation she was having with herself. She would not.

Because if she did, someone would ask questions, and then she'd have to come up with a reason that wasn't completely truthful. She couldn't, she absolutely couldn't speak those truthful words here. Or now.

Or at any time, really.

Eyes open again, she looked around the crowd, searching for something to get her mind off *that* topic. And her gaze locked with Eric's. He raised his glass of tea in a salute. She didn't want to respond, but his grin beckoned a smile from her.

It took him mere minutes to cross to her side. "I had no idea," he said, "that you could sing like that. Oh, I knew Darling used your songs, and I knew Brisa had inherited his voice, but I had no idea so much talent lived just down the street."

She could feel her cheeks heating. "Thank you."

Danny tugged on her arm. "You did real good, Miss Jeminy."

Relieved at the distraction, she bent toward him. "Thank you so much, Danny. Do you like to sing?"

"I guess, only I'm not so good. Kids at the home used to laugh at me."

The preacher had come up behind Danny and now leaned in. "You only got to make a joyful noise unto the Lord, young man. God will hear it as perfect."

Danny looked up at the large man. "You mean, like laughing?"

Jeminy caught Eric's eye again. The preacher chuckled. "Laughter is good medicine, sure enough, but you sing to God? That's a noise the Lord appreciates."

"I don't know how to sing to God."

"You don't? Well, you just get your Uncle Henry to bring you to church on Sunday. He'll show you."

Danny slid his hand into Eric's and tugged. Eric leaned in. "Can we?" Danny asked.

Eric shrugged. "Sure, why not?"

The preacher slapped Eric on the shoulder. As tall and strong as Eric was, he still looked as if he had to brace for the impact. "Good man. I'll look for you both." And then to Danny, he said, "And you'll see a passel of folks from here, like Miss Rita and her mama and daddy."

Danny looked confused.

Eric leaned down. "See that older couple chatting with Miss Tadie? That's Miss Elvie Mae and her husband, Mr. James

Whitlock. They live up there." He pointed to the stairs leading to an apartment above the garage.

"They do? How come?"

"From what I know," Eric continued, "Miss Elvie and Mr. James have been working for Miss Tadie's family forever, back when her own mama and daddy needed help."

"They're good people," Jeminy said. "I remember them from my childhood, coming here to visit."

"Yes, ma'am," the preacher said. "Real good people." He smiled at Jeminy. "You feel free to come to service any time."

"Thank you. I may need to take my nana to her church on Sundays."

"Well, that's fine. Long as you're in a house of the Lord where they preach truth, makes no difference which one."

She'd given a lot of thought to Darling's words. What sort of proposal did he have in mind? Curiosity had her jumping when her cell phone rang. She checked the caller ID but didn't recognize the number and clicked the phone to ignore.

It was Monday afternoon before she saw any of the partygoers again, and this time it was only Danny, sitting on their back porch steps and chatting with Nana.

"Hey, Danny, you here alone?"

"Yeah," he said, not looking all that happy.

"What happened to Brisa?"

"She wanted to go play with Jilly, so Mrs. Barnes said she could. Said I could, too, only I didn't want to. So I came to check on Jinx here." He stroked the tabby's fur.

Jeminy raised a brow. "Jinx? I didn't know he had a name."

"Your grandmother told me."

"She did, did she? Then I guess he does."

Nana smiled from her place on the swing. "He's a good kitty. He likes the boy."

"It seems he does." And to Danny, "How's school going?"

"Okay, I guess." But his shoulders slumped, and he didn't look up at her.

"Are you having trouble with the work—or the kids?"

"Work's easy."

Then maybe he didn't feel as if he fit in. "It's hard to begin a new school, isn't it? Meeting new kids…"

"Kinda." He hunched protectively over the cat, and what did that say about how he was feeling?

Maybe his responses had to do with his mother's death and being forced to move to a new place with a stepfather he hadn't seen in years. "How're you doing on the boat? Do you like living there?"

At that, his head jerked up, and he grinned. "It's real neat. We get to imagine going off on adventures, me and Eric."

So, not Eric or boat life. "I've always thought it would be amazing to cruise on a sailboat. Did you know Jilly and her parents sailed to the Caribbean and to lots of other places?"

"Yeah. She said it was super, only they gotta stay in one place now on account of Sammy needing to grow up more." Danny ran one hand down the cat's back and up his tail while the cat preened under his touch. "It's kinda fun. Brisa's got a dad with a boat, too."

"Do you guys talk about sailing together, all three boats? I've heard about people doing that. They call it buddy-boating." She'd actually read about two boats doing it while she waited for a dental appointment back in L.A. It had made her long to try out the lifestyle. Oh, maybe not for really long periods, but for a few months here and there. "It would be inspirational."

She didn't realize she'd spoken that aloud until Danny said, "What's inspi-inspiration?"

"Something that can give a person ideas, you know, like for songs or stories."

"Yeah, I guess." Danny concentrated on the cat again, rubbing behind its ears and down along its back. "I heard them talking, Brisa and Jilly, about what they could do on a boat, but they weren't talking to me. I'm just a kid."

Jeminy bit back a smile. "Maybe you should speak up next time. Let them know what you think."

"Don't think so." The shake of his head was barely perceptible.

"Ah, well, maybe someday."

Again the boy shrugged, and Jeminy changed the subject. "Nana, do you want some tea? Or some ice water?"

"Tea would be lovely."

"Danny?"

"I don't need nothing."

"Anything," Jeminy said automatically.

He wasn't looking at her when he spoke. "Don't need anything." Then he stood. "I better go."

"Thanks for coming by. I know Jinx was thrilled, and we always enjoy seeing you. Are you okay to go alone?"

"Just going back to Jilly's. It's right over there." With one last pat to the cat's head, he said goodbye and fled.

"I'll get your tea, Nana."

Nana pushed her shoes against the porch floorboard to get her swing rocking and merely smiled.

Inside, Jeminy set the kettle on the stove and stared out the back window. There was so much to think about, so much to set her mind worrying, but she tried to focus on the yard and her grandmother's garden. It still needed tending. More on the to-do list, a list that threatened to bend her back—and not from physical labor.

The problem was, all she wanted to do was sit with Gully and strum chords to see what came.

The kettle's whistle reminded her to turn off the flame and get a cup and saucer ready for the tea bag. She ought to go grocery shopping again and this time add some good herbal teas to her purchases. Nana would probably enjoy a ginger tea. And maybe it would let her sleep more soundly.

How did everyone else manage to consume glasses of sweet tea and walk around all peaceful and happy? It couldn't be the sugar because that would wear off. Did the caffeine balance the sugar or vice versa?

Odd thoughts to be having, she supposed, as she stirred Nana's sugar into the steeped tea. But worrying about tea and sugar was better than fretting about lawsuits and royalties.

When her phone rang later that afternoon, Jeminy checked the caller ID before she answered. Seeing it was Eric, she took a deep breath. And, no, that didn't mean a single thing except she needed a breath. Really.

She answered with "Hey."

"Jeminy. I just got a notice your ex-manager refused delivery of the certified letter I sent. That's two letters ignored, and our path forward may be the courts."

"Oh." Which would mean more money on legal fees. Jeminy chewed on her cheek and then her bottom lip. Money, it always came down to money.

"And," Eric continued, "we now know that Darling wrote to you a couple of times, offering a new contract the first of the year. Your ex-manager failed to inform you of this, which has defrauded you of income. The man has some answering to do."

He did, and she'd been a fool.

"I also met with Darling and have negotiated terms going forward. He has been very generous. He also left a letter for you. Any way you can come to my office to discuss this with me? I can't do more until I have your okay."

"Sure. When do you want me to come in?" She glanced at the

clock. "It's not five yet. I could come now." Because she'd like to see that letter.

"Maybe tomorrow morning? I'm free after ten."

"Ten, then."

She disconnected with a sigh, impatience gnawing at her. She needed to figure out what she would fix for dinner, but she'd just dash upstairs to check on her bank balance. What she saw when she went online made her huff in frustration because, no, it hadn't magically grown in size, and because, no, she still wasn't getting royalty payments.

Her father's call came in after dinner. She pictured him sitting in his den, his feet propped on his desk, the lights low. She'd seen him that way so many times, his fingers laced over his chest as he relaxed and contemplated life. Sometimes, he'd be praying. Sometimes, he'd have his Bible opened in front of him. Sometimes, he'd be looking out the long window at the woods behind their house.

"Hey, sweetie," he said now. He sounded weary.

"Have you spoken to her?"

"I have. Your mother keeps trying to convince me she's right." He paused, but Jeminy didn't speak. "I think she needs to confront you both, you and your grandmother, face to face."

"We did that already. It wasn't pretty."

"Yes, but perhaps if you do that with me there. A mediator."

"I don't think it will do any good." She sighed. "Tell me this, do you think she's on anything? Something that might make her irrational?"

"Other than alcohol? I don't know. I haven't seen any evidence of pill bottles."

"That could make her crazy, couldn't it?"

"There's some underlying cause, honey, and I think it's

spiritual. She began to drink more than usual after we lost Oliver, and she did a lot of pointing fingers everywhere."

"From grief?"

"Not normal grief. You and I experienced what I'd call normal grief. We still ache because he isn't with us because we loved him and hate his death, but we came to terms with it. At least, I think we did."

"I still dream about him."

"Good or bad?"

She gripped the phone. "Nightmares. Dreams of being there again, finding him on the path, trying to wake him."

"Oh, honey, I hoped you'd gotten over those."

His sympathy nearly undid her. "They… they don't come all the time, but I may never be completely free of the memory. He was my twin." Her beautiful, sweet, darling brother.

"I know." His voice was a whisper. She could imagine him thinking *and my son.*

She waited until she felt able to speak without tears. "So why does Mother have what you call an abnormal grief? Why do you think it's a spiritual thing?"

In the background, Jeminy heard her mother's voice calling her father. Mother sounded irritated.

Didn't she always.

"Let's talk about this later. Could you meet us, say in Goldsboro, for lunch on Wednesday? There's a lovely little restaurant, very quiet, just off the main street. I happen to know the owners, and I can get him to let us have one of the two tea rooms. Keep it private."

"Hang on." She dug in her purse for her little notebook and checked the calendar. "Nana doesn't seem to have any appointments, so that would work for us, I think."

"Excellent. I'm in town, and, as far as I know, your mother doesn't have any clubs or committees."

"I'll make it happen. Good luck on getting her to agree."

"Oh, she'll agree."

Really? That didn't sound like the mother she knew, but maybe Daddy had something she wanted.

She sat across from Eric after going over the contract and her accounts with him. Darling had promised to have his lawyers discover how much had actually been paid in royalties in the last six months, money that should have come to her.

"Once we have that information, we'll try to get a court order for Mr. Radcliff's records, and then we may need a forensic accountant to go over them."

"What about whatever the police are already doing out there?" She'd been so stupid, so naive. "Did I ever tell you how I found out Rand had hidden files on a thumb drive?"

"I don't think so."

"It was way too easy. I'd stuffed a desk drawer too full and one of my papers got stuck out the back, if you can picture it. I couldn't pull it free, so I got under the desk to try to unstick the drawer. The thing was taped right there."

"Why would he keep secretive materials where they could be found so easily?"

"Stupidity?"

"Or hubris," Eric said.

"Yeah, that sounds about right. I couldn't open it, though, so I found a match for it and taped the blank one back in its place. Then I asked around until I found a guy who could unlock and download the files. That's when I went to the police."

"Did anyone confront him?"

"I don't know. Money'd gone missing in dribs and drabs while we were together, enough that I finally asked him about it. He said it was needed for various business deals he'd been working on for me, but that didn't make sense. We had a business account and an accountant handling that. Rand shrugged and went on doing whatever he wished." On a sigh, she said, "I didn't have answers until after he walked out. I left it in the hands of the police, and I froze what assets I could still find."

"He was a busy boy, I take it."

"Very busy, and not just with my money."

"We may have to find you representation in California."

"I assumed as much. Can you help?"

"I'll do what I can." He slid an envelope across the desk. "While I go make copies of your account documents, you might want to read this letter Darlington left for you."

She held it for a moment before tearing open the seal.

Jeminy, I love your new song and would like to add it to my repertoire. I would also like to ask if you've ever thought of writing inspirational songs. I gave Brisa a CD of ones I've just recorded, and I asked her to play them for you.

No pressure, but this is a direction I'd like to take. God has done so much for me in the last months, and I want to give back.

Think about it, will you? I mean, I know songs have to come from the heart, and I don't really know where you stand on the faith spectrum— I'm still rediscovering the relationship I had with God as a child.

I look forward to talking to you in the future. Below is my cell phone number. Call whenever.

D

Tears threatened to spill, but she dashed them away before Eric returned and took his seat. He slid the original statements in a folder and passed copies to her.

She took them, but her thoughts were on the letter. "Did Darling tell you what he was writing to me?"

Eric shook his head. "No. And I didn't ask. Figured it was between the two of you."

"Ah."

With a slight smile, he said, "I'll let you know what I can

uncover and if I think we need to go the court route. I am afraid that may be our only recourse."

She was barely listening. Inspirational songs? If that's what Darling wanted, she'd have to figure out what that meant to her—if she could pull anything out of her befuddled mind—because she doubted Rose's words like "the wages of sin" were what he'd consider uplifting.

And, of course, that night the dream came again, but this time it segued from Olli to her lost little baby, her unborn child who kept calling her. His cries—or her cries, she never knew which—sent her running to find the little lost infant. But the babe could not be found.

When she woke, her own tears streaming down her cheeks, she cried to the God Darling had come to know, and begged Him for help.

27

RAND

Rand had interviewed three private detectives before he found one who wouldn't charge him an arm and a leg to find Jeminy.

Why was it so expensive? It wasn't like they had to go flying all over the country; they had the internet. Anyway, this guy said it shouldn't be hard as long as their quarry hadn't traveled under an assumed name.

Was Jeminy even smart enough to have thought of that?

In the meantime, he tried to keep Arthur happy with promises of new contacts, new artists to sign. He only needed to make that a reality.

He did have a couple of appointments next week. But he'd already had one refuse to meet with him.

Something about the word being out. Only, the man wouldn't be specific about what word.

She'd done something. He didn't know what yet, but he'd find out.

ERIC

Danny had seemed restless the last couple of days, not even wanting to play with his new friends. Becca Barnes said he'd spent time with Harvey, Brisa's dog, but not so much with Brisa and the others. Monday, she'd gone looking for him and seen him coming from Mrs. Warren's, where he said he'd gone to play with her cats on account of Brisa having homework she and Jilly and Louis were doing together.

"A project, they called it. I checked with Miss Jeminy," Becca told him, "and she didn't seem to mind. Matter of fact, she said Mrs. Warren got real tickled having him around."

Eric wasn't quite sure what to say to all that, but he did watch his son more closely when they got home Tuesday. Danny willingly helped stir sauce and dump noodles in water for a quick spaghetti dish, and he also set the table.

Plates in front of them, a few bites taken to stave off hunger, Eric asked about homework.

Danny stirred his fork around, shifting noodles off to one side and then back again. "Did it," he said, not looking up.

"May I see it?"

The boy mumbled something.

"What?"

"Already turned it in."

"You already turned it in." Eric didn't make it a question.

Danny nodded.

Did they do that here? Collect homework early? Because the way he remembered it, teachers went over homework in class the next day and then collected it.

"Tomorrow, bring it home, please. I want to see what you're learning."

Danny only shrugged.

When the child was ready for bed, Eric pulled out the book they'd been reading together and climbed in the v-berth next to his son. But as he tried to settle, he accidentally nudged Danny's shoulder. The boy cried out.

Eric sat up immediately. "What?"

"Nothing."

"You didn't cry out about nothing. Something hurt you."

"It's nothing. I just ran into a door at school."

"Let me see it."

"It's fine. You'll just make it worse if you go messing with it." Danny curled away from him.

Obviously, it was only one shoulder, and the boy had used his arm, so maybe it really was nothing. "If it still hurts in the morning, maybe we should put something on it. You could have scraped it."

"I'll be fine."

Eric hoped so. "You want to turn over so we can read?"

"Naw. I'm tired. I just want to sleep."

Eric hated leaving it there. He looked forward to this time with Danny, considered it a bonding opportunity.

"Okay." He climbed off the berth. "See you in the morning."

He was wiping down galley counters when he heard soft sobs coming from the forward cabin. Did Danny's shoulder hurt so much, or was he missing his mother?

Eric was wading in deep waters, going under when a wave hit, and he knew he'd have to figure out how to swim in this ocean called fatherhood if Danny were going to grow into the man Eric hoped he'd be.

He sat in the dimly lit salon and thought about his life, the mistakes he'd made, the choices he'd faced—and the ones he'd run from. These thoughts morphed into ones of his twin. Eric had had it easy, but not Henry. Henry, who'd always been considered less by their father, a man who couldn't see past Henry's cleft lip to the brilliant, precious boy who'd been such a gift—so much more than he, Eric, had been. Eric, their father's favorite. Eric, the one of value because nothing marred his outward appearance.

He hadn't been able to fix things for Henry, certainly not by always trying to rescue him. He hadn't been the catalyst for change in his twin.

No, that had been his brother's faith. Hen's reliance on a Savior to deliver him when effort alone kept failing.

And now look at him—married, a stepfather, comfortable in his own skin.

And Eric?

He shrugged off the thought and grabbed a beer from the refrigerator. He'd figure it out.

He had to.

In the meantime?

He pushed the beer to one side of the dining table, set his head in his hands and tried prayer. He desperately needed the God who'd set Hen free.

"Lord? Can you hear me?"

29

MR. JENKINS

Waiting to find the kid alone or with the man far from other folk was takin' all the patience Dalton'd ever gained from his years of doin' this. Town was too danged small with not nearly enough parking for him stake out places without being noticed.

Careful, that's what he had to be, that's what he was. Just needed to blend. He wore jeans, kind lots of locals wore, not dirty, not too clean. His plain shirts wouldn't draw attention, and he had a couple different ball caps. He'd grown out a short beard so he didn't look much like himself, and beards were common enough in town.

He kept his duffel in the black Chevy truck he'd found behind a Stop 'n Shop in Morehead, on account of the truck looking like a lot of others around town. He'd left his tan one a few blocks away, and sometimes he switched them out. No problem with the "borrowed" truck. He'd changed those plates for New Jersey ones he'd got from a friend down home.

Dalton never left anything in the flea-bag trailer he'd also "borrowed" from some absentee owner. Place didn't have lights, but it had water. Good enough, free, and he could get in with his flashlight, get out early enough not to be noticed. Park a ways back on an unkempt dirt drive. Easy peasy.

Wednesday morning, he arrived back on Front Street in time to see the school bus heading down the block away from the water, and Danny ducking behind shrubs to keep out of sight. Dalton's heart did a little tap-tap, hurrying to catch up with the excitement he felt.

Somebody must finally be watchin' out for him, Dalton decided. He pulled his ball cap low on his forehead, parked across the street, pocketed his gun, and climbed out of the car, keepin' his eyes on those bushes. Yep, there the kid was, running across a yard.

Question was, where best to nab him? Porches were empty, not much traffic. Dalton stayed on the water side of the street, trying to look like he belonged. And there the kid went, around the side of that house to the garage.

A door shut, a screen door, it sounded like. The kid ducked, hid at the side of the house. Then Dalton saw him try a garage side door, open it, and duck inside.

Oh, this would be a piece of cake.

He fingered his gun and turned deliberately toward the driveway and that garage.

30

JEMINY

"Do I have a tissue?" Nana asked as Jeminy reached the back door. "I always carry a tissue in my bag. And lipstick. I don't want to go anywhere without my lipstick."

"Let's check." Jeminy opened Nana's purse, which was stuffed with extra tissues. In a side pocket, she found two tubes of the lipgloss Nana used. "It's all there. See?"

"Do I have sunglasses? I'll need sunglasses. And what about a sweater? You young people always like to turn it cold."

Jeminy plucked sunglasses from the kitchen table and pointed to the sweater her grandmother wore. "I think we've got everything.!"

She hadn't told her grandmother they'd be confronting her mother. She'd save that until they were on the road and Nana couldn't argue. And once they were in a public place, Nana's manners would kick in. Whether or not her mother would behave was a different question.

"I don't drive anymore, so you'll have to do it," Nana said, sounding a little worried.

"I plan to, Nana. I put gas in your car the other day, so we're set." She had the car and door keys in hand and locked up after she'd led her grandmother onto the porch.

The garage door opened at the push of a button. "Can you see well enough in this dim light, Nana? Or do I need to back out first?"

"I'm fine. I can manage to get in my own car."

"Of course you can."

The only help her grandmother needed was in placing her bag. That done, Jeminy inserted the CD of Darling's new songs, which Brisa had dropped off, into the player. And they were off.

Nana commented on the view all the way out of town, especially when they crossed the high bridges and entered Morehead. Several big ships were at the port, and a tug maneuvered another one out in the channel. Nana found it endlessly fascinating, which made Jeminy realize how constricted her grandmother's life was now that she didn't drive.

"We'll have to come out more often, won't we?"

"Oh, yes. My husband used to bring me out to dinner here every week."

Surely it hadn't been that long since Nana had been out. But maybe it had. Well, she and Isa would have to do something about that.

By the time they'd passed the exits for New Bern forty minutes later, Nana had quieted. Jeminy glanced over at her.

"You sleepy?"

"I am, honey."

"Reach down on the side of your seat. There's a button to make the seat back recline and you can have a nice nap."

Nana fumbled with a few different buttons and then came to the right one, and back she went. "Oh, this is lovely."

Wasn't there a pillow in the back seat? Jeminy felt between the seats until her hand came to the small one she'd seen earlier. "Here, Nana. Put this behind your head. That's right, between you and the door. And yes, the door is locked, so you'll be safe."

"So nice."

"Good. I'll wake you when we get there."

"Hmm…"

With her grandmother asleep, Jeminy turned on the music and listened to Darling sing.

MR. JENKINS

Dalton cursed under his breath. He'd been *so* close.

He was on their tail now. He'd scurried to the black truck when the garage door had opened and he'd scanned the obviously empty space once the car backed out. It was a narrow, one-car garage with only a lawn mower, some gardening tools at the back. No kid. Which meant the kid was in the car.

Off he'd gone after them, always watching out for a place to force the car to a stop on an empty stretch of road. Traffic was heavy through Morehead, even on 70 all the way to Havelock. Either beach people or Cherry Point Air Station folk were on that blasted highway.

Oka-ay. His patience would be rewarded. It always was.

Things got a little better up around New Bern. Most everyone either got off the highway at the several exits or they sped way past that little car he was tailing. Soon as they got clear, he'd make his move.

Finally, the road on both sides was empty. He sped up alongside the car, saw the boy in back, and determined to get it over with and done.

3 2

JEMINY

Lord, O Lord, are You listening?
Do You hear? Are You near?

There was hardly any traffic on this stretch of highway between New Bern and Kinston, and Jeminy relaxed into the drive. She'd listened to as much of Darling's new music as she could manage and was left with a hollow feeling. She'd never be able to write the songs he wanted. Those songs spoke of a relationship with God she didn't have in spite of her early church-going days.

Was God really a miracle worker?

Could God actually be *for her*?

She'd certainly never known a God like that.

She was checking her mirrors, focusing on not choking up, on keeping under the speed limit, when a sudden gasp from the back of the car caught her attention. And there, in the rearview mirror, appeared a child's head.

Followed by a scream.

She whipped her head around to peer between the seats, just a quick peek because, of course, she didn't believe in ghosts. At the very moment she recognized Danny, a crashing explosion of sound came from her side window . Small chunks of glass shards showered her face, arms, and hands, and wind buffeted her. She inadvertently jerked the wheel away from the noise, and the car flew off the road, over the shallow bank, onto the flats, still at some speed even as she hit the brakes, even as a loud pop sounded, but she couldn't think, she couldn't do, she couldn't fix this...

Surely there were screams, and not only hers, in her ear, behind her, in front, all around, screams...

O God, O God, O Lord Jesus, help!

Jeminy clutched the steering wheel as the car bounced and rocked down, across, and onto a slight rise. It slammed into bushes, bushes that broke and crunched under them, stopping the car's forward advance just before it crashed into a pine forest full of big fat hard trees.

Thank God.

And "Amen." No trees. No airbags.

"Nana, Nana?"

Her grandmother turned and stared at Jeminy, her eyes huge and frightened. Her sunglasses had rocked right off her face, and her hands cradled her head.

"Are you okay? Are you hurt anywhere?"

Nana lowered her arms and continued to stare, speechless, while Jeminy ran hands from shoulder to wrist and reached to make sure the pillow still supported her grandmother's neck and head.

And then a moan came from the cargo section of the Subaru.

"Hang on," she said to her nana and to the boy.

Unbuckling her belt, she turned toward her door. The shattered window fell away as she forced open the door, pushing twiggy bits of brush out of the way. Her left shoulder ached, her head hurt, and she felt bruised all over, but it wasn't much, nor was it dangerous, and she ignored the pain as she scrambled to the back hatch.

Inside lay Danny, curled up against the seat back and whimpering.

"Where do you hurt, honey?"

He, too, just stared with those big eyes of his as he bit his lower lip and let the tears ooze out.

"Did you break anything? Can you move your arms and legs?" Nothing. "I need to know, Danny."

Okay, he wasn't talking, and she wasn't about to try moving him. "Stay there," she told him as she went to retrieve her phone from her purse, now on the floor of the back seat.

When the emergency dispatcher answered, Jeminy looked around helplessly and took a deep breath before she spoke the words aloud. "It… it looks like a bullet went through my driver's side window. A bullet, yes. I think it came out the windshield. There's a hole and cracked windshield in front of the passenger's seat."

"What is your location?"

"We're on 70 West, between New Bern and Kinston. Close to where you have to slow down."

"Was anyone else in the car with you?"

"My grandmother. I don't know if she's bruised, or if there's anything broken. I don't see any blood, but I can't get her to talk. I mean, she's awake, and she looks like she's in pain. And there's a seven-year-old boy who seems to have stowed away in the cargo area of the car—a Subaru wagon. He's crying but not talking. His left arm looks kind of out of whack, as if it might be broken."

Another car had pulled to the side of the road and a man was calling down to her. She waved to show she was okay as she listened to the dispatcher.

"Yes, ma'am. Somebody just stopped to help. Thank you. I don't want to stay on the line. I need to see if my nana or the boy needs anything. Yes," and she gave her name and phone number, as well as the names of her passengers. The dispatcher assured her a sheriff's deputy had just spotted the other car and would be there momentarily.

Jeminy returned to check on Danny, who was still curled out of her reach and whimpering piteously. By the time she'd climbed up next to him, the deputy was there, saying something and leaning in to check on her. He gave her a smile that he controlled so quickly she may have imagined it.

"My grandmother. Please see if she's okay. Her name is Georgina Warren."

He was speaking into his shoulder microphone as he went around and knelt at Nana's open door.

"Danny, honey, help is on the way. Can you move at all or talk to me?"

"I... I'm sorry," he said through choked back tears. "So... s...sorry."

"You mean for hiding in the car?"

He only loosed a little yelp as if he'd shifted and made things worse.

"Tell me where it hurts. Is it just your arm?" What if he had internal injuries or was bleeding someplace she couldn't see? "You'll be okay soon." Surely he would. *Please, God.*

An emergency vehicle arrived. She heard EMTs talking to each other, and then one of them was at the back of the car. "Ma'am, could you trade places with me, please?"

She scooted out and waited by the tailgate while the first EMT climbed in next to Danny and a second crouched next to Nana. The deputy approached.

"Was I right?" she asked. "Did someone shoot at me?"

"Looks like it. What did you see right before you went off the road?" He pulled out a small notebook.

"That's just it. I didn't. I mean, I'd been checking in my mirrors, and I knew there was another vehicle coming up on my left, but I didn't pay it any attention, other than to note it was a truck, black, I think."

His pen was poised. "Anything else? What about the child in the back of your car? Why wasn't he buckled in a seat?"

Jeminy blew out a breath. "I didn't even know he was *in* the car. The thing is, I'd just caught sight of him in my rearview mirror, his face flashing and a gasp coming from him, like maybe he'd seen something. I turned quickly to see if I was imagining him, if I'd really seen his face in the mirror, and that's when he screamed and when the explosion—the bullet, I guess—made me turn the wheel, and off we went."

"You think the boy may have witnessed the event?" The deputy's eyes lit as if that possibility would make his day.

"I don't know. But he definitely made a distressed sound just before it all happened."

He glanced around and said, "Be right back." He went to speak to the EMTs who were working together to load Danny onto a stretcher.

By now, a state trooper had joined the others and moved in to confer with the deputy.

Nana was able to walk, but the emergency technician wanted her to be seen at the hospital also. Jeminy agreed, especially as Nana still seemed too confused to know where or if she hurt. Both Nana and Danny needed her with them.

"Will someone stay with my grandmother until I make sure Danny is okay? He's bound to be terrified."

"Don't you worry about Mrs. Warren. We'll take good care of her."

"Nana, Eric's little boy is hurt, so I'm going with him to the hospital, and these nice people will get you there. Okay?"

"Little boy?" At least Nana could speak.

"Yes, Danny. The boy who likes to pet your kitties."

"He's a good boy."

"Yes, ma'am. These nice people will bring you to the hospital where I'll be, but I have to go with Danny now. I'll see you very soon. Don't worry, Nana. Please."

This was killing her, leaving her grandmother, making this choice. But it had to be done. Danny was only seven.

In a hurry, she called Isa. "Would you ask Eric to call me about Danny, please? I don't have his number and need to talk to him, I mean, like now."

"Sure, honey. What's going on?"

"We were in an accident. I'll tell you later. Just reach Eric for me, will you?"

Danny still looked scared and in pain. She moved up beside his stretcher and took his free hand. "I'm trying to reach your father. I'm sure he'll come to the hospital as soon as he can."

"He'll be so mad. I-I bet he'll send me back."

"Excuse me, miss." The deputy was back, the trooper at his side. "Son, did you see anything before the accident? Anyone trying to do something bad?"

"Un-huh. The gun. I saw the gun."

The trooper had his own notebook out. "Did you see the man?"

"I saw the truck."

"What can you tell me about it?"

"It was black, dirty. Kind of big."

"Anything else you noticed?"

"The truck, it was coming fast and then it slowed next to Miss Jeminy's car. I saw the man point the gun. I wanted to warn her, to say stop or turn or something, but the blast came too quick."

"Good, good." The trooper nodded toward the deputy. "You got that?"

"I did. I'll get the APB out."

"You have any enemies?" the trooper asked Jeminy.

"Me? Who'd want to kill me and my grandmother?" He didn't answer. "No. The only person who probably doesn't like me is my ex, but he's in California. He's a creep, but he's not physically abusive."

———

Walking toward the two ambulances, Jeminy punched in her father's number and explained why they wouldn't be meeting him. He wanted to rush to her side.

"No, no, please don't come." The thought appalled her. "If you were alone, that would be one thing, but I'm dealing with too much right now. I can't add Mother to it." She imagined her mother going on a rant, accusing her of endangering her grandmother. Lord, help them all then, the hospital staff, too.

"Okay," Daddy said, "but call me."

"As soon as I know more."

And then she switched over to take what she assumed would be Eric's call. He sounded grim when he said he wouldn't be far behind them at the hospital.

As she rode next to Danny, she imagined Eric racing to his car and then swearing as traffic meandered down Arendell Street in Morehead, especially when the speed limit kept him at 30 mph.

The emergency room was crowded for a small regional hospital, and although this was her first experience with an ER, she'd seen plenty of medical dramas with gunshot victims or bloody accidents, and all she could think was how glad she was she'd moved to small-town America.

While they wheeled Danny to a cubicle, Jeminy checked them in, handing over Nana's insurance card and her own, explaining that Danny's father was on the way.

It wasn't long before a nurse led her to a cubicle next to Danny's. "Let's look at that graze on your head. See what else is going on with you."

"I'm fine, really."

"Just humor me," the nurse said, preparing to clean where her head had hit something. "How does your head feel?"

"Achy. But it's more my shoulder, probably from the seat belt. At least the airbags didn't deploy."

"Good thing you didn't need them. I assume you didn't hit anything hard."

"Just bushes."

"The doctor might want an X-ray on that shoulder."

"I need to see Danny and my grandmother. Please. She came separately from us."

"Mrs. Warren? I believe she's just the other side of the young boy."

The nurse showed her. Both her nana and Danny lay draped in blankets. Nana's eyes were closed, Danny's round and searching as tears pooled. He looked so miserable and lost that Jeminy's heart broke for him.

She ran a comforting hand over his curls. "Your dad will be here soon, and the doctors will get you all fixed up." She trusted it wouldn't be too much longer before they actually did something for him.

The nurse stood at the cubicle's entrance. "You cold, honey?" she asked Jeminy. "I can get you a heated blanket. Another for the boy too."

"That would be great. Thanks."

"They keep it cold on account of the machines."

Which made no sense to Jeminy, but she accepted the blankets, draping one over Danny, who cried a little when it touched his arm. "I'm sorry, honey. It really hurts, huh?"

He nodded.

She wrapped herself in the other blanket and spoke to the nurse. "Can you get me an update on my grandmother? Is she okay?"

"I'll find someone who can."

Jeminy asked for directions to the bathroom, suddenly

overwhelmed by the need for one. And that was when the shaking took over, the horror of what had happened finally penetrating the busyness of rescue.

Someone had tried to kill her.

Her senses had dulled in spite of the noises from beyond the separating curtains. She allowed her eyes to close as she hunched into the blanket.

And then a woman's voice was followed by a man's. Eric. Jeminy straightened her back and glanced up. His face looked flushed, and a worry line drew his brows together. He carried his suit jacket; he'd be glad to have its warmth soon enough.

"Where is he?" Eric asked impatiently.

She wanted to tell him to calm down, but in his place she'd probably be just as upset. "They wheeled him to X-ray. It's all hurry up and wait around here."

"And your grandmother?"

"The next cubicle." She fluttered her hand to the left. "Over there. They've given her something, probably a pain reliever, but they don't think she has anything really wrong with her more than a few bruises. I imagine they'll do some tests. Eventually. Why don't you grab the extra chair by her bed? She should still be asleep."

He pulled on his jacket. "Ah, better. I don't know why they think frigid air more conducive to healing." He fetched the chair and then really looked at her. He nodded toward her bandage. "You okay?"

"Bruised. Shaken. It's not every day that someone shoots at you."

"Shoots?" He sounded grim. "Okay, start at the beginning."

She remembered that she'd only mentioned running off the

road, not the thing that caused it. She did her best, but he interrupted her. "Why was Danny even in your car?"

"I haven't had a chance to ask him. I don't know why he didn't speak up when I helped Nana in or when I backed out of the garage. I get that it was darkish in there, and the back windows are tinted, but if he'd said anything, I would have brought him right to you."

As he shook his head, that stray lock fell forward. "I thought he was in school."

Jeminy shifted her focus, speaking as she pushed off the chair. "And the school probably thought he was home sick. Excuse me. I need to check on Nana." She eased out and toward her grandmother, smiling at the sight of Nana in a deep sleep with her mouth slightly open.

Sweet thing. How fortunate that she could sleep through the wait.

"I'd really like to ask Danny a few questions," Eric said when she returned, but he didn't look her way.

She lowered herself to the chair and pulled the blanket back over her lap. "He saved my life."

Eric's gaze returned to her, his brows raised. "How?"

"Obviously, the bullet was meant for me, and it would have connected at least with my face, but I saw Danny in my rearview mirror. I tell you, he scared the life out of me. The last thing I expected to see was a boy's face staring at me with a panicked look. And he was screaming. So I whipped around to check it out. Under normal circumstances, that would have been stupid, taking my eyes off the road, but this time it saved me. I turned just before the bullet slammed into the window to my side." Telling it again brought the horror back, and she yanked the blanket up to her neck as a shiver raced through her. "Of course, I also steered off the road, but we survived. All of us."

"Thank God," Eric whispered.

"Yeah. Absolutely. Nana was saved because her seat was

reclined and she had a pillow between her head and the door. The bullet's trajectory took it through the windshield on the passenger side. There may have been a second shot, but I can't be certain. I didn't see evidence of another bullet, but I seem to remember another pop."

She saw again the boy's image, the cracking glass, the noise, her fright as they went off the road and down the bank.

"I'm sorry Danny was hurt," she said, "but I'm very glad he decided to stow away today."

"I guess you are. Hen would say that sounds like a God thing."

That's what Nana had said. "The good Lord was watching out for us today, sweet girl." In spite of shock and in spite of memory issues, her grandmother could hang onto her faith.

And it seemed as if she had reason to.

33

MR. JENKINS

Dalton wiped the sweat off his brow and looked for an exit off Highway 70 that would let him retreat back to Morehead. Time to ditch this black truck, get back in his own. Make sure no one could identify him and link him to this truck.

How had it gone so wrong? He'd aimed, shot, and the crazy woman had veered. How come? She hadn't seen him, hadn't seen his lowered window or his gun, on account of her not lookin' his way. His first shot and her veering had happened in a split second of each other. He'd pulled the trigger a second time. Bang, poof, nothing. Like there was something between his bullet and them. It didn't make sense.

He'd braked when her car went off the road and down into the bushes, but by then speeders had come into view, and he'd had no time to dawdle. He'd either had to look like help and get the kid or hightail it out of there. One of those speeders was bound to be a busybody who'd stop and get out.

Fine. He could admit he hadn't played that very well. He needed to get away and try another day. Strategize a little better.

After all, there was a lot of money involved. Enough to set him up for good, so he wouldn't be dependent on Stelle and that set-up she had going. He finished this job, and he could go far away, start over, find new clients, new ways.

34

ERIC

Eric blew out a breath and plowed his fingers through his hair. Danny wasn't going to be able to hold onto railings or navigate off his bunk easily with his arm in a cast, and holding on was an important part of navigating life on a boat, even if that boat was moored to a dock.

So, for tonight he'd get them a room at the Inn. And tomorrow he'd look for a small house to rent.

"You okay back there, buddy?" he asked. Danny was lying in the backseat, drugged up, fortunately, so the car's bouncing didn't cause him too much pain.

Eric hoped Danny's silence meant the boy slept.

His cell phone rang, and he picked up the call through his car's system. It was Mrs. Barnes saying Danny hadn't come home on the bus, and Brisa hadn't seen him since this morning. She was pretty sure he'd gotten on the bus with them, but he usually sat with other guys toward the back, and she and Jilly sat near the front.

"I have him with me, Mrs. Barnes," trying to speak softly so he wouldn't disturb Danny. "It seems he skipped school." He went on to explain what had happened and asked if she'd mind meeting

236

them at the Inn so he could leave Danny while he collected a few things they'd need.

"Thank the good Lord he's okay. I'll be there," she said, "and I'll bring Brisa along with me. I'm thinkin' Danny might like to tell his story to someone other than doctors, and she'd be a good audience."

"Thank you. I'll let you know when I have him settled in a room."

Maybe Brisa'd be able to figure out why Danny had skipped school. Eric hadn't been able to get the boy to talk, only shrug.

Traffic was minimal over the high-rise bridges and into Beaufort, and he pulled into the parking lot next to the Inn with barely a moan from Danny.

"How you doing, buddy? You okay to walk into this motel?"

"Mmm."

"We're going to camp out here tonight."

As he spoke, a knock sounded on the back window. He opened his door and climbed out to speak to Mrs. Barnes as Brisa peered in through the back.

"Come to see if we can help you settle. The manager, Darla,"— Becca Barnes motioned toward the office—"she gave me the key. Said you could take care of paperwork later."

"Mrs. Barnes, you're a gem. And hey, Brisa. You want to take some of this food on in?" He handed her the plastic bags.

"Smells yummy," she said, a note of hope in her voice.

"Yes, there's plenty, only maybe not enough milk for two." He opened the back door, helped Danny to sit up and slide out. "Watch yourself on the frame there."

Danny wobbled a little as he stood, so Eric braced him and let Mrs. Barnes lead the way. Once he'd settled Danny on one of the beds, and Brisa had the food spread on a table under Mrs. Barnes's capable management, Eric headed out, first to the office to hand over his credit card, and then back to *Escape* to load up a duffle with clean clothes and pajamas along with a couple of books, his laptop, and a few bottles of beer.

He dawdled, hoping Danny could be coaxed to talk when he didn't have to worry about reprisals from the parental unit, a man who hadn't a clue what to do next. Looking at the boy's bunk as he shuffled through books, and the weight of responsibility, of failure, felt heavier than he could have imagined.

If he'd ever needed help, now was the time.

God, if You hear me, would You give me some wisdom? How can I help this child when I don't even know what's wrong?

Except, of course, being orphaned and shipped off to live with a virtual stranger.

Danny still wasn't talking. It didn't seem as if he'd said anything to Brisa either, at least not as far as Mrs. Barnes knew. The boy looked so lost in that big bed, curled away from his broken arm and his other bruises, his eyes closed against interrogation or even the offer of a story.

Maybe he'd make headway tomorrow. Mrs. Barnes had said she'd keep Danny at the house with her if he didn't feel up to going to school. Eric thanked her. Between his two appointments, he planned to visit the school and see what he could discover. Something had to have happened to make a seven-year-old skip the fun things he himself remembered from second grade.

He carried his cell phone into the bathroom and called Jeminy.

"Eric, hey. How's Danny doing?"

"Quiet, pretending to sleep so he won't have to talk."

"Nana's awake. The scan came back clean, so we should be able to head home soon. Isa's on her way to pick us up."

"I had to bring Danny to the Inn for tonight."

"I hadn't thought of that. I imagine navigating up and down on your boat would be hard."

"Too hard. Tomorrow I begin my quest for something to rent on land."

"I'll keep my eye out. And ask Isa if she's heard of anything."

"Thank you. Anyway, let's keep in touch." Now, why had he said that? As if they were living in different cities and needed to keep the lines of communication open. In Beaufort, they'd be hard-pressed to ignore each other. Besides, she was his client.

"Sure," she said. "We can talk tomorrow."

Good news. Mrs. Warren and Jeminy had been spared, and Danny would recover. But what did real recovery mean for the boy?

Eric turned on the shower to let it warm while he shed his clothes, hanging his suit carefully in the closet and tossing his shirt on the floor. He'd already hung up a clean one, ready for tomorrow's appointments, neither of which would require a tie. If something came up while he was at work, he had a stash of upgrading supplies in one of his file drawers.

He'd better call and let Hen know where they were. Just in case his brother cared. Liking a town was all about finding friends, wasn't it? He, who'd always felt responsible for helping Henry navigate friendships, had only come to know these new friends through the connections Henry had made.

Turnabout, he supposed.

Two days later, he and Danny were still stuck at the Inn. Danny claimed he hurt too much to go back to school, and Eric wanted to give the boy space to recover and perhaps feel secure enough to talk. Mrs. Barnes continued to keep Danny with her during the day.

"We'll be just fine, Mr. Eric. Don't you worry yourself about me and the boy. And you know what? My favorite thing is to read, so we'll do a lot of that when we're together."

For now, that might be the best thing for his son, a way to increase his sense of a community caring for him.

Agnes had said she might have a lead on a sublet. And Clay called him at work to say the little house Annie Mac rented out was about to become available again.

"She'd be willing to let you have it short-term, if that's any help."

"Just might be," Eric answered. "Is it furnished?"

"Yeah, but we're not too sure about the condition of things. Day after tomorrow is the walk-through."

"Keep me posted."

"We'll talk," Clay said. "I also have something else in mind if the Beaufort house doesn't pan out."

Eric wasn't keen on living blocks away from the water. At least their hotel room gave them access, a view, and a short walking commute to *Escape*, work, and Danny's friends. Its appeal was limited because he couldn't cook in the room and it wasn't all that comfortable, so they would have to move. Agnes had offered them a guest room in her big house, but that sounded like a recipe for disaster, she and Hen newly married and Mrs. Barnes still living in the attic room.

He'd also called a local Realtor, who promised to let him know if a short-term rental came on the market.

When his cell phone rang with a call from Jeminy, he was between clients—very between, hours between—and he answered, grateful for the distraction.

"Can we meet?" she asked. "I've got to take a walk, do something."

"Sure. When?"

"How about now? At your office?"

"I'll be here."

He'd been hoping she'd suggest someplace other than the office. It was a gorgeous day outside...

And on that thought, he pressed the call button on his phone and said when she answered, "Can you meet me at the marina? I need to check on *Escape*, and it's so nice out."

"That'd be fun. I'm already on my way."

He spoke to AnnaLouise as he shut his office door, and then he hurried out to the sidewalk. Gorgeous out, warm but not hot, perfect for sitting on his boat and not in his office.

He led Jeminy down the dock to the finger pier of the slip where *Escape* lay still in the quiet of a barely-there breeze. After lowering the ladder, he boarded first and extended his hand to help her up.

She followed him to the cockpit and stood at the helm, looking forward. "What a beautiful boat."

"Come on down." He unlocked the companionway doors and hooked them open before preceding her down the steep steps. "Hang on here," he said, showing her the hand-holds on the way down.

"So cozy," she said, "with gorgeous wood. Teak? I bet it's even more beautiful in the lamplight." She pointed to the oil lamp hanging over the table. He had another one in the galley, along with LEDs to brighten the place.

"You want a cup of tea? Water?"

"Tea would be great."

He turned on the stove's propane switch, lit a burner, filled the kettle, and set it on to boil. "Green or black?" He used to have more variety for visitors, but he hadn't bothered to replenish his supply.

"Black's fine. No sugar."

When he'd filled the mugs, he carried them to the salon and handed her one. Sitting across from her, he asked, "So, what's up?"

Clasping the mug between her palms, she looked straight at him. "They found a black truck, recently washed down, abandoned at a gas station in Morehead. It had New Jersey plates, which gave nothing away as they certainly didn't belong to the truck. The VIN showed the truck reported stolen."

"They have any leads to the driver? Any proof it's the right truck?"

"There was a camera out back of the gas station, but the picture wasn't clear."

"So some guy turns around on 70, heads back to Morehead, dumps a truck after he picks you and your car out of everyone driving west and decides to shoot at you?"

Jeminy made an unattractive sound, almost a snort. He bit back a smile.

"Doesn't sound like it," she said. "But it's interesting that as clean as the truck was—no fingerprints that they could find, even on the license—there was a receipt for snacks from a station in New Bern that had ended up under the passenger seat."

"And?"

She grinned. "They checked surveillance footage from the date of the receipt. And there's a clear picture of some bearded guy— who is not the owner of the truck. They're running the picture through the system."

"Good. Maybe he's in a database somewhere, and there'll be something that'll link him to you."

"The deputy asked again if I could think of anyone who might want me hurt—or dead."

"And you mentioned your ex?"

"Sure, but why would Rand go to all this trouble—even if he learned I'd moved here? I haven't heard anything from the California police about an investigation. Unless word somehow got out and he's angry? But still, hiring someone to shoot me seems way over the top."

Eric had no answer to that. What he did say was, "It's possible the deputy told you what he did to see if he could jog your memory. Keep thinking. There must be something in your past that's linked to this unless it's mistaken identity."

"Wouldn't that be great."

"It's possible. There's a lot of anger and road rage out there these days, and no one is held accountable, so anything goes. Maybe you looked like someone who'd been mean to the guy. Or the color of your car triggered him. Who knows?"

He studied the range of expressions that flashed over her features. She was so lovely, especially when her disgust turned to hope and lit her eyes.

She was his client. He did *not* get involved with clients.

Ever.

Besides, she didn't seem at all interested in him as anything more than the lawyer who might help her out of this fix. Why should she, right after coming off a miserable relationship?

But, oh, man, look at her.

Fine, maybe she wasn't cover-girl perfect like Gabby'd been, but still… There were those long, long legs, long straight hair he'd like to run fingers through, and a smile that took up most of her face when she let it. A guy could get lost in that smile.

35

DEBORAH

Deborah kicked off her new high heels and massaged the balls of her feet. Stupid shoes must be the wrong size in spite of the labeling.

Someone had tried to kill her only surviving child, and no one knew why. Jeminy had lived in California, a state filled with crazy homeless people, but they couldn't have done this. Not here.

It had to have been a random attempt. Maybe a carjacking. Maybe the man was high on something and went crazy on the highway.

But he'd missed. Did that mean he'd try again? He'd been heading west, but how far west? Might he pick them next if they did what Larry wanted and visited Jeminy?

Larry was beside himself, worrying about his daughter, barely giving his wife the time of day. He should be worried about them, too, and not go driving along the interstate, certainly not until the gunman had been caught.

Instead, he was either on his phone or at a meeting, not checking on his wife, not sitting down to a meal with her or for a drink. "I'll just grab a bite out," he'd told her last night, as if he couldn't be bothered with even the pretense of a marriage.

She slipped her feet into a pair of satin slippers and stole down the stairs, hearing his voice from the slightly open door to his study. She wanted to know who was on the other end of that call. If it was the floozy, she'd have ammunition, and to win in this game, she needed more than accusations.

Stopping at the last step, she listened.

Larry's voice was tense. "What have you found out? ... Oh, really... No, that's excellent work. Can you scan the documents and send them to me? ... Good. Are the police on that trail yet?... Maybe it's time... Thank you. I look forward to hearing from you." He still sounded tense, but there was a different tone, more like a *gotcha.*

She was about to knock on his door, when he spoke into it again, stopping her where she was. "Hey, darling girl. How are you?"

His loving tone, *that* tone, was reserved for their daughter. *His* daughter. Unless he'd taken to using it for the floozy.

"I'm glad. You heard anything more from the police? ... Well, I've had an investigator working out in L.A... Yes, someone recommended to me... He did... It seems Rand has been paying on a life insurance policy for you. Did you know there's one for five million dollars with him still listed as the beneficiary?"

He was quiet for a minute. Deborah strained to hear every word.

"I know, love. I know. I'm so sorry... I should be getting copies of the paperwork from my investigator soon. Where do you want me to send them?... Okay. You want to give me the detective's name?... Great. I'll give him a call... Is everything else okay with you?... Your grandmother?... Excellent. What about the child?... Oh, really? I'm thinking of driving over to see you in the next few days. Would that work?... Great. See you soon, lovey."

Deborah waited no longer. She pushed open the door, not bothering to knock, and stood there, staring at her husband. "You think Rand tried to kill Jeminy?"

Larry seemed surprised to see her. "What, have you been standing out there eavesdropping?"

She didn't appreciate being on the defensive. "I heard you."

He rubbed a hand across his eyes. "I wasn't trying to hide. You could have knocked and come in."

"Sure. You'd have continued talking with me in the room." As if. "You never do."

Sighing, Larry said, "I don't know if Rand's behind this attempt on Jeminy's life or not, but that insurance policy seems like a smoking gun. Jeminy said she'd quit paying on it—and it had only been for one million—when Rand left. He must have forged her signature to get the amount changed and then continued making payments in her name. I think that's illegal on its own." He picked up his pen and began tapping it on his desk, something he did when he was trying to sort out something. "I wonder how he thought he'd collect."

"I'm sure you'll sort it out. Anything to do with Jeminy will have your full attention." And with that, she turned and left the study. Larry hadn't discussed anything with her, had he? Oh, no. He'd gone and hired a detective behind her back and was making plans to visit Beaufort on his own. He didn't need her, that was evident.

Well, she didn't need him either. She'd call JoAnn and they could have lunch at the club. Maybe she'd make arrangements for a mani-pedi on the way home. Her nails were a little shabby.

Or maybe she'd fit in a massage. A drink at the club, a massage after? Why not?

Fine, she'd postpone any lawsuit. With someone trying to kill Jeminy, now was obviously not the time to try to engage a judge's sympathy, but she'd figure out a way.

She had to. With Larry holding all the purse strings, she either had to find evidence of his infidelity or she had to toe *his* line. Neither option brought much peace, but at least the first would give her the means to live as she wanted.

Because she'd demand everything.

The next day, Larry called to say he was picking up Thai food for dinner and hoped she'd be home to enjoy it with him. It had been months since he'd offered to bring home something. She'd squinted at the phone, wondering what he meant by it.

Should she be pleased or worried?

Opting to pretend this was normal—on the special side of normal—she readied the table and set out linen napkins along with serving dishes. Then she poured wine for herself and waited.

He didn't behave differently when he carried the sacks in from the garage or when he joined her at the table. He asked about her day.

What was there to tell? She'd played tennis at the club where the pro had let her win, barely. She'd gone to Maxin's to have her hair touched up, but she only mentioned a trim. Larry said she looked lovely.

She bit back skeptical words because she would *not* antagonize him tonight. She'd wait for him to play his hand and not let him force hers.

He said he'd received photocopies of the investigator's first report and had sent them on to the detective in Craven County and to Jeminy, who planned to share them with her lawyer.

"Anything new in his report?" Deborah set her chopsticks down and spooned another small helping of her favorite mango chicken.

"Nothing yet. I'm hoping this insurance thing will get the local police looking toward California." His smile looked tentative. "I'm hoping to go to Beaufort after my next trip, and I'd like you to come with me."

"Me?" She wasn't sure what the smile meant or the suggestion that she go along.

"I've been giving this situation a lot of thought, and we can't go on as we have been."

She leaned forward. Did he mean he wanted a divorce? Did he want her along so they could tell Jeminy together? "What situation? What are you saying?"

"Between you and our daughter."

She huffed out a breath. "You think my going to Beaufort with you is going to fix anything?"

"Not really. I think the issue goes way deeper than you've been willing to admit."

Here it came. He was going to blame her for his own failures.

"What issue?" she asked, not really wanting to know.

He sat back. "Your rejection of our daughter after Olli's death."

His words took her breath away, and all she could do was stare at him. He waited, silent while anger lashed through her.

Finally, she pushed away from the table. "I don't know what you're talking about. It's not true. That is *not* true."

When the tears came, she didn't know if they were from the anger or from pain. Eyes closed tightly against the draining emotions, she saw him, right there, right in front of her, sheet draped, body cold, being hefted, touched, taken—

Her boy. Her darling boy.

Your fault.

She stood and fled.

———

She had no idea how long she lay there after deserting the fancied-up table and whatever was left of their meal. The bed creaked as he sat next to her. He didn't touch her curled body but merely waited silently.

His silence made her want to hit him. He should speak, apologize.

She must look a fright, red-eyed and blotchy. It wasn't fair.

Larry wore aging like a trophy, growing more and more handsome every year, while she had to go for color and facials, and next it would be to the facelift magicians. Even her boobs weren't as perky as they used to be.

Finally, he cleared his throat. "I've been unfair to you all these years, hiding out in my work, not wanting to deal with your pain because my own was so great. It wasn't fair to you when I didn't confront your neglect of Jeminy." He drew a hand down his face. "To be truthful—and I'd really rather not be, but the Lord has finally gotten through my self-absorption and told me I have to take a look at myself—I've taken refuge in my relationship with Jeminy. I reached out to her, which made her reach out to me, and her preference soothed my ego."

At this, Deborah sat up, shoving a pillow at her back and leaning against the headboard. Words formed in her mind, but they still held anger, and she was sober enough to recognize the danger of speaking them.

"I bet it did." Well, there went her sober silence.

"Yes, I'm sorry." He sounded penitent.

She didn't want penitent. She wanted a fight. "You've always chosen Jeminy over me. Over me *and* over Oliver, your own son."

For a moment, he remained silent. When his words came, they were spoken coldly. "How dare you."

She raised her chin. "You know that's true. You cuddled her more than you ever did him. As far as tickling matches went, it was you and Jeminy, never you and Oliver."

"The only time Jeminy got more attention was when you were clutching so hard to her brother that he didn't have a chance to play with us."

"Never!"

He shrugged. "I loved both children equally. Always. And"—his voice quavered, surprising her—"the loss of our son has left a hole in *my* heart, too, Deborah. No one can replace him. No one."

"You don't act like that's true. You blame me for his death, and you've been trying to punish me ever since, making up to Jeminy."

"Whoa. Why do you think I blame you?"

"You just do." She couldn't bring herself to say more.

"Deborah, are you sure it's not you blaming yourself?"

She shook her head vehemently, her eyes closed, her breathing shallow. He blamed her. He had to.

He touched her hand. "It was an accident, that's all. A horrible accident."

She started to shake off his touch, but she realized she didn't want to. Instead, she bit her lip to keep it closed. She couldn't speak. She wouldn't speak. Larry didn't understand.

And then, into her husband's silence, her lips opened and her mouth formed words. "If he'd waited. If I'd been on time. If it hadn't been raining. My *boy!*"

She dropped her head into her hands as the sobs took over her body. Her boy. O God, her boy.

Her fault.

Always and forever, her fault.

She felt the mattress depress even more as her husband moved closer and his arm went around her shoulders, drawing her to him. It had been so long since she'd felt his body next to hers, since he'd offered comfort.

Or maybe it had just been years since she'd accepted it.

JEMINY

Bumps and ruts and potholes, oh my;
Danger to the left, fear to the right,
How dare I close my eyes at night?

A week had passed since the accident—the shooting. Jeminy'd been fielding phone calls from all the local women, including Tadie, Hannah, and Rita, offering help, asking for news. She had none to offer, no reasonable explanation for a would-be murder, nothing except that Nana seemed fine and was focusing on the idea of finding a new car.

Maybe Nana didn't remember the incident that had made a new one necessary, but she was like a kid with the promise of a new toy. "You know that one was really pretty old."

As for Jeminy, she couldn't face dealing with the insurance company adjuster again. They ought to total the car, but if they didn't, she wouldn't be able to drive it without remembering.

"You don't need to," Isa said. "Your grandmother can afford a new car. And a new 'pretty' will be a good distraction for her. Why don't I take you car hunting in the morning?"

They made their plans, and set out the next day. Car shopping turned out to be more problematic than Jeminy'd imagined. "This is the first time I've considered comfort above economy," she said.

Isa smiled and said, "That's why you need to let your grandmother sit in the various models. Her comfort and safety come first."

Nana seemed happy with every new car they tried. Finally, they agreed on a barely used, safety-packed, pettable, small SUV in a silvery gray that would blend in with so many others of like design and not act like a magnet to crazies. Isa wrote the check, and they took a break for lunch while the dealer prepped the car so Jeminy could drive it off the lot that afternoon.

While Nana focused on her plate of Indian food, Jeminy and Isa continued their earlier conversation.

"If the guy picked me at random," Jeminy said, "he could try it again with someone else, right? And if he meant to come after me, well, why?"

Isa stirred chutney into her rice. "Maybe the question needs to be, who would benefit by your death? Do you have a life insurance policy? A will naming a third party?"

"My father hired an investigator. It seems he found a life insurance policy my ex has been paying for." An insurance policy that would make her hugely valuable once dead. An insurance policy signed for, paid for by a man who'd once said he loved her. Now a forger.

Sickening thoughts.

"Motive, then?"

"If they're tied together, the shooter and Rand."

Her father'd called the detective's office. Maybe the sheriff's deputy who'd been so forthcoming would call later with news.

Maybe.

Between worrying about men with guns roaming the highways and developing new life skills as a small-town homebody caregiver, Jeminy tried to write songs that Darling might like. As if she had any idea how to sing about faith. From ballads to Christian pop? How on earth was she supposed to make that transition?

I mean, really?

With a sigh, she inserted a replacement CD Brisa had given her of Darling's latest covers—the other was stuck in the Subaru—and hit *Play*. Maybe she'd be inspired by his voice and other writers' words because right now her thoughts took her everywhere but into creativity.

Leaning back against her bed's headboard, she closed her eyes and listened. Some of the words she recognized from a childhood spent going to church. Some, she'd first heard on that fateful drive toward a trigger-happy madman.

One of the new ones, *Way Maker,* was written by a Nigerian singer named Sinach. Musically, it was compelling, especially with Darling's voice giving it life.

Emotionally, it nearly knocked her to her knees.

The singer talked about God as the way maker, the miracle worker, the promise keeper. Said He was Light in the darkness. And then, the gut-wrencher, *"You mend the broken heart, You're the answer to it all..."*

O God, if only.

If only she could worship like that. If only He were her God, too.

Tears streamed from her eyes, and she turned on the bed to bury her face in the pillow, because He wasn't, and she'd never deserve Him anyway.

"Jeminy! Oh, Jeminy! Honey, where are you?" Nana's voice, coming from the bottom of the stairs. "Are you up there?"

She kept her eyes closed. *Please go away.* But she didn't speak, and, besides, she couldn't say such a thing to her grandmother.

"Jeminy, honey? You there?"

Yes, she was here. A mess, but here. She grabbed a tissue as she sat up and blew her nose on the way to the door. "I'm right here." Trying to reenter the real world of responsibilities as she opened to her nana.

"Your little phone, honey. You left it in the kitchen, and it's been ringing and ringing."

"Hang on. I'll be right there."

She headed to her bathroom to splash water on her face. Nana's voice came again. "Are you coming, dear?"

"Yes, Nana. I just need to use the potty first."

"Oh, I'm sorry to interrupt you. I only wanted to tell you about your little phone. It wouldn't stop ringing."

"Coming." With a shake of her head and a long, jagged sigh, she opened her bathroom door.

Nana extended her hand. "Here. I brought it to you. Because it might have been important, whoever was calling."

"Oh, Nana." All Jeminy's annoyance dropped off to be replaced by guilt. "You didn't have to come all the way up here to bring it to me."

"It might have been important, someone so impatient."

Her father. It had been her father trying to reach her. She listened to his voicemail and returned the call as she followed her grandmother down the stairs. "Hey, Daddy."

"I was just worried about you, darlin'. You okay?"

"I'm fine."

"Your mother and I will try to visit as soon as I can cajole her into the car again. She's acting as if the man who shot at you might have a vendetta against the family and come after her next."

That would be like Mother.

"Anyway, I've got to go out of town for a couple of days, but when I get back, I'll try to convince her that we're perfectly safe."

"I'd like to see *you*." *Alone, please.* But she didn't say that.

"I wish I could tell you I've made progress convincing her of anything."

When had anyone been able to convince Mother of something that went against her agenda? And how much had Daddy even tried? "Is she still talking lawsuit?"

There was a loud sigh from the other end. "Talking, yes. But she hasn't actually done anything about it. I'm working on that, too."

It was Jeminy's turn to sigh. "I suppose she's hoping Isa and I will just go away. But Nana asked for our help. She wants to stay here."

"I know she does, and your mother knows it, too. It's a heart issue, and only prayer can fix that."

"Not working all that well, is it?"

"Jeminy."

"Sorry, but it seems like you've been praying forever."

"God's in control, no matter what we see or feel. I try to align my thoughts and purposes with His Word, hang onto His promises, and trust. Remember what the Bible says about faith? That it's *the substance of things hoped for and the evidence of things not seen.*"

Something unseen and only hoped for. That about said it as far as her faith was concerned—hoped for. Not seen.

But growing, in spite of her doubts?

She *hoped* so. That word again—hope. Her laugh held no humor at all.

She'd barely ended her father's call when it rang again. "Hey, Jeminy. Tadie here."

"Tadie, how are you?"

"We're doing great. How's your grandmother?"

"Amazingly well, thank you for asking." Jeminy glanced toward the front of the house where she heard her nana's shoes on the hard floor.

"Look, I'm calling to invite you both to a baby shower for Annie Mac. You know her baby's due in a couple of months."

"Ah. Right."

"She and Clay are over the moon, getting ready for this new one. Ty and Katie, too."

Her heart constricted slightly. *Be nice,* she told herself. "Do they know the gender?" She hadn't known hers, had she? But she'd imagined a daughter, a sweet little girl…

Stop it.

"A boy. Ty's been strutting around with his little chest puffed out, talking about everything he and Clay will teach this little brother. And to top that off, he confided to Jilly that he and Katie are going to become Doughertys before the birth." Tadie laughed. "Clay's so proud. I mean, he considered the kids his from the very first, but making it official is good for all of them."

Times like this, Jeminy realized how little she actually knew of everyone's story. Becoming part of a close-knit group of friends meant she was going to find herself smack-dab in the middle of scenarios she'd rather avoid.

Like another woman's pregnancy.

Sweat had her sticking to the sheets. Jeminy opened her eyes in the gloom of dawn and turned to stare at the window's outline, at anything other than the faces inside her head. Olli's accusing eyes had morphed into that horrible doctor's. The doctor who'd entered the cold cubicle all businesslike and then had sneered—it had been a sneer, hadn't it?—as he'd dropped metal instruments against a stainless steel table, as he'd snapped off his gloves, as he'd said, "That's it."

O God.

Weak. She'd been weak, and she'd listened when she ought to have stood up and said she'd not be a party to… to…

She couldn't bring herself to call it by name.

But drawing her second pillow over her head didn't stop the voices. *Murderer.*

Worthless.

Damned.

All those "thou shalt nots" from childhood... *Thou shalt not, thou shalt not...*

If you do, you'll die.

Well, she hadn't died yet because legalized murder wasn't a capital crime. Although, perhaps, it should be.

Way Maker. Promise Keeper. Miracle Worker.

O God!

She tossed back her covers and stood. It was four-fifteen, which meant she could quit trying to sleep and get ready for the day. First, a shower, then coffee, breakfast, and an hour in the garden, readying it to lie fallow until she could find someone to work it, someone who knew plants and growing cycles.

Fallow? She wished she hadn't thought that word because what was she but fallow, empty of new growth, lying idle and unwanted, perhaps never to be fertile again?

She'd been reading gardening books so she could help her grandmother maintain the beautiful spaces she'd cultivated over the years. She'd known the term before, but it hadn't exactly been part of her normal vocabulary.

Sitting there, willing herself to activity, she slammed shut her eyes. If only she could slam shut her mind as easily.

Tomorrow, she had to take Nana to a baby shower. Today, they had to buy baby gifts.

Tomorrow, she'd have to see the pregnant belly, hear the oohs and ahhs that would never exist for her.

Not for her, a woman who'd killed her own child.

Please, God.

37

ERIC

By Sunday, Danny felt well enough to be up and about, and Eric decided to give him a taste of a more traditional church service. "You'll see a number of the kids you know."

"How come we have to go at all?"

"Church is good for us."

"Yeah, right. Mama said the God stuff wasn't real."

He could hear Gabby now, scoffing at faith. Well, she'd have had to be a scoffer to live the way she did and feel comfortable with her choices. He didn't want Danny to take after her.

"You were baptized in a church like this one, back in Charleston. At least your mother approved when you were a baby."

Danny glared at him. "I'm not a baby now."

"No, indeed. But at your christening, your mother and I both promised to teach you the ways of God. This is how we do it."

The boy shrugged, but he didn't object when Eric helped him buckle into his seatbelt. At church, it didn't hurt that Lewis and Ty and their families were already seated when Eric ushered Danny into the row behind them or that Will and Jilly slid in next to Danny.

Will leaned toward Eric. "Tadie's driving separately with Sammy so she can cut out in time to play hostess to this baby shower. You two want to join us for a guy's lunch after service?"

"I'm supposed to meet Henry…"

"Invite him, too."

The congregation stood as the musicians began the processional.

"We'll see," Eric whispered as he drew Danny to his feet.

From then on, it was up, down, and on their knees, and Eric was very grateful that Jilly had taken the seat right next to Danny's so he could copy what she did. When it was time for the kids to leave for Sunday school, she grabbed Danny's good hand and led him out of the sanctuary.

Eric had attended church here a few times, but this was the first chance he'd had to do it as a father wanting a good experience for his son. Interesting, he thought as he listened to the sermon, how much more focused he was on what might be happening in the children's wing than in the preaching going on right in front of him.

Best keep his head where it belonged.

The next thing he heard were James's words from the New Testament reading: *If any of you lacks wisdom, you should ask God, who gives generously to all without finding fault, and it will be given to you.*

Wisdom, exactly what he needed. Divine wisdom to cope with this parenting thing that had been thrust upon him.

For instance, why on earth had Danny skipped school? His teacher said he was doing well in reading and math for his age level, although she had put him in one of the lower groups for reading, to help him feel more confident and build up his skills, she'd said. "Lots of boys take a while to get comfortable reading. He's smart, so it'll come. And he's still getting used to a new school."

Fine, but Danny's actions had put the boy in a life-threatening situation. Eric found it hard to be patient when he worried Danny might repeat the behavior. He sure didn't want to play the heavy and walk the boy to and from class.

If the guys were going to lunch without kids, he might have a chance to ask their advice. Of course, the dads might be on babysitting detail.

He was letting his thoughts get away from him again and tried to refocus on the pastor's words. And, yes, he needed those, too, didn't he? The idea of peace from trusting God.

He glanced around at the other parishioners. Most seemed to be listening raptly, while he couldn't stop his thoughts from wandering all over the place or his insides from feeling about as peaceful as boiling soup.

At the close of the service, Clay and his wife, Annie Mac, approached while their children, Ty and Katie, gathered round the other kids and drew Danny along with them.

"Eric," Clay said, "you guys still closeted at the Inn?"

"Sadly."

"Well, look. We have a proposition for you. No obligation, mind you, but it might make things easier for a while, and you're used to small spaces."

Eric grinned. "You could say that."

Annie Mac spoke. "We know you've been worried about Danny staying on the boat, and with his arm broken, it's worse."

"So," Clay said, "we just bought one of those tiny homes and had it planted on the property. A fellow I know builds them, planned to use this one as a rental, but he got transferred out of the country and decided it was too much for him to manage."

"Tiny home?"

"Yeah, kind of boat-sized." Clay said that with a grin.

Annie Mac slapped Clay's forearm playfully. "It's got glass galore, so it doesn't feel really small, and we put it where it has a great view of the creek. We thought maybe we'd use it for overflow when guests come."

"How big?"

Clay nodded for Annie Mac to continue. "Well," she said, "there's a loft with not a lot of headroom, and then there's a bed that lowers over the sofa area. Danny could use that—or the sofa, which also makes into a bed—until he's able to climb up. I imagine he'd love the loft."

"Sounds a lot nicer than the hotel."

"And no fear of Danny falling overboard." That was Clay.

Annie Mac grinned. "I was petrified when we first stayed out at Clay's because my two couldn't swim."

"Yeah," Clay said, "swimming lessons became a must. First on the list, along with teaching Ty to sail my Sunfish."

"Would you like to see the space?" Annie Mac asked. "Maybe later today?" She looked at her watch. "Speaking of which, I'd better collect the kids and get over to Tadie's. I'll get Danny, too."

"Thanks. He'll like that."

"Come on," Clay said. "We're going to *No Name Pizza*. Plenty of room there for us to get a big table and hang out."

"And you can tell me more about this tiny house."

Henry agreed to join them, and Eric made sure to save a seat for his brother before he squeezed in next to Clay. Talking about the tiny house was on his radar, but he wanted to pick Clay's brain about step-parenting.

They'd ordered, the food had been delivered, and Henry was busy chatting with Will and Matt. When he brought up the tiny house, Clay said, "You'd better just come take a look. It may be too small for you and your son."

"That works. But about Danny... I need some advice, if you have any."

Clay raised a brow.

"I'm not sure how to handle this whole skipping school thing.

His teacher can't think of any reason for him not to want to come, and he won't talk to me about it."

Clay swirled a fry in ketchup. "You think maybe he had trouble with some other kids?"

"He won't say."

"You ask any of ours yet, see if they've heard rumors?" He tipped his head toward the other men at the table.

"I did. I mean, I asked Brisa and Jilly when they came by to visit him, and they said they hadn't seen anything on the bus."

"Isn't Katie in his grade?"

"But not in his class."

"Still, maybe she's witnessed something on the playground. I'll ask her."

"That'd be great. Thanks, Clay."

"Sure thing. I know it's hard, coming in as a single parent when you've missed so many years. At least I had Annie Mac as a sounding board."

"Yeah. Danny's got a slew of anger issues. I imagine he's going to need counseling."

Clay cleared his throat. "Listen, before we leave here, why don't you let us pray with you? God's got your back, but you need to get in contact with Him, if you know what I mean."

Eric shifted in his chair. It wouldn't hurt. Might even help, if he could get his mind wholly wrapped around trusting God.

***

After lunch, he picked up a tired Danny and took him back to the Inn for a rest before they headed down east. He didn't explain the purpose of the drive, except to say they were going to Ty's house. Signs directed him toward Harker's Island, over small bridges, past small houses and the occasional produce stand, and then the GPS got him all the way there.

When he turned into Clay's long lane, the creek opened up to his right, pine woods and a field to the left. A heron took off, and an osprey nest sat atop a post out in the water. As he slowed to give Danny a better view, an osprey soared from the nest as if to distract them from the babies whose heads could be seen over the top of the sticks and twigs.

The lane curved, and a tiny house appeared, nestled in a small clearing in the woods, all glass and wood, beautifully designed. He couldn't wait to get inside.

Danny's attention was glued to the creek until they'd driven another eighth of a mile to the end of the lane and what had to be Clay's house, where a boy ran around chasing a big Lab. "There's Ty!"

Danny barely waited for the car to come to a stop before using his good hand to unbuckle his seat belt and open the door.

"Slowly, kiddo." Eric watched to make sure Danny managed to get himself out before climbing from the car himself.

By then, Ty and the dog were welcoming Danny, and Clay and Annie Mac emerged from the deck, Clay with his hand under his wife's elbow as she and her pregnant belly made their careful way forward.

Eric waved. "Gorgeous place you have here."

"Thank you," Clay said. "Which do you want to see first, the big or the little house?"

"Oh, I'm eager to see that little one, if you don't mind. Fascinating design."

"That's what caught our attention when we saw it." Annie Mac smiled. "Can't ever have too much view, can you?"

"How did you get it here? I understood it wasn't built in place?"

"No," Clay admitted. "It was a tad tricky to move from my friend's place to here, but the crew knew what they were doing. It was originally built to be accommodated on a big trailer, but we wanted it to sit on pilings. Not that it floods much, but there's no telling when a hurricane might push a good wave or two up."

"What about wind, you know, hurricane force, with all that glass?"

"We've ordered big shutters, and the place is securely tied down. Trusting we won't have any storms come this way until the shutters are in place."

"Or it'll be plywood?"

"It will."

Annie Mac started waddling up the road. "Come on, boys, let's go see the little house."

"Where's Katie?" Danny asked as he came up next to Eric.

"She stayed in town with Miss Hannah and Mr. Matt so she and Linney could play a while."

"Oh."

"Yeah," Ty said. "Louis wanted me to hang out, too, only we knew you'd be coming."

That brought a smile to Danny's too-sober countenance. Eric caught Clay's wink and mouthed a thank-you.

Clay stood proudly in front of the little house. "Looks like it fits right there, doesn't it? Like it was designed to make the most of the view."

"It does. Love the wood combined with black metal and all that glass."

"Yeah, the metal was specially treated for use in salt air, and the wood's cedar, so low maintenance. The glass is rated up to hurricane force, although I'm not sure it would withstand a direct hit from a projectile."

"Hence the need for shutters."

"Yep." Clay led the way up the steps and unlocked the glass door.

They stepped in, and Eric stared in amazement.

The afternoon sunlight filtered in at an angle and illuminated the light wood of the cabinets and floor. Most of the interior was done in that same light wood in contrast with charcoal gray upholstery.

"Very manly," Eric said.

Clay laughed. "Annie Mac had ideas for changing that up, but then we thought of you two."

"Thank you. Appreciate that. I don't think I could cope with ruffles. Or pink."

"Or doilies?" Annie Mac grinned at him.

"You the doily sort, Annie Mac?"

Her grin turned to a laugh. "Not I. I might have added some color—no, not pink and not any ruffles either."

"Looks to me," Eric said, his gaze taking in the entire space, "like there's color in abundance from the light and the outdoors, which feels almost as if it's right in here with us."

"Mom, show them how that bed works."

"Why don't you do it, Ty?" Annie Mac waved him toward the settee.

Fourteen-year-old Ty, all arms and legs, bounded to that end of the space and started removing cushions from the back of the settees. Then he went to a switch on the wall and turned it on. Slowly, the platform above began to come down until it rested just above the couch.

"See? Isn't that cool? You can climb up to use it like a loft—and then you can make up a bed down below on the couch *and* up high—or you can have it down here and climb on that step there to get up."

Danny ran his hand over the covers. The bed came to chest height on him. "Cool."

"Still might be a long fall if you rolled off," Eric said.

"Netting?" Clay suggested.

"That would work. Like a lee cloth."

"Lee cloth?" Annie Mac asked.

"To keep things from falling off a bunk—or shelf—when a boat is heeling to leeward." Eric showed her with hand gestures, palm down, then tilted sideways.

"Oh. Right." Annie Mac seemed uncertain.

"I could have that one?" Danny asked.

"You could. At least until your arm heals enough for you to climb up there." Clay pointed to the steps to a loft high above the other side of the tiny house.

"What's up there?"

"A bed, mostly, along with some cubbies for storage."

"It's even cooler," Ty said, fingering the switch to lift the bed again. "I can't stand up straight, but there's a big bed and a window looking at the sky, plus windows all around so you can see everything, like being in a tree house. Dad said he wanted to close it off better…"

"For safety's sake," Clay said. "Maybe more netting up there if Danny uses it."

"The kitchen has everything you'll need, and there's even a washer-dryer unit." Annie Mac spoke with pride.

"Really? That's great. And a shower, I assume?"

"Yep," Clay said. "We had our guy come out and hook up to septic and water, also power, so you're good to go."

Eric turned to his son. "What do you think, Danny?"

The boy's eyes shone. "It's really neat. Kinda like the boat, only not so rocky."

"I guess we need to talk business," Eric said.

Annie Mac waved her son toward the door. "Okay, boys, let's leave the dads here to talk, and we'll meet them at the big house."

When they'd left, Clay replaced the back cushions on the L-shaped settee. "Have a seat."

Eric sat and looked out the big window toward the creek. "Really great view."

"Better than *Escape*?"

"Different. On my boat, I can change backyards, but while I'm in the marina, my view is of other boats, and I have to go on deck to manage even that. Here…" He waved at the space. "Here you've got almost a 360-degree aspect, either woods or water."

"We're pretty remote, but I think it's worth it."

"I understand that Katie's been attending the Beaufort school because Annie Mac teaches there."

"Annie Mac's going to take time off once the baby comes. I think she's hoping to get on at the local school next year, so there's a bit of uncertainty for Katie."

"I don't think Danny's going to want to make another huge change in terms of schooling. That is, if I can find out why he skipped school and hasn't wanted to go back. I told him he had to go tomorrow, but I'm expecting a recurrence of too sick, too hurting, too weak to go. If I can manage that and then keep him in Beaufort, I can drive them all in once Annie Mac goes on leave."

"That would be great. I'm not always available."

"Yeah, I get that. So, what do you want in terms of rent?"

38

JEMINY

*Good is as good does, but how does one get there
When bad's been the way?*

The baby shower turned out to be a lot less stressful than Jeminy'd imagined. Maybe it had been the welcome she'd received from all the other ladies. Maybe it had been watching her grandmother happily engaged with Rita Levison's mother.

Elvie Mae and her husband, James, lived above the garage at Tadie and Will's, and weren't they the cutest old couple in the world? James was a bit stooped, but she could tell by his build he'd been tall and probably muscled at one time, while Elvie Mae was a tiny little thing, full of life and smiles. James doted on his wife, which meant he was on hand to bring Nana something cool to drink when he brought one to Elvie.

She overheard Elvie explaining to Nana how they'd finally relented and let Tadie put in an elevator for them. "Got a bit too much for James, you know. His knees. Just before he had the surgery, the elevator people came along and made it possible for us to stay in our home."

"You must love your place," Nana said.

"Oh, we do. Indeed we do. Our view out to the water in front and trees out back. When Rita moved out, I even got me a sewing room. Who could want more?"

Jeminy stopped listening and turned her head to watch Rita approach her mother. Elvie Mae patted the hand Rita dropped onto her shoulder. "Hey, lovey."

"Mama."

"You know Mrs. Warren?"

"I do. Hey, Mrs. Warren, how're you doing?"

"I'm well, thank you."

"I've been telling her about our elevator," Elvie Mae said.

Jeminy entered the conversation. "If you ever need one, Nana, we could get one of those chair lifts for the stairs. Think how much easier it would be to get suitcases up and down."

"Let them ride?" Rita smiled at her.

"Why not? Save my back."

Nana reached for Jeminy's hand and clutched it. "You need to move your suitcase? Are you leaving?"

"No, Nana." Jeminy squeezed back. "I'm not going anywhere."

"I thought maybe… You said suitcases."

"Just remembering how heavy mine were. But they're put away in the attic, and I've unpacked everything."

"I'm so glad."

Hannah, best friends with Tadie and business partner of Isa's, pulled up a nearby chair. Hannah had reached out to her several times, especially since the accident, but Jeminy didn't know her well at all. "We're so glad you've moved to town," Hannah said. "I mean, there's not a one of us who isn't a huge fan of your songs, so we're just a little in awe. A little starstruck."

"By *me*?"

"Of course. You're the talent behind the songs Darling made

famous, right? I mean, he's got a great voice, but your words are what touch the heart."

"I've got to tell you, Hannah, right about now your words mean more than you can imagine." She paused, not ready to say more. "Darling wants me to write religious songs, inspirational, you know?"

"Really? He's taking that direction?"

"Seems so."

Hannah pressed her palms together and brought the tips of her fingers to her chin. "How wonderful."

"I don't know if I can do it. Because a songwriter's words have to come from the heart."

"Oh, I just assumed…"

"What, that I'm a believer because my nana is?"

"No, of course not. It's just, your songs have depth, soul."

"Yeah, well, I'm going to need a lot more to do what Darling's asking."

A silent Hannah turned her attention to the gathering. Jeminy wished she hadn't said anything because she'd obviously made the other woman uncomfortable. On the other side of the yard, Annie Mac was oohing over her gifts.

Jeminy was about to get up when Hannah finally spoke. "You know Annie Mac at all? Her story?"

"Nothing other than she seems nice."

"She survived so much, what with her abusive husband almost killing her. Now she's found happiness with Clay—and her darling children, too. I fell in love with them when I helped out while she was in the hospital."

"Ty and Katie, right?"

"Maybe you don't know, but I lost two babies, so my jealous heart nearly fell apart during those days. My two best friends, Tadie and Rita, were about to give birth, and I was left on the sidelines."

"Rita? I didn't know she had children."

"She doesn't. And can't ever."

"Oh?"

"Annie Mac's abuser ran Rita off the road and made her lose the baby—and her womb."

"Oh, Hannah, no."

"He was a horrid man, and the loss nearly destroyed her. And if you haven't met her husband, Martin, you're in for a treat. Such a kind man, a pediatrician. They support a number of orphans overseas, have even talked about bringing one or two here."

"Are your two adopted, then?"

Hannah sighed. "A gift from God Who saw my broken heart. And the broken hearts of those two darling orphans. Remind me to tell you the whole story someday." She glanced again across the yard. "But that's enough for today. Let's go see what's happening with everyone else."

These women, who'd seemed to have had such perfect lives, actually hadn't. That knowledge helped her see the tiny baby clothes without falling apart. Maybe she couldn't quite forgive herself, but she didn't leak tears when each little item was held up for inspection. And she didn't lock herself away in a misplaced jealousy. It seemed Annie Mac—and Rita and Hannah—all had regrets and pain that might not be visible on the outside.

Of course, maybe she ought to feel guilty for taking comfort in their woundedness.

Great, Jeminy. Perfect. You're a piece of work, aren't you?

The next day, Jeminy opened her door to find an unexpected visitor. Annie Mac smiled hesitantly and asked, "Have you got a minute?"

A minute for what?

"Sure." Jeminy stood back to let her enter. "Why don't you come into the front room. Nana's upstairs."

"It's you I'd like to see."

Okay… "Then, how about something to drink? Tea, water, lemonade?"

"Lemonade would be lovely, and why don't I follow you on back? We don't have to be formal."

Jeminy led the way to the kitchen where she filled two glasses with icy lemonade she'd made that morning. Annie Mac accepted one and lowered herself to a chair at the kitchen table.

Jeminy slid in across from her and waited.

"Thank you for coming to the shower yesterday," Annie Mac said. "And for the sweet layette set you gave us."

"Nana's choice."

"It will be perfect."

Jeminy couldn't help her grin. "Are you visiting all the guests to thank them personally?"

Looking slightly sheepish, Annie Mac said, "No, of course not. But—oh, this is so awkward…"

"What?'

"It's just… well, I caught an expression… I know it's none of my business, but you looked so sad. I mean, not all the time, but I'm sorry. I couldn't help noticing. And it occurred to me that I don't know anything of your history, and I want to be sensitive to… well, you know, anything that might be bothering you."

Jeminy knew about small towns and wasn't sure whether to be annoyed or flattered to be the object of concern. Annoyed came most naturally.

Annie Mac set her drink on the table. "Look, I get that my question's intrusive, but you've made an impression on us all—a good one," she said on a grin, "and that's why I wanted to reach out. Like the others did for me when I came to their attention."

"What do you mean?"

"Only that I never imagined I could fit into a group made up of people like Tadie and Hannah on account of my past, my horrible choices. But their friendliness sneaked in under my reserve, and then, of course, there was Clay."

"He doesn't seem like one of those bad choices."

"Oh, no," Annie Mac said. "He's about the best thing that ever happened to me. And my babies." She upended her glass and finished her lemonade.

Jeminy brought the pitcher over to the table and offered a refill.

"It's so good." Annie Mac settled the glass in front of her again, both hands wrapped around it. "Anyway, back to my reason for coming. Or one of them. It occurred to me maybe you don't have a lot of friends in town, and maybe you're missing the ones you left to come take care of your grandmother. Everyone's going to try to make you feel at home. They'll stick their noses in your business—in a good way—and not let you alone until you open the door to their help."

"That what they did for you?"

"They did. They wouldn't allow me to wallow in self-pity as I felt bound to do on account of having let a really horrible man into my life and the life of my children. I'm grateful they did because, at the end of the day, the healing I needed finally took hold."

"I let a bad man in, too." As soon as she'd spoken, Jeminy wanted to take the words back. She stood abruptly, scraping back her chair and almost knocking it over. She went to the sink and stared out the window, her back to her guest.

"It makes you feel real stupid, doesn't it? And worthless?"

Jeminy just nodded.

"Where's he now?"

"Maybe trying to kill me."

"Whoa." Annie Mac paused, then said, "You come back here and sit down, Jeminy. You can tell me more, but first maybe I'd better let you know about Roy."

Her attention caught, Jeminy sat again. "Roy? Your ex?"

"Yep. The scumbag who beat me and messed with my baby girl before killing a deputy, along with Rita's unborn—making sure she never could bear children again. He purposefully ran her off the road."

Jeminy could only squeeze her eyes as she imagined that pain.

"The folks here, Clay mostly, dragged me out of my depression. It's on account of them and the faith they live that I got past that horrible time and can look forward to having this baby."

"I had no idea."

"It makes me super sensitive to other folks' pain." Annie Mac reached toward her. "And it was pain I saw in your eyes."

Jeminy drew back her hands and clutched her glass, using it as a prop, something to look at, something to touch. "But all that happened *to* you. You didn't do the bad stuff."

"And you did?"

Jeminy nodded.

"I don't know anyone who's lived a while who hasn't done stuff they regret. I mean, I'm the one who married a man who could beat me and messed with my little girl, and that was after I believed a lying boy who got me pregnant, which got me thrown out of my home. That was all on me, but marrying Roy was the worst, on account of what he did to Katie."

And then out it came, straight out like Jeminy'd left her filter behind, the one that didn't want anyone else to know her secret. "I murdered my baby."

She stood abruptly and wandered to the sink because she couldn't face Annie Mac's disdain.

The other woman didn't speak. Telling someone—and someone she barely knew—was a dumb thing to do. Now she'd lose even this potential friend.

Finally, on a sigh, Annie Mac said, "That's a hard word, Jeminy."

She turned. Annie Mac was staring, but not unkindly. Jeminy

said, "It's nothing but the truth. No one made me go to that clinic. No one put me on that table. I'm the one who nodded and let them kill the life in me. That was my doing."

"You mean by abortion."

Jeminy nodded.

"I'm so sorry."

"Yeah, well, so am I."

"Is that what your expression meant?"

"You mean, at the baby shower?"

Annie Mac nodded.

Jeminy glanced out the window. "It's hard. I can't undo my choice."

"But you can make other choices from now on." The other woman approached and touched Jeminy's back. "And you can accept God's forgiveness…"

"I don't really know how to do that."

"It was hard for me. Hard to let go of my guilt and shame."

Guilt and shame. The weight of it settled like a stone in her stomach. Annie Mac's had been hard, but nothing like what she'd done. Being stupid wasn't listed on those tablets of stone. It wasn't a commandment, a thou shalt not.

Murder was.

She may not have plunged the knife, but she'd been complicit.

Guilty.

Annie Mac stood beside her and spoke softly. "God loves you, Jeminy. He's just waiting for you to come."

"Come where?"

"To the foot of the Cross. To the place where His Blood cleanses all who repent."

She pondered that. She got the visuals, but not the how. Not the path from here to there.

"I don't know if I can."

"You just talk to Him, honey. He'll show you."

Annie Mac smoothed down her loose top. "Gotta run. The kids are at Tadie's, and they'll be expecting me."

Jeminy smiled slightly. "If they're all playing together, they probably hope you'll forget about picking them up."

"Probably." She carried her glass to the sink. "Thank you for the lemonade. Will you come out to the house sometime? I'd love to show you where we live."

"I'd like that. Thank you."

"How about Friday? Bring your grandmother. Clay's got a half-day, and he's promised to grill an early dinner." She grinned and patted her belly. "All us kids like to go to bed early, so we also like to eat early."

39

RAND

You get what you paid for.

Nothing truer was ever said, Rand decided as he slammed that blasted detective's office door. Money down the tubes, that's what it had been.

If the man's overly muscled henchman hadn't been lounging in a ratty office chair, Rand would have happily choked the life out of the jerk behind the desk. Not that he was a violent man.

Not he. But there was only so much a man could take.

Promises, promises, and Rand's money pocketed with nothing to show for it. Oh, mister slicked-back hair said he was still waiting for word from his contacts, but Rand figured he was lying. He looked too smug, his lip curling as he leaned back in his desk chair, his attention focused on everything but his client.

Rand should have known better than to hire the cheapest. Anyone who cared so little for his surroundings had to be a liar and a cheat. Why hadn't Rand taken that into account when hiring someone? The faux-leather armchairs had actual tears—knife slits?—and the carpet was covered with stains of unknown origin, although the one in front of the desk held just a hint of red around the edges. Red wine? Blood?

He hurried down the two flights of stairs and pushed open the heavy glass door. After the stale air of that office building, the afternoon sunshine brought its own relief and the sight of his lovely little BMW reminded him he had much to fight for. Jeminy wasn't going to walk off with it all.

With nothing better to do that afternoon, Rand returned to the apartment that Jeminy had left for him to deal with. He'd paid the rent and had looked through the things she'd left behind, but maybe, just maybe, he'd missed something, some clue that would tell him where she'd gone.

He'd begun to suspect a return to Nashville where they'd met. She knew the town, and she'd be looking for somewhere to start over.

He was heading to the front door when the neighbor from downstairs called out from behind him. "Yoohoo!"

He smiled perfunctorily, and paused to ask how she'd been. She came up next to him talking about caring for the flowers along the walkway, how she enjoyed their scent through her open windows "just like dear Jeminy had."

"Lovely," he interrupted and held the door open for her.

"I've missed Jeminy. Such a sweet girl. I was sorry to hear she'd moved away."

"Ah. Yes." He was about to turn away when she continued.

"I didn't recognize the car that took her, but I remembered the young woman helped carry some of her boxes." The woman laughed that ridiculous way some old ladies had. "I did recognize her on account of having to let her in one time when Jeminy asked me to."

That stopped him. "You did?"

"Yes indeedy. She calls herself Maggie." She paused momentarily. "Nice young woman."

Nice young woman? Yeah, right.

Rand cursed under his breath all the way to Maggie's house and while he parked across the street, waiting for her to come home.

40

JEMINY

Confusion, convolutions, a straight line
Or a curve?

Her week continued to be one of revelation after revelation. Her father's phone call had set things in motion for the New Bern police—or more in motion than they had been—and she couldn't wait to get additional details.

Investigations, said the detective in charge, plodded toward the finish line; they never seemed to sprint. But she'd be the first to know when they had information they could share.

Brilliant.

No. Not that word. *Brilliant* was Rand's. In the beginning, he'd drawn her in with "You've a brilliant voice. Your songs are brilliant." As if he'd been watching British television and was mimicking their word choices. He'd just needed a "Darling" at the end.

Then, when things shifted in their world, he'd used it

pejoratively, his voice a sneer. "Brilliant, Jeminy." His lips had curled. "Just brilliant."

The memory made her want to scrub her mind, wipe his image from her thoughts until he was gone forever. Except, Rand might long for her death.

For that insurance money.

What a thought. She'd shared a bed with a potential murderer, even if the murder he'd planned had been vicarious. Worse, she'd offered herself to him. It had never been rape.

You're a mess, my girl.

Or, you were.

She pressed her palm against her roiling stomach and tried to shake off the horrible memories.

The surveillance cameras had shown a different face for the attacker, not Rand's, but he'd be the sort to hire someone else to do the dirty work, just like he'd never lifted a finger to make the money—only to "manage" it.

She shook off the thoughts. She couldn't fix anything, couldn't undo the past, had survived whoever'd shot at her from the truck, and she was here, with a job to do, with her nana to love. She wandered outside and found her grandmother near the shed, bending over a bush. When she drew closer, she recognized a stunted azalea.

"Nana, I think we need to transplant that so it can grow freely. Look how the bushes on either side are stunting it. What color is it when in bloom?"

Nana thought a moment. "I'm not sure. Maybe pink?"

"Let's think of where to put it."

Her grandmother smiled at her. "Thank you. But I need to go to the bank. I don't seem to have any money, and I'd like to pay you for all you do for me."

Jeminy backed up a step. "Nana, why would you want to pay me? I'm your granddaughter."

"I know you're my granddaughter, but you do so much."

"I do it because I love you. Aren't we having fun together? Don't we do well like this?"

"I do very well, but what about you?"

Jeminy wondered where this was coming from. "Nana, I love living with you. We're a team. And you're saving me huge rent payments."

"Oh."

"Besides, think of all the times you were generous with me when I was growing up."

Nana patted her hand. "Thank you, sweet girl." She turned toward the house. "Let's go have some tea."

"Yes, ma'am."

Jeminy'd just made the tea and given her grandmother a cup when her cell phone rang. Eric was on the line, returning her call. "Thanks for getting back to me. I have a lot to tell you."

"You want to do it by phone or in person?"

"In person?"

"How would you like to help me take *Escape* around to the boatyard so I can get her hauled and get the bottom painted while I'm not living on her?"

On a boat? Was there even a question? "I'd love to!"

"It's an incoming tide, so we'll have plenty of water, and slack hits in about thirty minutes. Can you meet me at the marina?"

"I'll be there. Do I need to bring anything?"

"Just a light jacket in case it cools off. I have everything else."

Nana's smile blossomed when Jeminy told her of the invite. "You'll get out on the water, and I'll be fine here. You've made me a lovely salad with ham, and I don't need anything else."

"Are you sure, Nana?"

"Sweet girl, of course. I can manage just fine. It's going to be a lovely afternoon, and I'm going to enjoy myself. I'm perfectly capable of managing on my own."

Jeminy bent and kissed her nana's cheek. "I know you are. The phone is on the stand and charged, and you know how to reach me if you need me. Or Isa. Her phone number is also right by the phone."

"Scoot. And don't you worry."

Jeminy grabbed her new yellow hat, sunscreen, and her summer jacket, and headed out to the marina. On the way, she called Isa to give her a heads-up.

"She'll be fine," Isa said. "You need to have some fun, too, you know. I'll call and check in with her, though, so you don't have to."

"Thanks, Isa. I appreciate it."

Jeminy had a spring in her step. Amazing, really, considering the news she had for Eric was so unpleasant. But the sun shone, the water sparkled, and she was going out on that beautiful boat— even if only from the marina to the boatyard.

Eric was waiting to help her on board. She wasn't certain whether her heart tap danced because she'd just stepped onto the deck of a boat or because his hand had touched hers.

It was the boat. It had to be the boat. She knew absolutely nothing about sailing, but she'd been out with her granddaddy on his fishing trawler all through her childhood, and there was nothing better than pulling away from the dock and feeling the breeze on her face.

"You need help untying or holding lines?" she asked once she'd stowed her things below—and didn't she long to peek in areas she hadn't seen before? Maybe later, once they were on their way. The tide waited for no one.

"I've got it, thanks. There's no wind or current to worry about."

He pointed her to a seat in the cockpit, started the engine, and then climbed down to the dock to uncleat the lines still tied. Ones on the port side already lay coiled on deck. Then he climbed back on board, holding one line still looped around a dock cleat, and put the engine in gear.

It was the smoothest exit she'd ever seen.

He kept their speed to the minimum as he steered past the

marina and through what used to be the Beaufort bridge, heading, she assumed, to one of the boatyards on the ICW.

"What a gorgeous day for this." She gazed from the light-speckled water to the captain.

Eric grinned at her. His hair fell a little long over his forehead, but he brushed it back and donned a cap he'd left lying on the steering station. "It's been way too long since *Escape* has left the dock."

"It must be frustrating having her and not being able to go out much."

"Way too frustrating. Do you sail?"

"I don't. But that doesn't mean I wouldn't like to learn." She patted a shiny winch sitting just outside the cockpit. "I'd love to know what you use this for, how you manage your sails. The idea of being able to propel a boat using the wind sounds magical."

He seemed surprised by her statement. "It is. I've never heard a non-sailor speak in those terms."

She shrugged. "My experience as a child was my granddaddy's big old trawler. I loved being out on it, but I wasn't a huge fan of the loud diesel engine." She paused to listen. "Yours doesn't seem bad."

"It's probably a lot smaller, for one thing. And a lot newer. We won't be hoisting the sails for this short run, but perhaps one day soon, when she's back in the water, I can take you out. It's a nice sail out to Cape Lookout."

"Oh, I would love that."

"It's a deal." He motioned to the companionway. "I've got water in the refrigerator if you want some."

"I would. How about you?"

He nodded. "Hang on to the rails on your way down and forward."

"Mind if I take a look around while I'm there? You showed me the main rooms before, but I'm nosy."

He laughed. "Make yourself at home."

When the wake from a passing speedboat rocked them uncomfortably, Jeminy tightened her hold on the handrail until the waves flattened. Then she went exploring.

Her fingers itched to touch everything, and she slid them along the gorgeous teak paneling of the walls and doors. Eric kept things shipshape, including what was obviously Danny's room at the front of the boat. She examined the bookcase over the settee and recognized a few titles, although she hadn't read any of them. The galley was efficient and attractive, the heads—he had two— were small but well set up, one with a real shower, one with a grated floor and an extension wand for the basin faucet.

All of this made for a very nice traveling home, and she bet he liked being able to go places in it. She could imagine anchoring in Turtle Bay just off Cape Lookout and waking to coffee in the cockpit, maybe a dolphin or two cavorting nearby, the wild banks ponies nibbling grass, a sea turtle swimming just under the surface. She'd been really young when her grandparents had taken her out for the weekend. To do that as an adult? It would be perfect.

She dug two water bottles out of the small refrigerator. Back in the cockpit, she handed one to Eric. "What a great boat."

"Thank you. I enjoy her, but it's a lot more fun with company onboard. Thank you for joining me today."

"I bet you have a lot of willing guests." She took a swig as soon as she spoke to hide the red she could feel creeping up her neck.

"Not since I had her docked in Charleston." He sounded casual, relaxed. Jeminy glanced back at him when he spoke again. "The partners and associates loved going out with me. One was a sailor without a boat, one a woman who liked that I gave her grandchildren the opportunity to experience sailing, and the others sport fishermen who enjoyed the variety."

"Oh? I'd love to hear about life there."

"Sure, but first you said you had something you wanted to talk about."

She told him what her father's investigator had discovered.

"You called the detective." He didn't make it a question.

"My father did first, and then I tried to follow up. The detective promised to keep us updated."

Eric blew out a loud breath. "Yeah. You've heard that before, haven't you?" Another powerful boat sped past, and Eric turned *Escape* so she would cross the other wake at a better angle.

When they were again pointing straight down the channel, he said, "Did they ever figure out who the guy in the surveillance photo was?"

"This detective was more interested in asking me questions than in giving me answers. He was only doing his job, but it was still frustrating. The shooter wasn't Rand, but that whole life insurance thing makes me think he might have been involved. It puts an entirely different slant on my quiet country life, doesn't it?"

Eric glanced from her to the water ahead and then back. "How would Rand have found you?"

"That's a good question. I mean, Rand would know where Nana lives and might guess I'd come here. I hadn't thought that likely, but he might have." Surely Maggie wouldn't have told him, and no one else knew...

"There's still a good chance it was random."

"I don't know if that makes me feel better—or worse."

41

ERIC

Eric pointed *Escape* toward the next marker, but his gaze kept returning to Jeminy, who stood, one hand on the rail, the breeze blowing strands of her long hair into her face. She brushed them away with those incredibly graceful fingers. He'd noticed her hands at their first meeting, the way she held them, the way she moved them. They were hands that strummed a guitar and gestured vividly when she spoke.

Don't get ahead of yourself. Concentrate on her words.

Those were unsettling enough. He asked his own question. "Did the detective you spoke to indicate they might call in the feds?"

"Would they?"

"If there's a link between Rand's activities in Los Angeles and what's been happening here."

She fiddled with her water bottle. "I hate not knowing."

"I get that. Waiting on others when you'd like to be up and doing."

She laughed. "Not that I want to be the one trying to uncover more of Rand's secrets. I've come across too many for my peace of mind, but even if he's guilty of nothing more than embezzling and maintaining an insurance policy in the off chance I die of natural causes, enough already."

Eric adjusted course, giving way as a tug approached pushing a barge down the channel. After they'd passed, he said, "I've been checking out the old contracts Rand had you sign and getting a new one to submit to Darling. I left the draft in my car of what I've put together for him. We'll finalize things if you approve."

"Thank you." Her expression seemed to have lightened when the topic shifted to contracts.

Good. She'd looked as if she carried the weight of the world when talking about the old boyfriend, and today was supposed to be about… About what? Getting to know her?

He focused again on the water ahead. They were here to move his boat and enjoy the water and the sun. Fun stuff. Yep. That was all.

"Lots of shoals," she said, shading her eyes and facing toward shore. "I guess you have to be really careful to stay in the channel."

"Yes, indeed. They're treacherous at low tide or on a boat like *Escape* with her fairly deep keel. You need to know how to read a chart and navigate the channels."

She leaned out over the rails. Maybe she was watching the small wake produced as the boat's hull pushed water out of the way. Straightening, she said, "My granddaddy used to say we had to learn the waters, to pay attention to the markers and to the shifting of shoals after a storm so as not to run aground. The markers are there to show the way, he said, only they don't tell the whole story, not when a hurricane can come along and change things so you could stay in what you think ought to be the channel and still hit bottom."

"That's especially true on the inside of Cape Lookout, which is why the Coast Guard uses moveable buoys."

"Granddaddy'd tell stories of ships that went aground and how sometimes local islanders would make ship captains think a certain way was safe. Then, when the ship broke apart on the shoals, they'd ransack the wreck for whatever they could take away."

"You're trying to make a point that has nothing to do with following charts, aren't you?"

"It's just interesting. I've never actually put these thoughts into words before." She paused. "Do you ever feel as if your life is like shoal-clogged waters? That your movement may take you—or maybe has already taken you—into water so shallow you're about to run aground? Or maybe you've already run aground and long to get free?"

He thought about her words. "We all face things that push us in one direction instead of another, that get us stuck in the sand or slam us against the rocks."

"I'm tired of being stuck, and I'm really tired of rocky bottoms."

He wasn't sure what to say because he didn't know exactly which issue had her most stuck. He wasn't sure how to ask—or if she'd think him intrusive if he tried—but he couldn't just stay silent. "Anything you want to talk about?" That seemed safe enough. Let her open up if she wanted. As her lawyer, he knew a lot, but maybe she wanted to go deeper.

With a shrug, she said, "Not really. I don't know why I went on like that. Just memories, and seeing how close those shoals are to the channel."

"I don't think you need to worry about us running aground in the literal sense, and if you're talking figuratively, it's one step at a time. We'll get you a decent royalty contract with Darling, we'll go after whatever money Rand stole, and we'll trust the detectives to do their job and find answers. I'm glad you're staying in touch with them, but you'd better keep your eyes open and be watchful."

"I'm sure the gunman is long gone by now. If I was even his intentional target."

"Be careful anyway? Until he's been caught?"

"Sure. Of course."

Maybe it was her enthusiasm for everything maritime and her willingness to lend a hand that attracted him. Maybe he responded to her fascination with the difference between his sailboat and her grandfather's fishing boat.

And maybe it was just that she was a beautiful young woman with whom he could laugh and enjoy a few hours of conversation —when not talking about potential murderers—during a time when he'd lost some of his perspective after the advent of Danny back into his life.

Oh, he loved the boy, but he was way out of his league, and having to focus his attention on a child with needs he couldn't fathom left him feeling alone and even slightly worried.

And then came a smiling woman, his boat on the move, and sun glistening off both *Escape's* teak rails and Jeminy's silky hair.

When had he last noticed a woman's hair or called it *silky?*

Yeah, a long time ago.

Anyway, he sure saw it now, and he wanted to touch it. To verify that it felt the way he imagined.

Only that. A quick test.

Hah. Delude yourself all you want, buddy, but why not admit you'd like to do a lot more than run a few fingers through that hair?

Enough.

"Will you take the wheel for a minute?" he asked. "I need to put the fenders over. Just hold her steady."

Her grin widened. "Happy to."

He set out the fenders, got the lines ready, and returned to the cockpit. "Thanks," he said, preparing to turn into the slip for the travel lift. Fortunately, the tide was still slack and there wasn't much of a breeze to inhibit an easy turn. A call to the yard, and he slid into place, lassoing dock cleats as the boat idled.

"Look at you," she said. "A regular cowboy."

He laughed. "I can only manage that in perfect conditions, which we happen to have."

"I'm impressed anyway."

Which, of course, had been his intention. And, yes, he felt a bit smug as he tied off and shut down systems.

The travel lift driver waved from the head of the dock. With him were a couple of other yard guys. While Eric waited for them, he unloaded what few things were left in the refrigerator into a cooler and grabbed it and whatever else he'd brought with him, along with Jeminy's bag.

"Off we go." He took Jeminy's hand and helped her to the dock, then offloaded the other gear into a waiting cart, which he wheeled out of the way. "You can go on up if you'd like. Wait in the air-conditioned office."

"I'd rather watch, thanks."

While the yard guys lifted *Escape* and maneuvered her into the yard, Eric phoned for a cab to meet them at the yard office. They power-washed her bottom before moving her onto jack stands, leaving Eric with nothing more to do until all the commissioned work had been completed. He'd check on the progress in a day or two, but now he ushered Jeminy to the taxi, loaded his cooler and other gear into the trunk, and gave the driver Jeminy's address as their first stop.

He glanced over at her grinning countenance. The grin pleased him, and he returned it. "Thanks for all your help," he said as they neared town.

"I didn't do much, but I certainly had fun. You're prepared in case a hurricane comes barreling up this way?"

"I will be. I'll head back out there in a day or so to finish securing everything so she'll keep while I'm land-bound."

"But not forever."

"No," he said. "Have you ever seen where Annie Mac and Clay live?"

"I haven't, but Annie Mac stopped by yesterday and invited us over for a Friday night cookout."

"They have a gorgeous house on the water, and they just added one of those tiny houses not much bigger than my boat, where Danny and I are staying.."

"Really?" She was watching him, her eyes wide. "Better than the Inn, I'd guess."

"Oh, man. So much better." He laughed, thinking of their time in that cramped room. "The place may be small, but the windows bring the outside right in."

"And Danny?"

"He's able to sleep on a bed that comes down from the ceiling, so he's pretty happy. I'm thinking of moving him to the loft once his arm's healed. I don't really like the idea of him being on the main floor by himself."

She took a moment to ask, "You thinking something might happen? He might go out alone?"

"I'm probably being overprotective, but I'd feel better if I were the first line of defense, you know, should an intruder try to enter. The house is pretty remote."

"Yes, of course you would."

"And getting down from the loft is tricky. Someone came to the door, I'd be hard-pressed to get there before a curious Danny would be up and peering out the window. Not a scenario that gives me a lot of peace." When the cab pulled up in front of Nana's home, Eric remembered the contract. "Look, I'll drop off the draft proposal soon, and you can call me with any questions you might have."

"Thank you." She grinned over at him as she opened the car door. "Any time you want crew to actually sail with you, I'm your girl."

He laughed. "I'll keep it in mind. Tell your grandmother thanks for sharing you. And I'll be eager to hear the latest developments in the case when you have news."

As she climbed out and headed inside, he asked the driver to take him to the marina parking where he'd left his car. There, he paid and allowed the driver to help him unload his stuff from the taxi's trunk and into his own.

He should be at ease now that *Escape* was tucked into her space at the work yard, but his conversation with Jeminy wouldn't settle. There had to be more he could do.

He drove to the police station and went inside. "Clay here?" he asked the woman behind the desk.

"He is. He expecting you?"

"No, ma'am. I'm Eric Houston. Maybe he has a minute?"

She made a call, and Clay soon stepped into the hall. "Come on back, Eric."

The lieutenant waved Eric to a chair next to his big, paper-strewn desk. "What's up? Everything okay at the tiny house?"

"Very okay. It's an amazing place to wake to." Eric leaned forward, resting one arm on the desk. "You talked to the detectives from Craven recently? The ones investigating that shooting?"

"I haven't. Sorry. We've got a few things going on with some new meth labs selling here in town."

Eric shook his head. "Hard to keep up with them, I guess."

"Never-ending. We get rid of one dealer, one supplier, and another slithers in to take his place. Anyway, what's the latest?"

Eric told him what Jeminy'd said. "That life insurance policy's strong motivation, wouldn't you say?"

Clay blew out a long breath. "I would. And this is the guy she used to be with?"

"He was her manager as well. She has me looking into her old recording contracts, anything he could be using fraudulently."

"Interesting."

"I'm wondering," Eric said, "if you could do a little digging, as a friend, apart from what the Craven folks are doing. Or maybe if you have contacts up there, you could check on what they know." He sighed. "I'm not sure the shooter's related to the issues with this Rand guy, her ex, but it would be good to know. They got the shooter's photo from a surveillance camera, and I know they were running him through the system, but shouldn't they send you and Morehead his photo, too? On account of the gas station being in Morehead and the truck stolen from there. It's possible he's known around here."

Clay stood up. "Hang on a minute. Let me see if anything's come through that maybe I haven't heard about yet."

He walked out of his office. Eric heard him talking to someone. When he eventually returned, he was carrying paperwork.

"We did get something. The Chief's been studying it and has asked the patrolmen to see if they recognize the man."

"Any luck there?"

"He got one yes. Said the guy looked like a man he'd seen down on Front Street driving a tan truck, not a black one." Clay handed over the paper that had the man's photo.

Eric studied it. Something about the face looked vaguely familiar. Where had he seen the man?

Clay leaned forward. "You recognize him?"

"I'm trying to place the face. He seems familiar, but the beard makes it hard. And the cap just about covers his eyes."

"Hang on." Clay walked back out and returned with a young woman, looked like a secretary. "Nan here does side work using computer software and photos. Maybe she can get rid of the beard."

"I can, Lieutenant. I'll scan in the image and give him a shave!" She laughed as she said it.

Eric gave her the picture. "Can you do it now?"

"I just have to get my program up and running."

Clay looked at his watch. "Annie Mac collecting all the kids, Danny too?"

Eric nodded. "She said she would. Danny's thrilled to be hanging with Ty."

"Can't hurt him to learn from Tyler. Annie Mac did a great job with those kids before I entered their life. Now I get to reap the joy of it all."

"Seems Ty really loves having you as his dad."

Clay grinned. "Yep. The two of us bonded right off. And Katie, man, that little girl just bats those lashes of hers, and I'm a goner. Seems Danny has compelling eyes, too."

"He does. Since he was born." And they'd been doing a number on Eric since then. He smiled at the thought and said, "And now you're going to have one of your own. The kids okay with that?"

"They seem real glad. I'm thinkin' Ty's going to get a kick out of having a little brother."

"Pretty special, the way that all worked out."

"God's been working on filling needs everywhere around here. Look at your brother and Agnes."

Eric sighed. "That one had me worried in the beginning. Hen with his issues taking on a woman with her own problems."

"Yeah, but isn't that how God's economy works? My rough edges get smoothed by yours?"

"Hmm." Was that the way it worked?

"I heard someone once suggest that when the shepherd boy David reached into the water for five stones to use against Goliath, he had to pick ones that had been rubbed smooth so they'd fly straight to their target. In the same way, he said, our rough edges need to be worn away by what they come up against so we'll be effective in the battles we need to win."

"Great image." It was, Eric decided. "I guess we all have rough edges that need smoothing out—our anger, impatience, whatever. It just never occurred to me that our relationships might be the things sent to rub them off." He smiled weakly. "Maybe that's one reason Danny's in my life. Because I'd gotten very comfortable in my single existence on *Escape*, happy to do what I wanted when I wanted. I was pretty selfish, or at least self-absorbed."

"Shot that right out from under you, didn't he?"

"Completely."

Clay's smile straightened. "How are you doing with him? Any headway on what's bothering him in school, why he skipped?"

"Your wife said she'd be listening to see if she can pick up on anything."

"Good. You can trust Annie Mac to ferret out whatever's there."

All this was good conversation, but he really wanted to see that picture. There was something about the man he was supposed to remember.

It wasn't long before Nan returned with the original photo in one hand and a reconstructed one in the other. "Based on how lean the man appears, I didn't give him a lot of flesh around the jaw. Does this look at all familiar?"

Eric studied the new rendition of the shooter's face. Something nagged... what was it? He thought back, trying to remember, hoping for something to click.

What if... he imagined a sneer on that face, the man standing on his stoop, watching them. And it fit. "I think his name may just be Jenkins. I don't know the first name, but he was Danny's foster father." Another image sprang into mind. "And there was an old tan truck in the driveway."

Clay nodded at the computer artist. "Thank you, Nan. Great work." Then to Eric. "Come on. You can tell the chief all you know. Supposition or not, we'll follow the first lead we've had."

He not only told the chief, but he was there when they phoned the Craven detective.

"At least we know who," Eric said. "Now we need to know why. He can't have come after us just because I took Danny away."

Clay nodded. "This case has just gotten a lot more interesting."

He wondered if Jeminy would think so. "Catch you later?"

"I've got an hour or so more before I take off. You need me to bring you guys anything? Annie Mac's always calling, asking me to pick up something or other."

"Why don't I stop at the store if you guys have a list? I'm not going back to the office today."

Clay held up a finger as he pulled out his cell phone. When Annie Mac answered, he repeated Eric's offer. "You sure that's all?"

When he disconnected, Clay smiled. "Seems she wants me to pick up pizza for dinner."

"I can do that. Give me your order, I'll get some for everyone."

Clay jotted down their choices, including the white sauce Annie Mac preferred during her pregnancy, and handed it to Eric. Then he fished out his wallet.

"Don't even think about it." Eric waved away the offer of cash. "I owe you guys plenty for making that place available, and Annie Mac for acting as transport and sitter for Danny. You need drinks, too?"

"No, thanks. Appreciate you taking care of that. She can keep a slice warm for me."

"I'll call it in—you normally use No Name Pizza?"

"Yep. Or Crossroads."

"I don't know that one."

"A good little place on the way home. They have Greek food too."

"Sounds interesting. Maybe I'll give them a try next time." At the door, he said, "See you later. And thanks."

He phoned in the order from his car. While he waited for them to prepare it, he called Jeminy. "You won't believe who the shooter is."

ERIC

Eric's phone pinged with a voicemail from his brother. He settled the boxes of pizza in the back seat, slid in behind the wheel, and started the car. His phone linked to the car's computer and he told it to dial Henry.

"How's the new place working out?" Hen asked.

"Great. You need to come see it. I'd invite you all, but it's a micro house."

"Like boat-living on land?"

"Similar, but I can't move it and it doesn't rock. I hauled *Escape* today."

"Yeah, I stopped by and saw she was missing from her slip. It's been too long since we've chatted, you and I."

"You've been honeymooning."

Hen laughed. "In place."

"When will you actually go somewhere with your bride?"

"We thought we'd take off during the slow season come winter. Find some lovely beach somewhere."

"Agnes interested in little umbrella drinks?"

"More like interested in a vacation of any sort, but neither of us is a skier, so a beach vacation seems like the best thing. Escape the cold. We have discussed going somewhere exotic, maybe the Far East, Singapore, Japan. Even Thailand."

"Wow. That would be incredible. I've always had a hankering to see Japan, and they say Singapore is one of the cleanest cities in the world."

"We both love good Asian food, so that makes Japan and Thailand really attractive. But we'd be totally dependent on translators."

"True. Fun to dream, anyway, right?"

"Amen."

"So how's Brisa doing?"

"Great. She loved seeing her dad at the wedding. He even left her a CD of what he's working on now. All inspirational covers. Amazing transformation from the man he'd been."

"Christian music?"

"Worship. And with his voice? Powerful, powerful stuff."

"He also sings Jeminy Buchanan's songs," Eric said.

"Yeah. I think he's planning to see if she'll also move in the direction he's taking now."

Jeminy hadn't mentioned this, so maybe that discussion hadn't taken place yet. Or maybe that's what Darling had talked about in the letter, the one that had made her go quiet in his office. "That should be interesting. She's a client of mine."

"A client, and your kid skipped school to hide in her car?"

Eric huffed. "Small-town interrelationships are interesting, aren't they?"

It sounded as if Hen had someone talking to him in the background. His next words confirmed it. "Look, gotta run. Chef needs me."

"Thanks for checking in. Let's work harder at finding more time."

"Will do."

As Eric turned down the lane leading to his and Clay's houses, he reminded himself that time was all he needed with his own issues. Danny would heal, in time, and he'd find answers to help the boy.

He pulled up in front of the big house and unloaded the three boxes of pizza that belonged there. The kids were outside, playing on a big rope swing—well, Ty and Katie were playing on it. Danny's broken arm wouldn't let him, so he sat on the edge of a big sandbox, creating what looked like a fortified castle.

"Pizza!" Ty shouted, and they gathered round.

"In the house," Eric told them.

Annie Mac waved from the deck. "Come on up."

He followed her inside, the kids on his heels. "Where do you want me to put these?"

"On the counter will be fine." She turned to the kids. "Hands washed, please. We'll eat soon."

Eric looked at his hopeful son. "I got some for us too. It's in the car."

"Danny, why don't you go wash up with the others. I want to speak to your dad for a minute before you go." She waved Eric back outside and closed the door behind them. "I thought you'd like to know what Katie overheard at school today."

"About Danny?"

"Seems so. Two of the bigger boys, not only older—as in they've failed a few grades—but also heavier, were trying to push a much younger and smaller student into the boys' bathroom. They didn't see Katie on the way to the office with papers from her teacher, and they had the boy up by his collar, his back against the door. They said he'd better come through—with what, she didn't hear—or they'd do to him what they did to the little colored kid. Danny."

Heat rose in Eric's face, and all he could think was that if those punks had been within reach, he'd have made them regret the day they'd touched his son.

"Katie hurried on to the office to tell someone what was

happening. They may have seen her then because one of them called after her. She ran."

"Did an adult intervene?"

"All she said was that a guard went racing down the hall when she said the little kid needed rescuing."

"Is she afraid?"

"I think she may be. I'm going to follow up tomorrow to find out all I can, but you may need to see if Danny will talk about what they did to him. Maybe even get some counseling if it was really bad."

"And maybe get him out of that school."

"There are bullies everywhere. You think you can protect him from them all?"

"I'd like to know what those boys were doing out of class and why the younger, smaller boy was there, too. Don't they have hall monitors anymore?"

"It's amazing how sneaky some kids are. Anyway, I'll find out as much as I can tomorrow and let you know."

"Thanks, Annie Mac. I'm glad Danny has Ty and Katie to take his mind off whatever else is going on."

He put his head through the door and called for Danny. "Let's go eat, son."

Danny hurried down the steps and raced to the car. Eric followed more slowly, climbed in, and they headed to the small house. He hadn't yet dubbed it theirs because it didn't yet feel like home, but perhaps it would soon. Perhaps.

He couldn't fault the view, he decided as he unpacked their pizza, got down two plates, and poured milk and a beer.

He waited until Danny'd finished one slice before beginning the conversation, trying not to spook the boy with too much too quickly. "It seems some big kids at school cornered a smaller boy and threatened him."

Danny glanced at him and lowered his gaze. But he didn't speak.

Eric took another bite, chewed, swallowed. Trying to keep his voice casual, he said, "The big boys used your name when they threatened the younger one. Said they'd do to him what they did to you."

Danny's shoulders began to shake slightly. His head was bowed; he'd begun to curl into himself.

"Son?"

"They… they said they'd… they'd kill me."

Eric scooted Danny's stool close and drew him into his arms. "Oh, son…"

Torn between rage at anyone who'd hurt his boy and a huge sense of pity for what Danny'd been dealing with, he held the child with one arm and used his other hand to smooth his hair. "I won't let them hurt you again. We'll put a stop to this now."

Danny pulled back enough to say, "I… I… don't want them to h-hurt anybody else."

"Of course you don't. Can you tell me what they did to you?"

Danny shook his head, focusing again on his lap.

"I can't stop them if I don't know."

"Can I just not go to school?"

"Not an option, buddy. Let's back up. Some bullies did something to you and threatened you if you told. You didn't, only now they're coming after another kid. Right?"

Danny squeezed shut his eyes.

"I have that right, son?"

He nodded slightly.

"How do you think we can stop them from hurting anyone else? By being quiet or by telling?"

He shrugged.

Eric stood and brought Danny with him, drawing him down next to him on the settee. "Here's the thing about bad people that you may not have considered. If no one has the courage to stand up to them and tell about the bad things, they will keep on thinking they're stronger and better and that they can win. And that sort of winning means someone else loses badly. Maybe gets hurt. Or has something taken from them." Eric bent over so he was level with Danny's face. "Are you courageous enough to fight for other little kids even if you couldn't stand up for yourself when it happened?"

Danny took a deep breath and for a moment continued gazing into his lap. And then he turned his head so he was face-to-face with Eric. "I guess."

"Will you tell me what happened?"

Danny nodded. "Yeah, I guess."

Eric didn't wait to hear from Annie Mac but called the school office the next morning. When they arrived to meet the principal, she ushered them in and asked them to sit down.

"How's your arm, Danny?" Mrs. Melborne spoke gently, not at all the voice of a disciplinarian.

"It's okay."

"Ma'am," Eric prompted.

"It's okay, ma'am."

"Your teacher and I have been concerned for you. I'm so glad you're feeling better."

"As I said on the phone, Danny has something he'd like to tell you, but he's been worried about repercussions. I assured him you won't let anything else happen to him."

She leaned forward, her expression solemn. "I'd like to hear what's been bothering you, Danny."

Danny bit his lip. Eric laid a hand on his good arm "Son, we talked about this. It's important that you say something. To protect others."

The child's big brown eyes looked from him to the principal. "I've been scared, on account of them saying they'd kill me if I told."

"But now you're being very brave," Mrs. Melborne said.

"I guess," Danny said, his voice small and worried. "Only I don't feel brave."

"Remember what I told you?" Eric said. "Courage isn't lack of fear, it's doing the right thing even when you're scared." Eric moved his hand to Danny's rounded back.

They waited for the child to speak again. Finally, he sat up and said, "It was two big boys. I don't know their names. But they had a knife."

Mrs. Melborne straightened and glanced over at Eric, her eyes wide. "What did they do with the knife?" she asked.

"First off, they stole my stuff, and when I got mad, they shoved me so I hit my shoulder on the john. I was real scared, but that's when they pulled out a real sharp knife and waved it at my face. Said they'd slice me open if I told."

Eric remembered the shoulder injury, the one Danny'd blamed on running into a door. "He came home with his shoulder hurting, but he wouldn't tell me what happened."

"What did they steal, Danny?" Mrs. Melborne asked.

His lips quivered, and when he looked up, his eyes had filled. "My mom's...my mom's special thing. It... it was... all... all I h-had."

"Oh, son, I'm sorry. What was it? Where did you have it?"

"It was in my... my pocket. They asked... if I had money. Made me empty my pockets."

"Can you describe the thing they stole, your mother's special thing?" Mrs. Melborne asked.

"It was a dolphin with a shiny eye."

Eric sat back with a heavy sigh. He'd given her that pin at the birth of her son because she'd loved dolphins. He hadn't thought of it in years. "I know that pin," he said.

Danny swiveled toward him. "You do?"

He nodded. "I do. I gave it to your mother when you were born. The eye was a diamond."

"A diamond?" Danny asked.

"Very valuable."

"Danny," Mrs. Melborne said, "Did anyone else see what was going on?"

"Wally. He came in. I was on the floor."

"Wallace Danes?"

"Un-huh. He's in my class."

"Thank you, Danny. Are you feeling able to go to class today?"

"Do I have to?" he asked.

She smiled at him. "Maybe you can have another sick day or two, but let me send someone to your classroom to get your assignments. Can you wait while I do that?"

"Un-huh."

"Mr. Houston, could you step outside a moment?"

A worried Danny shifted in his seat. Eric said, "It's okay, son."

"We'll be right back," Mrs. Melborne promised.

In the outer office, the principal asked the secretary to call down to Danny's teacher to ask for assignments and any paperwork Danny would need for a couple of days. Then she turned to Eric.

"I think it might be a good idea if Danny's not here while I deal with those two boys and their parents. I know who they are because we caught them bothering Wallace yesterday. But I'm going to have to follow protocol here. If it comes down to a police issue, do you think you can get Danny to talk to them?"

"Sure, if it's Lieutenant Dougherty asking the questions. We're renting a small house on Clay's property, and Danny's friends with his children."

"Good. As soon as you've taken Danny home, I'll call the boys' parents and set up a meeting with them. In the meantime, I'm going to get our security guard to go with me to check their backpacks." She sighed. "Maybe we'll find something to make this a lot easier than the testimony of two young kids."

"Will you call me and let me know?"

"I will. As soon as I discover something."

Eric did his best to soothe Danny's worries as they waited to hear from Mrs. Melborne. The boy didn't want Eric out of his sight, and during the hours he spent with Becca Barnes while Eric was at work, he refused to go outside, so fearful was he that the bullies would know he'd talked.

Knowing this, Eric left work early and was on his way home when the call finally came.

Mrs. Melborne identified herself and said, "I thought you'd like to know the two students have both been turned over to the authorities. We found a switchblade in the backpack of one and in the other's a silver dolphin pin with a diamond eye."

"Wow. I wonder how they imagined they could carry those things around and get away with it."

"Not the brightest two. They've been held back a couple of times." She hesitated a moment. "Danny and Wallace may have to speak to the police, though, because the one with the pin said he'd found it on the ground and no one could prove differently."

"I'll talk to Clay, see what he needs from Danny and his friend. Danny's going to be happy to get his mother's pin back. As far as I can tell, he doesn't have anything else to remember her by."

"I'm glad we found it."

Yeah. That was a good thing. Now they had to speak to Clay and see what he could do to protect Danny from any repercussions. In former times, those two hoodlums would have been sent away to reform school. Today, judges too often gave delinquents of any age a pass with an admonition and maybe some sort of community service.

Fine, he believed in second chances, but when it came to bullies, he wanted them miles away from his boy. Often bullies were bullies because they'd been bullied at home, and soft-peddling that with community service wouldn't do a thing about their underlying issues.

Issues that might cause their bad behavior to escalate and eventually get someone killed.

Clay stopped by the tiny house on his way home. Danny trusted him and spoke freely of the events. When they got to the part about the bullies taking his mama's pin, Clay glanced over at Eric.

"You know the piece? You can describe it?"

"Easily."

"And, Danny, did anyone else witness their violence or the theft?"

Danny leaned closer and whispered, "Wally."

"And this Wally, could he back you up?"

"He didn't see them take the dolphin pin, on account of they did that first off, before they punched and pushed me. I got real mad."

"What did he see?"

"I was on the floor next to the john. I was crying 'cause I hurt so bad." He paused. "And I was real mad. I kept saying to give it back or I would tell."

"Wally heard you say to give it back?"

"Un-huh. And he heard the biggest one—don't know his name or the other guy's—but he said some real bad words."

"What else?" Clay asked.

"He said the bad words about me and my mama and then he said if I wanted the pin back I could go do that, um, that thing. It's a bad word. Sorry."

Eric flexed his fingers to keep them from making a fist. He hated that Danny even knew bad words.

"Thank you for telling me, Danny. I'll be looking into it." As

Clay stepped toward the door to leave, he asked Eric to walk outside with him. "Just for a moment."

Eric followed, waiting for Clay to speak.

"Sheriff's deputies found Jenkins shacking up in an abandoned trailer. He'd shaved, but was using his own truck, for which we have plate numbers."

"And?"

"When they told him they had him for auto theft as well as attempted murder, he held out for a while, finally admitting he'd been sent to kidnap Danny. He hadn't meant to hurt anyone, just get them off the road. Sheriff did tag team with the detective from Craven. Eventually, Jenkins tried to shift blame to a customer. Promised to give over his name if they dropped the attempted murder charge."

"Customer?" Eric stopped walking.

"A big name in Charleston. A man who likes boys."

"He wanted to *buy* Danny?" Eric swallowed down the rising bile.

"The feds are involved now. Jenkins may get away with attempted murder, but he'll rot in jail for attempted kidnapping and sex trafficking charges."

43

GEORGINA

Georgie watched her granddaughter head upstairs to change out of her boating clothes. Her sweet girl must have had fun out on the water with that nice Mr. Houston. The smile on her face had said so, like the color in her cheeks and on her nose. Maybe she'd like something nice to eat when she came down.

Georgie toddled back to the kitchen. She'd take her time, give Jeminy a chance to finish doing what she needed, a shower maybe, and come on back down. At the refrigerator, Georgie opened the door and peered in. She stared for a minute, then reached out and drew her hand back. What had she intended to get? Something for someone, obviously.

An open refrigerator meant food, but what food? Had she come looking for something? She wasn't hungry.

Iced tea, maybe. Iced tea sounded good, and Jeminy'd made some, hadn't she? Jeminy was such a good girl, always thoughtful, wanting to help.

Did Jeminy want tea?

Did *she*?

Maybe if she stood here long enough she'd remember.

But it was cold in the refrigerator, and she mustn't let all that cold out. She closed the door and retreated.

Was Jeminy home yet?

Georgie went to the back door and looked out. Oh, both her cats were on the steps, waiting. She should feed them.

That must have been what she'd been doing. Getting cat food. Of course.

And with a smile, she opened the refrigerator door again and reached in for the cat food. But on the way, she noticed a plastic bowl filled with potato salad. Maybe Jeminy would like some potato salad.

She withdrew the bowl and set it on the counter. Then she took a small bite with a fork lying on the counter. It needed something. She thought about that for a while because she didn't want to add too much of anything.

When the phone rang, she was sitting at the kitchen table, a plate of potato salad in front of her, her fork toying with a bite she really didn't want. But she ought to eat. It wouldn't do if she neglected her health.

A cup of tea to go with it would be nice.

The phone rang two more times before it stopped. Georgie was real glad it had stopped. She didn't want to pick it up in case it was her daughter. Dee had said she was coming.

Hadn't she?

But she couldn't if Georgie didn't answer the phone. Dee wouldn't just show up uninvited. She wasn't a child anymore, thinking she lived here. Georgie knew that much.

The sound of footfalls on the steps brought her head up. Who?

Oh, right, Jeminy.

Jeminy'd been gone and now she was back. And Georgie was going to fix her granddaughter something to eat.

She glanced at the fork in her hand and the bowl in front of her, and tears filled her eyes. Pushing it all away, she dropped her head on her now folded arms and let the sobs come.

Someetime in the middle of it all, a crooning voice spoke. "Nana? Oh, Nana," and the girl's head bent to hers, the girl's body came near. "What happened, Nana?"

Georgie sniffled, trying for control. "I forgot. Oh, Jeminy honey, I completely forgot what I was supposed to be doing."

4 4

———

JEMINY

Forgetting the what and where and how,
Knowing the pain, the loss, the worry.
Will the day come, the moments of time, when even that fear will be
gone?

Jeminy bent low over her sobbing grandmother. "But, Nana, there is no *supposed to do*. You don't have anyone waiting for something important from you, and there's not a single thing you *have* to do."

Nana fumbled in her pocket. "But…"

"No buts. Really." Jeminy reached behind her for a tissue from the box on the counter.

After Nana'd wiped at her eyes and delicately blown her nose, she spoke in just above a whisper. "You sure?"

"I'm positive. That's why I'm here, to take away all those worries. Remember how you tended Granddaddy when he was sick and you told him he didn't have to fret about a thing, you were there?"

313

"I do. He was my husband. Of course, I did for him."

"Yes, and I watched how carefully you took care of him. Now it's my turn to tend to you when you need me."

"I don't need that kind of tending." Nana sat a little straighter in her chair.

"I know you don't. But it's what family does, isn't it? We take care of each other in ways needed, like you did me when I was little. This time, I get to give back in whatever way I can."

Reaching out, Nana patted her cheek. "You're a good girl, Jeminy."

"I learned it from you." Jeminy smiled, remembering all the times Nana had been there for her.

"You're my sweet, sweet girl," Nana said, dusting her palms along her thighs. "Speaking of sweets, we need some. I ever teach you how to make a pie? Peaches are still coming in, and there are still apples. We could make an apple pie. I'd love an apple pie, wouldn't you?"

"I would. You and I used to make peach pies when I came summers, and apple sounds wonderful. We may have to take ourselves off to the Food Lion to get supplies, though."

"That's fine. You make a list. Then we can go."

Jeminy'd just slid the two apple pies onto cooler racks when a knock sounded on the back door and a voice called through the screen. "Mrs. Warren? Miss Jeminy?"

"Brisa, hey, honey, come on in." Jeminy pushed open the door for her.

The child stepped inside and grinned at them both. "I just got another CD of my dad singing. You want to hear it?"

"Hang on. Nana's got an old player in the living room. Let me get it."

"You want me to come in there with you?"

"I'll get it. You sit down with Nana."

Jeminy slid Darling's CD into the player. He'd told her he was doing covers for a lot of Christian music, and she suspected these were more examples of those he planned to add to a new album.

Before the music began, his voice came through with a personal note. "Brisa, honey, I'm hoping you'll use your influence to convince Jeminy to join in this new work. We have new people to reach, and I'd like her on my team. What do you think? You, me, and Jeminy?"

Brisa reached over to hit the pause button. "I told him I'd be coming to see you."

Jeminy raised a brow. "And here you are."

Brisa grinned, pushed the play button again, and there was that million-dollar voice crooning songs of worship.

They listened in silence for a couple of minutes, and then Brisa joined in, motioning for Jeminy to sing, too. "I don't know that one," Jeminy said, although it wouldn't be hard to pick up the melody.

Nana's face glowed.

When Darling sang about the Lion of Judah, an image came to Jeminy of power and strength, of a God who could fight her battles if she'd just give them to Him. Rose's promises came to mind, her comfort, her joy, the sheen on her lovely skin and in her dark eyes when she spoke of her Lord, and Jeminy wondered again as she had then. Rose said the Lord had forgiven her, had healed her. And she promised He'd do the same for anyone who came to Him.

Darling's voice promised the same.

When the song ended, Jeminy was surprised to find tears sliding, unheeded, down her cheeks. She turned away and swiped at them, hoping Brisa hadn't seen.

The young girl's hand reached out to rub circles on her back, and Jeminy sighed. "Sorry," she said.

"Why? Because a song about Jesus touched your heart? That's

what worship songs should do, you know. It makes them real," Brisa said, a hint of pride in her voice. "That's what my daddy says, and Henry does, too."

Jeminy turned a puzzled frown toward Brisa. "Makes what real? Songs?"

"My daddy says we shouldn't just sing *about* God. We should sing *to* Him, and if we do that, the words have to mean something to us. Otherwise they're empty, clanging gongs, he called them." She paused. "No, I think I mean cymbals. Clanging cymbals. But he also said gongs."

Jeminy happened to know that scripture because it was spoken so often at weddings, and she'd been to her fair share of those when her college friends fell like dominoes into matrimony. "'If I speak in the tongues of men or of angels,'" she quoted, "'but do not have love, I am only a resounding gong or a clanging cymbal.'"

Brisa clapped and laughed. "That's it!"

"But that talks about loving people."

"Yeah, but my daddy says that you have to love God so you can love people the right way. And if you're singing about God, you have to also sing *to* Him." Brisa looked as if she expected a response, but Jeminy didn't have one to give her. The girl continued. "I know that doesn't sound like the way my daddy used to be. I mean, he wasn't so nice before."

"He certainly didn't talk that way."

"No, I know. But he said he came back to faith. On account of his grandma's prayers mostly, he says, and because of me. He used to sing only church songs when he was a kid, then his father got hold of him and made him famous."

"He is that. Famous, I mean."

"His grandma—my great-grandma, Mama Bea—said God purposed Daddy for great things and that hasn't got anything to do with money. God set him on a high place—fame—so Daddy would use it for God's purpose, not his own gratification."

"Big words and big thoughts, young lady."

Brisa giggled. "I know. But Mama Bea claims it made him so Mama could forgive him, and Henry even kind of likes him."

"I noticed that at the wedding. Amazing, isn't it? And much easier on you."

"I know." The grin lit Brisa's face. "Henry says Daddy's actions show he really has changed, so we should do whatever we can to support him in his walk."

"His walk where?"

Brisa had sobered, but at that she broke into another giggle. "His walk with Jesus, silly!"

"Oh, right. Like in his music."

"Un-huh. So we're hoping you'll help make his stuff even better, you know, because you're so good at it. At writing."

"Predicated on my faith level."

"What's predicated?"

"Based on?" Jeminy hadn't meant it to sound like a question, but Brisa's silence may have meant she didn't catch that.

"I don't know. I guess so, if you mean what my daddy says about worship."

Worship. Jeminy glanced away from the girl's sharp gaze. How could she worship God when she wasn't even convinced He cared —or could care for one such as she?

But was that true any longer?

She shook her head, mirroring her thoughts as they ping-ponged. Divergent thinking wouldn't get her anywhere this time, either.

"Jeminy?" Brisa sounded worried.

"I'm sorry," Jeminy said. "Just thinking too much."

Brisa's puzzled expression remained. "I can leave the CD for you. I have my own copy."

Jeminy focused, planting what she hoped was a reassuring smile on her face. "That would be great. Thanks."

"Okay, then. I'd better go." The girl headed toward the back door.

"Thank you again," Jeminy said.

She'd scared the girl away. Well, kids were resilient. She could make it up to her next time.

Maybe she'd try writing a song that went along with what Darling wanted. She should try, at any rate. After all, Darling was the singer who'd made her music famous.

She was still imagining that shift to inspirational songs when Nana interrupted with, "Shall I fix a cup of tea for each of us, lovey? And maybe a slice of pie. It smells real good, even from here."

"Oh, sure." *Focus,* Jeminy told herself. "I'll put the kettle on."

"Thank you, honey. I think a cup of tea would be very nice."

Jeminy opened the cupboard next to the stove. "Earl Grey or herbal?"

"Oh, I don't know." Nana sounded confused, so Jeminy took out the Earl Grey and waggled the box toward her grandmother.

"I think I'd enjoy this. Earl Grey. Shall I fix one for you, too?"

"Yes, thank you. Please."

While the water came to a boil, and then while the tea steeped, Jeminy tried to concentrate on the small task at hand and not on the larger issues waiting like a big cat honing its claws for the kill. If she worked on songwriting, she might be able to dodge the other nasties, like her own guilt or an ex-boyfriend with larcenous intentions.

They were supposed to go to Annie Mac's in a couple of hours. Nana was taking a nap, but Jeminy couldn't settle. Finally, she carried Gully, paper, and pen to the back porch.

She strummed and hummed and thought, but nothing came. She supposed nothing would if she didn't follow Brisa's advice—or rather, Darling's. She had to write from her heart, and her heart wasn't where it needed to be.

Setting the guitar down, she walked down the steps and out into the garden, which had begun to take shape. When she first arrived, there'd been a mess back here, debris and dead plants. Now things were coming back to life. She'd hired a man with a rototiller, and he'd done wonders to clear and clean and to showcase what had been struggling for life.

She couldn't help but compare the garden with herself, only she needed a lot more tilling before she'd bear fruit again.

That provoked a humorless laugh. Tilling? What would that mean exactly? Because, hey, tillers had blades. Sharp blades.

Not a pretty image.

Eric must have been watching for their arrival because there he was, helping Nana out of the passenger side and grinning across at her. "Ladies, welcome to the creek house!"

"We didn't know you'd be here."

"Take my arm, Mrs. Warren. The ground's a little uneven here." He looked over her shoulder to Jeminy. "Danny and I are hangers on." He nodded down the lane. "You passed the little house we're renting."

"So cute. Nana and I wished we could see inside…" She raised both brows, hopefully.

"Maybe after dinner you can stop by. Danny loves to show off his space."

"How's he navigating with his arm?"

"As if he's always had a cast to sling around."

"Amazing." She reached for one of the apple pies and carried it with her.

Clay manned the grill, kids were down by the water, and Annie Mac waved from inside the French doors. "Hey, Mrs. Warren, Jeminy," Clay said. "Come on up and have a seat. Maybe Eric can take your drink orders in to Annie Mac."

"We've brought a contribution, one of Nana's apple pies."

"The kind of guests we like best," Clay said with a laugh.

They'd eaten and Annie Mac was busy with the children. Nana had her eyes closed as she sat in a comfortable deck chair. Jeminy stood looking out at the creek when Clay spoke from behind her. "You have a moment?"

"Sure."

He nodded to Eric, and they led the way off the deck and down toward the creek. "What's up?" she asked when they stopped.

"The man who ran you off the road, Dalton Jenkins—"

"—The foster father from whom I rescued Danny—"

Clay continued. "They arrested him and eventually got him to confess. He was after Danny, and you got in the way."

"Why did he want Danny?"

"It's a rather long story," Clay said.

"I have time."

All her maternal instincts had been roused. Thank heavens, Eric had saved him from that foster family. And thank God, someone, something had made that man's bullets go astray, had taken him to a gas station where they had a working camera, had allowed Eric to identify him, had let the police trace his truck and find him.

All those coincidences couldn't just be luck.

Eric's gaze had locked with hers every time she glanced his way. Had he been checking to see how she'd taken the news? Or, she thought with a lift of her spirits, checking her out?

That's what she'd found herself doing. But, really? What were they, in high school?

She wasn't interested in connecting with another man, not after Rand—and certainly not with a man who knew so many of her secrets.

But, oh, when his eyes laughed and those crinkles showed up, both at his eyes and around his lips, or even when the smile stayed in his eyes, it did something to her insides. He'd age well, wouldn't he, those laugh lines adding character.

And, no, she wouldn't examine what that might mean.

Her discomfort didn't keep her from gushing over the tiny house Eric and Danny rented. By the time they'd left the Dougherty's, the light had faded to dusk, and the view had silvered but was still magnificent.

Eric had ushered her inside, and their hands had touched. Not good. Not good at all.

What had that zing meant? Had he noticed and felt it too?

"Lovely place," she'd said as she helped Nana back to the car for the trip into Beaufort and home.

She worried her bottom lip as she drove across Ward Creek, then North River. Her grandmother's voice sounded plaintive when she said she needed a bathroom. "We're almost there. Can you hold it?"

"I should have gone before we left. I shouldn't have waited." Poor thing sounded panicky.

She didn't like the thought of pulling off on the side of the road, so all she could do was continue to reassure Nana and hope for the best.

"Jesus, Jesus, God help me," Nana'd whispered in a voice that Jeminy heard clearly.

"Yes, please."

When she finally led her nearly frantic grandmother into the house and to the downstairs bathroom, Jeminy said a quick *Thank You.* From then on, she decided, she'd remember the need before they ever got in a car.

45

RAND

Rand clicked off his laptop and sat back in his padded desk chair, a whistle of satisfaction the only sound in the room. He'd found her.

Amazing how everything turned up on the Internet if you just kept searching. He should never have wasted time and money with that shyster investigator. All he'd had to do today was type her name in the search engine, and there she'd been, front and center of an investigation into a drive-by shooting incident.

And didn't that just serve her right? Too bad the guy had missed.

This discovery shifted his focus from Maggie, whose phone number he'd been calling from various aliases—thanks to that delicious app that let him use multiple numbers from the same phone. Badgering Maggie had felt like payback, even if it hadn't given him what he wanted.

No, he'd gotten that from his own efforts.

A feeling of euphoria washed over him. This would be the turning point. He knew it.

He headed downstairs to pour himself a beer. Arthur should be about ready to quit work, and wouldn't he enjoy the tidbit

Rand had unearthed? Arthur's last words before he'd gone to a meeting in the city had been ominous and had sent Rand back to his search. "You fix this, Rand. I'm not going to have my name smeared along with yours."

Arthur was going to be thrilled because he, Rand, was on the way to doing just that. Jeminy was such a weakling. She'd bend to his will again.

As he poured his beer into a cooled mug, he forgot that Jeminy'd been the one trying to topple his castle. She'd been the one to sic the police on him.

The staff had left for the day. Arthur didn't like people who might sell secrets lurking around in the evenings; for parties, he had them prepare everything early and then come in for clean-up in the mornings. They didn't even question his relationship to their boss; Arthur'd given him his own bedroom, a friend staying for a while.

That rankled, but, as those in the "know" knew the truth and he got to live in the luxury of this house without having to spend a penny of his own, he'd kept his mouth shut.

Although, he hated it when Arthur brought home the occasional double-X-chromosomed beauty. "To keep up my image," he'd said, smiling maliciously at Rand's scowl. "After all, you enjoyed Jeminy all those years."

Rand shrugged. He had, until she'd stopped being the cash cow he'd needed because her music had turned all melancholy after the abortion. What a wimp. But he wasn't about to let her have some kid that would tie him up financially for years to come.

The front door opened and closed again. Rand leaned against the granite counter and waited for Arthur to call out.

Keys dropped on the marble top of the hall table, and leather soles slapped against the hardwood until they hit carpet.

"Arthur? That you?"

Arthur walked in and handed him an envelope. "Yours, I believe."

Caught by the stiffness in Arthur's tone, Rand pocked the letter without looking at it.

Arthur opened a cupboard and took down a glass, still not looking at Rand, and then dropped in a few ice cubes before pouring Scotch from the decanter at the bar.

Finally, he turned, his black eyes blazing. "I got a call today from a client." He took a long swig. "A very influential client. One who has made me a good deal of money."

"Oh?"

"Can you guess what he said?"

"How could I?" Rand tried to sound relaxed, carefree. He was pretty sure sweat had started to bead on his forehead.

"He mentioned some documentation the police have in their hot little hands. Some rather damning papers."

"Really?"

"I told you to take care of things."

"I'm working on it. As a matter of fact," Rand said, trying to infuse his words with conviction, "I have located Jeminy. She's gone back to her grandmother's in North Carolina, and all I have to do is get her to admit she falsified those papers. Whatever papers she gave the police."

"All you have to do…"

"Yes. Considering I know nothing about other accounts or whatever, she must have been the one to lie. She probably wanted me out of the picture so she could take all the money."

"You think?"

"I do. That has to be it." He had to make Arthur believe him. After all, the accounts were very well hidden.

"Well, let's just say that how you solve that is between you and her. I'm afraid your time here has come to an end."

"An end?"

"I believe I spoke in English."

"But…"

"I expect you packed and out by the time I've showered and

changed. That should give you just under an hour." He began to leave the room, then stopped, still with his back to Rand. "Leave the keys on the hall table on your way out. Good thing you haven't unloaded all those items from your old apartment. I'm pleased you have somewhere to go."

And with that, Arthur carried his glass upstairs. Minutes later, his bedroom door closed.

Rand stood rooted in place for long minutes, contemplating his next move. How on earth was he expected to get his clothes, his computer, his *stuff* out in an hour?

First things first. He went to the den, grateful that once upon a time Arthur had been looped enough to tell him the combination to a locked cabinet. From this, he took out a small jar Arthur kept filled and the handgun Arthur hid there. Unregistered, Arthur had said. Untraceable. For just in case.

Rand hadn't asked what the "just in case" might be, but he figured he had more need of that insurance than Arthur, now that so many "just in cases" seemed to be lobbing bombs at him.

Next, he went to his bedside table and collected his stash of meds, stuffing them in the suitcase he pulled from the back of the closet before adding his clothes. He'd never fit them all in this one case, so, cringing, he got a plastic garbage bag for his shoes and another for items that wouldn't wrinkle.

He'd never forgive Arthur for this. It was one thing to break up with him. It was quite another to make him resort to garbage bags.

It was dark by the time Rand unlocked the door to the apartment he'd shared with Jeminy. The place hadn't changed since he'd searched for clues to her whereabouts. Anger rose, and his blood pressure surged. This was all her fault.

Every single thing that had gone wrong in his life had started with that pitiful waif he'd rescued in Nashville.

Fine, maybe "waif" was a misnomer for someone whose height almost matched his. He should have guessed she'd turn into a whiney brat when she didn't get her way.

She owed her success—all of it—to him and his salesmanship. If he hadn't come along, she'd still be singing and trying to peddle her songs in those dives with too much competition banging on the same closed doors.

She owed him.

So, he'd taken what he was owed and maybe topped it off, but she couldn't prove a thing. And neither could the cops.

Now, she'd ruined things with Arthur, just as the two of them were making an agency comeback by signing new talent, some he'd found. *He,* not Arthur.

Arthur was taking them all. "My agency, my rules," he said a few days ago when Rand had asked to be made a partner.

Everyone used him. Jeminy. Arthur. His own family. Used and tossed.

At least he'd taken some of his back from Jeminy.

Too bad, really, that crazy driver who'd shot at her had failed. Rand would be rich now if she'd been killed.

If he could only find the guy, he'd thank him for at least getting her name in the papers and thus enabling him to locate her. Not that it was likely to do him much good unless he could figure out a good payback.

So, she owed him.

He rolled his suitcase to the bedroom, leaving the trash bags where they sat in the living room. What a mess. She'd left the bed unmade. She could at least have cleaned up the packing material scattered on the floor.

He almost felt sorry for the grandmother, having such a slob move into her house. He bet the old lady wouldn't put up with Jeminy's ways for long.

Unless Jeminy put on a good show to get some of the loot he was pretty sure Grandma had. That would make sense.

Move in, take over, maybe even hurry the old gal's demise. Not hard to believe.

Not hard at all.

His first order of business was to take a hit or two, then call for pizza delivery. Both would take the edge off, one for his nerves, the other hunger.

He didn't remember the envelope until he undressed for bed. He was feeling a tad hazy but not muddled enough to impair his reading ability.

The letter inside was from the insurance company he'd been paying for that policy on Jeminy, a cancellation notice.

It seemed Jeminy'd found him out.

He dropped his head and then fell onto the unmade bed. He needed to sleep. Forget.

Until tomorrow. Then he'd come up with a plan.

If only that drive-by had finished her off.

46

JEMINY

I love you, I love you not,
I leave you, I come running back.
Trust me, my darling, whether you've reason or not.
Trust me, my darling.

As of that afternoon, Jeminy'd received three phone calls with no one on the other end. It could have been a telemarketer unable to make his computer line work. Maybe. Or three wrong numbers. Not likely.

She blocked each number anyway. And then she heard from Maggie.

"You okay?" Maggie asked.

"Other than surviving a madman shooting us off the road? Yeah, I'm fine."

"Tell me." Maggie would want details.

When Jeminy'd finished the telling and dealt with Maggie's suggestion that she move out of North Carolina as fast as she could, she asked what had been going on in Maggie's life.

"A lot of the same. Except Rand keeps calling. I block one number, he comes up with another one. He's seriously looking for you. And—"

Jeminy stopped her. "Hold on. I've been getting random calls with no one at the other end. You think he's behind those?"

"Could be. From what the gossip mill says, Arthur threw him out."

"Do the gossips say why?"

"Hints only, but Rand's name has been bandied about as being a *persona non grata.*"

"He's not going to like that."

"Which might make him dangerous."

"What are you saying?" Jeminy'd had those same thoughts, but to hear it from Maggie jacked up her nerves.

"I don't know, but if he's losing clout because the police are investigating him, he may become desperate. And, think about it, if there's a record of that shooting incident, he may be able to find you with a little effort."

"Thanks for the warning." Jeminy sighed. "I'll let the police here know he's looking for me."

"Good." Maggie let out a low whistle. "And you thought you were moving to the sleepy south where not much happens. Just goes to show..."

"My nana needs me."

"Just stay safe and alive to take care of her then."

"Thanks for the heads-up. If you find out anything more, will you call?"

"Of course."

After they said their goodbyes, Jeminy phoned Clay and gave him the update. And tried to forget the messes fomenting around her. After all, what good had worry ever done her?

She worked in the back garden, sat on the back porch with Nana, tried unsuccessfully to write a song for Brisa and Darling, napped, cleaned, cooked, returned to the garden, strummed her guitar… The Internet offered nothing, and she didn't even have the sort of girlfriends she could invite over for coffee because the friends she'd made all had very busy lives, and not a one of them was single.

By the time her phone rang again, she had a good funk going. She was ready for a fight. With anyone.

"What?" she said, putting mad behind the word.

"Hey, babe."

Him?

Rand's smarmy voice tried to sound conciliatory, but that wasn't going to work. He oozed something. "I've been thinking about you."

She wanted to gag. "Oh yeah, why?" Because your guy failed to kill me? Because you won't get that insurance money for my death?

"Oh, maybe because I miss you."

"You miss me. Really?"

"Absolutely. Biggest mistake of my life, moving out."

"Rand. You didn't just leave." She would not scream. Instead, she said, "What, did your big shot lover toss you out? Did he discover you couldn't bring enough to the table?" She paused for emphasis. "Or that you steal."

"No, of course not. I left him when I realized how much you still mean to me." His voice sounded as if he'd swallowed lubricant before phoning.

Pretty picture, that. "You're a liar. Oh, and that insurance policy you had on me? Canceled. The police were very interested in that piece of the puzzle." She grinned. This felt good. "Bye-bye now."

"Police?" Up went his voice, two octaves up.

"What did you expect, Rand? Hmmm?" She waited one beat and repeated, "Bye."

"Wait, Jeminy, honey, hang on."

But her thumb was already touching the disconnect button.

When he called again, she silenced her phone.

And smiled.

———

Yesterday, it had been Rand's call. Today, her father's, and she'd told him the highway shooter had been arrested and charged.

Her father had then said they were driving over to see her. Both of them. Would be there that afternoon.

Jeminy flicked a dust rag over one of the living room lamp shades and distracted herself from thoughts of a confrontation with her mother by picturing Rand peeking out the window of whatever dwelling he now inhabited, worrying about being watched and caught for whatever nasty scheme he had in the works. She hummed, she grinned, she actually chortled.

It was about time he paid for his corruption.

She'd made it to the kitchen when the doorbell chimed, and all she wanted to do was hide. They were here.

Daddy had promised Mother wouldn't kick up a fuss or upset Nana, but he'd never been able to control her before, so what made him imagine he could now? Had he threatened her? Taken away a toy?

What a thought to have about one's parents.

Nana, sipping a cup of tea, looked up at the sound. "Who is it?"

"Daddy, I think." She wouldn't worry Nana by mentioning anyone else. "I'll go find out."

She opened the door and grinned at the sight of the tall, strong man who stood before her. "Daddy."

He stepped in and grabbed her. "Sweetheart, it's so good to see you."

Forgetting everything and everyone else, she hugged him back, wincing only slightly from her bruises, leaning in close to his neck. Even if she'd been blind, she'd have recognized him by his scent, a dry citrus mixed with clean. "Oh, Daddy, I'm so glad…" she began until tears filled her eyes and words wouldn't come.

"Sweet girl, I'm here. How are you? Hurting still?"

"A little. Nothing to worry about."

His arms tightened once more, and then she peered over his shoulder. Her mother was climbing out of the car.

Nana shuffled in from the kitchen. "Who is it, Jeminy?"

"It's Daddy. With Mother."

Nana directed her smile from Jeminy's father to the woman approaching behind him. "How lovely to see you both." Manners and grace were bred in Southern women like Nana. They should have been bred into Nana's daughter, but at least her grandmother didn't seem to remember any tension.

"Would you like to come in and sit a spell? Perhaps Jeminy would get us some tea."

"Thank you," said Mother, "that's lovely of you to offer, but I'd prefer ice water for now. We stopped for lunch and Larry flooded me with tea."

Daddy's arm went around Mother's back as he answered. "Water for me, too, honey."

"Nana, why don't you take them in, and I'll be right back."

Jeminy set plates and slices from their second apple pie on the tray, along with Nana's reheated tea and ice water for the rest of them. All she had to do was keep her smile pasted on and be polite while she served drinks and pie.

"I shouldn't." But Mother accepted a plate and forked a bite. "You always could make a better pie than anyone else, Mama."

Nana beamed over her teacup. "Thank you, sweetheart. I made it just for you."

Which was a nice thing to say, but not a true one. Still, that might be what Nana imagined had actually happened.

Mother queried Nana on her garden and, when they'd set their empty plates down, asked Nana to show her what she'd been doing with it.

Nana popped right up. "Oh, yes."

Daddy cleared his throat, and, in response, Mother sighed and said, "I remember."

"Will they be okay?" Jeminy moved closer to her father after the back door closed.

"I think so. Your mother has promised not to upset your grandmother. And she has agreed to see a therapist as long as it's couple's therapy."

"Really." The same mother who'd said she never would and didn't need to see anyone but her tennis instructor?

"Couple's therapy, the counselor told me, means meeting with us separately, too, and that's where I'm praying your mother will actually be able to find truth."

"Wouldn't that be a treat." Jeminy didn't make it a question. "She has lived in some delusional alternate reality for so long, I'm not sure she'll recognize truth if it hits her head on."

"Maybe not, but I'm trusting this will be able to help her get to the root of her obsessions and guilt."

"And get over the idea you're cheating on her?"

"That, too. She needs to learn trust again, but that's probably the harder thing to achieve and may take a while."

Yeah, Jeminy could believe that. She wasn't doing so well in the trust department herself. "So what about the lawsuit thing?"

"On hold." He looked down at his hands.

On hold—what did that mean? "What, is she stopping to take a breath? Waiting on something else?"

He shrugged.

"Money?" Jeminy stared into his face. "You put the brakes on?"

With a sigh, he nodded. "I had to get a little heavy-handed."

"Money does seem to be her language."

"And loss of it puts her in a panic. You'd think that would make her a hoarder. It hasn't."

"Why, I wonder. I mean, Nana and Grandpa always had

enough, didn't they? She wasn't starving or anything. What made her the way she is?"

He shook his head. "I wish I knew. I was aware when we married that she was very taken with my family and the comfortable life she could expect, but I never thought much of it. I suppose you take for granted what you've always had."

"Yes, but she'd always been comfortable, hadn't she? Maybe this house wasn't as big as some of its neighbors, but I never heard of anyone going without." Jeminy shook her head. "Enough wasn't enough for her, I guess. She wanted prestige, and Beaufort doesn't offer much of that—or only what can be found within its limited society."

"If your grandfather hadn't left plenty, would your mother be so worried about that inheritance falling into the wrong hands?"

"Like mine and Isa's." Jeminy blew a huff of air between her lips. "Whatever. I think Granddaddy invested wisely for his and Nana's old age, so maybe he didn't spend as freely as his children would have preferred. He grew up on a small farm and was the first to graduate from college. I remember his stories about his family and how proud he was that he'd made it this far. Occasionally, though, he mentioned he could have risen to prominence if he'd stayed in Raleigh." She paused for a moment. "He still seemed happy to me, but, then, I was just a kid."

"I never heard him complain," her father said.

"Sometimes he'd sound wistful, but he loved being here, where he could go fishing whenever he wanted, instead of being always tied to his desk in the city." Jeminy remembered sitting on his lap as he drove his boat out the channel and thinking this was a great life, the wind in her face, the sun shimmering on the water, her granddaddy laughing when they bounced over another boat's wake or when he helped her reel in a fish, no matter what its size. How could her mother have needed more? "You think Mother and her brother picked up on those moments of longing and missed the moments of fun?"

"Could be. It's always about choices, isn't it? Your grandfather chose his boat and his view even if he could have made more money in a big firm in Raleigh. Maybe what seemed to be longing was merely appreciating what he had as he weighed it against the other. Your nana seems to have been contented here."

"She was. And she is. Mother always said she was glad she'd gotten out of Beaufort. And Uncle Andrew felt the same way when he was alive. He was always too busy. I know it hurt Nana."

"She's never had a bad word to say about either of them, not that I've heard."

"Or about anyone."

Jeminy glanced out the front windows before turning back. "I'm sorry you've had to deal with this. Sometimes Mother makes me so angry."

"She has failed you, and that's on her, but it's also because she has a hole in her heart that only God can fill."

"Mmm." She didn't need more of her father's excuses for a mother who loved only herself.

Daddy smiled sadly and patted Jeminy's hand. "I know you think she's beyond change, but I don't. Anything is possible in the Lord."

Jeminy shrugged. "If you say so. I've never seen it."

"I love your mother, but I'm not blind. Sometimes it's hard to like her." He sighed heavily. "I hope, honey, that you find a partner who can be your best friend, one you can trust to respond with humor instead of anger when things get tough. Marrying merely because you fall in love is sometimes hard going, but I made a lifetime commitment, which means sticking to my vows in the hard times as well as in the easy ones."

She shot him a quizzical look. "Did you guys ever have easy times?"

"In the beginning. Many a time since then I've had to ask God to love your mother through me because on my own, love seems to leak right out."

"Interesting way to put it." It was, the idea of love leaking. Because hers for Rand hadn't leaked; it had flooded. All she'd been left with was guilt and regret. "What if I'd married Rand? Would I have been expected to love him after he deceived me?"

"Rand made those choices on his own, and I can't help but think you didn't marry because you were being spared that additional grief."

Had she been? "If so, I wish the sparing had come earlier, before I met him."

His laugh held no humor. "If wisdom only came before we had to learn it through mistakes," he said, a wistful note in his voice. "Have you learned anything from your mistakes with him? Would you ever be tempted again to fall for someone whose moral code was so different from yours? From the way I taught you?"

"I hope not. But I don't know when, if ever, I'll want another relationship."

Daddy patted her hand. "First things first. Let's make sure Rand is out of your life, and then you can think in future terms."

"Yes, sir." She looked toward the back of the house. "You think we ought to check on them? Make sure everyone's okay?"

"We can. Or we can make plans for dinner out and trust your mother to behave herself."

She sighed and then pecked his cheek. "What a lovely thought. Out and about on the town."

ERIC

"Maybe we should have called ahead," Eric suggested when Clay pulled up behind a car he didn't recognize. He'd come at Clay's request, but he didn't want them barging in on company.

"Let's see," Clay said. "

Jeminy opened the door to their knock, her eyes lighting when she saw who it was. "Hey, guys. What a nice surprise." She waved them toward the parlor. "Come meet my daddy."

A distinguished looking older gentleman with a definite twinkle in his blue eyes greeted them. When he learned how they fit into Jeminy's world, he was especially welcoming. "I've spoken to your counterpart in Craven County, Lieutenant. Is there more news?"

"Come, take a seat." Jeminy sat down beside her father and leaned forward as if eager to know what they had to say.

"May we speak freely?" Clay asked.

"Of course," Jeminy said. "I don't have secrets from my father."

Clay nodded. "Although we have Jenkins under lock and key, we're continuing to look into your friend, Mr. Radcliff—"

"Ex-friend."

"Ex, right. I've been in touch with the detectives in L.A. about the case they've been building against him. I understand he also fraudulently continued a life insurance policy, which you have recently canceled."

Jeminy straightened. "And Rand emptied what had been the household account of twenty-some thousand dollars by using a POA I must have given him once upon a time—although I have no memory of doing so. Still, he was obviously good at forgery, and he probably had contacts to work the notary thing."

"Why didn't you go after him for that money?" her dad asked.

"I should have done something right away, but he made me so sick, I only wanted to be rid of him." She nodded toward Eric. "That's why I hired Eric to cut all those ties and help me get my life back."

Mr. Buchanan draped an arm around his daughter and pulled her close. "Sounds like you're reclaiming some of that strength I remember."

"I hope so, Daddy."

"Seems to me," Clay said, "Mr. Radcliff may have outsmarted himself right into a prison sentence for a whole slew of crimes." His gaze moved to each of them, returning finally to Jeminy. "Can you think of anything else that might help build the case against him?"

"Not really. I hope I didn't mess things up by telling him the police know about that insurance scam."

If Eric hadn't been watching Clay, he might not have noticed the swift control his friend exercised over his expression before he spoke. "He phoned you?"

"I think his boyfriend kicked him out. He made some excuse about having left Arthur because he realized how much he missed me."

"I assume from this that he knows where you are," Clay said.

Jeminy looked stricken, and her father patted her fisted hand where it lay on her thigh before saying, "Rand is a man with no morals and a lot of ambition."

Eric agreed. "Exactly. The paperwork I sent out for Jeminy coupled with her new contract with Darling—if he learns about that—has to be making him fear for his financial future. And without a sugar daddy, what's a man to do?"

Voices came from the back of the house. Jeminy's father said, "My wife has been outside, inspecting the gardens." He glanced at his watch. "For a woman who hasn't a single green finger, she's shown remarkable patience." And then ruefully, "I hope."

Eric raised his brows at Jeminy. Worry lines creased her face. "Is that likely?"

Mr. Buchanan answered him. "Deborah promised not to upset her mother. We'll see."

One voice sounded loud in the hall. "Let's go sit in here, Mama."

Mrs. Buchanan stopped abruptly at the room's entrance. Her husband had moved to greet her. Eric and Clay both stood in front of their chairs.

"Come, let me introduce you to Jeminy's guests."

"Mama," Mrs. Buchanan said, ignoring him and pulling Mrs. Warren to her side, "why don't you sit down here, on the couch. Or perhaps that gentleman will change with you so you may have your very own chair." She frowned at Clay.

"Of course." He moved quickly toward the fireplace, out of the way.

"Oh, no," Mrs. Warren said. "I'm comfortable anywhere, please."

"Well, Mama, you're always telling me you like to sit where you can watch outside, so let me help you."

Jeminy's lips were drawn in a tight line as her mother hovered and propelled. Her father stepped in. "Deborah, Georgina's fine. Come meet these gentlemen."

Her smile showed teeth when she met Clay, but it thinned at

Eric's name, and she glared through slitted eyes. "My mother's lawyer?"

"Yes, ma'am. I have that privilege." Kill her with kindness?

"He's also my lawyer, Mother," Jeminy said. "Did you and Nana have fun in the garden?"

Mrs. Buchanan pulled a second chair close to her mother's. "I see you've been helping her tidy it up."

"I think it's time I got back to work," Eric said. "Clay?"

"Coming."

He turned to Jeminy. "Let me know if you have any questions —or just want to talk."

"So you can add to your billable hours?" Jeminy's mother was a piece of work.

"Mother."

Mr. Buchanan extended a hand. "It was a pleasure to meet you, Eric." And then to Clay, "Thank you both for coming."

Clay shook his hand. "If you find out anything more, let me know."

"You, too, please."

Jeminy followed the men to the front door. "Thank you. Call me?"

"I will," Eric said. And then, more quietly, "How long's your mother staying?"

Jeminy's father stepped into the hall. "We're taking the ladies out to dinner, then it's home to Chapel Hill."

"Have a safe trip." Eric walked out with Clay to his car. "Now we've met the dragon. Do you think her husband's up to her weight?"

"Good question. He seems to be a man of faith, so that's where our hope has to be, certainly for Jeminy and Mrs. Warren."

"Either that, or you and I will have to play St. George and raise our swords to slay the dragon."

Clay laughed. "Or perhaps we should speak words of peace and prayer to send the demons back where they belong."

"Ah, yes. Your faith speaking. I'm working on mine, but I've had very little practice."

"The Lord's bigger than anything the enemy tries to bring against us, so He's the one we can trust with everything we confront."

"Like bullets coming for Jeminy."

"Like those. I admit it's sometimes hard in my job to keep God at the forefront, and I have to spend a lot of time in prayer so I don't get in the way of His purposes."

"Thank you for your encouragement." Eric glanced up the street. "I'll walk back to my office. See you later." He waved and set off. Then he turned. "Let me know what you find out."

"Soon as I know more and am free to talk about it."

4 8

JEMINY

The truth, the truth, to know and see and hear it,
If only she could learn it,
With no more hiding out.

She watched from the door's sidelight as Eric waved Clay on his way. She couldn't let Eric just leave like that—although she wouldn't ask herself why not. "Daddy, I'll be right back."

He shooed her. "Don't worry about us."

Eric was halfway down the block when she got to the sidewalk. At her call, he turned and waited. She didn't run, she wouldn't, but she did pick up her pace, glad now for long legs that cut the distance between them quickly.

"What's up?" he asked when she got to his side.

She tried not to blush. She'd practically run after this man, and now what? "I-I'm sorry about my mother."

He shrugged. "You knew she wouldn't be pleased with either of us."

Jeminy looked down at the sidewalk. "It's hard, having your own mother hate you."

"I doubt she hates you. I imagine it's more that she hates herself."

She raised her head. "That's what my father said. Maybe it's true, and if so, it probably got worse when my brother died."

"Your brother?"

"My twin. Oliver. We called him Olli." She paused. Would she ever get over the hurt of that loss? "Mother was supposed to pick us up from school if it rained, but she was late. Olli rode his bike through the woods, and he skidded, flew off, and hit his head. It was the night of our twelfth birthday."

"I am so sorry." He took her hand. "Come. Let's sit a few minutes." He led her to a bench looking out over the water and turned toward her as they sat. "I know about having a twin. If something had happened to Henry…"

"Yes." She'd forgotten they had that in common.

He paused a moment. "I like your father."

His words surprised her. Not that Eric liked her dad, but that he segued there from talk about twins.

"He likes you, too. I know he's glad you and Clay are helping."

"And God, it seems."

She grinned. "Isn't that wild? That idea of God's timing during that shooting incident—Danny showing his face at that moment so that I turned the wheel?"

"It is. Everything that's been happening keeps pointing to trusting in the Lord." He seemed to be struggling for the right words. "I feel as if God is trying to get my attention. Starting with Danny."

She'd been feeling the same tug, hadn't she? "Tell me more about your son."

"When his mother took him away and wouldn't let me see him, my heart nearly broke. Not from loss of her. I mean, I'd been willing to try to make the marriage work." He shrugged before continuing. "She wasn't interested. But that little boy had stolen my heart from the moment of his birth."

"He's a real cutie. And smart."

"I'm still learning how to be a dad, but when I look at him and see him smile, it feels pretty amazing."

"You saved him."

"I think we were both saved. I was pretty self-absorbed before Danny. Now I can't be."

"Kind of like me having to come home to take care of Nana. Interesting, both of us forced to look past our preoccupations to care for someone else."

His hand moved to her shoulder, and he squeezed gently. "You know, don't you, that I'm attracted to you."

Oh, my. Words. He'd put it into words.

What was she supposed to say? She couldn't look at him. "Mmm…"

He waited. Finally, she braved a glance at his face, into his eyes, those startlingly blue eyes.

"I know. And I to you. But—"

"It's too early for you."

"It should be. I've made such a mess of so many things." And he didn't know the worst. Here they were, talking about God, and God hated what she'd done. The abortion. On that thought, she stood. "I should go back. My parents…"

"Yes, of course." He followed her back to the sidewalk. "May I call you later?"

She should say no. She should. "I guess. Sure."

"I'll watch to see you get home safely."

At that, she grinned. "How gallant. Thank you."

He smiled back. "We wouldn't want to test those angels if we don't have to."

She didn't have far to walk back to the house, but it was time enough for her stomach to wish it were empty of whatever stirred within.

He was attracted to her.

She'd known it, seen it. She'd even returned it.

But it couldn't be. He was good and kind and intelligent and free of the baggage she carried. He also seemed to be a man growing in faith, which soon would have him talking like Clay and all that crowd. Like Rose and Daddy.

She didn't deserve Eric or any of them.

She pressed a fist against her belly, trying to push out a pain that made her worry she'd lose her stomach's contents right here, in the bushes. She hurried into the house.

A raised voice from the kitchen stopped her. She peeked into the parlor where Nana sat with her eyes closed, her head leaning back against the chair, her hands peacefully in her lap. At least the voices hadn't roused her.

Jeminy didn't want to walk in on her parents arguing, so she tiptoed upstairs to her room. Her father had tried to get Mother to behave. Obviously, she'd run out of being-good steam and had reverted to her former self.

Jeminy felt sorry for her daddy, but not sorry enough to interfere. She had no desire to go out to dinner with her parents, and from now on her mother could stay home if she was going to behave badly. Daddy could either manage her or not, but Jeminy had enough going on in her life and didn't need the added stress Deborah Buchanan brought to the table.

She kicked off her shoes and lay down on her bed. She'd just close her eyes for a little while, and maybe when she woke, only Nana would still be here.

If only. She couldn't sleep, and her imagination was busily peopling the back of her eyelids with memories.

Images flittered of Olli catching tadpoles in a stream back behind their house and trying to convince her it was fun; of Olli's big glasses sliding down his nose and Daddy trying to fix them so they fit better; of her standing in front of her slighter brother in the face of bullies who'd sooner push her down than turn from their quarry; and of Olli telling her brilliant stories he'd written while she talked of how proud she'd be when he made the bestseller lists. She would sing and he would write and they'd live together forever.

She swiped at tears that dampened her pillow. At least she'd remembered good times and not the last time.

"Rose said you're in Heaven waiting, sweet brother of mine. If I can figure out how to get there, I'll see you then. I will."

She spoke the words quietly, wishing there were some crack in the realms between earth and Heaven that would let him hear. The idea that he was someplace real and waiting, along with her baby and all the too-soon-dead children made her long to know this God of Rose's. The God of her daddy and Clay and Darling.

Jesus, who supposedly cracked dimensions with an invisible shield that deflected those bullets. Jesus, about whom Rose had told story after story to her willing self when she'd been young.

Why had she turned away?

Because she'd wanted her way more than she'd wanted God's? Because of the promises of a care-for-nobody man?

Had she been weak or had it been something else?

A knock on her door interrupted these thoughts. "Jeminy, honey?" her daddy called.

She sat up, wiping her cheeks with her fingers and grabbing a tissue from the bedside table to finish the job. Swinging her legs off the bed, she said, "Come in."

Her father pushed open the door and entered. "How are you feeling?"

"Okay. I don't really want to go out to dinner, though, if you don't mind. I'm sorry."

"I'm sure your mother is sorry for her outburst."

"I'm sure she is, if you say so. But I don't think I can sit across the table from her and pretend, Daddy."

He sat down next to her, his expression sorrowful. "Maybe the counseling will help. I hoped for a miracle, but she's battling things that are deeply seated."

"It's not your fault."

"It's mine for letting it go on this long. I remember when you were little we had a child-rearing book that suggested we draw lines in the sand early to stop bad behavior. I should have drawn a line in the sand for your mother years ago, with consequences for crossing it."

Intrigued, Jeminy asked, "What would have been the line? I mean, for a wife?"

He laughed without humor. "I know. It sounds a little dramatic, doesn't it? We don't live in a time when wives have to obey their husbands. But she made life hard for you—and for me—after Olli died. I should have insisted on counseling for all of us, individual and as a family."

"You were dealing with his death, too."

"I know, but as her husband and your father, I had an obligation to act like the head of the household. I failed. I've been working through all of this in a men's group I attend, and getting counseling on my own. And I have a lot to make up for."

She reached out and took his hand. "Not to me."

"Yes, to you, too, honey. If I'd done what I needed to push your mother to get help, she might have learned how to forgive herself and to show you love. I regret that deeply." He sighed. "Instead of being the husband your mother needed, I allowed her to find other ways of coping."

"Like drinking too much."

"And growing bitter and jealous. I'm deeply ashamed."

Jeminy wrapped her arms around him and laid her head against him. "I love you so much."

His arms encircled her. "And I love you. Do you think you can have patience with your parents while we figure things out?"

"Of course, Daddy."

"And will you pray for us both?"

She backed away and looked at him. "You think God hears my prayers?" Wasn't there something in the Bible about sin blocking the way to God?

"Of course, He does."

"What about if you do something really horrible? Can He hear you then?"

"God hears and knows everything. If we sin, he wants us to confess, to admit we've done wrong, and to repent. Repenting doesn't just mean saying sorry. It means to quit the behavior, to go in the opposite direction. We also have to forgive others who hurt us. These things will free us to hear Him and be in a right relationship to Him."

That was about as clear as mud. "Right relationship?"

"Think about it. When you were little, if you did something you knew was bad, you were afraid to look me in the eye, right? You were worried I'd find out and be angry, maybe even punish you, and you hid from me. But when you came to me and said how sorry you were you'd done that thing, what did I do?"

"You asked if I planned to do it again."

"And when you said no—that 'repent' part I mentioned—what happened then?"

"You held out your arms and showed me how much you loved me."

"Were you then able to come to me openly?"

She grinned. "Yes, sir."

"Same with God."

If only she could believe that. "I hope you're right."

"Oh, honey, you think if I'd come to the realization of my

faults in a vacuum I'd be able to stand here before you and confess them without falling apart? If I hadn't already taken them to the Lord, I'd have a hard time bringing them to you—or to your mother. I know I shocked her when I told her what I'd realized, but it was a beginning, I think, to healing for us. I hope for her, too."

"You're amazing."

"No, but I have an amazing God who loves me and you and your mother, and He wants each of us to be free and healed."

"Will you give me ten minutes?"

"You mean, you'll go to dinner with us?"

"Nana would enjoy it, and I should try, right?"

He leaned over and kissed her cheek. "I'll go make sure your grandmother and mother will be ready to go when you are."

As he closed the door behind him, Jeminy shut herself in the bathroom and stared at her reflection in the wall mirror. "You, my girl, have some thinking to do."

Perhaps intentional thought would work better than her mind spilling images of mistakes and regret.

Perhaps.

48

DEBORAH

She'd been good. She had. One glass of wine with dinner, polite conversation only, and a little attention to her mother, which seemed to make everyone happy, even if she'd been bored senseless talking about dying plants and whatever else her mother'd wanted. It hadn't been much better at dinner, but what had she expected?

It's what came from living in a backwater town like this. Her mother'd cut herself off from any worthwhile society, and while Chapel Hill didn't offer much, there were powerful people who belonged to the country club. Didn't she play tennis with the lieutenant governor's wife?

She certainly hoped Larry didn't expect her to make a lot of these visits. He was being so stingy these days. She didn't know what had come over him, but it wasn't making life at home a piece of cake, especially after that phony apology of his.

During dinner, Jeminy'd answered her father's queries about her music and contracts, but Deborah hadn't really listened. The girl was talented, no doubt about it, but so had she herself been in her own way. Oliver, too.

She bit the inside of her cheek to press down thoughts of her boy, the only one who'd ever truly loved her. Not Jeminy, who'd been a daddy's girl, always and forever. And now that her boy was gone? There was no one. And the only one who'd stick up for her?

Exactly. Herself.

No one else to tell her anything, to include her, to take her side in any argument. She'd had to walk in on that discussion about the shooter. They hadn't thought to bring her inside to hear about her own daughter.

All that time, she'd been outside, letting her mother drone on and on. It hadn't taken Mama long to tire and start forgetting things, like names of the plants. Then she'd wanted to sit in her back porch swing to talk to the cats—at least the tabby. The other cat had only his nose peeking out from under the porch.

Deborah hated cats, although she hated dogs more.

Anyway, by the time she'd been able to coax her mama inside, the others had finished their visit. Larry had told her they'd been talking about the drive-by shooter, some crazy man who'd missed his target. Now everyone was saying only God could have saved Jeminy.

Good. God had saved her. Yippee.

Why hadn't He saved Jeminy's brother? What kind of God would let that sweet boy be taken? Because if He had the power to save one, why not the other? Why not the good one?

Really, Deborah? You'd rather God have taken your daughter than your son? What kind of mother wishes something like that?

She closed her eyes and leaned her forehead against the side window. Who *was* she?

The tears seemed to fall of their own accord, and Deborah turned to face out so Larry wouldn't know. She couldn't let him see her weakness.

Her fear.

Unable to staunch the flow, she grabbed her purse and rifled through it in search of a tissue, two tissues, twenty, the whole pack. Where were they?

She was sorry. She was. A terrible mother had to be sorry.

She was.

She barely registered the turn signal or Larry pulling off the highway. She assumed he needed gas—or something.

Her eyes remained shut, and she sniffed, too caught up in her misery to care what he was doing. And then the car stopped, he shifted into Park, and the only sound was that of her hiccuping.

"Tell me." His voice was quiet, gentle.

She shook her head.

A big hand squeezed her shoulder. She kept her face pressed to the glass.

"Deborah, I'm your husband. I want only the best for you. Please, talk to me."

"I was good, wasn't I? I-I tried, just as you asked." She wished her voice were steadier.

"Most of the time."

She whipped her head around. "What? Can't you give me credit for anything? You're always against me."

His hand slipped down her arm and moved away. "I'm not. I know you believe I always sided against you, and I've asked your forgiveness for making you feel as if you were less—"

"You blamed me for his death! You turned from me!"

"Oh, honey, I didn't. I never blamed you."

"Yes, you did. Everyone did."

"No, only you did, and because of that, you've closed yourself off from your daughter and from me. I might have been complicit in allowing the estrangement, but you need to stop playing the victim."

Victim? She didn't *play* the victim, she *was* the victim!

Deborah bit her lip and looked away again. There wasn't much to see except the lights near the convenience center, one she didn't recognize.

"We should just go," she finally said. "Talking isn't doing us any good."

She almost hoped he'd insist they talk more, really talk, but he rarely did that. His modus *operandi* had always been to close himself off and go to work or take a work call—or to go on a trip.

Alone?

She squinted as the headlights pointed back to the road and the car headed west again. But she didn't speak, not then and not during the several hours they were on the road. She'd tried to sleep, but as soon as she began to relax, a bump in the road snapped her awake.

Larry pulled his car into the garage next to hers and turned the key. She could almost feel the weight he seemed to be carrying, and for a moment she felt sympathy, especially when he held open the house door for her. But that emotion dissipated when he turned from her and walked toward his study, as silent as she.

50

JEMINY

How does a person stay holed up at home for days on end without going stir crazy? That was the question Jeminy put to Eric when he called two days later to check up on her.

"Do you want company? Danny and I could bring dinner over, if that would help."

"That would be great, but why don't I cook? It's not like I have places to go or people to see, and Isa was kind enough to take Nana out to the supermarket yesterday, so we have a lot of food."

"Thank you, we'd like that. Home-cooked as opposed to bachelor food sounds incredible."

"Do you have a preference? Some food you and Danny like best?"

"He's a lad of simple tastes, and I'm happy with whatever."

"How about spaghetti? I can make a sauce with lots of veggies

354

hidden from the view of a boy who might not eat them if he knew they were there."

He laughed. "What time?"

"Whenever you want. I'll work on the sauce this afternoon so Danny won't catch me chopping and grinding the vegetables."

The house was spotless because what else had she had to do on rainy days like today and yesterday or when she'd done all the staring at nothing she could bear? Her guitar sat idly under fingers that strummed and plucked and quit because motivation had dried up. Her notebooks weren't filling, her score sheet pile was woefully skinny. Her creative juices seemed to have dribbled out.

And so she began early to chop and whir and toss and heat and blend the sort of sauce Rose used to fix when they'd turned up their noses at broccoli and spinach, but busyness didn't silence her thoughts, which kept returning to the visit from her parents. Dinner had been tense and elongated because Nana ate so slowly. Finally, Jeminy had asked for a carry-out box and convinced her grandmother she could finish her shrimp and grits later because Mother and Daddy had a long drive home.

Even now, Jeminy was having trouble swiping away images of her mother the way she swiped screens on her phone—unwanted, poof, gone. The only way to manage a brain wipe was to concentrate on replacing the unwanted with something else.

She knew what she'd prefer to imagine: another day on *Escape* with Eric.

Wind had begun to blow rain against the window panes as the storm moved through. She hurried upstairs to unplug her computer in case lightning struck.

Nana sat in her favorite chair, her head back and her mouth hanging open. Beside her seat was her half-empty teacup. Jeminy laid a light coverlet over her grandmother and bent to kiss the soft forehead. Nana opened her eyes for a moment and smiled.

"I'm getting the spaghetti sauce ready. If you need anything, will you call me?"

"Fine, lovey. I'm fine." And she closed her eyes again.

It was a sleeping kind of day, Jeminy decided, wishing she could find oblivion as easily.

As she poured in another can of tomatoes, her unhelpful brain saw the red as blood, and she had to stop and shake herself. She hadn't seen the blood on the operating table that day, but surely there'd been some. Blood and death, a body, a baby.

She dropped the spoon and stood, rigid, mentally swiping, finally physically running her hands down her face, trying to get rid of the pictures so she wouldn't scream and scare her grandmother as the rain slashed from the darkening sky.

O God.

Please forgive me. Forgive, forgive...

The floor was hard when she fell onto her knees. Crying out, she repeated, "Please, oh please forgive me."

She didn't deserve forgiveness or a second chance.

Rose's voice seemed to chime in. "Grace is undeserved. None of us deserves forgiveness, but God, in His mercy, sent his Son to pay the price."

If only she knew what that meant. Rose used to read the Bible to her and Olli and then just to her so she wasn't completely ignorant of what it said. But she'd left her own copy at her parents' home when she'd finally moved out. It hadn't seemed at all relevant to her life.

She'd been wrong. On so many levels.

She finally rose from the floor and washed her face at the kitchen sink. She had time to find one of Nana's Bibles that were all over the house and that she'd placed on shelves or tables in her attempt to organize things.

The first she came to lay on top of a short bookcase in the living room. She flipped through the pages, her gaze catching on the word forgiveness in the book of Ephesians. *In Him we have redemption through His blood, the forgiveness of sins.*

Not some sins. All sins.

She read more, finding words of comfort, words she clutched tightly to herself. Forgiveness. Mercy. Grace.

The mantle clock chimed, and she jumped up, replacing the Bible and returning to the kitchen to finish meal preparation.

Finally, they arrived.

She focused on them during dinner and on her nana and filled her mind with listening and doing to make them all feel happy and relaxed. Danny was a darling, full of stories of playing with Ty and Katie at the creek house, of liking school now that the bullies were gone, of his latest math test and how he'd had the highest score, probably on account of his dad making him do speed drills for his times tables. Did Miss Jeminy know the nine's tricks?

When Jeminy admitted she had no idea there were nine's tricks, Danny proudly told her about them, how when multiplying nine, the tens place numbers get bigger and the ones place numbers get smaller. He asked her to write factors on paper and showed her how the digits all add to nine.

"Pretty cool," Jeminy said. "I'd like to know why no one bothered to tell me those secrets back when I was in school."

Danny looked over at Eric. "Teachers weren't as cool back then," Eric said. "We had to figure those out for ourselves."

"Yeah, well, speak for yourself. I didn't."

Danny's grin was priceless. "Lucky me!"

Jeminy's thoughts focused away from herself while they

visited, which was exactly where they needed to be. And then their guests left, and she helped Nana to bed.

Wash, brush, change, pick up a good book, climb in bed. That normally worked to let her drift into sleep.

Not tonight.

She'd known she would have to come to grips with those minutes in the kitchen, the scriptures she'd read. It seemed she'd have to do it by heading once again to the floor, kneeling this time beside her bed. She remembered Rose telling her to do that when Rose taught her—and Olli—how to pray. She'd told them about Joshua falling on his face because he was on holy ground, so Rose reckoned they should also be respectful.

In the kitchen, Jeminy'd gone straight to her knees without any help from her own volition—sort a whoosh/fall sequence. This time, she'd start from the down posture so she didn't land there involuntarily.

Fine, she was on her knees. Now what?

She closed her eyes and waited, but all she heard (or imagined she heard because it was all in her head instead of being audible, right?) were the words, "You're a fake. God doesn't really care that you said *sorry*. It's too late. Forget it." And then, "Might as well get up and get to bed. God hasn't forgiven you. Why should He?"

That couldn't be true, could it? Hadn't both Rose and her daddy said God forgave? That all she had to do was confess and turn away from her sin?

She gritted her teeth and pressed the heels of her hands against her closed lids. She wouldn't listen to the voice in her head.

But it was loud and grating, and she couldn't seem to shut it out. "Hasn't God said he hates murder? You can confess all you want, but you can't turn away from what you did. That life is gone. Poof. Dead."

She brought her hands up to cover her ears, to swipe down her face, to press against her leaking eyes, but the voice wouldn't hush.

Staying on the floor became uncomfortable, and so she rose, retreated to the kitchen to brew some soporific tea, and carried it to the back porch. There she sat, sipping and staring at the moon as it made its slow way up over the trees and into the sky.

The moon illuminated the yard, bringing shadows into sharp relief until a cloud obscured the light. She waited until the cloud passed. In the brightness of the moon, she felt a tug on her senses.

Focus, she told herself. What did she know to be true?

She'd start with the *who.* She knew Rose was true. Rose had lived the words she'd spoken and continued to live them. She'd used the same words Daddy had, the same idea of repentance and forgiveness. Jeminy could remember watching the moon climb over the trees when she'd been with Rose, when Rose's soft hands had smoothed Jeminy's hair back, had wiped Jeminy's tears, and massaged Jeminy's tense muscles. Rose's words had brought Jeminy back from many a brink when despair wanted to crush her.

And Jeminy heard those words now, spoken once upon a time in Rose's voice. "Peace I leave with you, My peace I give to you…" She'd been telling a story of Jesus, of what He'd done on the Cross and by rising again. Of His promises. And then Rose had said, "Jesus told those listening not to be afraid. We take in His words, lovey, and they'll heal our heart. I know yours is broken, baby girl, but you just hold on to Him. He'll see you through."

Jeminy watched the moon here on Nana's porch and whispered, "Will You?"

She thought she heard an answer—or maybe she only felt the answer. *Do you believe?*

"I want to," she said aloud. "I want to."

Lay down your sorrows.

"I don't know how."

Give them to Me. Trust.

And even though she didn't know what that meant or how to do it, she suddenly felt sleepy enough to climb the stairs and crawl into her bed. And she slept.

JEMINY

Moving into darkness, hiding from the light,
Who will win at hide-and-seek,
And who will be found out?

Another week passed before word came from Clay. Jeminy had been walking tenderly around the thing she'd encountered. It was all so new to her—not the hearing *about* but the hearing *from.* Had God really, truly spoken to her?

Had she really, truly been forgiven?

She wanted to ask someone, but Rose was out of cell phone range somewhere in Africa. She thought of phoning Eric, because he seemed to know more about God than she did. But she put it off.

And then Clay called. "The folk keeping an eye on your ex in L.A. seem to have lost him."

"Lost him? How do you lose a person you're watching?"

"My bet is they didn't have enough personnel to give it priority. They might have said they'd keep an eye on him, meaning if he did anything else that brought him to their attention, they'd let us know."

"So he could have skipped town, flown—or driven—across either border or to another state, maybe even fled to Mexico?"

"He could have just found another residence. We'll stay alert in case he has indeed become violent and escalated from theft. If he's trying to drive across country—"

"He wouldn't. He hates long distance driving and only does it when he can stop at a fancy hotel early and leave late."

"We have a picture of him from the old website he maintained for you. We'll distribute that."

"Thanks, Clay. I guess that's all you can do. I'll try not to worry that a man as crazy as he might change his appearance."

"Relax. Enjoy life. This will come to an end very soon." He was trying to soothe her. If only she could feel it. "And, Jeminy?" he continued. "We're all praying for you and for your safety. God really is in control."

"Thank you."

She disconnected and wandered into the kitchen where Nana stood staring out at the still-soggy back yard, all from last week's storm and a series of afternoon showers. The ground had absorbed about all it could handle.

"You okay, Nana?" Jeminy asked, draping an arm around her grandmother.

Nana leaned her head on Jeminy's shoulder. "Yes, sweet girl. Can we go out for a long walk? Do you think we could?"

"I do. Why don't we walk down to *Samantha's?*"

"Ice cream?" Nana asked.

"Absolutely."

"We won't get wet?"

Jeminy opened the back door and looked at the sky. "It's blue and clear, so I think we'll be fine. Why don't you head to the bathroom down here, and I'll dash upstairs to put on some walking shoes. Then we can go."

Nana checked out her Merrell-clad feet. "I have my walking shoes."

"Yes, ma'am. You do."

And out they headed, Nana smiling at passersby, Jeminy grateful to have something else to occupy her thoughts. Because she wanted desperately to believe that God really was in control and that she had nothing to fear. Maybe, when they got back home, she'd be able to put her worries and her budding faith together in a song for Darling to sing.

If only.

She found another letter from Rose when they returned, and after she settled Nana in for her afternoon nap, Jeminy tore it open and began to read. Rose and her team had been in place somewhere in the wilds of Africa for several weeks and had experienced the power of God in ways Jeminy'd only read about in the New Testament.

I wish you could have been here, darling girl, to have seen what we saw. Yes, the team has done a lot of good medically speaking, but it's the miracles we've witnessed that have had the greatest impact on everyone and have spurred one of the team members, who's a preacher back home, to call for daily worship times. These have grown so that people are coming from miles around because they've heard what our great Lord Jesus has been performing. I saw a blind man's eyes opened, a lame man walk, and a witch doctor delivered of demons. And those are only the ones I personally witnessed. Other team members have come back from villages with their own tales. God is so good!

Jeminy read Rose's words, and something inside her clicked into place. If anyone other than Rose had written those things, she'd have doubted the truth of them. But Rose had never lied to her nor made up stories. She'd listened to Jeminy's doubts and acknowledged having once had some herself. But now she was saying that Jesus Christ was the same today as He'd been in biblical times—the same God Moses knew, the same God the disciples experienced, the same God Rose and her daddy and her new friends here worshipped. This was a God she wanted to know.

She sat down and tried to write a song expressing the emotions that almost overwhelmed her. She wasn't sure how to pray, but maybe her song would do it for her.

A string broke on Gully, and then another. The phone rang with Eric checking up on her. "I'm fine," she said, but curtly because two lines of the chorus had just come together. She turned off her phone and sighed when her nana kept interrupting with one question, repeated three times with three queries of "I'm not interrupting anything, am I?"

Eventually, she set Gully down and went to fix Nana's dinner. When she picked up her guitar again, the house phone rang, but it was a wrong number. Writing songs was never an easy process, and maybe this one was particularly hard because she was so unsure of herself and what exactly all this meant in her life. Faith seemed so easy for everyone else, so uncomplicated—they chose to believe and bang, they believed. They could even talk about it freely.

She, instead, decided God loved and forgave her, and an hour later, doubts assailed her. That voice in her head reminded her that when folks knew what she'd done—when Eric knew—that would be the end. He'd turn away, disgusted.

Exhaustion hit her early that night, and she turned out her light just as soon as she'd been assured Nana would stay in bed and sleep. Then, as dawn approached, the dream came. She knew the time because she'd awakened and then fallen back to sleep.

When the baby whimpered, she raced outside into the morning mist. "I'm coming, I'm coming," she cried, and she saw his face, baby eyes imploring her, baby arms flailing. She reached out to pick up the child, speaking soothing words to stop his cries, but he wasn't there in flesh she could touch, no matter what her eyes told her, as if he were a ghost baby, come to haunt her.

"Please, I'm so sorry... So very sorry," but her words changed nothing, and she woke to tears sliding down her cheeks onto the pillow.

She supposed, with all she'd been experiencing lately, that she shouldn't be surprised to find Eric at her door before eight. It was early, way too early for anyone to be up and about on a Saturday, but there he stood, handsome in his awkwardness.

"I'm sorry. I know it's early, but something compelled me to come."

She held open the screen door. "Come on in."

"Your grandmother?"

"She's still asleep."

That seemed to relieve him.

"Can I get you anything? Tea, coffee?"

"Only if you're having something."

She led the way into the kitchen. "Tea."

"That's fine."

He sat at the table while she took down two cups and various teas. "Water's already hot." She held up the tea choices.

"I'm not picky," he said.

She chose two teabags of Earl Grey, poured water over them, and set both on the table before she slid in across from him.

"You said you felt compelled to come here."

He dunked the tea bag a few times before looking up. "I was looking out over the creek this morning and thought I heard weeping, but no one was there. Danny was staying overnight with Ty, and the place was empty. When I closed my eyes and asked the Lord for help, I saw you, Jeminy, and knew I had to come."

"You saw me?"

He nodded. "There's been something growing in me. It started as mere attraction, but I believe it has the potential for so much more. And I think that's why the Lord propelled me here, knowing you needed something and that I was supposed to give it to you."

"God?"

"Yes."

"But what? And why?"

But she knew. She had to come clean before this went too far. She might long for the more he mentioned, but she couldn't let it happen without him knowing the truth. As much as it hurt her, as much as it would destroy the possibility of more, he had to know. Wasn't that why God had sent Eric here?

She blinked at the tears forming. She'd had enough of crying. But they wouldn't stay gone.

He reached a hand across the table. "What is it?"

She only shook her head, and the tears came in a burst of sobs.

She felt cloth against her fingers, and she took it to wipe her face, pressing it against her lips. When she'd calmed somewhat, she tried to still the rage inside her, a tidal wave of emotions that she finally loosed with the words she had to speak.

"I… I killed my baby."

ERIC

He crouched beside where she sat with her head lowered. "I'm so sorry," he said.

She didn't look at him. "God must have wanted you to know so you'd back off."

"Why would God want that?"

"It's a big deal, murder."

"So is hatred, envy, adultery, lying—the Book of Romans lists sins but doesn't rank them. Remember what the Word says, that we have all sinned and fallen short of the glory of God? The only sinless man was Christ Jesus."

Think, Eric told himself. *Lord, give me the words to help.* "God says that if I hate my brother, I'm a murderer."

She shook her head. "That's not the same as actually killing a living being."

He stood and pulled the chair around so he could touch her. "Let me tell you a story," he began. "I hated my father for years, not only because of what he did to Henry, but because of his treatment of me, both the negative and the positive. I was the lucky son, the one unmarred, and so he gave me the most and always expected great things from me, his perfect child."

She continued to stare at the table.

He was trying to make her understand that everyone had issues that plagued them, but he seemed to be making a mess of it. He set one hand on hers. "I helped destroy my own brother."

She withdrew her hand. "Did you? Did you really? Or are you just wrapping things up in a neat bow because you didn't suffer as he did? Maybe have some survivor's guilt."

"That's possible. Part of me liked the attention and the achievements, but the treatment my father gave Henry helped propel my twin into addiction and created the spiral Hen barely escaped. He was beaten and rejected, while I was lauded and praised. I hated the man who'd been my father."

"And now?"

"We never did make things right before he died, but Henry has helped me let it go. Our father was a product of his own upbringing and the lack of real love in his life."

"Now, that's a mouthful."

"It is."

Her look turned disdainful. "You sound like my daddy trying to explain Mother's bad behavior. I mean, I get that she's carrying a lot of junk around because of what happened to my brother, but, hey, so are we all. And why should that give her permission to quit being a decent person? Sorry, but I'm not at the forgiving stage yet."

"Henry said if I wanted to be forgiven for my own sins and failures, I had to forgive those who had hurt me."

"Even if they don't ask for forgiveness? If they never apologize?"

"Even then."

She let out a sigh. "It feels impossible."

"Not impossible, just hard."

"And you wanted to be forgiven enough to go through with the whole forgiving thing?"

"Yeah, I guess so."

"It's a lot to think about."

"A lot to take in and so contrary to what we hear all around us."

Jeminy pushed her chair back and stood. "Thanks for coming by."

He stood up next to her. "I care."

At the same time, she said, "I'm sorry I burdened you with my horror story…"

"Wait." He reached for her hand. "When I said I care, I meant it. I'm not going to judge you or your choices because there's not a one of us without baggage of one sort or another."

"Yours is nothing. Nothing's as bad as what I did."

"Remember. Hatred is like murder. I spent many years so angry I wanted my father dead. And then he was, and I'd never forgiven him."

She stood, silent.

"Since then, I've had to. That hatred was keeping me from experiencing all I could of God's love." He laced their fingers together.

When she still didn't speak, he leaned toward her and brushed her lips lightly with his. "Remember," he said as he backed up, "the Lord sent me here, which means His purpose is being done. He loves you, Jeminy."

He wanted to tell her he was falling for her, but it was too soon. Way too soon.

53

JEMINY

In a world of color turned to gray, madness and horror are kept at bay.

Jeminy wasn't certain what woke her. More rain was forecast, but for now, Beaufort was as asleep as she'd been minutes ago. The small bedside clock read 12:35.

She closed her eyes and tried to relax. Maybe it had been someone's car door down the way, a late-night worker. Just a normal sound in a normal night.

Then a floorboard creaked. She'd left her door open in case Nana needed her, but Nana would shuffle in her slippers and not try for quiet.

It could easily be nothing. This was an old house, and just because there'd been one attempt on her life didn't mean there'd be another, especially not with the shooter in jail and, here, all the doors and windows locked on the first floor. It couldn't be Rand.

Too bad Nana didn't have a dog. A big, snarling dog because her granddaddy's guns were locked away in what had been his den.

370

Jeminy barely breathed as she waited for another creak to sound, all her focus on the open door and the slight light from the hall's nightlight. For a moment, all was silent.

And then a muffled groan came from another of the old boards. She recognized the sound. She and Olli had known exactly where to step to creep undetected when looking for a midnight snack. With her eyes closed, she tried to pretend that what she didn't see wouldn't be real, like they'd believed about closet monsters when they'd been little. Back then, staying hidden under the covers kept the monster from finding them.

She was being absurd, but still…

Stop it. She wasn't a child. She had to look. She had to know.

She opened her eyes and stared at the rectangle that was her doorway.

Why hadn't she thought to put a big flashlight on her night table, a big, heavy one she could use as a weapon, with a strong enough light to blind anyone who approached? Because she was witless, that's why.

The nightlights worked, she noted stupidly when the figure stood silhouetted in her doorway.

She clutched the sheet, stifling a scream that came instinctively. Nana would hear and be in danger. She had to act quietly.

Act?

How did one *act* without a weapon, with her phone out of reach, when she was vulnerable, alone, and a man was tiptoeing into her room.

Should she pretend sleep? Let him pillage and pray he didn't rape, too? Or murder?

God! She sent the cry up soundlessly. *Please!*

He smelled as he always had, although now it was coupled with something sickeningly sweet.

She sat up abruptly. "Rand? What are you doing here?"

She would not let him frighten her. She'd lived with the creep. He was a coward.

He sat down on the side of the bed and pulled something off his head. A mask, she supposed. She reached over and turned on the light.

He looked around, then went to the windows to close the blinds. That wasn't encouraging.

She tried to slide her phone off the table, but he saw and grabbed it on his way to the side window. He sat back down on the bed, this time drawing a gun from his pocket. "You've caused me no end of trouble, Jeminy."

"So you planned to kill me?"

"Why, no, I haven't done any such thing. But I may have to now."

"Oh, really?"

"Arthur found out I was being investigated by someone—who did you sic on me, my pretty?—and he threw me out. Then the police came. What really puzzles me is how you found out about that insurance policy?"

He made it a question, but she didn't answer. Instead, she tried to come up with an escape plan.

He had a gun. Did Rand even know how to shoot? Of course, at this range he probably just had to point and pull the trigger.

She'd imagined she knew the man. So full of lies. So narcissistic and manipulative. He'd always been so pro gun control, ridiculing the NRA. So sophisticated and remote. And now look at him.

Keep him talking. The thought made her feel even more desperate because how did you engage with a madman?

She nodded toward his lap. "I thought you hated guns."

His smile looked off-kilter, pasted on. "Oh, I do. This?" He wiggled the gun at her. "*My* insurance plan."

"In-insurance?" Her voice squeaked that out. She cleared her throat. "Please point it away from me."

"Well, Jeminy honey, you and I are going on a trip. I've been doing a little investigating of my own, and I know you have a power of attorney for your grandmother, who, I also discovered, has a lot of money."

She backed away until she hit the headboard. "No, no. You have it all wrong because my POA doesn't allow me to access anything without approval from her other attorney-in-fact. We can't take money out on our own. It's... it's set up to protect Nana."

He smirked. "Well, then, we'll just have to get the other one involved, won't we?"

"You can't."

"Watch me." He stood, pushed her legs over the side and grabbed her arm. "Up. Now."

She might have been tall, but Rand was strong, bulging-muscles strong, and before she knew it, she was stumbling to her feet. His fingers dug like claws in her biceps. She bit her lip. She would not give him the satisfaction of hearing her whimper.

"Get some clothes on."

"Why?"

He lifted the gun he still held in his left hand. "Because I said so?" He wagged it at her to show he hadn't been asking a question.

"Fine. I need to use the bathroom first."

"I'll just join you in there. It won't be the first time." His smirk, almost a leer, was back.

Fear clawed its way back up to her throat. He'd changed so much from the carefree man she'd first known into this possibly deadly person before her that she'd better tread very, very carefully.

She grabbed a set of loose sweats that would slip on easily and be comfortable for going out and about with a potential killer because who wouldn't? They also camouflaged her figure because she didn't want him getting any ideas of her offering access.

"Would you at least turn around?"

"Why should I?"

"I'd like to pee."

"Fine. But don't try anything."

She used the time to change quickly behind the open door. He could probably see part of her reflected in the vanity mirror, but at least he wasn't leering over her.

He had the brawn and the gun, but she had brains, if she'd stop thinking ridiculous thoughts and begin using her wits to come up with a plan. He wasn't stupid, but she ought to be able to outsmart a narcissist, surely. It seemed she also had at least one angel on guard. She shot up another prayer that the angel would be motivated to help here, too.

"Where are we going?" she asked.

He didn't answer but instead waved her out the door. He'd gathered her purse and then stopped. "Maybe we should invite your grandmother along," he said as if the thought had just occurred to him. His cognitive processes seemed slower than normal, making her wonder again what he'd been using. Something had made his body odor change.

"She'll just be in your way, Rand. Take me. I'll help you convince the other person who has Power of Attorney."

"My guy didn't mention this other POA. Who is it?"

Think, Jeminy. "Eric Houston. Her lawyer."

"A lawyer?" He narrowed his eyes at her. "He the one who sent those papers to me?" He didn't wait for her to answer. "He is, isn't he? Well, your Mr. Houston is going to get a visit from us. Where's he live?"

Why had she dragged Eric into this? That's what came from imagining she was so smart.

"I don't know. He was living on his boat, but he moved recently."

"Living on a boat? What, he couldn't afford a house? Like those squatters who tuck up in a marina to keep their property taxes down, I bet." He let out a puff of air and shot her a look of disgust along with an ugly curse. "They're all over California." Another word she'd rather not have heard. "You have his number? Call and tell him you need to see him now." His fingers trailed down his face. "No. That won't work. You both registered at the bank for the old lady's accounts?"

She couldn't tell Rand the truth, but just maybe—please, oh please—she or Eric could come up with a plan.

"Yes. Both of us are needed for any action. In person."

"Of course. You'd have to make it hard." He looked at his watch. "Okay, here's what we'll do. Your grandmother can stay where she is as long as you don't wake her. She wakes, she comes with us. She's pretty deaf, you said?"

When had she said that? Well, it didn't matter. She could agree easily enough if it would protect Nana. Jeminy nodded. "Where are we going?"

"We have a few hours to kill before the bank opens, so you're going to fix me a cup of coffee and something to eat." He pointed her toward the door. "First, though, you go check on your grandmother. Make sure she's asleep."

54

GEORGINA

Georgie always woke a couple of times a night to go to the bathroom. Right after they'd bought the house, Gerard had converted a small bedroom into two baths, one opening into their bedroom and one into the room next door. He knew she liked convenience. He'd been so good to her. Two smaller bedrooms across the hall had shared a guest bath. And, so, tonight when she slid her feet into slippers, she didn't have far to walk.

Maybe the walls weren't that well insulated between the baths because she was sure she heard voices. In her house. And they were the voices of a woman and a man. Jeminy used the other bathroom.

Jeminy was here. But a man wasn't supposed to be in the house with her, and certainly not in Jeminy's bathroom. In Georgie's house.

That was *not* to be allowed.

Georgie crept up to the adjoining wall. There were definitely people, at least two. Her nightlight lit her path, so she tiptoed to the partially open hall door. She wouldn't go out, not yet, but she'd wait and see.

Better hide behind the door. No telling who was out there.

Her heart was beating hard, but she wouldn't let it be fear. No, ma'am. If something wrong was happening, she was the one to fix it. This was her house, and she was the grandmother. Only, she had to be smart and think, not act like some crazy old lady.

She was *not* crazy. And she'd do what needed doing. Whatever that was.

The voices weren't quiet. And the man's didn't belong.

Think, Georgie, think.

The phone. Yes, that was it. She needed to call for help. Because her Jeminy wouldn't have invited a man into the house, which meant that man didn't belong.

She tiptoed back to her bedside table and picked up the phone, then she carried it with her to the bathroom to dial 911. She didn't turn on the light. Her nightlight was enough. When the lady answered, Georgie tried to be very quiet. "There's a man in my house."

"May I have your name and address? And can you tell me what this man is doing?"

"I don't know what he's doing," Georgie hissed. "But he doesn't belong!"

"Please, ma'am, what is your name?"

"Georgina Warren. Shh, I hear them."

"Them? Ma'am, is there more than one?"

"Hush. Don't talk. Let me listen." Georgie set the phone on the counter and opened the door.

The man's voice was saying to check on her. Georgie scurried back to her bed and climbed under her covers, slippers and all, so she wouldn't be caught. She could do that much, but she couldn't control her breathing. Whoever was checking would hear her breaths coming hard and fast, and he—or she—would know.

Footsteps came near the bed. Someone bent low. She could tell it was Jeminy, and she heard a whispered, "Do not come downstairs. No matter what, Nana. Stay up here."

Georgie opened her eyes wide and nodded. She lay still and

silent as Jeminy left, closing the door behind her. The voices were muted, but the man seemed satisfied because the stairs creaked as they descended.

As soon as she judged them safely down, she climbed back out of bed and returned to the phone.

Jeminy needed her.

"Are you still there?" she asked the dispatcher. And yes, she remembered she'd called the 911 dispatcher. She straightened her shoulders. Jeminy needed her. God would keep her mind clear.

"Yes, ma'am."

"I had to pretend to be asleep, but my granddaughter came in and she leaned down to warn me not to go downstairs."

"Do you know why she'd have said that?"

"She told me 'no matter what' to stay here in my room."

"Did she sound frightened?"

"Yes. People have been shooting at her. You need to ask Clay Dougherty. He knows."

"Lieutenant Dougherty?"

"Yes, him. He knows."

"Will you stay on the line, Mrs. Warren, while we contact him?"

"I will stay right here. Jeminy told me to."

"What's Jeminy's full name, Mrs. Warren?"

"It's Jeminy Buchanan. No, it's Jemima. We call her Jeminy."

"Okay, hang on."

She sat on the toilet seat lid and waited, while downstairs some man had Jeminy.

Maybe with a gun. Georgie froze. *Another gun.*

Her knees wouldn't let her fall to them, not with the arthritis and the creakiness, but she bowed her head over the phone in her lap, and she talked to God because only He could save them and only He could deliver them.

If God wanted to use the police, He could. But if there were a gun, they'd need angels. Lots of angels. And the Sword of the Lord to do battle.

"Ma'am?" the voice on the phone said, loudly enough to penetrate the space and get to Georgie. The voice continued.

Georgie stared at receiver, and then she picked it up. "What?"

"I said I can't understand you."

"You don't need to. I was talking to God."

"Oh, right. Good idea." She paused a moment. "They've reached Lieutenant Dougherty. He said he's on the way."

"You tell him to be careful. The man might have a gun."

"Yes, ma'am. He knows that. You stay on with me, okay?"

"I will. Long as I can."

55

JEMINY

Evil enters, slithers through the keyhole, presses its advantage:
You cower. But wait, think.
Good shushes the lies, speaks to Truth.
Overcomes.
And wins. Surely, Truth wins.

Jeminy'd had evidence that Rand didn't have the sharpest intellect, but his behavior here just didn't make sense. He had to be on something that was making him delusional because if he thought his gun made him impervious to someone else's cunning, he was definitely going to find himself behind bars before this night was over.

Once they called Eric to meet her at the bank, Eric would call Clay, who'd call in backup, and rescue would be right around the corner. Rand's only hope would be holding that gun to Nana's head, but how'd he imagine he could get away once he had the money? Especially as he couldn't shoot either of them first, not if he hoped to get something from the bank. Taking them hostage would require he hide them and himself somewhere unknown to the police, but where might that be in Beaufort?

Either he was too stupid for words—and she'd always thought him cunning, at least—or he was hallucinating some alternate ending to this.

Or… what?

Or nothing. Stupid and delusional were both frightening because neither involved linear thinking, which meant it would be very hard to anticipate what might come next.

They were sipping the coffee she'd brewed at his direction, the dining area illuminated only by light from the kitchen. He'd wanted to wait away from the light, just in case, he'd said.

In case what? Someone was peering in the windows?

Rand stared at his empty cup. "Fill it back up. And bring me something to eat." He reached into his jacket pocket and pulled out a pill bottle.

She didn't ask what the bottle contained or why he needed more now. The last time she'd queried him about his drug use, toward the end of their relationship, he'd slammed his fist on the table and told her to mind her own business.

"What do you want?" she asked. "Eggs? Toast?"

"Sure." He wiggled the gun toward her chest. "Don't try anything. You do, your grandmother will be toast." He huffed out a laugh. "Get it? Toast?"

Exhaustion slowed her as she pushed off the chair.

He grabbed her forearm. "You hear what I said?"

"How could I not?" She yanked her arm free.

"Then acknowledge it, Jeminy." Another gun wave. "Now."

"I heard you. I won't try anything."

"Or your grandmother will be…?"

"Toast. I got it."

"Good. Now fix me something to eat."

As she cracked eggs in a bowl and began to whisk them, Jeminy glanced out the back window into a night darkened by rain and low clouds. She wished someone were out there who might see her standing here and somehow be able to break the spell. That's what it felt like, Rand's gun weaving and wrapping her until she succumbed. Had she done this before, been his obedient slave, fearful of upsetting him?

If so, what did that say about her?

But that was the old Jeminy, not this new person who was learning to stand up for her nana and for herself. How much of her movements could Rand see? Could she get a knife, hide it somewhere until she could use it?

A knife versus a gun, a gun against a knife. She'd bet on the gun unless she could somehow distract him. And then what? Could she use a weapon against him?

She thought again about Rand's state of mind and hoped his dumb-drug wouldn't wear off in the immediate future. She needed him to remain inattentive—unless whatever he'd taken roused him to violence and compelled him to use that gun.

A flash of lightning illuminated the sky. Jeminy stared out, letting her focus recede so she might catch movement on the periphery of the yard. She'd seen something, hadn't she, a shadowy something?

But that was too much to hope for, rescue in the middle of the night when no one knew they needed help. The house phone was only five feet away, but Rand would be able to see her pick up the receiver. She'd never get away with it.

"How soon's that going to be ready?" Rand called from the other room.

"Putting it in the pan now."

God, will you help me and my nana? Will you have mercy on her? And even, maybe, on me?

Rand was edgy enough. She couldn't take risks, not with her grandmother's life, but maybe God would show her the way.

She set the plate of food in front of him.

"You have any ranch dressing?"

"I think so. Maybe."

"Go get it. These eggs look bland."

Nana kept all sorts of condiments, and, yes, she had a half-full bottle of the dressing. And next to it, was a small bottle. Its label seemed to flash potential: Ipecac. She remembered throwing up and up and up when Rose gave her the emetic after she swallowed enough sugary cough syrup to have stopped her breathing. She opened the dressing and upended the Ipecac into it.

"What's taking you so long?"

"My grandmother has lots of bottles in here, but I found it. I'm coming."

She shook the dressing to mix in the emetic, hoping the color and taste of the Ipecac would be camouflaged enough for him not to notice it—and that it would work soon and make Rand so sick he'd lose control of that gun. She only needed one minute to grab it away and point it at him, to gain control of the situation.

For the first time in their relationship.

It was her fault she hadn't done that before, but maybe it wasn't too late, considering her nana's life was at stake.

Rand poured the dressing onto his eggs. "Not very white. How old is this stuff?"

"I don't know. It's been in the refrigerator, so it should be okay."

"Better be."

"I'm going to clean up the kitchen." She waited for his response.

He glanced up. "Just remember."

"Can't forget," she said, working on meek and obedient.

And then, standing in front of the sink, she turned on the water, looked at the bleak sky, and again prayed.

Lord God, please, if You're the One who showed up in my kitchen

*and by my bed, I need You. Nana needs You. I'm desperate. Only You
can fix this.*

Was there more she should do?

Rose's face came to mind, her teachings. "Honey, God wants all
of you, everything you are." Amazing, wasn't it, how well she
remembered Rose's exact tone and words? As if they'd been so
deeply branded into her that, even when she'd tried hard to ignore
them, she'd found it impossible.

And now they'd surfaced.

O God, Lord Almighty...

Jesus.

Yes, Jesus.

I'm so sorry for it all, so sorry... so sorry.

"*I told you I wanted you, Jeminy. You.*"

God?

"*I AM.*"

Jeminy clutched at the edge of the counter to keep her legs
from folding under her again, to keep from falling on her face.
Because... *God.*

Again tears flowed unbidden and unwiped down her cheeks.

She heard Rand push back his chair, and she tensed, but he only
went to the window. The curtain slides moved on the rod, but he
wouldn't see anything. Only rain.

She eased close to the open doorway. He was mumbling
something that sounded like, "Better get going. Better check...
better... better." And then he returned to his seat and she ducked
back out of the way.

He had to be on drugs.

The lights flickered, and then went out. She listened closely.
He seemed to be searching for something—probably one of the
phones. And then she heard a clunk against something, maybe the

other phone, and then two thunks sounded when they, something, hit the wooden floor.

He cursed loudly. "Jeminy! Get your skinny behind in here!"

She tried to hide in the darkness and remembered the pantry closet. Grabbing a knife out of the drawer, she dashed inside but left the door ajar so she could keep track of his movements.

"Sneaky fool woman." He must be crawling around on the floor, searching for the phones. He found one and flicked on the light. He'd probably gotten the gun, too, and now he'd come for her.

The phone's flashlight beam panned the room as he entered the kitchen. "Jeminy, you might as well come out now, wherever you are."

He tripped on a small rug but caught himself.

"Not going to miss my chance on account of your foolishness. You hear me?" The beam closed in on the closet door. "Snakes, all of you. Arthur, you. But I promise you this. I have to come get you, your grandmother's in big trouble."

He yanked open the door and found her cowering inside, the knife poised. Backing up a step, he sneered. "What, you think you can fight me with that puny thing?" He waved the gun toward her. "You suicidal tonight?"

Her hand wavered.

"Drop it. Now."

The moment she did, he reached in and grabbed her by the neck, hauling her out and to the floor. Her head hit the door jamb on her way down. "That was a stupid move, Jeminy. A real stupid move."

She didn't budge.

He kept the light on her face. She turned away from its beam. "I... I didn't mean anything..."

"The knife?" He bent to pick it up. "You were going to use that to pick the lock or something when you left the door cracked open? What do you take me for?"

She raised her head on a moan. She was going to have a knot on one side.

"Time to go check on Grandma."

He checked out the back window as lightning flashed. "Your grandmother's locks aren't worth squat. Get up and let's go."

He must have noticed the wall phone then because he grabbed the receiver, yanked it off, and tugged the unit from the wall. "Is there another one?"

"I use my cell phone." Jeminy stood cautiously. She wouldn't mention Nana's bedside phone.

"That's not what I—"

Lightning struck something not very far away, followed almost immediately by a crack of thunder. The storm was on top of them.

ERIC

Eric hit *End* on the call with Clay. Then he grabbed his clothes, climbed down to the lower floor, and quietly went into the small bathroom. When he came out, dressed in jeans and a casual shirt, he sat on Danny's bunk.

"Hey, buddy, wake up."

"Huh?" The sleepy eyes opened. "What?"

"Miss Jeminy's in trouble, and Mr. Clay and I have to go help her."

"Me, too?" Danny tossed off his sheet, alert now.

"I appreciate that, but Miss Annie Mac is going to take you to the big house. It's real early, and you can go back to sleep with Ty. Can you do that? Stay safe with them while I go?"

"Yeah. I guess so." He sounded disappointed. "Is the trouble bad?"

"Nothing Mr. Clay and his team can't handle. Everyone will be fine."

"You mean, the police will be there? Will there be guns?"

"Not in my hands," Eric said, ruffling the boy's hair.

"Then how come you gotta be there?"

"Well, Mr. Clay thought I should."

"On account of you being Miss Jeminy's lawyer? And Miss Georgie's?"

"Maybe on account of that."

Clay's horn sounded. "Gotta go, buddy. Miss Annie Mac should be right behind him."

"Daddy?" The little boy voice actually called him *Daddy?*

Eric's throat filled. "Yes, son?"

"You be careful."

He pulled Danny close. "I love you, buddy. And I'll be very careful. See you soon."

"Okay. Daddy." He said it more confidently that time, not as if he were still trying out the name. As if he remembered all those years ago when that had been his favorite word. *Daddy.*

Eric's heart nearly burst as he grabbed a light jacket and closed the door behind him. Annie Mac's car had just pulled up. She waved as Eric climbed in the Jeep, and then, with barely an acknowledgement, Clay accelerated.

"Who's with her?" Eric asked, buckling his seat belt.

"We don't know. Mrs. Warren only said there was a man and that Jeminy wanted her to stay in her room no matter what."

"What's the plan?"

"Officers are to approach the house carefully, staying out of sight. Avery Grainger's on duty. He'll keep the situation under control and not do anything until we get there."

"They'll make sure no one takes Jeminy?"

"Absolutely. Anyone leaves the house, they'll step in."

Why had Clay brought him into this? Had Clay seen something Eric hadn't been willing to admit even to himself? An attraction that was more than attraction? A *caring* that meant he, Eric, should be at the center of any rescue because it would involve a woman he... what? Loved? Wanted?

It seemed so.

And how had that happened? He thought it might have begun when he'd first been involved with Rita Levinson in helping secure Brisa's future because he'd listened to Darling's recordings —and an entire album had been full of Jeminy's songs. He'd even heard Brisa sing some.

And then, at his brother's wedding, she'd been up there with Brisa, singing her newest. The feeling that had slammed into him hadn't been only admiration for talent. It had been almost an acknowledgement of *there she is.*

As if his whole being knew something he wasn't willing to admit. Because, hey, *now?* With Danny just arrived and his need for stability? No way could Eric add in a relationship with a woman.

Besides, Jeminy had just come from a miserable affair with a man who wanted her dead.

Yeah, that was really going to work.

Fine, Clay saw it, but surely no one else had.

But he'd told Jeminy, hadn't he? And she'd admitted to the same attraction.

And said she wasn't ready.

She needs you.

Huh? Okay, she needed them all right now, but later? After?

And you need her.

He happened to agree with that last.

They didn't talk as Clay's Jeep hurtled into town, his light set on top of the car and flashing to alert the four other vehicles on the road at this time of night. A storm shot lightning to their left, and thunder boomed.

"Gonna be messy in a couple of minutes," Clay said. "There's an umbrella back there, and I keep an extra slicker with me."

"Good thing Annie Mac got Danny back to your house when she did. Here it comes."

A curtain of rain closed over them. Clay turned on the wipers, and the swish/click of them competed with the slosh and splash of the tires.

———

He parked out of sight of the house and passed the extra rain gear and umbrella to Eric before pulling his own rain slicker over his head. "The umbrella would just be in my way. You stay back with that until I need you."

Sure. Like that was going to happen.

But Eric didn't comment. He just pulled the second slicker over his head, ignored the umbrella, and followed.

While Clay strode up to a man standing behind a tall hedge just outside the front yard, Eric picked his way through the neighbor's yard until he could peer into Mrs. Warren's house. An arm shot out and stopped him from going further.

"No closer," the officer whispered. Then he looked at Eric. "Who're you?"

"I came with Clay. Lieutenant Dougherty. Family friend and lawyer. What's been happening?"

"Lights were on in the kitchen, but I didn't try to get close enough to look in. And then they went out. We'll see what the lieutenant says."

They didn't have long to wait. Clay approached quietly.

"Mrs. Warren is still in her room, so that's good. We have an open line to her. What do you have to report, Henley?"

"Kitchen light until just a minute ago, no movement outside. You want me to get closer?"

"I know the house. You stay here."

Eric wiped his face and nodded. "You should be able to get a view of the kitchen through the half-glass of the back door, but if they're not using candles or a flashlight, I don't know how much you'll see. I wouldn't risk the porch steps. Old wood."

Clay rounded the hedge. Following him, Eric crept as far as he could go without getting in Clay's way or creating a stir that might alert whoever had Jeminy.

There were no voices. Jeminy was in there, possibly hurt, probably scared, and her grandmother...

He wanted to storm the place, break down the door, break the guy, maim him... whatever it took. He wished he had a gun. Unarmed against an armed man, a gun pointed at Jeminy? Impossible.

He'd have to use brains, not brawn.

He should be carrying at least as backup for Clay's guys. He knew how to shoot. His father had made sure of that, taking him hunting at an early age, taking him to the range so he'd be comfortable with all sorts of firearms. But since his father's death, Eric hadn't wanted anything to do with his father's choices.

Clay reappeared. He'd thrown his hood back and water dripped down his face. "Curtains are drawn in the dining room, totally black, except there seems to be a flashlight illuminating a doorway. Kitchen looks empty." He turned to the uniformed officer. "Keep to your position. Let me know if there's any change, any light moving in."

Clay headed back up front to speak to someone he called Avery. Eric moved close enough to hear to the low words. "Is the line still open inside?"

"I just got off with dispatch. The line's dead."

"That means," Clay said, his voice hardening, "whoever's in there discovered Mrs. Warren was keeping it open."

"Or," Eric said, "she forgot what she was supposed to do and hung up. Of course, if it's a landline..."

"Oh, boy. Either way, it's not good. If she forgot the phone, maybe she left her room, and he's got them both."

The wind had picked up. "Storm's not abating," Eric said to no one in particular. "Maybe it's distracting them inside."

Rumblings were louder, and the time between the lightning

and thunder could be counted in a few seconds. Eric couldn't see beyond the road.

And then the lightning and thunder collided above them. Eric wished he had a gun and actually believed in using it against someone. If anyone deserved to be taken down, it was that creep inside who was threatening two defenseless women.

GEORGINA

Thunder pealed outside, and Georgie opened her eyes. She wasn't afraid, and she generally liked the sight of lightning flashing in the sky over the ocean. It wasn't quite as pleasant when it hit so close to home, but she was tucked up well in her house. She lay in bed for a few minutes and then threw back her covers. Sliding her feet into her slippers and pulling on her robe, she set off for her bathroom.

And then she heard voices, one very loud one, where there shouldn't be any. Who had invaded her house? Whoever was there wasn't bothering to be quiet.

What did that mean? If only she weren't alone up here. She missed her husband something dreadful.

"Gerald, I sure could do with some of your strength about now, you armed and ready to scare off any intruder." Georgie whispered to her dead husband so whoever was making that noise downstairs wouldn't hear her.

She picked up a brass candlestick, minus its candle, and held it at the ready. No telling who was there, but whoever it was didn't seem to mind being heard.

And then it occurred to her maybe she'd forgotten she had

guests. Closing her eyes, she did her best to grab a memory that would clear this up. Because wouldn't a housebreaker be quieter? He wouldn't know there wasn't a houseful of men ready to take him down.

Unless he was a local who actually knew her.

No, that wasn't possible. The locals, at least the locals she dealt with, were protective, not out to hurt her. This was all very strange… and very frightening.

"Get hold of yourself, Georgie. You're not helpless."

No, she wasn't, was she? She might not have a brain full of memories, but she could still think. So that's what she'd do.

Glancing down at the heavy candlestick, she stopped. Candlestick? What did she think she could do with that as a weapon? She wasn't strong enough to use it with any force.

Or strong enough to do much of anything.

She backed up to the edge of her bed and lowered herself, laying the candlestick on the downturned comforter.

The storm continued to rage, lightning streaking the sky outside, and thunder shaking the windows. She'd just begun to think how close the last had been when the electricity went off. Without nightlights, she sat in total darkness.

"Lord, please help," she whispered. And then she said it out loud. "Lord, help. Please."

JEMINY

The night grows dark, and hearts fail with it
While peace grows silent, waiting, waiting.

Jeminy tried to ignore the pain in her arm where Rand's fingers dug into her flesh. She'd tried to convince him to stay in or near the kitchen, telling him she'd make him more coffee or more to eat, that it would be the best place to wait out the storm until daylight, until it was time to call Eric about the bank and, if she played it right, to alert him. She'd planned out what she'd say to override any disclaimer about that power of attorney. Eric was smart enough to catch on, and once he did, he'd rally the troops.

She hadn't seen a clock since the electricity went off, but dawn had to be drawing near. On the way up the stairs, she had a few more words with God, a few more *we need a miracle* cries.

Rand pulled her to a stop outside her grandmother's door. "Open it quietly," he hissed. "Don't want to deal with anyone else unless I have to."

She inched it open and stuck her head in. Nana's curtains let enough light in for her to see her grandmother sitting upright on the bed, focusing her attention forward. *Please don't let her speak. Please don't let her move.*

Jeminy closed the door behind her and shook her head before leading the way back into her bedroom. Rand waved the pistol and light toward the bed.

"Sit," he said, swiping a forearm along his forehead. "And don't let me hear a sound from you." On a groan, he pressed his hand against his stomach. She bet his face was starting to look bleached out. Sickly.

She didn't say a word.

He looked frantically around and started yanking open drawers, finally grabbing one of her long silk scarves. "Lie down. Put your arms over your head." He set the gun just out of her reach and grabbed her wrists, lacing them one over the other to a newel post on the headboard and knotting the end of the scarf.

As he tightened it, he suddenly lost the contents of his stomach, barely missing her. The ipecac had worked, although she wished it had waited until he was in the bathroom. He grabbed his gun and carried it and the phone with him to the toilet, where the rest of his dinner/lunch/food left him retching violently. He'd barely finished one bout when another slammed him.

Jeminy tried to breathe through her mouth to keep her own bile down, but the stench was horrific. She bit her lip, shifted her hands to ease the dig of the scarf, kept her eyes closed, and tried to picture a good end to this.

She wasn't positive there was one.

Still… *God, are you there?*

59

GEORGINA

*G*et up, Georgie.

She looked around the dark room. Someone spoke to her?

Why was she sitting up in her bed? Why was the big candlestick next to her? What was happening?

Panic brought her close to tears.

Georgie, I need you to get up and go to the window.

Go to the window. Okay, she could do that.

She pushed off her bed, slid her feet into her slippers, and walked to the window. Lightning flashed and something moved. Was that a flashlight? What was she supposed to see?

And then she glanced to the left. A car door opened, and the interior lights shone for a moment, just a moment, but long enough that she recognized the person standing there.

Why was the lieutenant in front of the house next door?

And then she heard something from Jeminy's room. Voices. And that clicked her memory into gear.

That's why she was sitting up and waiting. There'd been voices. And Jeminy'd wanted her to stay quiet, only that was before.

Before the person with Jeminy took her downstairs. And after she'd called 911.

That meant the lieutenant was here on account of her.

Lord, please keep my mind focused and guide me.

Maybe, if she was really, really quiet, she could tiptoe downstairs while the man had Jeminy in her room, and she could open the door for the lieutenant. She knew the way, no matter the dark. All she had to do was follow the wall with her hand and then grab the railing and hold on. One step at a time.

Oh, my, what was that strange noise? It didn't sound good, which meant she had no time to waste.

Please, Lord, please. Lead me.

She knew where the bad board was, but all that noise from Jeminy's room or bathroom would probably keep them from hearing her. At the foot of the stairs, she felt her way to the front door. All those years in this house meant she could pretty much find her way blindfolded.

Another strike of lightning, another peal of thunder, and she turned the lock and flung open the front door. She wasn't afraid of a little rain or a little thunder, not when Jeminy needed saving.

At the porch steps, a gust accompanied by slanting rain forced her to pause for a moment. But not for long. God was with her. God wouldn't let her fall.

Down she went, one sloppy step after another, her slippers soggy and floppy on her feet. Her arms circled her front as she shuffled toward the gate. Then she was out on the sidewalk and a man was running her way, throwing a raincoat over her shoulders.

"Miss Georgie!" He kept his voice low, leading her away from the house. "What are you doing out here in the rain? Are you okay?"

"You gotta go. Right now. He's upstairs with my girl, and you've got to go save her."

The lieutenant handed her off to someone else and spoke to another man before they ran up the sidewalk and into the house.

60

DEBORAH

She'd had dreams before, bad ones that clawed at her through the night and then held her captive even when morning came. But this time she woke screaming.

"Honey? Deborah?" Larry's voice from beside the bed finally penetrated her cries.

She shook off his hand. It felt vise-like. What could he offer, this husband who wasn't really a husband, who loved their daughter best and probably loved that floozy, too. Or if theirs wasn't love, it certainly was something he withheld from her.

He'd turned on the bathroom light, which let her see the jumbled sheet, the pillow she'd tossed aside. "Go away." Her voice quavered when she'd meant it to sound brusque, unwelcoming.

"Can't I help? Tell me what's wrong."

"Nothing. Just go."

She glanced over at his bent form as he perched on the side of her bed. Hers, not theirs. No longer theirs.

His eyes were closed, but his lips moved silently. Of course. He was praying.

That just made it worse. She hated him thinking he could

control her by talking to or about some unreal being. She knew better. The power was *in her*, not out there.

"Stop that." This time she'd sounded just as definite as she'd meant to, just as decisive.

His eyes opened, and in the dim light she thought she recognized compassion. Or, more likely, pity. She did not need or want him to feel sorry for her. Once it might have been love, but that had obviously died along with hers for him. Now all he offered was the means to her independence. A means she never wanted to be without.

Especially as she'd lost her mother's, what with Jeminy playing the victim and cajoling that whole town into thinking she was someone special. The lawyer, the police lieutenant, who knew who else?

She'd reconsidered things since her conversation with JoAnn. The more she thought about it, the more convinced she was Jeminy would get it all if she couldn't figure out a way to stop her before it was too late.

She thinned her lips into a smile and pressed her other hand to her forehead. "I'm sorry, Larry. I was having a nightmare." Pause, deep breath, more smile, and "Thank you for checking on me. I'll be fine."

"Will you?"

She nodded, resting both hands on the bed. "I'll go wash my face and go back to sleep. The dream is over."

"Do you want me to stay?"

There was that puppy-dog look again. It made her want to gag.

"Probably not tonight," she said with as much regret as she could put into her voice.

Or ever again.

But she didn't say that.

As he left, she scooted off the bed and retrieved the bottle she kept in the hamper and carried it to the bathroom and her empty "water" glass. A little clear liquid with a kick and she'd sleep like a baby.

61

JEMINY

Into the black, a tiny light glimmers, a pinprick, a circle,
To shatter the darkness, to bury the fear.

A breeze wafted up the stairs, as if the front door had opened. She kept her eyes closed, her foxhole prayers going up as best as she knew how, and hoped Rand wouldn't come to check.

Whatever malevolent spirit propelled him now brought him, armed and ready, out of the bathroom. He was a little woozy, if the wavering of the flashlight was any indication. He'd been turning it off intermittently, probably to save the battery, but it had to be running low by now.

He paused at the entrance to her bedroom and listened. Even she heard it now, a stealthy creak of boards, but if rescue were on the way, whoever it was would be slaughtered by Rand's bullets if they tried to come up the stairs. He knelt on the floor, pulled from his left pocket what looked like an extra magazine. Great. More bullets meant more possible deaths.

This did not bode well for anyone out there, and it was all her fault. She'd led this madman here, and now he not only threatened her, but also whoever was on the stairs. Could Nana have gone down to fetch something or to look for her? Would he shoot without checking to see who it was? Shoot an innocent old lady?

"What are you doing?" she asked.

"Hush." He whispered it with a wave of the gun toward her.

Jeminy had to free herself and even up the odds. If she called out a warning, Rand was crazy enough to put a bullet in her.

She twisted her hands, tried to make them small enough to slide out of the restraints. He'd tied her in a hurry. Surely she'd be able to undo the knots or slide her hands out. People did this all the time in the movies. They curled their thumb over their palm and bunched their fingers to narrow their hand.

Right one first. She inched her body up the headboard to relieve some of the tension on the knots. Then, ignoring the pain, she tried to slide one hand out. The fabric eased slightly on her right hand and tightened on her left. It wasn't going to work.

Lord, are You there? Please do something to stop Rand. Take him down before he takes down someone else, please... please...

Without pause, lightning flashed and thunder crashed, as if God wanted their attention. He had hers, but Rand now crouched at the doorway. And then, suddenly, he moaned, cried out, and dashed back to the bathroom.

What, he didn't want to spew whatever was left of his dinner on the hardwood floor? Or maybe he was afraid of being a target if he were sick right there.

While he was too busy upchucking to shoot her, she called out, "I'd help, Rand, but you tied me so tightly I can't get to you. You okay in there?"

At that, feet pounded up the stairs and down the hall, stopping outside the bedroom. One policeman, wet but fully vested and armed, entered slowly, shining his light around the room and taking up a position beside the bathroom entrance, his nose wrinkling at the stench. Clay followed. When Rand moaned, the first cop sidestepped and, pistol ready, eased open the door. They heard what sounded like a gun sliding across the floor.

"Lieutenant, our man is too ill to fight." The hilarity in the patrolman's voice made Jeminy grin.

"Ipecac," she said. "I put it in the salad dressing."

On a laugh, Clay holstered his gun and radioed someone named Avery. "Suspect disarmed. Send someone up to help Lee get the man out, and someone else to help with cleanup—"

"No, no," Jeminy interrupted, "I can see to that if you'll just untie me."

"Oh, and tell Eric to bring Mrs. Warren inside."

"Nana's out there? In this?"

"Brave woman. She's the one who let us in. We have her in a car with the heat on, but she can't be comfortable." As he spoke, he was trying to work the knots free around her wrists. "Mind if I cut this?"

"Please do."

He pulled out a pocket knife, and as he released her arms, they fell to her sides. She worked her fingers to get rid of the numbness and then eased off the bed, avoiding Rand's mess on the floor. More noises came from the bathroom.

"So, Mr. Radcliff, not feeling so very fine?" Clay said as he poked his head around the door.

Rand mumbled something.

"Sorry, didn't catch that."

"… Poisoned me."

"Oh, I don't think so. If she'd poisoned you, you'd be dead about now."

"'Tempted murder… arrest… arrest her."

"Read him his rights, Lee."

ERIC

One of the officers took charge of getting Mrs. Warren inside. Eric couldn't wait for them to move. Fortunately, the electricity came back on before he even reached the front hall.

Dashing up the stairs, he prayed Jeminy was okay, that the cretin hadn't hurt her.

And there she was, rubbing her wrists. He surprised a glad light in her eyes when she saw him.

That was all he needed. He opened his arms, and she flew into them, her arms circling his neck as his closed around her. "Oh, honey, are you okay? Did he do anything to you?"

"No," she said, but the word was muffled against his shoulder.

"Thank God," he said, his hold tightening.

That was when he became aware of a horrible stench pervading the air. He didn't want to let her go, but he had to get them away from it.

Amid shuffling noises and a few grunts and groans, Clay and one of the officers brought out a miserable looking man with a sallow face and bleary eyes. "Eric," Clay said. "You may want to get Jeminy out of here. It's pretty nasty."

"What happened? Somebody kick him in the gut?"

"Ipecac," Jeminy said, standing back. "I need to clean up the mess he made."

Man, somebody'd better. "Where's a bucket and cleaning stuff?"

While he cleaned—better be some brownie points for this one—Jeminy helped her grandmother change into a dry gown and climb into bed again. He'd just about finished by the time she rejoined him.

"Oh, Eric, I'm so sorry you had to do that."

She looked beat. And was that a bump on her head?

"You get hit?" he asked, pointing to her hairline.

"It could have been a lot worse. I made him mad."

"Just let me get my hands on the creep." He had another word in mind, but he wasn't going to say it.

"I think maybe he's got regrets enough."

Eric grinned. "Ipecac was a smart move."

She smiled back. "I'm glad I noticed it in the refrigerator. I don't know how old it was, but Rand was so ravenous, he barely noticed it in his salad dressing." She eased down on the side of her bed. "He was on something that made him completely bonkers. You won't believe his crazy idea for getting rich this time."

"Tell me," he said as he set the bucket, rags, and plastic bag in the hall.

He sat down next to her while she spoke. When she'd completed her tale, he pulled her toward him. "I'm so glad you were so quick-thinking. In that state? No telling what he might have tried."

"And Nana. She was the real heroine of the night."

"She was indeed. You should have seen her coming out the

front door, straight at the police cars, ignoring the rain. She was amazing. Seems she got the police here by calling 911."

Jeminy leaned on him. "What brought you? I mean, I get Clay and all…"

"Clay thought it might be important to me."

"He did, did he?"

"Annie Mac came for Danny. When we got here and I stood outside, unable to do anything, I was glad I wasn't armed because I badly wanted to break down the door and murder whoever was holding you hostage." He sighed and smoothed a hand over her head. "You didn't need us after all, you two intrepid ladies."

She sat up and giggled. Actually giggled. "We did pretty well, didn't we?"

"Very well." He stood up. She had to be so exhausted. "You need to climb in that bed and try to sleep.

She stood with him and glanced around the room. "You know, I think I'll sleep in one of the rooms across the hall. Tomorrow, I'll air out this place completely."

He sniffed. "Just smells like disinfectant to me."

"Even that's too much right now. I'll take care of it tomorrow." She led the way from the room.

He followed her downstairs and to the door. "I hope you can get some sleep."

"Thank you for coming."

They stared at each other for a moment, a little awkwardly, because somehow the emotions of the night had taken them to a new level of intimacy. And then he pulled her close, kissed her, and backed away.

"I'll call you," he said, glancing at his watch, "in about five hours."

"Okay."

"Lock the door. Back door lock's busted, but Clay said they boarded it until we can fix it tomorrow."

"Thank you."

"Goodnight." He opened the door and stepped out.

"Night." She stood there until he'd reached the sidewalk.

He heard the door close softly as he headed down Front Street. He'd better call Clay, see when he might be able to hitch a ride home.

JEMINY

The time has come, the time has come,...

"I won't stay any longer, sweet girl, but I had to hug you for myself, see that you're truly no worse for wear." Her daddy's big hands cupped her cheeks. "At least it's over, finally, and you can go about your life without worrying what's around the corner or who might be hiding in the bushes."

"Thank God for that," Jeminy leaned into him when he lowered his hands, and she hugged him hard.

"Amen."

"I love you, Daddy. Thank you for coming all this way."

"Any time. Always. I'm sorry your mother wasn't willing to make the trip. She said it's hard on her back."

"She has back issues?"

Frustration showed in his eyes. "So she says."

"I hope she feels better soon."

"Yes, well, I'd better get on the road. I'm likely to hit traffic around Raleigh this time of day." He turned to Nana, who was sitting in her rocker. "Georgina, it was lovely to see you."

Nana glanced up. "Thank you. It was kind of you to visit. Do you have everything you need?"

"I do. Thank you again." And with a quick kiss to Jeminy's cheek, he was off the porch and headed to his car.

Nana didn't speak until he'd pulled out of the driveway. "That man looks very familiar. Do we know him?"

"Yes, we do, Nana. That was my daddy."

"Your daddy? Are you sure?"

"I am. He is wearing new glasses."

"I haven't seen him in years, but we used to know each other quite well." Nana pointed to the other rocker. "Why don't you sit a spell?"

Jeminy sat and studied the puffs of white dappling a bright blue sky. She and Olli used to lie on the grass, side by side, pointing out cloud images. "There's a horse!' or "I spy a dragon!"

Oh, Olli. "I miss you, sweet brother."

She didn't realize she'd said the words aloud until Nana spoke from her own rocker. "He's waiting for us."

A short time ago, Jeminy wouldn't have been able to relate to that, the promise of a heaven she'd thought mythical, the idea she'd be reunited with her twin.

Or her baby.

But now? Her time with her grandmother and her new friends had shifted her focus and her belief system. After last night, a night that could have gone so wrong and yet hadn't, a night that had brought some sort of closure to her past, Jeminy had tried a more full-blown faith on for size. The choice she'd faced had been to believe and follow or to wallow and wonder. Wallowing hadn't done even the tiniest bit of good, and either the Bible and God's followers spoke truth—or they didn't.

Now, she didn't just hope. She knew.

What an odd concept, that one could *know* God lived. It was as if she'd walked to the edge of the water and a voice had said, *Step in.* She had, and that step had let her enter the realm of faith. What did the Bible say? Faith was *the substance of things hoped for, the evidence of things not seen.*

She'd hoped for something more than the life she'd lived, a life that had left her empty and hurting, but with a hope that had held no substance. It had seemed out of reach without evidence to back it up. Now? Now, she'd stepped into that water and believed. Now, her hope had substance and her faith provided the evidence of things she couldn't see.

It was miraculous, really.

"Nana, do you need anything?"

"I'm fine, honey. Just fine. I may just sit here and put my head back. I'm kind of tired today." She reached out to touch Jeminy's extended hand. "I had so many strange dreams last night that kept me awake."

"It was a strange night, wasn't it?"

"Maybe I'll just take a short nap."

Jeminy stood. "There's a nice, light breeze, but if you'd be more comfortable inside, you can come with me."

"I'm fine right here. You go on." Nana settled back, her eyes still open.

"I'm going to work on my music."

"Oh, look, honey. A sailboat."

A small sloop motor-sailed up the channel, its sleek lines outlined against the marsh on the other side of Taylor Creek. Jeminy sighed. "Lovely, isn't it?"

"Why don't you come sit a while? It's so nice out."

"Thank you, Nana. I'll be back out in a while. Is that okay?"

"Of course, honey. You do whatever makes you happy."

Gully was where she'd left him on the couch. After tuning up, Jeminy began strumming, only to be interrupted by the ringing of her cell phone.

"What's this I hear about excitement at your house?" Isa asked.

"Word travels quickly, doesn't it?"

When she'd answered Isa's questions, she hit speed dial for Annie Mac's phone to thank her for all she'd done to get Clay and Eric here. "I was so frightened." Tears threatened at the memory.

"That's one reason Clay thought to include Eric," Annie Mac said. "It's obvious you two have something going on."

"I guess we do. Anyway, thanks again."

Other calls would have to wait. She reached for Gully, but a knock sounded at the front door. Brisa stood on the other side of the screen, along with her best friends.

"Hello," Jeminy said as she stepped out onto the porch.

"Oh, Miss Jeminy," Brisa said, a little breathlessly. "Is it true? Did a man with a gun try to rob you?"

Jilly piped up with, "Danny here said his dad had to come save you."

Tyler, it seemed, wasn't to be outdone. Tyler matched Brisa in height, and now he stepped forward, a smug expression on his face. "He only came with *my* dad. My dad's the one who got the bad guy's gun."

Jeminy laughed. "Hey, hang on, guys. Both fathers came to our rescue. Both were equally important in saving Nana and me."

"Did they *save* us?" Nana leaned forward in her rocker, worry in her voice.

"They did. Last night when the bad man was here. You remember you had dreams about it."

"Oh. Well, I'm glad then. Thank you, children."

"It wasn't us," Danny said. "It was our dads."

"Oh." Confusion registered on her grandmother's face.

"It's okay, Nana. All is well now."

"That's good."

"He's been 'rested." That was the girl with Down Syndrome. What was her name?

"Absolutely," Jeminy said. "He won't hurt anyone any longer."

She sincerely hoped that was true and that Rand would be locked up for a good long time.

"Linney and me," said the shorter boy with glasses, "we didn't know about it until we went to Jilly's. Hope you don't mind us coming to ask you."

What a sweetie. "I don't mind at all—" She paused because his name hadn't stuck either, but at least he'd told her his sister's name.

"Louis. I'm Louis Morgan. Miss Hannah and Mr. Matt adopted Linney and me."

Now she remembered. She smiled at him. "Thank you, Louis. I apologize that names sometimes escape me."

"Oh, that's okay. It happens to a lot of folks."

"Louis," Jilly said, speaking to her and her grandmother, "is smart. I mean, really smart. He's way ahead in school."

"How lovely." Not that *lovely* was the appropriate word, but Jilly's pride in her friend seemed so touching—the way all these kids looked out for one another.

Brisa reached out to get her attention by touching her arm. "I wanted to ask if you've written more songs. My dad and I, well, we've been hoping."

"The thousand-dollar question." Jeminy was about to continue when Danny said, "Thousand-dollar question?"

"I mean," Jeminy said, "that while I've begun a new song, I'm not at all sure when it will be ready for anyone to hear."

There was a chorus of *ohs* and nods.

"But I hope it will be ready for you to sing with me very soon," she said.

"Oh, goody!" That from Brisa. She started to usher the other kids off the porch. "Come on, guys. Let's leave Miss Jeminy alone so she can write her song. My dad says he *really* wants it."

"Tell him I'm trying," Jeminy said as she watched them go.

"What nice children," Nana said.

"Yes, ma'am. Very nice children." Jeminy turned toward the

door. "I'm heading back inside. Have you had enough of sitting out here?"

"I think I need a nap." Nana pushed herself up and waited a moment before moving. Jeminy stood ready to stabilize her if she needed it, but her grandmother's steps were firm when she finally moved.

Jeminy read the words she'd scribbled and recognized their power, but something stopped her when she tried to begin writing again.

Her sins were washed, but the memories hadn't been. How could she possibly go on when they still had the power to set her back?

She longed to talk to Eric about the God thing… and other issues… but she hadn't heard from him since last night. Maybe he was running fast and far. After all, her choices had made the mess that had put her grandmother's life in jeopardy. It didn't matter that the shooter had been a crazed child-abuser selling kids out of the foster-care system, because the rest, Rand following her to Beaufort with his own probably drug-induced delusions, had been on her.

Eric wouldn't want Danny put in such a position.

Not that he would be now that Rand and that nasty Jenkins were behind bars. Rand probably wouldn't stay there long, not the way the courts were letting criminals run free every day. But Jenkins was a different matter. Attempted murder and child trafficking would likely keep him locked up for years.

She'd told Eric about the abortion, and he'd tried to comfort her, but the memory of that was bound to come haunting them both again.

She checked on her sleeping grandmother and headed out the door to the sidewalk. Maybe clarity would come as she walked.

If only.

Blindly, she found her way down Front Street to a bench that hid her face from onlookers. Only the marsh and the water would see her weeping mess or hear her sniffles.

She searched the pockets of her shorts and withdrew the only tissue she carried. It was useless in minutes, and she wiped her runny nose with the back of her hand and tried, desperately, to stop the flow.

He didn't speak as he lowered himself beside her, but he did pull out a bandana and place it in her hand. She didn't look at him, but hoped her nod let him know how grateful she was. As the tears slowed and finally stopped, he asked if he could help.

She shook her head, but maybe it was his stillness, his silence that gave her permission to relax. They seemed cocooned on that bench. No one else came by, the normal traffic stayed downtown.

6 4

DEBORAH

She'd had time to think as she sat sipping a cup of latte at the island counter. Larry had barely paused to shower before he'd dashed off to Beaufort to be there for Jeminy.

Fine, Deborah got it. His daughter had been held at gunpoint by a man that same daughter had brought into their lives. As always, Daddy would hurry to the rescue.

Deborah was tired of it. She was tired of worrying about Carole, tired of playing second-to-everyone in her husband's life. And she was sick and tired of having Larry use money to control her.

She picked up her phone and called Dave.

She walked over to the French doors leading to the garden, but anger kept her from seeing much beyond a riot of green. When Dave told her North Carolina was not a community property state, she tightened her lips against the words that came to mind. But they'd been there, just beneath the surface, as Dave continued with the bad news. "The court will insist on an

417

equitable division, Deborah, and only property obtained during the marriage is considered in the division. If he can prove you overspent or wasted the resources, the judge might give him a bigger share."

He talked about other things, and none of them boded well for her if Larry decided to be unpleasant. It was up to her to figure things out so he'd cooperate.

"What about the lawsuit against your mother and the other two? You still want to follow through with that?"

It would be costly, and she might not win. "I doubt it. I mean, I don't want to deplete Mama's assets any more than my daughter and that woman will. Besides, that's not something you'd do on a contingency basis is it?"

"I can't do that."

"Not even for me?"

"I'm afraid not, as much as I value you as a friend."

She longed to push against the glass in front of her, push against something—Dave's balding head?—to change his words, all of them. He was useless. "I'll get back to you if I want to pursue a divorce."

He cleared his throat. "May I speak as a friend and not just your attorney?"

She turned from the door, surprised. "Of course."

"I've known you two a long time, and financially you'll be a lot better off staying in the marriage. Don't you think you can manage that?"

"If it weren't for Carole…"

"Deborah, listen. Carole may be interested in becoming the next Mrs. Lawrence Buchanan, but Larry's not about to mess around with her."

Sure, right, what did Dave know? She just wanted off the phone. "Maybe, maybe not. Thanks for your help."

"Any time."

The silent house felt like a tomb. Larry would probably eat

something on his way home from Beaufort, if he didn't decide to stay overnight with Jeminy. What did he care if his wife ate alone?

She could order something. Put on a movie. Fill at least one room with noise.

She phoned the best Japanese restaurant in town and asked them to send the chef's recommendation. Sushi, a drink, and a movie might take her mind off the messes that seemed to require a decision, one she wasn't ready to make.

Her meal arrived forty minutes after she ordered it, but she hadn't minded the wait. She'd opened a new bottle of white wine and was sipping slowly as she set up a tray with silver, a good pair of chopsticks, and her best china. There was no reason not to indulge just because she was alone. She'd never be able to use her lovely pieces if she waited until she had company, even the company of her husband.

She picked out a romantic comedy to help her forget that her life held no romance and very little comedy, and when the food arrived, she mixed a dollop of wasabi into a small bowl of soy sauce. There was nothing better than perfectly prepared food, dipped in perfectly seasoned sauce. But first, a little more wine. Perhaps she should bring the bottle to the den with her so she wouldn't have to get up during the meal.

It was delicious. As she toyed with the savory pieces, she watched Meg Ryan act ridiculous. The story and Meg might have brought a smile to her lips at any other time, but she was soon distracted by thoughts of her conversation with Dave. Had his tone changed when she mentioned divorce? She knew he'd been attracted to her before—a woman can always tell—but did her acknowledging a failed marriage pique his interest?

Maybe he'd suggested she stay married to Larry because he didn't want a second marriage. Dave had money, and although he was balding and had a slight paunch, he was attractive enough. But did she really want to be with any man ever again?

After Larry? She didn't think so.

But there was the issue of money.

The front door opened, closed, and Larry called out. She waited for him to look for her, and when footfalls sounded at the den's entrance, she glanced up. "I didn't order for you."

"I wouldn't have expected you to. I picked up barbecue on my way home." He headed to the stairs. "I'll be down in a minute."

By the time Larry returned, she'd finished her sushi, turned off the movie, and carried her tray and the wine bottle to the kitchen. She poured herself another glass to sip as she rinsed her plate. Larry eased past where she stood and filled a glass with filtered water from the spout in the refrigerator door.

Then he headed to the living room. "Do you want to hear how your daughter is?" he asked over his shoulder.

She watched him over the rim of her raised glass. "Of course. Although if she weren't fine, you wouldn't have returned home, would you?" Settling her nerves took a good two swigs, two hefty swigs.

Larry eased down into his favorite chair. She really didn't want to follow him, but she had to play nice, at least until things were settled between them.

He scowled. "What will it take, Deborah? What do you need to make you happy?" He added a barely heard, "Other than God, that is."

"Oh, stop with the God-talk. I mean it, Larry. God's never done a thing for me," she said, heading back for a refill.

"He's done things you never acknowledged because you're unwilling to see the good in anything. You focus on what you lost and not on what you have."

She whirled around. "What do I have? Hmm? A daughter who lived like a slut with a man who almost killed her? A husband who'd rather be anywhere else, with *anyone* else, than with me? You talk about the love of God, but you don't know the first thing about love. You never even loved Olli!"

She threw her wine glass against the brick hearth, and, with tears streaming down her cheeks, she fled, yelling, *"I hate you! And I hate your God!"*

It was after nine when she made up her mind. She heard the television babbling at Larry in the den and entered without knocking on the closed door. Larry glanced up.

"Turn that thing off, please."

He did, but he didn't speak.

"I need to get away."

"Oh? For how long?"

"I don't know. I thought I'd start with a two-week spa visit. You know that place I went before? The Wholeness Healing Center?"

"After Olli?"

"Yes. They have counselors and yoga teachers. They'll help me get centered again."

"You really think that's wise? They practice really off-the-wall stuff."

"What, because they believe in living in the now and know how to awaken consciousness?"

"Deborah, you're an educated woman. What does that even mean?"

She sat down across from him, unable to keep the excitement out of her voice. "I know you don't believe in what they do, Larry, but the woman I worked with before has the most amazing guide who shows her how to get in touch with the spirit world. Maybe this time I'll be able to reach Olli."

Larry's head fell against the back rest. "Oh, honey."

"It'll be good for me, and I really need to get away for a while."

He turned his head and looked beseechingly at her. "How about another trip to Paris? Or Greece? You loved spending time there."

Deborah stood. "I've made up my mind. I need to go to the Center." She sighed. "Look, you've chosen your path, all that God-stuff, but I get to choose mine. And I choose this."

"Do you plan to come home after the two weeks?"

"I don't know. When I decide, I'll tell you."

65

JEMINY

Melody in minor key moves to notes in major C,
The time has come, the time has come, to praise the Lord.

She really didn't want to be interrupted, not as close as she was to a breakthrough with her music. But he stood on the other side of the screen door, worry lines marring his forehead, his hands jammed in his front pockets. "You busy?" he asked.

She stared at him, trying to imagine what might be worrying him. "I was trying to write."

"Not going so well?"

Not so well, she might have said. Or, not yet. Instead, she shrugged. "The operative word is *trying.*"

"May I come in?"

"I really want to get this song finished."

He glanced behind him and then back at her. "I guess I can come by later."

He looked so pitiful that she opened the door. "You're here. You might as well come in."

His movements were so unlike the confident man she was beginning to know. Not like the man who'd comforted her and drawn her close. He was still standing at the room's opening when she eased down next to her guitar.

"Sit, please."

He took the chair facing her, bending forward, his forearms resting on his thighs. He glanced around. "Your grandmother napping?"

"Isa took her out, said they'd have an early dinner."

"Jeminy," he began.

She waited.

"I need to tell you… I know it's too soon. I mean, my own life's just coming under the semblance of control, what with Danny and all, and you're still recovering. I know that." His babbling efforts should have endeared him to her, but her fingers itched to touch the strings of her guitar.

"Well, the thing is," he said, "It's been coming on me for a while now. I tried to ignore it. Actually, I tried to pretend it away."

Had he been drinking? She'd never known him to drink at midday—or ever, although he probably had the occasional beer, maybe wine. But, after all, she barely knew him. "What are you talking about?"

He acted as if she hadn't spoken. "I wanted it to be mere attraction. I mean, I told you I was attracted, and a simple attraction would have made things easier for both of us. Friendship, you know?"

"But?"

He sat straighter. "Well, I sort of got hit over the head. God."

"God hit you?"

He laughed, but it seemed humorless. "I mean, I've been praying and asking God what it is, what I'm to do about it, and I keep getting the impression that I'm to tell you."

What on earth was he trying to say? "Eric, I hate to ask, but are you on something?" Because his behavior resembled some she'd seen in California.

"*What?* No, of course not. Nothing. Sober as can be."

"Then, what are you talking about?"

He ran his fingers through his hair and then pulled at it. "I'm making a mess of this. But, look, I'm falling for you. I shouldn't be. You're my client. But we've been through so much together, and I can't seem to keep you pigeonholed as a client." For the first time, he grinned. "Besides, it's what the Lord seems to be telling me."

Besides that. Right. She closed her eyes and took a deep breath before expelling it and whispering, "You can't be."

"It seems I can."

"Then," she said, standing, "*I can't.*"

"Oh, okay. Sorry." He stood also and brushed his hands down slacks, his expression hard to read. For several moments, he didn't say anything. And then he sighed. "Maybe I imagined I heard from God." He headed into the hall, turning back in the doorway. "I shouldn't have spoken."

She remained rooted in front of the couch. She should call him back. Apologize—or at least explain. But what could she say?

As the door closed quietly behind him, tremors began in her legs, moved upward. He'd said he was falling in love with her. How could that be?

She didn't deserve him. She *couldn't* deserve him. There were all her mistakes, mistakes that would take a toll on any relationship. She was better off staying single until enough time had passed to take the edge off her guilt and to make other memories to cover the horrible ones.

"Love isn't about deserving. It's a gift."

The voice in her head startled her, so unexpected were the words. Fine, she'd been listening, talking to God while she tried to craft a song, but she'd also let frustration in.

And she'd heard the Lord answer with his *I forgive you,* but that still seemed so hard to believe. Now God was saying she didn't have to deserve love? It was a gift?

He loved her in her unworthiness. It was still too much to believe. She sent her query heavenward. *A gift?*

"How would you feel if your offering were rejected? That's how I feel when people refuse my love and my sacrifice."

God? You?

"Rejection hurts, doesn't it?"

She nodded.

"Call Eric back."

She ran to the door, flung it open, and saw him sitting on the edge of the porch, his head in his hands. He didn't look up.

"Come back?" She spoke it as a question, soft and hopeful.

He turned his head to look at her. His expression cautious.

"Please?"

He pushed up and slowly approached. "Why?"

Now what?

"God told me to?"

"Really? Why?"

God? She waited, but the voice in her head remained silent. She guessed she was on her own. "I'm sorry."

"For what?" He stuck his hands back in those pockets, his shoulders rounded.

"You offered me a gift, and I rejected it."

"Yeah, well, you have the right to reject anything you don't want."

"Can we go in?" This was so awkward. *Lord, help, please.*

He waved away her suggestion. "Just say what you want to say, and I'll be on my way."

She recognized the protective mode he'd adopted as one she often used. "I didn't..." She cleared her throat. "I, well, I... I didn't mean to say I don't want the... um... gift."

He still didn't speak.

In a rush, she finished. "I do. I mean, I would. It's just I don't feel worthy." *Breathe.* "I know… I mean, God's been telling me that worthy isn't the issue because none of us is worthy enough. I guess I've hated myself for so long because of that big thing I did, and so I can't imagine someone knowing I killed my own baby and still being able to love me." She cleared her throat. "I mean, how?"

He came closer and reached out a hand. She stared down at it for a moment before placing hers in it. He squeezed gently.

"Jeminy, we have so much to learn about each other and about God's love for us, but I'd like to try doing it together. Slow and easy will be fine—for now—but will you at least let this thing between us have a chance?"

She backed up to the screen door, still keeping her hand in his. And she nodded. "Please."

He leaned in, touched her cheek with his free hand, and stared for a moment at her lips. In that pause, a tingle focused her attention on what he was doing, was about to do. As her breath quickened, she closed her eyes and felt the gentle brush of his kiss, a brush that brought her hands to his shoulders as he drew her closer, as his kiss went from barely there to more.

The more she'd always wondered about and never felt with a man before, a treasuring of her lips. Of her.

And so, with his promise of slow and easy, her arms slid around his neck, and she kissed him right back.

EPILOGUE

JEMINY

I am still confident of this: I will see the goodness of the Lord in the land of the living. Psalm 27:13 NIV

"Here's to us." Eric raised his glass of water in honor of their anniversary. "To my beautiful wife and—" he saluted her very pregnant belly "—to the babies who will soon be with us."

Henry had prepared a sumptuous meal, and Jeminy longed to eat more than the few bites that fit in the space not occupied by their unborn twins. She slid her plate a few inches away.

Agnes brought her a to-go box. "Honey, I'll be over first thing tomorrow to see what you need done."

Eric stood and gave her a quick hug. "Thanks, Agnes. Tell my brother the food was delicious, as always." Then he helped Jeminy into her coat, a coat that barely closed over her bulging middle.

She waddled out of the small restaurant, grateful to be up and moving. Outside, she took Eric's arm for support on the short walk home.

She barely slept that night. Her back ached. She got up several times to use the bathroom and felt cramps that she assumed were Braxton-Hicks. She left the bedroom quietly and went to the kitchen to make herself a soothing cup of herbal tea. That didn't work.

So she decided to do some cleaning and organizing in the already clean and organized kitchen. By the time Eric got up with Danny, she was ready for a nap. "I'm sorry, love. Do you mind?"

"You sure you're okay?"

"Just a little insomnia. I'll be fine if I close my eyes and rest for a while." She crawled back under the covers.

"I'll make sure Georgie's fine," her saint of a husband said as he tucked the comforter around her.

A couple of hours after Eric and Danny had left, she realized the cramps were morphing into something closer to the real thing. She lumbered out of bed, fluffed her pillows and laid them over the inexpertly tucked-in comforter. Eric may have spoken prophetically when he suggested the babies would be born early.

By the time Agnes showed up with Annie Mac and Tadie to help get the house ready for the holidays—insisting Jeminy was *not* to climb ladders or stress herself—she recognized full-blown contractions for what they were.

Fortunately, the tree was already up and the lights strung before her friends arrived. Tadie and Agnes helped Nana hang ornaments, while Annie Mac acted as Jeminy's temporary labor coach. Tadie had made the call to Eric's office, promising to phone again if things progressed more quickly than expected. He'd promised to get home as soon as possible.

Jeminy listened to the chatter and tried to relax between pains. At the next one, she rubbed her fingers in circles over her belly and breathed in rapid whooshes.

"Are they getting closer, lovey?" Nana asked, worry lines etching her forehead.

More powerful, anyway. "Mmm..." was all she could say. Maybe Eric ought to hurry it up.

Annie Mac panted with her. "Slow down. That's right. You're doing great."

As the contraction waned, Jeminy closed her eyes and leaned her head against the padded chair. "Is this—are they okay? So early..." Because she couldn't help her fears. "These babies shouldn't be coming until after Christmas.

"You'll be fine," Annie Mac said, squeezing her hand. "You're only a couple of weeks ahead of schedule. They're big enough. And soon they'll be crawling around."

"With your boy." Agnes grinned over at Annie Mac. "And then mine."

Jeminy felt tears well behind her closed lids. *What if?* The pregnancy had come so soon after marriage, and that had come so soon after she'd committed to thinking about a relationship. *Thinking* about it, not doing it. Being open to faith and love.

Learning how to trust was so hard. She opened her eyes and looked around. "I don't deserve—"

"Don't you dare finish that sentence." Agnes spoke from beside the tree where she was choosing an ornament. "It's not about deserving."

Tadie chimed in with, "Amen. The Lord has shown each and every one of us He's all about pouring blessings into our lives and restoring what we've lost. Not about condemning us for our failures."

Jeminy sighed. He'd given her so much, a husband, a young son, these friends. How could she be worth something as huge as two healthy babies on top of all that?

It's not about your worth. It's about His grace.

"Honey, we all love you, but that's nothing compared to how much the Lord loves you." Annie Mac laid a gentle hand on Jeminy's belly. "Get ready."

Jeminy nodded. "Love you," she whispered while she still could. Eric needed to get himself home. They should be at the hospital.

Nana shifted closer. "Is she okay?"

"She is, Georgie," Tadie said. "She's getting ready to bring your great-grandbabies into the world. Don't you worry."

"With us here, of course she's fine." Agnes said.

Tadie's phone rang. Once the contraction passed, Jeminy tried to stand. Not only was she restless, but her back was on fire. She braced her hands on the arms of the chair and pushed her ungainly self up. Annie Mac, head and shoulders shorter than she, reached out to help.

"Don't. I'd just drag you over."

Tadie waved her phone. "That was Eric. He just dropped Danny off at your house, Agnes."

Agnes nodded. "So he'll be here momentarily."

"What do you think?" Tadie asked her. "You about ready to go to the birthing center?"

"More than. I need to be sure everybody's okay."

"You having back pain?" Agnes must have noticed her pressing against the wall.

"That last one especially."

"They'll probably give you an epidural, make things easier."

Jeminy shook her head.

Agnes squinted at her. "Your choice, honey, but don't forget, you have two to push out, and you haven't seen anything yet, far as pain goes."

Tadie waved off Agnes's words. "It'll pass soon enough, and all will be forgotten when you hold those babies." Pointing to the packed overnight case near the door, she said, "I added a sandwich for Eric, and any one of us will bring more food if he needs it."

Jeminy raised her brows. "You thinking this is going to take a while?"

"Will was thrilled with the food Matt brought in when I was in having Sammy." Tadie paused a moment. "Did you imagine when you married a twin that you'd end up carrying one of each?"

"I never thought about it." Jeminy massaged the place over her right hip. "Should have. Twins from both sides."

"I guess I'd better consider it," a barely pregnant Agnes said. Then she laughed. "Wouldn't that be fun? If my next were two?"

"Lots of cousins," Jeminy said and braced her back against the wall.

Tadie waved her away from the wall and pressed her hands where Jeminy's had been. "Both sides?"

"Yes, please."

By the time she'd panted through another one, Eric had thrown open the door and was by her side. "How are you? How often?"

"Five minutes." It was Annie Mac who answered. "They're expecting you at the hospital."

Eric picked up her coat and held it out so she could slide her arms in.

Nana went to the hall closet. "I will come with you. I can help."

"Georgie." Tadie tucked her arm through Nana's. "Isa's on her way over, and we promised to finish decorating. Get the house ready for their return."

Jeminy leaned over to kiss her grandmother's cheek. "Don't forget the box of special decorations we found. Olli's paper chain."

"Paper chain?" Nana sounded confused.

"In that shoebox by the table." Jeminy waved toward it. "Nana, you helped Olli make it when he got sick and couldn't go with Grandpa and me to get the tree."

Nana beamed. "I wrapped it in tissue every year. And I think there are a few you made in that box, too."

"Let's go." Eric picked up the hospital bag and steered her toward the door. "I'll call as soon as we have news."

There was a chorus of: "We'll be praying hard," and "Love you."

Annie Mac reached over with a quick hug. "God's been with you through it all. You can do this."

At the door, Jeminy turned. "Thank you all for being here. I'm so blessed."

Another chorus of "We love you!" followed them to the car.

An ice storm was forecast overnight, but it wasn't supposed to begin for a few hours. The stoplights cooperated as they drove through Morehead City. She'd read that bouncing in a car helped things along, which would be really great about now, although she reconsidered when they crossed a bump during a contraction.

"Hold on," Eric said, reaching out as she panted. "Almost there."

And then they were. He pulled into emergency parking and got out to help her to her feet. Jeminy leaned into her husband's arm. Before she knew it, she was sitting in a wheelchair in front of the receptionist's window and her water was breaking.

"Sorry," she said as soon as she had a voice again.

The woman laughed. "Don't you worry, honey. We're used to things like that. You just hang on right there, and we'll get you up to your labor room."

Eric followed the chatty person wheeling her along. And soon they were in a room, being assisted by a nurse, and Jeminy was changing into a hospital gown. Good thing they'd packed a robe.

"Honey," the nurse said, "you get into that gown and we'll be in to check you out."

"Her water broke," Eric said. "And she's having twins."

"The doctor will be with you in a few minutes, and I'll alert the anesthesiologist too."

"She'd rather not have an epidural."

"Doctor's going to want to have her ready in case there's an issue with the second baby, but you take it up with her."

The doctor allowed labor to move forward without the meds, and it was all pant-breath-moan, with monitors and the occasional exam and encouraging words. Jeminy wasn't surprised by the pain, although there was no minimizing it. But at least it was going remarkably fast.

Or so said the doctor.

It didn't feel fast to her.

Eric leaned over and whispered another prayer as he wiped her brow. "You're so beautiful," he told her.

"Thank—oops." She went back to her breathing routine, leaning forward so Eric could massage her back and pant with her.

The urge to push followed soon after. Two nurses were on board, one for each baby, and when the doctor said it was a go, she began pushing and panting and pushing until finally a pink bundle of wrinkly baby girl pushed her way out. Seven minutes later, a little more slowly, with the need for a little more help, their son arrived.

"Thank You, Lord," Eric whispered. Were those tears in his eyes?

Jeminy swiped at ones leaking from hers. She hadn't had to be sedated, and there'd been no rush to a C-section. Those baby cries… how lovely were those baby cries.

"Good lungs," one of the nurses said as she wiped and weighed their boy child.

"Well done, Jeminy," the doctor said. "Your size probably helped you carry them as long as you did, and they're both healthy."

Soon, both were on her chest, skin-to-skin. "Oh, Eric."

"You did great," Eric said, bending over to kiss her. "They're perfect. Look at that dark hair on Rose."

Exhausted as she was, she couldn't help but gloat a little. "You noticed Rose was not about to let her brother come into the world first."

"But, my precious wife, Ryan means king and his other name, Oliver, is associated with peace, fruitfulness, and dignity, so we'll see how those sibling wars play out. Besides, there's nothing scrawny about that boy." His laugh was filled with pride. "I don't know how you carried them both."

"They're beautiful, aren't they?" She ran her hands down their backs. Just touching them made her heart leap. "Maybe they'll be as precious to each other as Olli and I were."

"They'll have parents working for that—and praying."

"Yes." Yes, they would. What an amazing thought.

They were so beautiful, their children. She and Eric took turns holding each one, going skin-to-skin with each as the nurses suggested. Finally, Jeminy said, "Do you think it's too late to Facetime Hen so Danny can see his new siblings?"

Eric checked his watch. It was a little after ten o'clock. "I think it's a very civilized time for such an announcement. Henry and I were born in the wee hours."

He drew out his phone and called his brother. Henry answered right away. "News?"

"Here they are, Rose and Ryan and a very tired mama." He showed both bundles and then a smiling Jeminy.

"Hang on, let me wake Danny."

"Oh, not if he's asleep."

"Eric, you must know your son. He's been camped right here in front of a movie, trying to prop open his eyes. I need to wake him so I can get him into bed."

Danny jumped up and grabbed Henry's phone. "Which is which?"

Eric showed him. "Blue hat for Ryan, multicolored for Rose."

"They're real little."

"They are indeed. But they'll grow, and they'll be so excited to have you as their big brother."

"How long 'fore they can play with me?"

"It may take a while. You'll have to be patient."

"Okay. When are you coming home?"

"I'll let you know."

"Okay."

"Good job, guys." Henry came back into view. "We won't be far behind you."

"Cousins are always a good thing." Eric centered the camera on Jeminy.

"See you soon, Henry. Give everyone a hug."

"Will do. Night all."

Next, Eric texted Isa. She wrote right back. "Facetime?"

Technology, what would they do without it?

He dialed and waited. She picked up and oohed when Eric panned the faces of the babies and Jeminy.

"Georgie, can you see? The babies are here."

"Where?"

"Right here on the screen. Eric's showing us the babies."

"Oh, my, look at them. Jeminy, honey, you had two?"

"I did, Nana. Rose and Ryan."

"I knew a Rose once. She was lovely."

"Yes, and she's going to be so excited about her namesake."

That didn't even seem to register, which was just as well. Jeminy didn't have the energy to carry on a longer conversation.

"When will you be coming home?" Nana asked.

"Soon, Nana. I'm hoping tomorrow. As long as the babies do well tonight."

"I'm going to bed now. We waited. Isa and I. We wanted to know."

"Please sleep well. We'll see you very soon."

Jeminy sighed. "Texts to Tadie and the others?"

Eric took his phone. "I'll tell your dad we'll chat tomorrow." His fingers typed out the good news, and then he turned to her. "One just came back from Tadie. Says she'll pass on the news, we're to expect the girlfriends to gather sometime tomorrow."

"Not too early, I hope."

He grinned. "Please."

"I'll be glad of the help when we get home." She touched a little forehead. Then the other's. "Two, Eric. Two!"

"Our mothers had live-in help."

Jeminy gave a satisfied smile. "Annie Mac said they've made up a schedule for someone to come by every day to help change, cuddle, and do a little cooking."

"Good folks."

"And everyone has promised to have Danny over so he won't feel neglected. This town has been good for him, hasn't it?"

"The town and you."

"Danny just needed a loving family and a dad who keeps his word." She glanced up at her strong, wonderful husband.

Eric picked up the baby closest to him, Rose. "I can't believe how tiny she is. As for Danny, my bet is we'll have to peel him away from these two—"

"Until he gets bored because they don't *do* anything fun."

He laid them, one at a time, in their bassinets. "I'm going to take advantage of that pull-out couch in a little while. You need to get some sleep, too, while these two are quiet."

"I love you, darling man."

Bending over, he brushed her lips with his. "I love you more."

"Thank you for the babies."

"Sleep, love, if only for an hour."

"You, too," she said, closing her eyes.

Eric dimmed the lights, tucked her blanket around her, and stood over his children. Jeminy's eyes drifted open.

"Remember when you wanted to run from us because it was all happening so quickly?"

He turned back to her. "That was you. I popped the question and you freaked out."

"I didn't. Did I?"

He grinned. "We were dining on the boat, lamps lit, a little wine, and I told you I wanted to spend a lifetime being with you."

"Oh, right, that."

"Your expression was priceless, panic written all over you."

"Eric, no."

Now he laughed. "Yes, indeed."

She tried to picture that evening. Danny'd been staying over with Henry and Agnes, and Isa was having dinner with Nana. She'd been exhausted from a particularly hard day with her grandmother, who'd seemed very needy. Isa'd thought Nana might be coming down with a bad cold, which might explain her attitude. But it had worn Jeminy out, and all she'd wanted to do that evening was relax and not think about much at all. Certainly not about future plans.

She nodded. "I remember. You're right. I wanted to run away from everything that day." She reached toward her husband. "I'm sorry. You got the brunt of my frustration. Thank you for not giving up on me."

"I'm glad I finally realized what was going on and waited for a more propitious moment."

Jeminy laughed, a little tiredly. "I'm glad you did."

Her eyes drifted shut but opened again when his lips touched her forehead, and he said, "Sleep, love. I'll be right here."

He turned toward the babies, his profile visible. In the dimmed light she heard quiet whispers and a prayer. Oh, yes. She joined in, silently giving thanks for the abundance of love poured out in her life.

O God, thank You. Thank You for my just-borns, for my circle of friends, all of them who've become like family, and especially for Annie Mac. How blessed it's been to learn to laugh again.

Who'd ever have guessed that life could be this abundant when only eighteen months ago it had seemed bleak and empty?

It was hard to comprehend the goodness of God, but it overflowed into her heart and her mind and her spirit. She'd been too cowardly—or too selfish—to give birth to her first child, but God had more than restored the years the canker worm had eaten, even if she'd been the one to let that worm invade. Forgiveness was an almost unfathomable gift, along with a love bigger than the human mind could imagine. But she'd found it.

She could only whisper *Thank You*. And again, *Thank You*.

JEMINY'S SONG

It is time, it is time, for the words to be unleashed,
It is time, it is time, to set the music free.
Melody in minor key moves to notes in major C,
The time has come, the time has come, to praise the Lord.

Your truth crushed lies that tied me down,
By Your promises I am unbound,
I believe because You live in me,
I believe, O, I believe.

It is time, it is time, for my heart to be unleashed,
It is time, it is time, to set my spirit free.
Melody in minor key moves to notes in major C,
The time has come, the time has come, to praise the Lord.

By Your Love, the Cross has set me free,
By Your Love, my sins were washed from me
And I believe because You live in me,
I believe, O, I believe.

Melody in minor key moves to notes in major C,
I believe, O, I believe.

All praise and honor go to Thee,
O Mighty God and holy King of Kings
I believe because You live in me,
I believe, O, I believe.

I worship You, O holy One,
As angels and all Heaven sing,
The cloud of witnesses proclaim
That You alone are Lord of all.

It is time, it is time, for the words to be unleashed,
It is time, it is time, to set the music free.
Melody in minor key moves to notes in major C,
The time has come, the time has come, to praise the Lord.

JEMINY'S SONG WITH CHORDS

<pre>
      C/C   C/E   F/F   C/C
It is time, it is time, for the words to be unleashed,
      C/C   C/E   F/E   G/G
It is time, it is time, to set the music free.
   F/F   A/Am   Bb/Bb   F/A
Melody in minor key moves to notes in major C,
   G/g   GG   F/C   C/C
The time has come, the time has come, to praise the Lord.

      G/G   F/A   G/B   C/C
Your truth crushed lies that tied me down,
     C/E   C/F   C/G   F/F
By Your promises my mind is now unbound,
       G/G   G/E   F/F
I believe because You live in me,
           G/G   C/C
I believe, O, I believe.

      C/C   C/E   F/F   C/C
It is time, it is time, for my heart to be unleashed,
      C/C   C/E   F/F   G/G
It is time, it is time, to set my spirit free.
   F/F   A/Am   Bb/Bb   F/A
Melody in minor key moves to notes in major C,
G/G   G/B   F/C   C/C
The time has come, the time has come, to praise the Lord.

       C/C   C/E   F/F
By Your Love, the Cross has set me free,
   F/D   F/F   C/G-G/G
By Your Love, my sins were washed from me
     C/E   C/F   F/D
And I believe because You live in me,
           G/G   C/C
I believe, O, I believe.

   F/F   A/Am   Bb/Bb   F/A
Melody in minor key moves to notes in major C,
           G/G   C/C
I believe, O, I believe.

      G/G   G/B   C/C   C/E
All praise and honor go to Thee,
   G/G   G/B   C/C   C/E   F/F
O Mighty God and holy King of Kings
   G/G   G/B C/C   C/E   F/F
I believe because You live in me,
           G/G   C/C
I believe, O, I believe.
</pre>

PAGE 2 SONG WITH CHORDS

G/G   G/B   C/C C/E
I worship You, O holy One,
G/G   G/B   C/C C/E
As angels and all Heaven sing,
G/G   G/B   C/C C/E
The cloud of witnesses proclaim
F/D   G/G
That You alone are Lord of all.

C/C   C/E   F/F   C/C
It is time, it is time, for the words to be unleashed,
C/C   C/E   F/F   C/G
It is time, it is time, to set the music free.
F/F   A/Am   Bb/Bb   F/A
Melody in minor key moves to notes in major C,
G/G   G/B   F/C C/C
The time has come, the time has come, to praise the Lord.

Words by Normandie Fischer
Music by Sherry Malcolm

PRAISE FOR NORMANDIE FISCHER

A wonderful voice in southern women's fiction. ~ Barbara Claypole White, bestselling author

Normandie Fischer has created a series of novels richly populated with fascinating characters... [with a] strong sense of place... and great heart in every story. ~ Jennifer Fromke, *She Talks Books*

[She] has mad skills. ~ *Books and Bindings*

Normandie Fischer can illustrate loneliness as if she has lived through it herself. ~ Linda Yezak, Author/Editor

Normandie Fischer anchors her readers so she can set them on a course full of twists, turns, and unforgettable characters. She digs into the human condition and pulls life's richest moments out, allowing the reader a chance to sail away and dream the impossible. ~ Linda Glaz, literary agent

ACKNOWLEDGMENTS

So many people contribute to my writing world that it's hard to thank them all. First must be my husband who is always my greatest cheerleader as well as a primary consultant on things engineering or armament related.

My vigilant critique partners prod me to dig and improve. Thank you to Jane Lebak for her lengthy and valuable critique. She has incredible skills. Jennifer Fromke took time out of her busy life to make valuable comments, and the brilliant Robin Patchen is always there when I need input from someone whose publishing skills have far outstripped mine. I couldn't manage without these three, and any accolades for this story will bounce back to them. My editor, Ray Rhamey, pushed me to make this a better book. He made me work hard for every word, and I am grateful for his insight. Thank you also to Judy DeVries, of Judicious Revisions, LLC, for proofreading the manuscript.

If I look good on social media, thank the very talented Tanya Eavenson for her gorgeous memes and other help. I feel so privileged to have her on my team and as my friend.

And there are my encouragers without whom I'd be flailing in a sea of a writer's worries. Thank you so much for kind words and lovely smiles.

For my tribe at Women's Fiction Writers Association. I've been missing in action for a while, but you're always there to encourage and inspire.

And you, my readers: you mean the world to me. Your letters

bless me and your continued support keeps me writing. If I've forgotten anyone, it wasn't intentional. I love you all.

As a plus, the brilliant Sherry Malcolm took Jeminy's song and put it to music. Included here are the chords, but I've heard it on the piano, and it sounded wonderful. Thank you, Sherry, for blessing us with your talent in so many ways.

ABOUT THE AUTHOR

Normandie Fischer lives in coastal North Carolina with her husband, their doodle dogs, and two once-feral cats. If only her two adult children and two adorable grandchildren lived within hailing distance, life on land instead of on their cruising sailboat would be just about perfect.

Normandie's Website: www.normandiefischer.com

Sleepy Creek Press: https://www.sleepycreekpress.com